THE

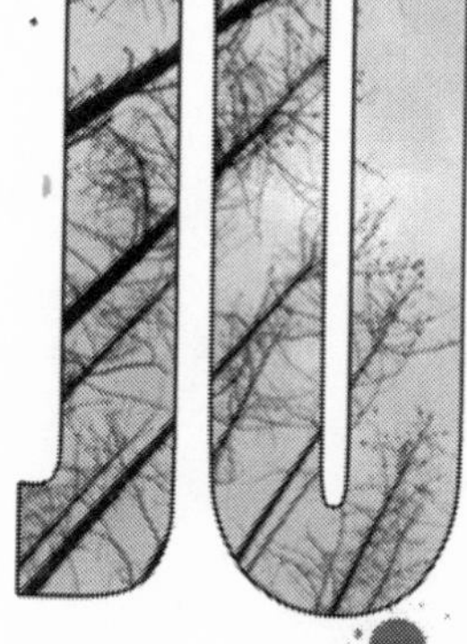

JUDAS SYNDROME

Trilogy

MICHAEL POELTL

This trilogy is a work of fiction. The characters, incidents, and dialogue are drawn from the author's imagination and are not to be construed as real. Any resemblance to actual events or persons, living or dead, is entirely coincidental.

FIRST EDITION

ISBN 978-0-9813168-5-7

The Judas Syndrome

The first book in the series

Michael E. Poeltl

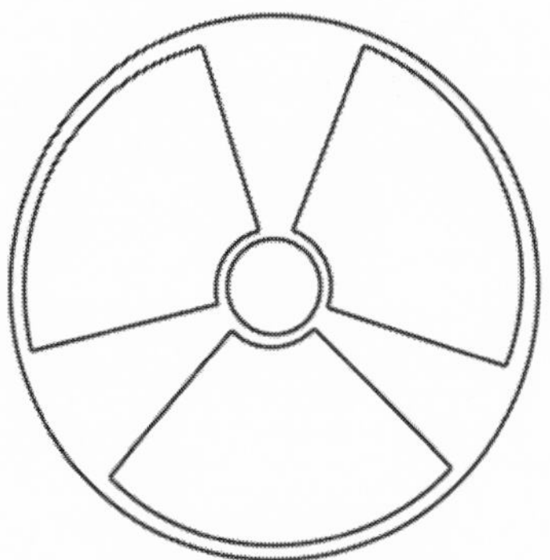

To the future

May you be kind...

The more rapidly a civilization progresses, the sooner it dies for another to rise in its place.

Havelock Ellis, The Dance of Life

Joel Speaks….

My name is Joel. Ever heard the expression; Shit happens? It hardly does justice to what's happened to me, but in a pinch it will suffice as a summation of my life these past few months.

I know now that a single action can put in motion a series of repercussions. Should that action be positive, the repercussions are rewarding, but when that action is negative, so too are the events to follow. A single action can change you forever. Sometimes, if the deed is large enough, if the intent evil enough, the results can be disastrous.

My friends can attest to this. My friends have always featured prominently in my life. Some helped shape my earliest memories while others I only met in high school. But as much as my friends have shaped my past, no memories can compare to those of the last few months as we struggled to survive. Their actions changed me and the way I lived as much as mine shaped their day to day lives. For those of us who made it out of this thing alive, the rewards were bittersweet. We kept our lives but lost our innocence and our faith, the lack of which can empty your existence like water evaporating under a merciless sun.

And for the rest of us…

Chapter One

The Apocalypse came quickly. Growing up in a small northern town located over two hundred kilometers away from any major city left me impervious to such global threats as war, famine, disease, and vicious dictators. I watched the news every night and knew the world wasn't right, but I never suspected just how wrong things were getting.

*****

Three weeks before disaster struck, I was planning to go to the beer garden at the town park. Remembering past events, I suspected there would be a few fights throughout the evening, but nothing too brutal unless some yahoos from another town decided to show up and make a play for our beer and girlfriends. I tried to steer clear of such free-for-alls unless a friend was getting the worst of it.

That friend was usually Sonny. Much as I loved the guy, drinking with him was a risky undertaking, for me as well as him. Big, beefy, and fearless, he attracted idiots like flies. Whiskey-fed farm boys, frustrated by a week of shitty work for shittier pay, would try to score a reputation by taking on Big Sonny. When he handed their asses to them, they'd try the strength in numbers routine and come back with some friends. That's when I had to get involved, whether I liked it or not. The morning after, it was hard to tell which hurt worse- my hangover or my bruised ribs. Wincing at past memories, I stocked up on aspirin.

My buddy Connor pulled into my driveway shortly after four-thirty that afternoon. The sky was bluer than it had been for days, and I was in the front yard, trailing my bare toes through the lawn pond. The goldfish were strangely agitated, darting for cover instead of swimming to the surface for food as usual.

"Just got off work- thank God!" Connor had a summer job with a landscaping company, so he'd spent the day sweating under a blazing sun and listening to hovering housewives whine out instructions and warnings. "If you're done with the goldfish pedicure, let's go get some beer for tonight!"

"Beer? What for? We're going to the gardens."

"No, we're not, buddy. Our plans have changed."

"What are you talking about?" I wasn't sure I liked this. I DEFINITELY didn't like missing the opportunity to hook up - you were as likely to stumble into some hot action as you were a fight on a night like that.

"Listen, you like a little excitement in your life, right?"

"Sure, unless it gets me in jail or family court." I chuckled.

"Good, then you're in." He started to roll his window back up.

"Not so fast. Let's assume I'm interested. What's the new plan?"

Connor smirked. "Be ready to go at six o'clock."

"Sonny's expecting me at the gardens. He'll kill me if I don't show."

"We have the rest of our lives to pull Sonny out of the fire. He won't miss us."

*****

I had to admit that I was intrigued. If Connor was willing to forgo the beer gardens, then his plans must really be something. True to his word, he picked me up at six, and we headed off toward parts that were, for me, unknown.

At the beer store we ran into Ruby. It was rumoured that she had slept with the entire senior hockey team. Two years ago she was Connor's girlfriend, now she was regularly coming between the jocks and their straps.

Her brows arched at the sight of us. "What are you guys doing in here: getting some drinks to warm up for the gardens?" I let Connor answer- I was too busy staring at the way her melon-sized breasts were trying to push out of her blouse.

"No, we've got other plans. Can't tell you what we're doing, but it'll be better than trying to keep up with the fall-down drunks at the beer gardens."

I added, "He won't tell me either, and I'm going with him."

"Oh, well, I just thought I'd see you guys there. Maybe get to dance with you or whatever."

The whatever part had sweet possibilities. I was wondering if it were too late to change my mind when Connor nudged me.

"Sorry, another night. Come on, Joel."

We bought the beer and went back to the car, where I finally blurted, "Are you going to tell me where we're headed, or what?"

Connor smiled and beckoned for me to get into the car. When we were both seated, he reached into his shirt pocket and pulled out two acid hits.

"We don't want to be at the beer gardens while we're on these," he grinned. While I peered closely at the stuff, Connor added, "I've only done it a couple times, in Grade Eleven, but they were the wildest trips of my life."

"You sure, man? I've heard some insane shit from people who've had bad trips on this stuff."

"No doubt. It's pretty crazy, Joel, I won't lie to you. It's not the Sweet Bitch." Sweet Bitch was our pet name for his dope pipe. "In fact, it's going to mess us up something huge. You'll be seeing hotter chicks than Ruby on an acid trip, my friend."

If anybody could make me see the lighter side of an otherwise risky situation, it was Connor. I'd done mushrooms once and enjoyed the trip, and he explained that acid was "mushrooms times ten." I hated math in school but liked that number, so I forgave him for ruining my sex life and said, "I'm in."

Settling into my seat, I closed my eyes and let him drive.

*****

Fifteen minutes later, we were at a spot that every local pothead, underage drinker, and horny couple without a room knew well. It was the crest of a hill that overlooked the distant city to the south and everything in between. The cops rarely came up, preferring that we break the law here instead of in the streets, where we'd be forcing them to get out of the donut shop and do their jobs.

"The perfect place to start up the summer, don't you think, old fella?" Connor, busting to drop his hit, dug into his pocket.

"Not a bad call," I allowed. As I handed him a beer from the backseat cooler, I added, "You know, you should have planned this better: no ladies up here."

"Don't be too sure I haven't taken care of you, old man." He gave me that knowing smile, and I had to grin back. There might be more to this night than met the eye.

He popped his hit under his tongue and held mine out to me. "What the hell, let's party."

Five minutes passed.

"Can you feel it yet, man?" Connor was buzzing so much that I could almost hear it emanating from his head.

"I can't say; it might take some time, right?" Then bang. I was hit. My head reeled and my perspective went beautifully ape-shit. "B-i-n-g-o." That was all I could say.

I studied my hands for what felt like the first time in my life. There they were, irreplaceable, attached to my arms at the wrist. With all of their digits and movable joints and feelings, they were so sensitive to the touch; that's it! Touch was born of the hand, of its fingers, my fingers, they were my own, and they were priceless.

I spun around in slow motion, still marveling at the dexterity and beauty of my hands. Connor was lying on the ground with his mouth wide open. Watching me, he started to laugh and I followed.

Suddenly a voice broke my psychedelic reverie. I watched it all shatter like stained-glass to make way for reality.

"Someone sounds like they're having way too much fun."

Sara and Julia were coming up the hill, each upward step making their denim skirts ride higher up their thighs. I'd known both girls for years, and when their smirks and coy greetings clued me in that they were joining us by prior arrangement, I realized that this was what Connor had meant by taking care of me. I could have kissed the stoned bastard, as I'd had a crush on Sara for months, but didn't want to risk sending the wrong message to the girl I'd admired so long from a distance.

"Want a beer?" Shit. It was all I could think of to say.

"Thanks, guys, don't mind if we do." Sara, flirtier than I'd ever seen her before, settled on the grass beside me and took a swig from my bottle. I watched her red lips draw tight around the bottle head and thanked God that she dumped her deadbeat boyfriend two weeks ago.

Hours later and ten beers into the night I found Sara pushing me down, her beer-sweetened breath in my face. Beside us, I think that Connor and Julia were doing something similar, but at that point I honestly did not care. Sara remained my focus: her mouth, her eyes, her hands.

Chapter Two

Light brightened the eastern sky and crawled across the hilly terrain. We shook the morning moisture out of our clothes, got dressed, and drove back to my house. Sara and I took her car. Last night she admitted that she'd had the hots for me for months. We weren't yet sure that we had anything in common, but if that department turned out to be a dud, we were sure compatible naked.

When we arrived at my place, I gave her a tour of the house, and she made breakfast. We were alone: Mom was still in Australia and Kevin, who rented a room from us, was at work. When we finished eating our fried egg sandwiches, we retired to the family room to watch some TV.

The Grimm Reaper was in the news again. This anonymous maniac had everyone on edge with his vows to create a better world by kyboshing the old one. He first made his presence known last May, via a website that went through so many proxies that its source was indecipherable. He claimed to have acquired some thirty nuclear missiles from Iraq, employed by Saddam's secret service, smuggling them out before the small country had agreed to the lengthy UN weapons inspections. He released messages to the media threatening to inflict worldwide nuclear devastation should the various governments not heed his 'suggestions', which included destroying schools and houses of worship, both of which he accused of turning people into automatons. No one knew exactly who he was and whether he was serious or full of shit, but a report had been leaked that the UN was searching for missing warheads, and that was enough to make the Grimm Reaper a 24-7 news feature.

"You know, if that Grimm Reaper is for real, we're pretty much screwed." Sara looked uneasy.

"I think the government can deal with this chump." I put my arm around her, noticing that she had gooseflesh under her blouse. She rested her head against my chest, her perfumed hair fluttering each time I exhaled. We both closed our eyes and drifted off.

*****

When I awoke, it was four-thirty in the afternoon. Sara was gone, but had left a note on the coffee table asking me to call her later. I smiled and made a mental note to thank Connor when I saw him again.

The house was too silent, so I turned on the radio. The news was on, but instead of yet another Grimm Reaper broadcast, they were airing an investigative report on a new drug that had proven to be over eighty-five percent effective in the treatment of depression. I laughed and swigged some orange juice. A drug like that would go over big time in the face of the world's current problems. Shit, they should just dump it in water supplies everywhere. Then, if the Grimm Reaper struck, we would fry happy.

The sudden crash of thunder drowned out the commentator's voice. Grinning in anticipation, I ran to the front door, opened it, and stepped onto the porch. The skies were the colour of slate, creating an unreal backdrop for the vibrant green trees and hills. I wasn't sure what I loved the most about thunderstorms: the unearthly stillness that preceded them, the glorious shout of thunder, or the freaky lightshow in the sky. I was still pondering the issue when my roommate Kevin pulled into the driveway.

"Joel!" he shouted as he vaulted out of his pickup. "It's going to storm-close the windows in the addition before my paintings are wrecked!"

Before I could react, the skies opened up. Kevin was soaked before he reached the door. He tore past me, running up the stairs three at a time. I heard the frantic sound of windows being slammed closed. Then he came back down, his glasses dotted with rain and 'Pro Painters' t-shirt clinging to his bony frame.

"Shit. That was close. I need a drink." He reached into one of his deep pockets. "I brought some whiskey with me. Do we have any ginger ale left?"

"Yeah there should be some in the fridge. Make me one too. I'll be there in a minute."

Thin and pasty white, Kevin was often asked whether he was sick or just on drugs full-time. Amused by the attention, he played up to his audiences by wearing tight clothes, slicking back his thick brown hair, and sporting black framed glasses. The whole visual effect was calculated to make him look like the classic heroin-chic, starving - yet successful- artist.

The studio above the three car garage also doubled as his bedroom; he'd arranged to rent the space from my mom while she was away. It was perfect timing: if she'd been home, his all-night binges at the easel would have made her insomnia worse and eventually left him homeless.

That would have added to the artist mystique, but I wasn't about to pass on the idea.

*****

That night Sara came over. Before we went to bed, I decided to introduce her to a ritual I'd always cherished.

I guided her onto the overhang just outside my bedroom window. The storm long past, the night sky was beset with stars. Pointing upward, I asked her to pick a point of light and stay with it. Then, standing up, I eased Sara to her feet and whispered, "Have you ever stood under a star, staring intensely, and felt the earth move under your feet?"

I was showing her something that I'd discovered one starry night many years ago. I'd been leaning against a pine tree in the woods behind the house, gazing at all the famous constellations: Big Dipper, Orion, and others. Suddenly I felt as if I were moving, although my feet had not budged. I later learned that the sensation was the earth rotating, something the average person did not notice until the stars provided a point of reference. A smile came to Sara's face as she experienced the same thing now, in my arms. Connected…

*****

After breakfast, Sara helped me study. The coming week meant exams for everyone, and the commencement of summer jobs for most. I would start working in another three weeks. I'd told the interviewer that my exams were over then, when in reality I would finish school in a week. I just wanted the extra fourteen days to relax, drink, party, and have no commitment to anything except my own pleasure.

Little did I know that two weeks from now, my summer job would be the very least of my inconveniences.

Chapter Three

The Grimm Reaper was mentioned on the radio again. I listened to the broadcast while shaving. Hostess Samantha McGinnis was grilling some military figure about the magnitude of the Reaper threat. The guest assured her that the media had taken yet another psycho's threats and blown them out of proportion.

"There is no possibility of anything coming of this," he said calmly. "No single individual has the resources to pull off an operation as large as he's suggesting. It is absurd to believe so and unfortunate that this man has the ability to instill such fear into so many via a tool like the Internet."

I changed the channel and started dinner. Moments later Connor breezed through the front door with a box of beer in hand.

"I've got a great idea for our last weekend before you start working, Joel!"

I popped the case open and helped myself to a beer. "Let's hear it."

"Let's get everyone together, I mean everybody, and go up to the lake for a couple days. Camping, canoeing, a little fishing. We'll go to the same spot we did two years ago with Ruby and Jill." He stopped to grab a drink. "Only it'll be way better this time. Get Sara and Julia to come, you know?"

Sounded good to me, but before I could say so, Sonny appeared behind Connor. Both of us jumped at the sight of him.

"Shit! Sonny, you scared the life outta us!" I complained. "Can't you knock once in a while?"

He didn't answer. Face grim, he grabbed a beer from Connor's pack, but didn't open it. He kept flexing his fingers, as if the beer can was a neck he longed to break. "Someone's been fucking around out in the field with our pot plants. Any ideas as to who I should beat on?"

"What happened to them?" We'd cultivated some twenty plants along the farmers' field the length of my property line.

"It looks like half the crop has been torn out. At the roots! Pisses me off, man." He opened the beer can, took an enormous swallow, and sat down. "Well, I have to hurt somebody over this." He paused, and then brightened. "Hey, I hear you and Sara from Cedar Links hooked up!"

When I nodded, he winked and turned to Connor. "What are you doing with a girl like Julia anyways, Connor? She's not your type."

"Maybe we're coming up in the world. You should try it."

"Bite me. After Ruby, dating a hooker would be coming up in the world."

He had a point there. We all chuckled and clinked cans. Then Connor said, "Sonny, what do you say to camping up at the lake next weekend?"

He shrugged his massive shoulders. "Yeah, sounds like a plan."

Our buddy Earl joined us an hour later. Earl was the human equivalent of a dynamite stick: light his fuse and disaster would follow. He always wore a baseball cap jammed over his shaggy red curls, and he was a gun nut, which wasn't a good match with his temper. But that evening, I was happy to see him come in with his rifle slung across his shoulders. Maybe he would finally shoot that damn skunk.

*****

I'd first encountered the skunk almost two weeks earlier. Earl and I spent the afternoon cruising along the forest trails on dad's five-wheeler. I was driving. Earl saw the skunk first, planted firmly in the path ahead. He yelled at me to stop, and I did, but the sudden motion sent him flying off the vehicle. He landed on his shoulder and rolled right into the little black and white bastard, who did what all skunks do when they're pissed off. I remembered Earl's .22, which we'd brought along for target practice, and threw it to him, backing the five-wheeler up frantically as the stench became intolerable. Before Earl could even take aim, the skunk, which was missing its left front foot, hobbled off into the bushes that lined the trail. I'd been seeing it on my property ever since: on the front lawn, beside the pool, in the garage. It seemed to stare at me with those beady black eyes, but perhaps I was imagining this. Either way it made me almost as nervous as the Reaper. Though I had been prone to panic attacks since my father's untimely death, I couldn't explain why this skunk played on my anxieties.

*****

Earl was soaking wet and annoyed. "I can't shoot a skunk in this shit!" He gestured toward the window, which was streaked with rain. The weather had taken a turn for the worse during dinner.

"You can't shoot a skunk at all!" Sonny reminded him. We laughed.

"Nice, Sonny, thanks." Earl laid the rifle carefully against the wall and peeled off his wet shirt and jacket. "Well, if I see that little prick here tonight, Stinky will find out that all skunks don't go to Heaven." His scowl was replaced by a sinister, anticipatory grin.

"Here, Earl, light this up for us." Connor passed him a freshly rolled joint. We smoked it and retired to the addition. Surrounded by Kevin's art, we sat and listened to the rain pound on the roof. This was a real powerhouse of a storm. We were safe though, we reveled in storms such as these. I felt safe in my father's house.

*****

Earl was up first on Saturday morning, being the resilient party animal that he was, so when the doorbell rang, he answered it.

Jake Sanders was sitting on the stoop. Jake was the sort that just showed up at parties, the kind of guy you saw once in awhile, which was good considering we could only take him in short spurts. Jake was a casebook addict, strung out on my doorstep and looking for a hit. I was willing to bet that he was the one who stole our crop, though I would never have told Sonny that. Jake used to be one of us, one of our best friends. Then he began chasing the dragon, and now he just ate, slept and did drugs.

His mother had been killed along with my father on the way home from their joint business venture in the neighbouring town. Our families were partners in a hardware store. Maybe that was why I felt like I should try to understand and help him instead of turn my back as so many others had. His dad turned to the bottle after the accident so there wasn't a whole lot of support at home.

I had come downstairs in response to the doorbell, and invited him in for coffee. When he came into the kitchen, Sonny stared him down as if sharing my suspicions about the pot theft.

"Drink this, Jake," I said as I poured a glass of O.J. "We were just going to shoot a skunk that's been hanging around here. Want to join us?"

"Can I just stick around here?"

"Sure, I'll hang back with you." Although too ashamed to admit it, I worried that he might steal something to feed his habit. I waved the rest of them off to hunt the elusive skunk.

When Sonny, Earl, and Connor walked out the back door with loaded rifles, I poured Jake a coffee and asked, "Want something to eat?"

He nodded, so I started cracking eggs into a bowl. Scrambled was my specialty.

"They won't be good like Connor's, but I'll do my best." I forced a smile. Jake was my age, but I felt like I was babysitting a three year old.

While I was stirring the eggs, Kevin came in, struggling with a massive board. "I'm taking it upstairs for a painting," he explained.

"That's cool. Come back down for breakfast."

"Will do!" He ascended the stairs carefully, the board wobbling in his grasp. "I brought my dog- she's just outside."

Hearing that, I ran out to the balcony and warned Earl and the guys that Kevin's dog was loose. She wasn't black and white, but she could rattle a bush or two, and accidents happen. They gave me the thumbs up before disappearing into the woods.

Jake ate only a few bites of breakfast, and spent the rest of his visit smoking weed. I was relieved when he wandered off at around 3 o'clock, leaving me alone with Sara and Julia, who'd dropped by for a swim and a beer. The hunting party returned to home base soon after 4:00 p.m. Earl was pissed off that they couldn't find old Stinky, but I just hoped that Dali, Kevin's dog, wasn't more successful in that department. We were debating whether or not we should risk a barbecue under the darkening skies, when rain suddenly came pelting down.

"Again with the rain!" Julia complained. "Damn it, history had better not be repeating itself." Last summer had been a complete washout, literally, with over twenty-eight days of rain. The ducks had been happy, but we humans had to deal with flooded roads and backed-up sewers. Still swearing, she took Connor's arm, and hurried inside with him.

Sonny pulled his van keys out of his pocket. "Alright, I'm hitting the road. I have a lot of crap I gotta take care of at home. See you guys in a bit." He pulled the magazine he had been reading over his head and jogged around the corner of the house.

"I'm out of here too." Earl ran after him. "Call you later, Joel."

I waved goodbye, then turned to Sara, who had just climbed out of the pool. "Coming in?"

"Joel, I thought you said you loved staying out in a rain storm. Let's stick it out for a while. Could be killer, didn't you think?"

Man, was this girl for me. I wished that we weren't going separate ways come the fall. God, I was pathetic, already experiencing separation anxiety.

We walked down to where the lawn met the wild, rollicking field and laid down on the soft grass. The rain intensified, and then thunder boomed, driving Sara to wrap herself around me. We remained open to the elements until the cold became too much and we started shivering. Springing to our feet, we raced each other into the house, where we towel-dried our hair and threw bathrobes over our swimming gear.

Connor and Julia were lounging on the living room sofa, munching sandwiches. The news was on, and as usual it was ominous. Sara shifted uncomfortably next to me as the Grimm Reaper took center stage yet again. Before I could reassure her, the phone rang. It was my mom, calling from Australia.

Apparently everyone down under was as obsessed with the Reaper as we were, because Mom asked me if I was holding up okay. She also wondered if I needed her to come home early. I told her that I wasn't bothered, and that I'd rather she enjoyed her well-deserved vacation. We discussed my exams and college applications. I told her that report cards hadn't come in yet, and I'd cut the grass tomorrow.

"Well, you have my number here, Joel. Call me when you have a minute. I love to hear from you. Love you."

"Bye, Mom. Have fun, okay? Love you too. Bye."

I hung up. An eerie feeling overwhelmed me.

"What is it, man?" Connor called. "Is everything alright with your mom?"

"Yeah, she just got a little worried about that Reaper shithead." I pointed at the television. The most recent post from his website scrolled across the bottom of the screen. "She was wondering if she should come home."

My heart sank. I was suddenly nauseous and I didn't know why.

Chapter Four

Sunday came and went. I wrote my first exam on Monday, and four more on Tuesday, Wednesday, and Thursday. Thanks to Sara's coaching, I thought that I did pretty well. My world seemed to be a perfect one, outwardly at least. Inside, my mind periodically raced with the anxiety the Reaper had instilled in me, in all of us. I hated him for that.

My chief concern was for my mom. I just wanted her to enjoy herself. Managing Dad's business had worn her out, especially with Jake's dad constantly screwing things up. At least she could relax with Connor's older brother running the place while she was gone. He was a godsend. That was what she called him.

Mom missed Dad terribly- that was why I liked her to get away from it all once a year and just live. But now this asshole Reaper was messing that up. God, I hoped that they would get him soon. It would be awful if he really had the means to carry out his threats. Maybe that was why the government didn't appear to be concerned about him; maybe his claims were so ridiculous that they couldn't possibly come to pass. That was a comforting thought.

On Wednesday afternoon I took my mother's car into town. I thought I might as well pick up what groceries I could for the camping weekend and save us from subsisting on the overpriced chips and hot dogs that the country stores tried to sell to campers as perfect outdoors food. When I returned home, rain began dotting my windshield. Again! "Why doesn't it let up already?" I wondered.

I rolled down my window and yelled up to the addition. "Hey Kev, get out here and help me unload the car." I saw his face press against the rain-streaked glass, followed by a thumbs-up.

When everything was put away, Kevin led me into the addition to study his newest piece. He wasn't happy with it. He was on a dark symbolism streak that began in school, and even though he'd been accepted to Art College, he couldn't seem to shake the dire imagery.

"If you're having trouble coming up with disturbing shit to paint, I should let you get inside my dreams."

"Do tell Joel, what sort of things are you dreaming about these days?" So I told him, and predictably, he was quite taken by the imagery of skunks and storm clouds. "Would you care if I used those? I've got great visuals in my head for them."

"Sure. You can copyright them for all I care."

I left Kevin frantically sketching in his book, and went out to the back yard to cut the grass, as the rain had tapered off for the moment. Just as I was starting up the ride-on lawnmower, I saw the three-legged skunk standing only thirty feet from me, staring. A shiver ripped down my spine.

"Okay, this is really starting to freak me out," I said aloud. He broke his stare and began hopping toward me. Jesus- was that thing rabid? I threw the mower into high gear and fled. Glancing over my shoulder, I saw Stinky gaining on me. Suddenly the mower stalled. I jumped off, slipped in the wet grass, and fell on my face. It was just like something out of a bad horror movie. I looked back, and there he was, right beside me. Now I was sweating. What the hell was I supposed to do?

Suddenly Kevin's dog barked from the house. Stinky looked up and bolted. Blessing that dog and her future generations, I scrambled to my feet and ran into the house, where I made a beeline for the liquor cabinet and poured myself a stiff drink.

"Do I smell a skunk?" Kevin came into the kitchen.

"What!" I lifted my wrist to my nose and sniffed. I didn't remember getting sprayed.

"Whoa, relax, Joel! I'm talking about my beer. Here, smell it. I think it's past its prime."

I took the bottle and inhaled. "Yikes! Yeah, that's nasty! You must have gotten a bad bottle. Sorry if I freaked you out just now. I ran into old Stinky outside and he almost got me. I swear, I am having nightmares about that thing."

"Speaking of your nightmares, I have some roughs done for you to see. Come on up."

That should be interesting. We went upstairs and into the addition, where he handed me his sketchbook. Flipping through it, I suddenly stopped cold. There, on the page in pen and ink, was a scene that I'd been seeing in my dreams for almost a month.

A cross stood alone on an empty desert terrain. The moon cast a long red shadow of the cross, like a red carpet rolling off the edge of a cliff. My face darkened. Kevin, thinking that I didn't like it, asked if I was okay.

"Yeah, yeah, I'm fine. Kev, this one in particular is phenomenal. It's exactly what I've been seeing."

"Thanks, man. I'm going to do huge canvas of it. I call it 'The Path to Hell is Paved with Good Intentions.'"

"Perfect." I breathed deeply and willed myself to relax as I sensed a panic attack rising in my chest. "I don't know what's wrong with me, man. Everything seems to be freaking me out lately. I think I'll go lie down for a bit and see if that helps."

I left the addition, shaking my arms to release the anxiety that was creeping into my waking world, leaving Kevin with more questions than answers.

My bedroom had always been a refuge for me, so I went there. After closing the door, I approached my oldest friend, who watched me from his post on my desk. Rex was not a person, though, or even a pet. My long time confidant, the one party who knew me better than my mom and Connor, was a Popsicle-stick Tyrannosaurus Rex.

I made him for my dad at summer camp when I was six. He stood a foot high, was painted green, and represented my proudest childhood achievement. If Rex could have talked, he would have spoken volumes about my life, but he couldn't, so I told him everything. You can't trust your closest friend with secrets. That's what my dad used to say. He knew how much I loved my dinosaur, so he urged me to use Rex as a sounding board whenever I needed to express my deepest thoughts or sweep out my darkest corners. "He'll never question or judge you," Dad said. Talking to Rex would be akin to holding a conversation with your conscience, with yourself. I didn't quite grasp the concept at the time, but Dad knew it would sink in later.

Sitting on my couch, I looked Rex in the eyes, eyes I had chosen to colour a bright piercing red. I took a deep, concentrated breath.

"Something's going on with me. This Grimm Reaper – the skunk, I'm on edge."

I picked Rex up and bounced him nervously on my lap.

"My nightmares – they started the day I heard about the Reaper. It's gotta be bullshit. But I can't shake this feeling."

Just as I finished my thought, Connor walked in.

"Joel? Talking to yourself? Freak! Just stopped in to grab my bag, I'm crashing at home tonight."

"I'll walk you out." I glanced at the clock on the wall as we descended the staircase. It was only 7:30 p.m., but I was exhausted. After seeing Connor off, I returned to my room, saluted Rex, and collapsed onto my water bed, the water sloshing around me. The bed had seemed like a good idea when I was twelve. Now it was just a noisy, nauseating pain in the ass.

Kevin peeked in. When he saw me stretched out, his brow furrowed. "Joel, it's only seven-thirty. Are you crashing now??"

"I thought I might try an early night. Today's been intense, man."

"Okay, I'm off to paint. See you tomorrow then."

He took his leave. Later, I could hear music through the walls, something instrumental, a beautiful lullaby. Kevin took much of his inspiration from music. Said it helped him create. I liked it.

*****

I spent most of Thursday preparing for our camping weekend and involuntarily listening to the Grimm Reaper updates. The media loved this guy because he was such a ratings booster. The more scared people got, the more they hovered around the television and radio.

The latest news was that the Reaper had a following of religious crazies who agreed that it was time for the planet to be "cleansed." These followers called themselves the Church of the Four Horsemen. The four horsemen of the apocalypse, no doubt. I wouldn't disagree that the world was a ruthless place where money and self-interest took priority over everything, but it had been that way since the dawn of civilization. The only way to change things would be to rip humanity up by the roots and plant new seeds, so to speak. I just didn't see how it was possible unless….

The music station I was listening to in the garage while polishing Dad's car suddenly interrupted its programming with a news flash. "This just in off the Reaper's web page," the announcer declared. "Money is not the root of all evil. Possessions are. We as a society strive to have more of everything. More than our neighbour, our brothers and sisters. Money buys us these possessions, and if we do not have the funds with which to purchase these material things, greed and want pushes us to steal in order to possess. In many instances one man will kill another in the attempt to possess that which he does not have." She stopped. "I don't know about our listeners out there, but that really hits home for me. Just yesterday a couple in my building had a break-in, and the man was beaten beyond recognition." She paused. "Is anyone else out there starting to like this guy?" Suddenly music came back on- the management must have stepped in.

I shook my head as I resumed polishing. "Sounds like the Church of The Four Horsemen just signed up another member."

When commercials started out-numbering music, I tried other stations, but half the time, I'd just catch another news broadcast about that shadowy son of a bitch. Speculation abounded on the subject of the Reaper's identity. One theory was that he was not a single individual, but a façade created by the Chinese or North Koreans to draw attention and accusation away from themselves when they commenced nuclear warfare. Others thought that he might be the Internet face of a group of Islamic extremists. Who would know before it was too late?

Chapter Five

It was now Friday morning and my duties pertaining to the weekend were finished. All that remained for me to do was wait for Connor and the girls. The rest of the crew would meet us up at the lake that night.

I had about four hours to kill before they arrived in Connor's four-runner, so I decided to lounge at the pool to escape any more media shit on the Reaper. The day couldn't have been more perfect. The sky was an intense blue, like the water. A soft breeze fluttered through the forest. My palm stroked the grass as I sat cross-legged on the lawn. My anxiety diminished.

Connor and the ladies arrived right on time.

"Ready to roll, Joel?" Julia sat on the diving board and splashed her feet in the water.

"Just say when."

"I loaded all the stuff you had in the front hall into the back of the truck, buddy," said Connor. "Beer in the fridge?"

"Uh, yeah, it's in the basement fridge. There wasn't enough room in the kitchen." I closed my arms around a smiling Sara and kissed her.

"You ready to go, lover?" She grinned.

"I'm ready if you are." I stared at her face- such beautiful green eyes set above high cheek-bones and full lips.

"Oh, I'm ready," she answered. She turned toward the truck, but I caught her hand and spun her back to me.

"You know, you'll never want to leave. Nobody ever does."

"Then maybe we never will."

Once the truck was loaded we paused for a beer, and soaked in the sunlight, faces angled upwards, eyes closed. Then we were on our way.

I settled into the front passenger seat. Just as we were backing up, I glanced toward the side of the house and saw the three legged skunk. He was staring at me, singling me out as if to say, I'll see you when you get back. I'll be here, waiting. It almost made me sick, literally. I turned to Connor. "Let's get the hell outta here."

"I hear that, old man, I hear that." He backed out and took the corner just a little harder than usual, and I left the skunk and the Reaper and thoughts of report cards behind me. I'd deal with all that later.

*****

The drive seemed longer than I remembered, but I willed myself to be patient. Soon we'd be setting up camp and opening our first pints around the lake. The thought made me smile with anticipation. God, how I needed to get away.

Finally we approached the long-hallowed spot. The lake glistened as the moon rose and the sun was put to bed. Trees surrounded us: we passed one that I knew bore my and Jill's initials. Jill had been a sweet girl, but Jesus, what a temper! And jealous! She blamed our breakup on another girl. Of course she did- she never considered that her attitude might have been the issue.

Connor found the perfect parking spot and we eagerly hopped out. The full moon illuminated our way as we ran to the lake's edge. Pines towered above us, leaning precariously over the water, their roots strangling rock as they dipped their branches into the lake. The air smelled of fresh dirt and sweet pine, and all was still and quiet save the loons calling in the distance. Stopping where water met land, we stood and silently reflected.

"This is the place!" Connor finally shouted at the top of his lungs, arms stretched out as if to pull it all in. A smiling Julia joined him and rested her head against his shoulder.

I took Sara's hand and walked the last few feet to the stony beach. Reaching down, I cupped the water in my hands and splashed it on my face. "Refreshing." I straightened and turned just in time to catch Sarah lunging to push me in. I chuckled and caught her wrists.

"You want to play that game?" I laughed. Picking her up was easy, as she couldn't weigh more then 110 pounds, but she was a feisty one and nearly kicked out of my arms twice. In a third and final attempt to break loose, she sent us both tumbling into the water.

"COLD!" She shrieked as she splashed for shore. I dragged her back in and ran. Laughing and coughing, I stripped to my boxers and tossed my wet clothes onto the rocks. Sara followed suit, dropping her outer garments on top of mine. God, she was a vision. I tried not to look too impressed. "Don't stop on my account," I teased as I threw her a towel.

Connor and Julia had unpacked the tents and begun setting up a few feet from his rear bumper. Sara and I hopped into the truck to change. When we emerged in dry clothes I offered to dig the fire pit while Sara collected rocks to rim it.

I used Connor's army shovel to dig. He was in love with army stuff. All of his wilderness gear was from a used surplus store in town, so he liked to brag that everything he owned had seen 'action' at one time.

The shovel's story should have started here, at this spot, where so many new stories would begin, stories of struggle, horror and survival, stories of war.

*****

The evening cooled down quickly, enough to warrant starting a fire before the others showed up. Seated on our blankets, we shut off the radio and tuned into nature's own special brand of acoustics. I lit a Bob Marley joint I'd rolled on the way up. It took me the better part of twenty minutes to roll it: the monster consisted of ten papers and almost a half a quarter of pot.

Connor put out his hand. "I'll light that bad boy up for you, old man."

I handed the blunt to my friend and tossed him my lighter. The buck was passed around our small semi-circle several times before it simply had to be put out.

An hour passed. Then we heard vehicles laboring their way through the last stretch of road. Connor and I staggered to our feet and ran to greet the new arrivals. I broke open one of our flares and waved it. Horns went off in response and everyone rolled down their windows as if on cue. Like a chorus, the occupants broke into excited war cries and screams. They parked beside us and joined the party, camping gear in one hand and beer bottles in the other.

All the tents were erected around the crackling fire, which offered us light, warmth and, of course, the means to cook, which came in handy once the munchies had taken hold. Hot dogs, popcorn, sausages, and toast were prepared: someone even cooked eggs and bacon. Fire really meant life, but it had to be respected: it was a force, and an unpredictable one at that. I knew how quickly something good could turn bad.

Wincing, I shook my head to derail such thoughts. Why be so morbid? I was with a solid group: many of us had been friends since the sandbox. All were the best kind of people, the type you'd want to spend your last time on earth with.

Kevin showed up at ten, and with him came someone especially unexpected. Uninvited was a better word, and for good reason: no one wanted to babysit a drug fiend during one of the best party weekends of the summer.

Jake.

Kevin explained sheepishly that he'd felt bad for the guy. "He was just sitting there on your front porch, wondering where you had gone. I would have lied right off if other shit wasn't on my mind. Anyway, he looked so pathetic I panicked and figured 'what's the difference', and invited him to come up with me. I had no passengers, so I thought maybe it would be nice to have a little company, but the guy slept the whole way up here."

I started to laugh. "What were you thinking, man? Connor! Could you fix Kev a strong drink? He's had a long drive." A thumbs-up sent Kevin hurrying gratefully toward him.

Sonny arrived a little later with Tom and Sidney. Tom was a good guy. Not much to look at, or so the girls told us, but a stand-up person, pale, thin, with ears that stuck out a little too far. He and Connor had known each other since kindergarten, but I met him only two years ago. A shy kid, Tom made you feel kind of awkward in a one-on-one situation. He and Sonny got along well, though. We figured that Sonny liked having someone to protect, and guys like Tom just seemed to attract bullies through no fault of their own. Suffice it to say that no one in our school had the nuts to insult Tom to his face, knowing full well they would incur Sonny's wrath.

"Hey, Joel." Sidney approached, a handsome, light-skinned African-American with a bulldog build and infectious smile. Two days ago he had returned from England after taking part in an exchange program. The 'bloke' our school got in return was cool and the ladies loved the accent, but we missed having Sid around last semester.

I slapped him on the shoulder and helped myself to a pint from Sonny's cooler. We spent several minutes comparing the finer points of foreign women. Then nature called, so I excused myself and headed for the woods. I was still bleary-eyed, so unbeknownst to me, I walked through the fire's smoldering edge, emerging with a lit shoe. Not noticing the small flame burning a hole in the toes, I continued to the edge of the trees to relieve myself. Ten seconds into a good piss, I finally saw what had onlookers in hysterics and kicked the shoe off before putting the fire out with what remained in my bladder. Honestly, that's the last thing I remember of that night.

*****

The group began to surface early the next morning, cooked out of their nylon ovens by the heat of the day. John and Caroline emerged first, toweling the sweat from their brows. They had been a couple since the ninth grade, and were straight shooters: they rarely drank, never mind smoked-up. Caroline was a classic beauty. Blonde, blue-eyed and the High School's head cheerleader. John was 6' 2" and solidly built. He was one of those rare youths who knew exactly what he wanted from life and went about getting it without hesitating. Find the hot girlfriend, *check*, manage his credits and courses to be an A student, *check*, enter University and become an architect. Though his last goal would never be realized, through no fault of his own, John was living out his perfect life.

Next were Gil and Seth: these two were inseparable on weekends. All they did was fish. Between them they'd bought a canoe for the express purpose of fishing.

Seth had come to our school late in our second last year. His family had moved from the boroughs that bordered the city to the south. It was pretty obvious right out of the gate that Seth wasn't straight, and once Gil had befriended him, the mystery of Gil's own sexual preference was pretty much put to bed.

Gay or straight, we couldn't care less, but the subject had come up. Gil suffered a terrible beating last year over it, and when Sonny found out he dismantled the assailant with his bare hands. I approved wholeheartedly of the vigilante justice: high school is tough enough without having to dodge hate-crimes.

Freddy had been up earlier than anyone, riding his mountain bike through the endless trails and old logging roads. Binge and purge: that was his motto. Freddy was our star athlete, and heading to an Ivy-League school in the fall on a Track and Field scholarship. He did everything as well as he could, and that was usually better than most.

Connor crawled out of his personal hothouse with Julia behind him. "Set me up," he said, pointing a shaky finger at the frosty pints in our hands. "That tent's a hotbox in the morning."

Before we could continue our conversation, we heard Earl's truck roaring toward us. We knew it was Earl: his truck was as distinctive as he was. Sounded like he was still in third gear, not exactly a recommended gear at this point in the drive but Earl was a bit of a speed freak.

He stopped just short of the campsite, spilling dirt over everything and everyone. The girls were furious and with good reason, as they were just in transit with what might have been breakfast. As Earl jumped down from the lifted truck, we applauded his successful negotiation of the ancient roads, and he took a well deserved bow.

I guess that the noise of Earl's arrival woke Jake. Either that or the blistering sun. He dragged himself out of Kevin's car, where he had spent the night passed out across the back seat, and joined the circular feeding frenzy. Sara set him up with a burger and orange juice.

"Screw the O.J." I snagged him a beer. "Take this, Jake."

He perked up a little and accepted the gift. Others eyeballed me, silently reminding me that Jake was an addict and giving him alcohol might create problems later in the day.

"Thanks, Joel." He cracked it open. "I owe you one. I've got lots of pot and shrooms on me- you guys can dig into my stash." He took a shaky sip of the beer and focused on the ground, declining to look at or talk to anyone but me. Jake knew he was unwelcome here. God, I felt bad for him. I hated that he had become this person.

After lunch, I grabbed the inflatable from the back of Earl's truck. He insisted on being the co-pilot. We took all of five minutes to pump it up and load a few beers into his backpack.

"I want to make it to the little island, set up there for awhile, and smoke a big fat joint," I said.

"Hell of an idea, Joel," Earl replied. "It's good to go."

We carried our gear to the lake. After waving to the remaining group at the fire, Earl and I tossed the dingy into the water, put our bag in, and pushed out into deep water before hopping in. We each picked up a paddle and headed for the island Connor and I had visited on our last trip.

The weather was perfect for the first twenty minutes of our voyage. However, northern storms tend to blow in rather quickly and violently, and the one we were about to face did just that.

Earl enjoyed the odd cigarette when under the influence, and pulled out a pack he'd bought especially for the weekend. I told him to wait until we'd made it to the island. He became somewhat ornery and threatened to stop paddling until I handed him a light.

"Earl, shut up and paddle the damn boat to shore!" Now I was getting pissed. Rain was starting to fall and we were a good distance away from any land. Earl was drunk, so debate and logic were lost on him. If he was ignoring the approaching storm, then he wasn't going to listen to me. Next came the white caps, and I began to worry.

"Alright, you moron, here." I passed him my lighter. "Light that thing and start paddling."

Too late- our dingy veered perilously to the right, and without Earl countering my own paddling, a wave hit us hard on the side and tossed the boat over in seconds. Our beer, his cigarettes, and my joint vanished beneath the choppy surface. We swam the remainder of the way to the island, towing the boat behind us, and made it to the rocky shore just as the rain really started to fall. Finding shelter under a tree, I quickly assessed our position.

"What the hell are we doing under a tree in a storm? Let's get in the open and pull the dingy over us." Now I was yelling: the thunder crashes were right on top of us. With the rubber boat firmly held over our heads we sat out the weather.

"If that damn smoke didn't mean so much to you, we'd have been set."

A sudden shiver overtook him. "Could be worse," He said, unapologetically.

"We could've drawn you asshole." I wasn't going to let him off too easily. We'd both lost any trace of our former buzz, and a whole morning and good portion of the afternoon was lost thanks to our nautical disaster.

It was a good gale though. Of course, this was not how I liked to approach a storm of this magnitude, but I did enjoy it. Thunder crashed overhead again and I yelled, "Is that all you got?"

Mother Nature answered immediately. The sky opened up and sent down great balls of water the size of marbles. The downpour lasted all of fifteen minutes. When the big black cloud trailed off into the distance, we crawled out from under the dingy, peeled off our soaked shirts, and began exploring. As fate would have it, Gil and Seth were on the other side of the island. They'd tied the canoe to a pair of trees to keep them dry as they rode out the storm.

"You guys were over there?" Seth asked, popping open his cooler and handing us a couple of beers. The island wasn't large, but the trees and brush in the middle were dense enough to have hidden us from each other.

"Yes, freezing our bags off," added Earl. We took the drinks and sat down. "Gil, you got a cigarette for me?"

Gil handed him a butt from his plastic bag- what a Boy Scout. We sat for a while, watching them fish as the sun reemerged, warming our skin and soothing my temper. Seth had caught two fish already, one perch and one large-mouth bass. An impressive pair too, fatties.

"If we catch a few more we'll feed the whole crew tonight," declared Seth.

We fished for another hour, as Gil had two extra rods to lend. I never caught a damn thing but Earl rivaled Seth's talent for the hunt. The day was back on track: we were well into our fourth beer and the sun had burned away what precipitation remained on our rocky shores.

"Joel, grab the net!" Gil cried.

I leaped into action when Seth dropped Earl's catch into the bucket and handed me the net. I ventured into the water up to my knees to get some leverage on the approaching fish.

"Can you see it, Joel? As soon as you do, scoop him up. It's a big one, man." Gil was leaning his full weight into the struggle, the rod mimicking the arch in his back.

"I see him now, Gil, reel him in a little more..."

The fin was showing and the tail began to whip back and forth violently just above the surface. Suddenly the fish hurled itself out of the water and headed right for Gil's face. Flinching, he dropped the rod and raised his hands to protect himself from the sharp fins. The fish sailed past him, landed in the water just beyond a large boulder, and continued swimming with the hook still firmly in its mouth. The rod was hung up on some foliage. Gil reached over to cut the line with his Swiss army knife.

"It was the right thing to do, man," I declared. "That fish fought the good fight; I'd have let him go too."

Gil peered over his shoulder at me. "Hey, I just didn't want to lose any more line," he smiled, and we both started laughing. I knew why he did it: we all did.

The lake was calm again, offering a smooth paddle back to the mainland. Earl sat in the mid-section of Gil and Seth's canoe as I lay in the dingy being towed behind them, hands clasped behind my head and staring up at the warm blue sky as I wondered whether life would always be this perfect.

Chapter Six

Back at the camp, everyone was relieved to see us. Gil and Seth skinned the fish on a large rock slab a few feet from the fire. Blood ran off the stone and was swallowed up by a thirsty earth below as though we were appeasing an angry god. Shirtless and huddled around the stone, wielding knives like ancient priests at a sacrificial alter, Gil and Seth seemed to transform before my eyes. Suddenly they were wearing feathered headdresses and loincloths, and had painted faces. I turned away, blaming the vision on whatever we'd smoked out on the island, and began stoking the flames and preparing the pans.

As dusk set in, conversation around the fire progressed from mellow dinner talk to a confrontation between Earl and Caroline over world issues. Caroline disagreed with him on the necessity of war as the great leveler. Practically every time we had a weekend away, Earl got into a debate with someone on this subject.

"Earl," I said, "we're not on this again, are we?"

He smirked, took a sip from his pint, and kept up the discussion with Caroline.

"Do you think this'll lead into his infamous end of the world speech?" I asked Connor.

"Is the pope Catholic?"

It didn't take Earl long to find the opening he'd been waiting for. I heard Caroline say, "You actually believe we need world wars, famine and disease? You think we need these things, things that extinguish the human race?"

"Do you really think that with all of the pollution we pump into the atmosphere and the theft of the planets natural resources, it wouldn't fight back to rid itself of the disease that's killing it? Like a surgeon cutting out the cancer?"

John attempted to speak but Earl raised his hand and continued.

"With all of the new diseases popping up, earthquakes, forest fires and tornados, you have to see that the world is actually fighting back. It's karma. There are too many people on the planet with no respect for what it can do for us. What it is doing for us. Nature's a bitch, 300 million killed off in the 20th Century from smallpox alone, the Spanish Flu wiped out nearly 100 million during the Great War, the Black Death, 75 million over the course of 300 years." He paused again, hand still up. His index and forefinger started to wiggle. "Jake, set me up with a butt."

Jake threw a cigarette to him without missing a beat. Earl lit it and continued. "And we're not much better, nearly 60 million people killed during the second world war. Horrible statistics - but necessary? You bet! With fewer people to shelter and feed, the planet isn't hit as hard by mankind's abuses. Right now there are too many people on earth, so you can expect to see one of two things happening soon: war or global retaliation. Read Malthus man, it's all there in black and white. My money's on war. Look at the history of the world – did you know that in all of recorded history there have been only seven days of peace? And that's seven in total, combined, taking an hour here, a few minutes there. War has been controlling population ever since we learned to fight.

"So in answer to your question, Caroline: yes, we do need world wars. Imagine the damage the planet would unleash if we didn't have them. The unfortunate thing about a world-wide war right now is that most life on earth would be devastated. That's why we never see countries that have nuclear weapons use them in battle. They're too efficient, too final. And the political implications of using a nuke could just as easily propel the planet into a world war. Every shithole country on the globe has a half-ass copy of the bomb now and won't be left out if someone decides to light one up."

"It looks as though we have a member of 'The Four Horsemen' among us," Julia commented. The whole group laughed.

Caroline staged a rebuttal. "So, Earl, with the shape the world is in right now, you're suggesting that another war is imminent. Beyond population densities, on what do you base that profound prophecy?"

"Think about it Caroline, everyone…" He paused for effect. "You've all heard of Revelations, in the Bible and the 'seer' Nostradamus. Not to mention the others who've seen the future, the dark future. They've all seen a third world war. Some say that the 'war on terror' is the third and final installment of world wars. A third global war with nukes would be the end of the world as we knew it. Radiation would permeate the soil and the air. The lucky ones would be those who happened to be at ground zero when their city was hit. With history, fact and the Bible backing up these arguments, I think I've pretty much covered my ass."

"I think you mean history, fact, and fiction, Earl. The Bible?" Connor shook his head. "Alright, I'm leaving this conversation." He struggled to stand.

"Connor," Sara broke in, annoyed, "the Bible is the most real thing in this conversation. I believe in the Revelations. I don't want to think it'll happen in my lifetime, but I believe it will one day."

"It's not a cop-out, Connor," added Earl. "It's as valid as anything you'll hear on the news these days."

"It's ancient history, I mean fictional history. It's a piece of fiction. What can you draw on from the Bible that can make sense of the state of the world today?"

"It's not all fiction, Connor. It's steeped in historical fact and to see into the future you have to look into the past. It's that simple."

"I think we're all a little too high right now to continue this line of thought," I declared.

"Joel!" Sara hissed. "I'm serious. Read it some time. I guarantee you'll shit your pants."

"I was just saying that we should mellow out a minute. Don't get all jerked off over nothing. You're not exactly a Bible thumper."

"I don't have to be a Bible thumper to believe in something, Joel!"

"Chill out," I went to grab her hand, but she pulled away. "Settle down."

I stared at Connor, amazed at Sara's attitude. He nodded and waved me over. On our way to the cooler, he settled me down with a show of acid.

"Just let her cool off, old man. You must have struck a chord or some shit." We snagged a beer each and sat on a large, protruding rock. "Do you want to do a hit?"

"I didn't know you brought this shit up." I licked my finger and dabbed it on the paper holding the acid. Connor followed suit with a mischievous smile. While we waited for the drug to take hold, we listened to Kevin arguing with Sara over the 'faith' she had in the Bible.

"Faith is the key word there, Kevin." Her voice became louder. "That's why religions are also called faiths. Faith requires no particular proof." I followed her shadow with my eyes as the fire projected it ever closer to our position. "Faith is everything. I believe in heaven and hell with little more proof then the Bible can give me. I believe because I want to."

Kevin went silent. Sara was blowing this way out of proportion.

Sidney broke in. "Maybe you should read the Bible like Sara said. I skimmed through it once in a hotel room when I was traveling and the end of the book is in essence the end of the world." With this said, the whole group exploded in conversation.

"Intense, man," Connor sighed as he studied the stars. "We wonder why wars break out over religion, and these people are friends. Man, everyone has their own ideas on how someone else should live." A melancholy mood struck us both. I glanced over at him, and saw him regarding me with vacant eyes.

Oh shit, not again.

For as long as I'd known him, Connor has had what some called a 'second sight'. He could often sense that something was going to happen before it did. He told me once that his grandmother had had the same ability. He'd never predicted anything that spooked me, at least nothing that he told me about in advance. Whenever one of those premonitions struck him, his expression would go blank and he'd stare off into space.

"Shit, Connor, if you're going into fortune-teller mode, keep it to yourself. I'm too buzzed to handle it, good or bad. Call me when it's over." I turned to leave, but was unable to see in the dark and banged my head on a low-hanging branch. "Shit!"

He jerked as if electrocuted, and watched me rubbing my forehead, his eyes slowly focusing. Then he started laughing. So did I, relieved that he was back and apparently without grim news. We wandered off into the trees, moving further from the noise, not stopping until the fire was a distant flicker. Finding a dry spot, we sat. Connor got cozy with the tree behind him, wrapping an arm around its trunk and resting his head against its rough bark.

"This is a good tree. Put your hand on it, Joel."

I did, and the experience blew me away. A rush of energy shot through my body as my hand breached the tree's aura, an aura I swear I could see. Connor watched the expression on my face change as I connected with nature. "Good?"

"Insane." That was all I could say. Connor knew what I meant. I got up and began touching as many trees as I could. The phrase 'tree hugger' had just clicked. I giggled.

"Let's start a fire of our own," he suggested. "What do you think?"

"Good call, but I think everything is wet from the storm this afternoon."

"We'll find dry wood somewhere." He rose with a grunt. "These are birch trees. We'll peel their bark for kindling. It burns good. You got a knife?"

"No, but I have a lighter."

"No worries." I could hear the bark being pulled apart as I resumed my tree loving.

A skunk crossed my path a moment after I left Connor. Not a bizarre thing in the north woods, but this was no ordinary skunk. My brain, still working on some instinctive level, recognized the threat in front of me. I froze. Raising my hands slowly, I massaged my eyes and prayed the image would fade away. "No, no, no...."

Unfortunately, the scene did not diminish. In fact, it got more freakish as my vision cleared. The skunk had positioned itself on a dead stump and stared at me with an urgency that sent me reeling. My heart stopped as my gaze fell upon the animal's distinctive and familiar abnormality. One front leg was shorter than the other.

He stood on his hind legs, like a puppet. Suddenly light from an unknown source illuminated his stage. "Joel, you know who I am," he said. "You need to know why I am here. Please don't be frightened, I am only a vision."

I cut him off.

"You're right about that!" I pointed an accusing finger. "You're nothing more than a vision. And a bad one at that."

I'd lost any ability to move and in trying, fell to my knees. Now face to face with the talking skunk, sure I had lost my grip on reality, I could only listen. It was all so very real, palpable. I giggled at the thought, shaking my head. "Joel, please, you must know. You must be prepared...."

Before he could say more, Connor's voice broke the spell and the skunk ran off.

"Joel! Where the hell did you go?" He slapped me on the back and knelt down beside me. "Freaking out a little bit? Don't love it too much, man."

Feeling had returned to my legs, so I stood. "You have no idea, buddy. No idea. I just had a conversation with a skunk. Explain that to me."

"Cool. Acid agrees with you. The night of the beer gardens you followed your hands around as though they were blazing a path for you." He led me back to our new fire. "What do you think? There wasn't a lot of dry wood, but it's cooking now, old man."

I sat. Then, pondering the events that turned an otherwise good trip into something of a nightmare, I clutched my stomach and threw up all over my shoes.

Chapter Seven

"Whoa, you sick, Joel?" Connor, now laughing, picked me up and assisted me to the water's edge. Taking off my shoes, I threw up again. "Let's get you back to the camp."

"Sorry, man," I groaned. "That vision messed me up." I remained by the lake while Connor went back to extinguish the fire. Feeling confident that I'd finished puking, I dragged myself to dry land and disrobed.

Back at the camp, the group was going strong except for Jake, who was lying in someone's lawn chair, a bag of pot on his lap. Sonny, John, and Caroline had pushed their chairs together and were howling over some joke. Freddy crawled into his tent with a beer and a magazine. Sidney and Julia both looked at a newspaper while Tom stood close enough to be part of their conversation but not have to contribute to it. Kevin lingered at the water's edge, chatting with Gil and Seth while Earl concentrated on keeping the fire hot.

"Look who's back!" Earl announced. "Thought we'd lost the two of you."

Everyone turned. Sara's head poked out of our tent. I waved, wiping my mouth. Then I looked down at myself, remembering I only had my boxers on.

Noting everyone's stares, Connor spoke in my defense. "What? He went for a swim." Leaning toward me, he then whispered, "Why don't you throw on something dry. I'll set us up with a night cap." I shook my head. I wasn't ready for bed yet.

After assuring Sara that all was well, I joined the diehards at the fire. The group, now quiet, gazed at the night sky. I followed suit and picked my star. I noticed something strange though- tonight the earth seemed still. The mood was right and the sky was clear, so I should have been cruising through the universe on my little planet, secure in the passenger seat. What was wrong? I felt panic set in again. Next black soot began to fill my field of vision, floating silently down all around me, like a dirty snow. I swatted at the flakes as they fell on my shoulders and in my hair.

Was it from the fire? No, no one else was being bothered by it, though it fell on them as well, on their shoulders, their laps, at their feet. I closed my eyes hard. Opening them again, I saw that all had returned to normal.

"I could see it too," Jake said to me.

Shivers ripped through my body. I sat up, slowly. "See what?"

"The... snow?" He paused. "The black snow." He pointed a hesitant finger above my head.

"You saw it?" I was floored.

Jake rubbed his eyes hard. Then he massaged his face roughly. He was now waking from his drug-induced nap. He steadied himself and lit a cigarette. Seeing that the drink at his side was still full, he took a nervous swallow. Scanning the ground and the group, he began to realize what he experienced hadn't actually happened. "Just what the… what did I see?"

I retreated tactfully. "Jake, I was just messing with your head, buddy. I don't know what it is you're talking about." A forced smile followed the lie. Jake squirmed a bit in his seat. Then he began to laugh.

"I must really be over the edge tonight, man." Jake continued to laugh, chalking the vision up to substance abuse. "I'm FUCKED!"

Sonny scowled. "Yeah, we know you're fucked, you idiot. Now shut up before I knock you out. You're ruining my trip."

Connor was now staring at me from across the fire with that damn look on his face, that knowing look. "Something going on? You want to tell me anything, man?"

Get outta my head, Connor. That's what I wanted to say to him. Actually I would have loved to tell them all about what I'd just witnessed, but doing so would have gotten me tagged as a whack job, or an asshole. No thanks. For all I knew, I was just having a bad acid trip.

"What would I have to say about anything, Connor? Jake was just freaking out at something he thought he saw. I'm fine." I could tell that he wasn't buying it, but he let it go.

Connor's pipe came out next, the Sweet Bitch, and made its rounds. Remembering my last vision, I quickly shifted my attention to the soil surrounding my bare feet. Playing with it soothed my soul.

Gil, Seth, and Kevin returned from their nighttime stroll in the forest. "We spotted a nasty cloud south of our position, blacker than the sky," Seth reported. "We should bear down for a crazy storm in about an hour or so."

Gil nodded as he gestured at a fine mist that was drifting off the water into our midst. "The wind's picking up off the lake, blowing this fog to shore. The cloud has blotted out the moon."

"You should be pleased, Joel," added Kev, remembering my love of storms. "This one's going to be a competitor."

Connor challenged me. "Going to ride this one out? Sounds like a rough one." He was pushing my buttons. If I could stay up for another hour I would fight it. I shook a lame fist at the sky. Nature's power. I respect it, that's why I challenge it.

*****

Gazing up at the ominous sky, I remembered a time, not long ago, when I was in the forest behind my house, facing a storm of similar size and fury. With me were Connor, Earl, and Jake - before Jake had ruined his life. The wind was wreaking havoc on the treetops and screaming through the fields, ushering in the rains. We stood our ground, leaning into the powerful gusts, shielding our faces with our hands and shirts as breathing became a chore.

We'd been playing war games all afternoon. No one had successfully ambushed anyone else the whole day, so I tuned into channel three on our communications gear and directed everyone to emerge from their positions to rethink our game strategy. They came, trigger fingers ready, when BOOM! Thunder crashed in the distance. We flinched. A wind pounded through the trees, knocking Jake on his ass. This gale had twister characteristics, so we planted ourselves.

"So, what do we do? Stick it out?" Connor asked. The rain was getting thick, making it hard to see the person in front of you. It was even harder to hear anything. About ten seconds later, the wind changed direction drastically, now pulling rather then pushing. Then it all came to a screeching halt: the wind, rain, all of it.

Drenched to the bone, we looked at the devastation around us, wondering how in the hell we'd managed to survive it unscathed. The forest was a mess. All around us trees were split or uprooted – only the very largest or the youngest remained. Yet not one of us incurred a single injury. Later we learned that we'd survived a mini-twister that killed five people and injured twenty others in the area.

It made you wonder. Ever since that fateful day I'd adopted the practice of challenging every storm that came my way. Connor was the same. Earl considered himself lucky but didn't invest any deeper meaning into it. Jake, I think, just got the shit scared out of him.

*****

Half an hour had passed without a word from the circle. We listened to the wind sweep the fog past our camp. Thunder soon broke our trance, obscure and still very distant. I glanced in the direction of my tent as Sara wandered out. Looking around and rubbing her eyes, she noticed me rooted to my chair. I smiled. She came over and planted herself on my lap, wrapping her warm arms around my neck. I kissed her exposed shoulder while she pulled her fingers through my matted blonde hair. We were back.

The rain never arrived. It could be heard on the far side of the lake, keeping its distance. We joked about how the storm didn't want to challenge us to a fight tonight. Waiting made everyone tired. Some slept in their chairs while others made it to the safety of their tents. Ending the weekend was tough; no one really wanted to be the first to crash on the last night. It was hard to let go of a good thing.

Chapter Eight

We awoke to a sticky, humid morning. Fog still hung at knee level, but at least we could see. A heavy grey cloud had replaced yesterday's stunning blue sky. Wiping my face in a desperate race to keep the sweat out of my eyes, I acknowledged that the humidity was absolutely brutal.

Sara and I had completed the task of loading the truck and now awaited the others. Kevin was attempting to wake up Jake who, we suspected, could end up dead one morning to no one's surprise. Gil and Seth had been up for a few hours- they were down at the lake catching and releasing their last few fish while Tom and Sonny made coffee for the crew. Freddy was out purging himself, as unbelievable as that might seem on a day like this, while Sidney, John and Caroline loaded up John's car. Earl was busying himself with his truck, fixing a leak: always something wrong with that truck. Connor and Julia returned from a nature walk, reporting a Freddy sighting.

"As he darted by us he said he'd be back in a half hour. One more lap around the forest, I guess." Connor shook his head, giggling at Fred's determination to be the picture of health. I shook my head.

"Jesus he can't be serious. It's so humid."

Gil came back from the lake, fishing rod in hand. "No fish today." He looked puzzled. "I can't understand it. We did so well this weekend."

I bit my lip as my heart skipped a beat. Gil added, "And that damn cloud's still hanging in the south." He pointed in its direction.

A pain in my chest ignited an anxiety attack. I squeezed Sara's hand a little too tightly. She pulled free, rubbing the reddened skin. "Joel, what's the matter?"

"Sorry.... I didn't mean to..."

"You need some down time, Joel. I think this weekend took a lot out of you." She smiled. "When we get home, I'll make you some soup, run you a bath, and tuck you in, alright lover?"

"Okay." I relaxed. We kissed. A hug followed, long and deep, melting us into each other. She was such a comfort.

The group was ready to go by 12:30, so we reluctantly began the long ride back to civilization. The fog cleared as we drove further from the lake. Pulling out of the forest and back onto the main road which would take us home, we spotted the dark cloud, hanging ominously overhead.

Silence reigned during the drive. Connor's radio picked up only static, and we were all too tired to talk much. An hour into the three-hour trip, we pulled into a gas station. Anyone with a full bladder took advantage of the facilities as we all gassed up. I wandered into the store to talk to the attendant and hopefully get an update on the Reaper's activity.

"Nope, can't say," replied the old man behind the counter. "Our t.v. and radio have been all screwy since I got up this morning. Must have something to do with that storm cloud there." He pointed out the window. "Not a lot of traffic either, not since yesterday. Come to think of it, yesterday I saw more people pass through here, headed north, than I've seen on most long weekends."

"Alright, thanks." I pushed through the heavy glass door, disheartened at the lack of information, and approached Connor, who was still pumping gas. "This guy's radio is out too, man. He's blaming it on the cloud." I paused. "I'd say he's right."

"No worries, buddy." Connor was in good spirits. "Get in the truck. I'll pay the man and we'll be on our way."

When we were on the road again, I fought the urge to tell Connor to turn around, to take us anywhere but home. I couldn't explain it. I told myself that the hovering cloud was the product of an early summer storm, that what the skunk had told me was nothing more than acid-induced bullshit. I fidgeted in my seat, feeling hot and anxious. Connor agreed that it was unusually warm and turned on the air conditioning.

Another hour and a half and the cloud was on top of us – that's when huge flakes of what looked like snow began to fall. Connor's wipers fought valiantly to clean up our field of vision as the flakes became thicker. The cleaner steamed as it hit the windshield, lubricating the wipers and muddying our view. Connor finally pulled off the road, got out, and tried to clean the window himself with a rag. After a couple of futile wipes, he hopped back into the truck.

"What is this shit?" He brushed it out of his hair and collar. "It's hot too, did you see that? Look at how my wipers are dragging along the windshield. Everything's so hot and the visibility is really starting to suck." The sound of the wiper motor struggling suddenly became audible.

"It looks like ash," Julia said. "Not to alarm anyone, but when I was in Costa Rica and the Arenal Volcano erupted, this is exactly what it looked like a few minutes later. Maybe there's a forest fire somewhere, burning out of control." She reached out the window, collected some of the downpour onto her palm, and studied it. "This is some pretty big ash, though."

Sara's voice trembled. "Just don't go back out in it unless you have a rag or something to put over your mouth and nose. We don't know what this stuff is. It could be from a chemical plant that burned down somewhere."

We stared at each other, anxiety and confusion visible on our faces as we tried to figure out what was happening. The silence was finally broken by John knocking on Connor's window.

"I'm not going to ask you guys what the hell's happening here, but I will suggest we get to cover as soon as possible." He glanced back at his vehicle covering his face and head with his hands.

"Shit. Okay, let's all go to Joel's house and wait this out. We can call our houses from there. That cool, Joel?" Connor looked at me.

"Sure, my place is closest. Let's do it."

John nodded. "I'll tell the rest of them."

Sara handed him a t-shirt from her bag. "Put this over your mouth, John, to be safe."

He thanked her, then ran back to his car, jacket pulled over his head, t-shirt pushed into his face.

Trying my best not to panic, now sure of what had happened, knowing the source behind the dirty snow, I turned and forced a smile at the girls. "It'll be alright... We're almost home."

Connor stepped on the gas and we rocketed back into action. During the final approach home we ran into a type of traffic congestion that only a farming town could throw at you. A herd of panicked cattle was pouring onto the road, pushing into one another as they squeezed through the narrow opening in the driftwood fence. Once again our motorcade was forced onto the shoulder. The stampede ended quickly enough, thank God, and soon we were moving again. I thought of my neighbour- did he know that his livestock had broken free? The trees were on fire behind his house: perhaps that was what spooked the cows. What if my forest was going up in flames? Or my house!

"I gotta clean the window again." Connor pulled over and got out while the rest of us remained in the car, craning our necks to see out the windows. A deafening sound came from above. I spotted a low-flying plane, a fat-bodied military one. A Hercules? Water poured out of its belly, smothering the flames behind my neighbour's house. That was a reassuring sight. Then we saw six more flying just over the tree line, heading north. They too released a huge payload on the forest just behind my house, and continued on.

"See that!?" shouted Connor, throwing himself back into the driver's seat. "Must be some serious forest fire causing this cloud!"

"Maybe that's all it is," I heard myself say. "Let's get to my house and turn on the generator. I want to see if we can get a channel on the tube. There has to be a station covering this." Our caravan sprang back into action, plowing through the heavy ash that had collected on the roads.

The yard looked slightly scorched but otherwise normal. But my house! My house was burning! Wait, no, it wasn't. It was just steam billowing off the clay shingles. I made a mad dash for the front door. Inside, everything was as I'd left it, except for the acrid smell of smoke that pervaded the rooms. The others still assumed that the culprit was a large forest fire. Not me. I knew differently. I knew, but didn't want to believe.

As we piled into the house, Connor rushed to the basement and immediately turned on the generator.

All of my friends lined up for the phone, as none of their cell phones had any reception. Nobody got through the first time around. Fear crept into our circle – I could see it in their eyes. I left the group at the phone and hurried to my room, where I looked out the window.

Seeing the devastation in the back woods sent my heart racing. Several large trees were stripped of their branches, naked to the soot and falling ash. I figured that the water from the planes tore the smaller branches from their trunks. While I watched, an inky darkness crawled over the sky, turning afternoon into night. What the...

Someone was calling for me from the main floor. Turning away from the alien view, I went downstairs.

"The phone doesn't seem to be working, Joel," said Caroline. "I think we'll have to go home to see what's up."

"Alright." Raising my voice, I addressed the troops. "If you guys want to head home and make sure everybody's okay, then go. I'll wait here, but come back tonight and let me know… so I know."

Freddy spoke up. "Personally, I don't think it's very smart to go back out in this shit. Not until the smoke clears."

"Well, I'm worried about my family. I need to know they're alright," Caroline insisted.

"It's only a twenty-minute drive to any of our houses from here," John added. "I think we'll be able to get safely there and back. Then we'll know..." His voice trailed off, his anxiety was audible.

"Maybe, but if you want, you're welcome to stay here. I'm going to try the TV." I passed through the crowd into the living room, wiping the endless stream of sweat from my face, and turned the television on. Nothing. Not even the local station was on the air. The satellite was obviously affected by the heavy ash in the atmosphere. Switching to antenna didn't help. "Damn!" I turned to Connor. "Try the stereo."

He fiddled with the switch. "Nope. Something's up. I think we'd all better go to our parents' places and see what we can see...." He pushed past Gil and Seth, and they followed. I was close behind.

"If something bad has happened, promise me you'll all come back here," I pleaded. I hugged Sara tightly before sending her off with Connor and Julia. Shaking Connor's hand, I added, "Come back before too long, either way, you know?" He nodded and the whole crew exited.

Since I was now alone, I tried the television again, leaving it on a single channel, just in case. If nothing more, the white noise would suffice as company. It was then that I remembered the internet: odds were that it would still be functioning! But as I sprinted for my room, I realized that if the phone line was down, there would be no way of accessing the Internet. "Damn it!" My stomach tightened into a fist.

Another possible resource came to mind. The paper- perhaps there had been some kind of warning. After all, the old man at the gas station had mentioned seeing heavy northbound traffic yesterday. We had the local paper delivered daily, so the Saturday edition should still be in the mail box at the end of the driveway. I put on a heavy jacket and raced outside, pressing a dish towel against my nose and mouth. Sure enough, the paper was stuffed tightly into our box. I pulled it out and ran back to the house.

After throwing the ash-flecked jacket off, I went to the kitchen, where I slammed the paper down on the table and sifted through the bloated inserts from the new super store. Then my worst fears were realized. I had that moment of terrible clarity, when my future and the future of those remaining were set out before me.

The headline read "The Reaper Cometh". I now knew that this was it, and that my friends would return with dire news of their own. I read on. The Reaper had confirmed that he had more nuclear missiles in his personal arsenal than first feared. The story also went on to explain what one should do if the Reaper followed through on his threats: where to go, how to stay safe and how to fight against the radiation poisoning that would be sure to follow.

I knew it had happened, but I still had hope. After all, we were all still alive. The worst-case scenario flashed through my head, and I did what little I could to control it. Wait and see.

Waiting for the door to open was agonizing, so I kept myself busy with mindless chores. Finally my attention returned to the paper. A new statement had been posted on The Four Horsemen website, this one directly from the head Horse's mouth. "Blame your Governments, blame your greed, blame your ignorance and your ambition. Blame yourselves for your end." It was absolutely chilling.

A bout of nausea struck me, sending me to the bathroom. I just knelt there, hugging the toilet and staring into the bowl. Like Nostradamus looking into his bowl of water to see the future, I sat looking at mine. Finally I stood and slowly made my way back to my room.

The clock on the wall read four in the afternoon. Funny, it felt like midnight in the seventh circle of hell. How long would it remain midnight here? I passed my parents' room on route. I still called it their room, as though Dad were still alive.

Stepping into my own room, once a sanctuary, I went to the window again and pressed my hands against the glass. It was warm. I pulled away and rubbed my palms together, never breaking my gaze. A feeling of hate overcame me. The Reaper was responsible for this, that piece of shit had thrown the world into the gutter! Who the hell did he think he was? I could feel my face tighten. "Fuck!" My fist hit the wall beside the window. "Fucker!" I sank to my knees, continuing to punch the wall on my way down. When I reached the floor it became my target until the mood left me, on my knees, slouched over, crying for all things lost.

After several minutes, I pulled myself together and got up, but in doing so, stumbled and knocked over Rex. When I picked him up, his tail fell off. I tried to reposition him, but he would no longer stand without the tail in place. Sighing, I sat Rex next to me on the bed.

Then I surveyed the rest of the house for damage. My rounds began with the bathroom, where I made sure that the toilet flushed and we had running water. Next stop was the addition, where I observed that Kevin's paintings remained intact. My gaze fell on his latest piece, the one from my recurring dream. It sat unfinished on his easel.

Back in the living room, I tried again to access a radio broadcast. No luck- maybe the reception was still messed up. Or maybe I was just full of wishful thinking. But there had to be other survivors in the area, right? We saw the planes in the sky- that was a definite sign that others made it too. I turned away from the radio and mused, "Actually, they may have seen us driving here as they put the fires out, and they'll come looking for us!"

I settled on the sofa, cherishing the image of a brilliant rescue until I was relaxed enough to sink into a restless slumber.

Chapter Nine

I dreamed, although all I could remember afterward was disjointed imagery. I saw body parts: first a leg, then an arm. A torso and a hand. The wing of a bird. A horn, like that of a mountain goat. When I tried to make sense of it, my initial thought was that my subconscious was trying to reconcile man and nature.

My throat tickled as I sat up. When I coughed, something dark and thick spattered onto my hand. I'd inhaled some of the crap that fell from the sky- maybe that was to blame for the messed-up dream. As I ran into the bathroom to spit the rest of it up, the front door opened.

"Joel!" Connor shouted. "You alright?" His voice cracked, as if he'd been crying. "Sara's here too, so is Julia."

I wiped my mouth and hurried to meet them. Connor was setting his bags on the entry hall floor while the girls hovered in the open doorway, clinging to each other. "Looks like we'll be staying here," he said. His head dropped, and my heart sank.

I squeezed his shoulders, assuring him that he didn't need to say more, that I knew. Then I approached Sara. I wanted to rescue her, to erase the haunted horror from her eyes. She released Julia and clung to me.

"Oh Joel," she half-sobbed. "It's awful, it's so awful...." She began to weep. I held her a little tighter. Julia hugged Connor from behind, her cheek resting against his back, but he seemed stiff, unresponsive. Like he was in shock.

"I've got to get the rest of our stuff out of the truck," he said in monotone before going back outside.

"They're all dead, Joel," whispered Sara. "My family, the whole town..." She broke down again.

It was hard to keep my own tears in check, but I managed. "I'm sorry, Sara, I'm so sorry.... but we'll be alright. We'll be alright." That seemed like such a weak thing to say, but it was all I could think of. "Look, would you mind giving Julia a hand? I have to take care of something."

She understood- I needed to go to Connor and snap him out of the shock that had him acting like a robot. Releasing her gently, I took a heavy parka from the front hall closet and threw it on to protect myself from the ash.

I found Connor in the truck, just sitting in the driver's seat, staring blankly ahead. Climbing into the passenger side, I asked gently, "Connor, you okay, buddy?"

He didn't move his head. "It's brutal, Joel. The roads are all congested, full of cars that don't go anymore. People are dead in the streets. I couldn't find anyone at my house, maybe they got away." He finally looked over at me.

"Maybe," I said. Then I turned away, studying the windshield. "The Reaper did it, man. He did exactly what he said he'd do. The local paper picked up the last thing he'd written on the net. This isn't the end though, Connor. The military planes, the ones that put out the fires, they saw us. They'll probably be back to pick us up. They might have even picked up your parents and brother."

My words seemed to have an effect. Some life warmed his eyes, and his rigid expression relaxed. "Yeah, maybe. Yeah…."

"Let's get this stuff into the house," I suggested, gesturing toward the back of the truck. Anything to keep him from slipping back into a funk. We loaded up and hurried back inside through the curtains of ash.

"The others should be here soon," I said to everyone after closing the door and dropping my load on the floor. "Let's keep busy. Sara, take your stuff into my room. Connor, take yours and Julia's into the spare. We've got to make room for everyone." While they complied, I remained on the main floor, lighting candles, mind racing.

Our tasks complete, the four of us sat coupled up on the pull-out chairs in the living room. None of us wanted to be alone. Connor and the girls recounted the horrors they'd seen on the streets and in their homes. Outside was a war zone. Death surrounded this house now.

"We went to each of our houses together, so none of us had to be alone." Connor wiped his eyes. "I covered up the ones we found, the dead. Then I took the stuff I thought we needed. Only what we needed."

Julia whimpered into Connor's shoulder. He put his hand on her head.

"There's more useful stuff out there, in other people's houses, in the stores. We should check it out before..... Well, we should check them out soon."

I nodded, knowing that he meant before the bodies started to decompose and the stench became unbearable. "The others will bring supplies too. Then we'll take stock, see what else we need."

No more was said until the door again opened. Earl could be heard bitching to himself as he pushed his way into the house.

"Joel, Connor, you guys in here?" He spoke clearly: nothing in his voice hinted that he'd endured the horrors the others had. We rounded the corner anxiously to greet him, sliding on the tile in our socks.

"Earl!" I took a box from him while Connor helped with the bags. "Nobody left at your house either, I take it." What else could I say?

Earl sat down at the kitchen table. "Oh, there were people alright: dead people. But people all the same."

Connor put a hand on his shoulder and led him into the living room. "Sorry, there's no good way to state the obvious. You want to talk about it?"

"No. But we need to start thinking about tomorrow." I thought I heard a light giggle escape him. "I got more shit out here if you want to help."

"Sure man, be right with you." I replied. When Earl left the room as quickly as he'd entered it and ventured outside, I beckoned to Connor. "What was that? Should we be seriously concerned about him? That was really creepy."

"Hey, what do we know, right?" Connor raised his palms. "Everybody's going to react differently to this."

Sara spoke up. "That response was not normal, Joel. I don't think he's all there."

"I know, but he's dealing with his family's death. He'll snap out of it."

"We have to get him to talk. To grieve is the only way to get past it. It's unnatural to block it out. It'll blow up in his face."

"Sara, let it go." I squeezed her shoulder gently. "It's his call, not ours to make for him." After kissing her, I helped Earl with his baggage, which included a mini-arsenal.

"Jesus, Earl, getting ready for that third world war?"

He stopped and gently pulled me aside. "Joel, look around you, the war's over." He pointed toward town. "This cache is for the continued survival of our group. I won't end up like the others; I am not ending up like that, Joel, poor fuckers. I raided the gun shop on Elm: figured the stiffs in there couldn't use 'em no more, so I grabbed everything I could carry."

"Well, let's hope we never have to use them. A good precaution, though."

"Oh, I was going to get more. There was a lot more than this: guns of all types, bows and arrows, crossbows, animal traps. Shit, Joel, I'll have the perimeter of your property so well guarded a squirrel won't make it in."

"You hearing this Connor? Earl's calling martial law." I picked up a gun and pointed it skyward. "Shit..."

Suddenly we heard a car skidding to a halt on the wet gravel outside, followed by a snapping sound. We rushed to the garage entrance but visibility was poor.

"Can you tell who it is?" I asked.

"We'll have to go out there to see," Connor replied. "That didn't sound too good."

We adjusted our parkas and ventured into the smoke. Just then three figures approached from the darkness, bags in hand.

"God damn it!" It was Freddy's voice. "Earl, is that you?"

"Damn straight. Who else have we got here?"

"It's me, John, and Caroline's with me too." They were close enough now for us to see them clearly.

"Hi guys..." Caroline was a mess. Ashes streaked her hair and face, and she clutched a backpack for dear life. "Are Sara and Julia here?"

"Yeah, they're in the house. Come on in."

"What the hell happened to your brakes, John?" Earl asked as we filed inside. "Sounds like you almost missed the place."

"John drove that piece of crap like a champ all the way up here," Freddy declared. "We almost went off the road ten times. His brakes aren't shot, it's the roads. That ash - it's brutal."

Kevin and Jake were the next to appear. Bags in hand, their faces were indelibly marked by what they'd seen. Soon afterward Gil and Seth showed up. They were crushed, we all were, but Gil seemed to show it more intensely. There was a black melancholy about him that made you uneasy. He chain-smoked, hands quivering, while Seth spoke.

"There are definitely survivors out there, but that's not necessarily good news. We saw two guys beat another one to a pulp. I'm pretty sure it was Danny and Donny Jinks, dicks. People like that are going to use this as an excuse. We saw people pouring out of the church on Wellesley too. Not sure if it was a riot or what. Then there were the shots fired in the distance. I'm afraid the violence is escalating out there and that we'll have to be just as ruthless to stay alive."

Sara broke in. "That sounds like we'll have to kill to survive." She was as white as… as a shroud.

"I just know that if we can't do the same - if only in self defense – we're already dead." Seth scanned the group as though looking for a weakness in our lines. "They're killing each other in the streets! We have to defend ourselves."

"Agreed." Earl didn't need persuasion. "We have to accept that people will not be the same after this. I brought the guns and ammunition here for that very reason."

I lifted my hand. "Let's just settle down a minute here. What Seth and Gil witnessed tonight may only be people's initial reaction to the situation. However, it does make sense that people who are hungry and frightened will do anything to remedy that. We can't take on any more people here other than Sonny, Sidney and Tom. We don't have the resources, so yes, we will have to defend our property from those who would take it from us." I looked at Earl. "I want you to scope out the best positions in the house to monitor any outside movement. "

He jumped out of his seat and went to work. I then addressed everyone else. "I want you all to keep watch but also keep your heads. We're in a pretty obscure spot up here and I doubt we'll ever meet up with anyone else, with the hopeful exception of the military. I still believe they saw us pull in here today and will return to help us."

Connor spoke up. "The fact is that we don't know what's in store for us, and the more prepared we are for the worst the better off we are in the end. Gathering supplies and hoarding food and water should be top priority tomorrow morning. Meats and dairy won't be edible in a couple days if we don't get it back here and in the cold cellar."

"Good thinking," I agreed. "We should go back to town and see what the grocery stores can offer."

"How was it at your house, Seth?" I asked. "Was anybody left behind?"

"Not a soul, actually. I'm hoping they got out with the others who went north."

Gil kicked the wall and lit up another cigarette. Seth placed a soothing hand on his arm. "I'm afraid Gil's experience didn't hold out as much hope for his family," he said. "My house was empty, but Gil's was full. I mean, it was like half the town had come to his place - just to die."

Gil whimpered. Caroline hugged him.

"My parents were in bed when it happened." Kevin's voice broke. "I don't know, maybe they suffocated or something. Just died in their sleep. I wrapped them as best I could, made them comfortable. My sister was at her boyfriends the night before last, I didn't see her. I left Dali with her before I came up to the lake so, I guess she's still with her..."

Then Julia volunteered the details of her own nightmare. "My parents are divorced, so I only found my mom," She spoke slowly, like she was still in shock. "I kissed her face. She was still warm but I guess that's just because of the heat…" She trailed off. Connor's touch brought her back. "My dad lives hours from here. Maybe he's still alive. My baby brother was with him this weekend. They have to be alive..."

"I think they all went quickly," Sara said. "I know my family did. We covered them up when we arrived. Remember, Julia? Remember how peaceful they looked? It's as though they never saw it coming. Like Kevin's parents, went in their sleep." She sank her face into my chest.

"When John, Caroline, and I first visited their houses I was praying that somehow my house hadn't been affected like the others." Freddy clenched his fists. "Goddamn..." His fist shot through the drywall. "Fuck!" He took a deep breath and then surveyed the damage. "Aw, Joel, I'm sorry, man."

Before I could respond, we heard someone come crashing through the door downstairs. It was Sonny, and he was alone. No Tom, no Sidney. Earl had to pick him up off the floor. He was black with ash and trembling all over.

"You alright, Sonny?" Earl asked.

"The hell kind of a question is that? I can barely breathe." He was the picture of an angry man, not one who'd just seen his entire life taken away, not a man who had the images of dead family fresh in his mind. "Where's Joel? I need to tell him something."

"I'm right here, big guy, what's up?" I helped him get his balance. Jesus, he was heavy.

"There's a group of people not far from your house. They're coming this way." A pause. "They got guns."

Earl's expression turned grim. "So do we." He headed for the garage, followed by Connor and John. When they returned, Earl passed me a pistol.

I checked the clip. "Where are Sidney and Tom?"

Sonny stared. "They're not here yet? They left town way before I did. I stayed back to get my dad's van for the ride back here. The two of them were supposed to come here together in Sidney's car. That was a good two hours ago." Wiping the sweat and ash out of his eyes, he went on. "The damn van broke down on me about a kilometer from here, so I dragged most of my shit the rest of the way."

"Well, they've never shown up, so something must have gone wrong on their way back." I glanced out the window, but all I could see were swirling ash and darkness. "How long before that group gets here, you think?"

"I figure about ten minutes. I passed them on the road up. Rowdy bunch-they shot at me."

"Let's just hope that Tom and Sid didn't run into those guys."

Sara approached me with gun in hand. "Earl's showing everybody where to position themselves. He's asking for you."

I found Earl cracking open the south window in my parents' bedroom. He beckoned me over. "Stay right here, Joel. I'm going to set the rest of our crew up around the house."

"Only fire if fired upon, okay, Earl? Promise me that. We don't know who they are. I know they shot at Sonny, but they're desperate... and they may have Sid and Tom."

Earl nodded, and continued placing the troops. We were at war: the Reaper's actions were only the beginning. Now that we were facing our first possible battle, anxiety gripped me, testing me. I reminded myself that it wasn't just me; we were all fighting the same fear. "Breathe, just breathe, Joel," I told myself. I focused on the sweat as it dripped from my nose. I wiped it away. Okay.

"Joel, I'm with you." Jake tiptoed into the room. "Earl won't let me have a gun: he thinks I'm too screwed up. He doesn't trust me, so I'm gonna stay with you."

"Jake, what are you sneaking up on me for?" I motioned for him to sit by the wall. "Where is he placing the girls? Where's Sara?"

"I think she's in the addition- he's got half the crew in there." Jake pulled out a smoke and lit it up. "Earl says that it's the best defensive spot in the house. He says we'd be able to hold off an army from up there."

He was obviously quite taken with Earl's ability to command a situation like this. I was impressed too. But right now I needed something to cool me down- I was still shaky. Gesturing toward Jake's cigarette, I said, "Set me up with a drag off that, will ya?"

Jake handed it over. "You can have a whole one if you want. Me and Kevin filled up on them before we came back. There must be a hundred cartons in his car."

"Don't get me hooked on one of your bad habits." I took a deep drag and handed the cigarette back. "Thanks."

"Fuck it, Joel, live it up, 'cause it don't look like we got much livin' left to do." A twisted giggle escaped him.

"Don't say that, Jake. We're going to be saved: the military will come for us. Until then we'll defend ourselves and wait."

Jake just shook his head, as if he didn't understand where this optimism of mine was coming from. Frankly, neither did I.

"Joel!" John shouted from the main floor. "Joel, get to the addition!"

I ran across the hall, Jake close behind me. "What, what is it?"

"They're here!"

Chapter Ten

Earl flew around the corner and headed up the stairs toward me. "It's go time, buddy!" he declared. Grabbing me by the arm, he guided me into the addition.

"Can you see them?" He pointed to the end of the driveway while the others frantically blew out the candles. We peered into the dimness and saw some shadowy figures approaching the house. "They can't see us, not with our lights out."

Sonny's lips moved as he counted. "I think I saw six guys in their group when I passed them, but it looks like they've got eight or nine now."

They drew closer. I kept praying they'd turn back, but they continued. Just as I was on the verge of shouting a warning, a familiar voice called out.

"Joel! Anyone there? It's me, Sid."

Behind me, everyone sighed with relief. Thrilled to know that another friend had returned safely, I opened the window further. "Is Tom with you?" I shouted back.

"Tom was with me, but we got attacked and I lost him. Listen, I'm coming in. I'll tell you everything in a minute."

Connor and I opened the front door with guns in hand. Sid staggered in while a dirty bunch of strangers remained on the porch, eyeing us warily.

"God, am I glad to see you guys!" he exclaimed. "Look, do you mind if we set these people up with some water? They've heard there's a migration of sorts headed north and only want to stop for a drink. They saved my life, man."

"Sure. Bring them in."

We set them up with a large cooler of water, which they gratefully accepted. Before leaving, they told us that a northbound pilgrimage was in progress, and they wanted to join it. I recalled that the military planes had flown north. They could be setting up a huge compound, collecting survivors. But how would these people know about it? What was driving them north? These questions hit me after the party departed, forcing me to go without answers.

"So what happened? Where's Tommy?" Sonny asked.

Sidney sat down at the dining room table. He looked exhausted. "After we left you, Sonny, we went to the grocery store to pick up what we could. Tom was having a real hard time. You know Tom, he's a wreck. Well, nothing was easy to look at or accept especially after we saw his house, right?"

Sonny nodded. "It was a total loss. We couldn't salvage anything."

"Yeah, well, I wish my house had burned to the ground too. Would have saved me from seeing what I saw." Sid swallowed hard and continued. "So, we were having a rough time with the bodies and all that on the street and in the store, but I was keeping it all down right? Tom couldn't, he kept on puking 'til all he had left were the dry heaves. So he's off puking for the tenth time as I was working the canned goods aisle, hoping to bring back some food for the house. Next thing I know, Tom's running out the far door, yelling for me to follow. Naturally, I high-tailed it out of there. When he finally stopped and I caught up, I asked why we were running. He tells me he'd seen the bodies of dead people get up and lash out at him. He said they were grabbing for him. I just chalked it up to paranoia in the face of all that was happening; I think I might have even laughed. That's when he really froze, and I took a look around me. We were being swarmed."

"So what next? You both ran in opposite directions, and that's the last time you saw him?" Sonny asked, his voice tight.

"Hey, I reasoned with them best I could." Sid looked offended. "When they got close enough I recognized two of them. I'm sure one of them was my third year soccer coach from years ago. I pleaded with him to back off. Used his name and everything. Then I saw Mrs. Klein, from the library. She was spouting some biblical bullshit. So we're getting backed into a corner. I finally got through to Mr. Banks, the soccer coach. He explained they only wanted what I had, the box of food. I told him to go get blown. There was plenty to go around. He grabbed for it and I hoofed him in the nuts. What I hadn't counted on was Tom bailing on me."

"You know he can't stand conflict, he probably just ran for cover..."

Sid cut Sonny off. "Don't you turn this on me, Sonny. I looked for him. I thought maybe he went back to your house, so I started for there. Then the pricks rushed me! I ran north, leaving the car behind and dropped the box of food. Shit, I felt bad about it, but Tom was gone, man." Sidney was losing his composure. "Then a shot rang past my ear and they ordered me to stop. So I did." He rubbed furiously at his eyes. "Before they could do their worst, the group who brought me here came and saved me. They told me where they were going and invited me to come along. I asked them to take me here instead. Sonny, we fired at you thinking you were one of the assholes who attacked me and Tom. You almost ran us down."

Sonny shook his head. "Sorry Sid, I couldn't see."

Sid plowed his fingers through his hair. Wet ash made for one hell of a mess, especially in Sid's short dreadlocks. "Listen Sonny, Tom'll show up… He just got scared and ran." He pushed his chair back and stood. "All my stuff is still in my car in town. I'd really like to get it back. Are there any plans to go soon?"

"We were planning on going there tomorrow morning," Connor replied, "but with all these freaks running around, I guess we'd better be armed."

I agreed. "Five of us can go to town and the rest can stay here to protect the house. Sound good?"

"Perfect," Earl approved. "I volunteer for the trip. Who else wants to go to town?"

"I'll hang back," I said. "Get some work done here." I didn't know if I was ready to stomach the reality of the situation yet.

"I'll stay here too," Connor decided. "It's important that nothing happens to this house."

John, Sid, Sonny and Seth all volunteered to return to town, leaving the defense of the house to the rest of us. We did a time check after the meeting was considered over, and I suggested that we start taking showers one at a time being as many of us were covered in the filmy black soot.

"No longer than three minutes each. That way water won't be wasted. We're on a well here, but keep in mind that it's not bottomless." My mind raced with instructions, what to do in a crisis. "Keep the hot water to a minimum too, we need to conserve what fuel we have for the generator."

"Meanwhile, let's get a schedule made up for 24 hour guard duty," Earl suggested. "It's important – for our defense."

And our survival.

*****

Freddy, Gil, and Sara took the inaugural guard shift while the rest of us went to our beds and couches and collapsed. The following morning, I prepared for the 8:00 a.m. watch while Earl and the boys collected their gear for the drive to town. Julia insisted that they tie wet rags to their faces to act as filters.

"Good luck, fellas," I said. "I'll see you in three hours." Then I added, "Come home with Tom..."

Sonny shot a thumbs-up. "Count on it."

After they departed, the rest of us spent the morning taking stock of what we had to work with and noting what we needed. Fuel was key to our survival, and conservation of our present supply would be paramount. We would only turn the lights on when absolutely necessary. The fridges and freezer would run day and night as always. Anything else that used up batteries or made the generator consume more fuel would be carefully monitored.

What struck me as bizarre was the amazing sleep I'd enjoyed the night before. The mental and physical stress combined had knocked me right out. Any dreams or nightmares that might have tormented me were not carried over into my waking memory. This made me almost feel like my old self again.

At 10:30 a.m. Connor approached me with the e.t.a. for our 'Away Team.'

"Half an hour more, Joel, and then I start to worry, right?" He wiped the sweat off his bare chest with a towel. I was going shirtless too. The girls had adopted a no-bra rule because the heat was just too much. There were no complaints from any of the guys.

I checked my watch. "Don't sweat it yet. Pun intended."

"Trying not to. What are you doing?"

"Trying to find some stuff we can use." I gestured at a dusty pile of boxes I'd pulled from the hall closets.

"Yeah, it's good to keep yourself busy." He stood over me, one leg shaking to an invisible beat. He was clearly nervous about something.

"You need to talk, Connor? You know I'm here for you buddy, just let me know."

"No, it ain't nothing. I'm going back up to see if Freddy needs anything."

"You're sure, man?"

He lifted his hands as if to say, "It's all good." Then he left.

Upstairs, Freddy yelled that the boys were back. Connor hadn't made it halfway up the stairs before he was blazing a path back down. I opened the door. They were still exiting the vehicles, bags slung over their shoulders. I started a head count while Connor looked at me anxiously.

I shook my head. "Shit, I can't count them. It's too dark."

"Hey! Did you find him?!" Connor called out.

No answer, so we waited. The troops finally trudged toward the house, heads down and shoulders hunched against the pounding wind. When they came in, I managed a head count. Five, only five.

"Where's Tom?"

At first they didn't answer. They glanced at each other and then at us, faces marked by discouragement and, yes, grief. "It's no good," Earl finally said. "We looked all over."

Sid lowered his head and grabbed his stomach. "Shit..." Pushing his way past us, he ran to the bathroom.

Sonny clenched his fists. "I'm going back! I'm not finished!"

"Are you going back out right now, Sonny?" I asked.

"I wouldn't have even come back if I had taken my own car." He never took his eyes off of Earl. I half-expected him to start swinging, so I moved between them.

"Alright, I'll come with you." I guided Sonny into the front door and started suiting up for the nasty weather. "Give us another three hours."

After I hugged Sara and promised to return on time, Sonny and I left the house. As we sprinted to Connor's four-runner, I felt the hot ash blowing on my neck. Breathing was difficult in this heat even with the wet clothes on our faces.

The truck didn't start on the first try, but I'd driven this pig enough to know its quirks. The uneasy moment soon passed and we were on our way.

Chapter Eleven

"Any new ideas on where we should look?" I asked, keeping my eyes on the road ahead.

"One." Sonny rubbed his hands together. "There's this place on the east side I remember him telling me about, behind one of those horse barns on the town line. He'd go there to think or some shit."

"So we'll go there after we make a pass through town." I took a turn slowly. The ash build-up on the roads demanded caution.

Passing through town was a nightmare. The visual picture I had created from the others' descriptions did not do justice to the reality I now witnessed. Emotion almost got the better of me as we coasted past the twisted metal and fallen trees. Everything was scorched or burned to the ground. So many landmarks which had helped shape my young life were no more. I saw no movement through the shadows and smoke. Had everyone fled north? How would we ever find anybody in this? It seemed hopeless.

Sonny shook his head at me as our eyes met, scanning the debris. I accelerated and turned up Concession Ten at Sonny's urgings.

We reached our destination after another twenty minutes on the road: a barn off the town line. It was then that the rain started to fall, black and heavy. Sprinting the final few meters through the devastated field, we despaired of finding Tom there, until we noticed a mechanical hum from the barn.

Sonny pushed his way in first, helping me as I slipped in the mucky downpour. Once inside the barn's fragile shell, I removed my gloves and wiped my eyes clear. Sonny retracted his ski goggles and joined me at my side.

There was a veritable pot factory in here, with hundreds of plants growing in their own bio-bubble. Tables lined the full length of the barn in several rows, and high intensity lights hung low from the rafters, supported by chains.

"Eden!" Sonny had said a mouthful. I had to smile. The tell-tale leaves of the marijuana plants stood several feet above the wooden tables. These were full grown specimens. The buds were huge and their sweet scent permeated the barns interior.

We walked softly on the concrete floor, careful not to disturb the perfect ambiance we'd stumbled into. It was an experienced set-up. Whoever did this had to be growing for a government-ordered medicinal supply; that was my first impression. On closer inspection, I realized that these plants were being fed more than hydroponics. A well-known drug used to treat depression was also being pumped into them via labeled tubes hanging from the rafters.

Plastic tubing ran the length of each table, feeding the planters the cocktail of water and anti-depression drug. The hum we'd been drawn to - we discovered - was a generator, situated in the corner of the barn. It was connected to a large gasoline tank, similar to what we had at the house, vented through a small hole in the side of the barn.

"We should take all of this back," I blurted. "It's a lot of weed, man. No one else is going to smoke it."

He agreed eagerly. Then, remembering why we had come here, he shouted, "Tom! Where the Christ are you?" I nearly jumped out of my skin. His cry broke the otherwise tranquil aura we'd enjoyed since entering the barn. Such a pained last attempt was his call that I felt compelled to join in.

"Tom! Are you in here?!" No response. My heart sank.

After a few moments of eerie stillness, I set to work on our second objective by collecting the buds. After about seven or eight batches, I realized that my jacket couldn't hold more and stopped. Sonny noticed and began to gather some of his own.

"Might as well get something outta this trip," he said, his voice catching in his throat.

I found a bunch of clear plastic bags under a discarded trench coat and handed some to Sonny. We collected as many ripe buds as we could carry, and then drove back to the house.

Despite the mass disappointment over not finding Tom, everyone was curious about our discovery.

"How much weed have you got??" Connor asked.

"Thousands of dollars' worth," I speculated. "And there's more in the barn, a lot more. The best place for it is in the dry storage."

Connor discouraged this plan as he informed me the dry storage was now full of food from the first mission to locate Tom.

We decided to put them in the garage instead. After clearing a dry shelf and stashing the bud on it, I grabbed enough to guarantee a couple days of buzzed bliss.

"I was wondering when you were going to pull it out," he grinned. "I could smell it a mile away." He picked some off my palm and rolled it in his fingers before elevating it slowly to his nose and inhaling deeply. "Shit, that's some serious dope."

"What do you say to a big smoke show up in the addition? I think we could all use some time away from..... Well, we could use some time away."

He understood. "You want me to rally them up? I'm sure they'll all be more than willing. We got booze too; Earl hit the liquor store today."

"Okay then, let's do it!"

Half an hour later, we gathered in the addition, eager to force aside the bewilderment and fear that threatened to overwhelm us at any moment. Sitting in one of the few chairs, I packed the pipe, a beer at my side-warm, but a beer all the same. The others were drinking and discussing the day's events. On the surface, that we carried weapons now was the only distinguishing factor that this get-together was any different from the dozens we had enjoyed in the past. The guns reminded me that this was just an attempt to punch holes in the darkness that enveloped us now.

I noticed Connor staring at me. I invite him over with a wave. He kneels beside me and nudges my arm with his elbow.

"You know you're our leader, right? They've all decided. We had a sort of vote while you and Sonny were gone. I for one couldn't sway them to vote Jake in but it was close." He smiled and took the pipe from me. "Why don't you say a few words for the troops? This is your party, Joel, your show."

I take a moment to let the news sink in. I hadn't even considered making any one person the *leader* of our tribe. It meant a lot to me hearing it from Connor though, the one person I would have voted for were I here. I stood up.

"Can I have everybody's attention for a second?" I spoke slowly, distant.ly. This weed was very different from what I was used to.

My friends assembled around me. My head started to hum and I felt the skin of my cheeks tighten as a huge smile tattooed itself to my face. My eyes closed slowly. I began to scratch my face and hair lethargically. The smile remained but transformed into a grotesque satire of itself. My scratching became more violently uninhibited, extending to my legs. I was completely unaware of what was happening around me now, interested only in the elusive itch. Not another word escaped my mouth for what I perceived to be five minutes. Then I sighed. "How long have I been scratching that itch?"

The laughter seemed to explode in my head. It was beautiful. I was the man. The Sweet Bitch did her job, now it was up to us to keep it unreal.

*****

The reasoning behind getting high tonight couldn't be disputed; it seemed almost ridiculous that we ever did it before. Before this end I saw drugs as an escape, but that begged the question: what was I trying to escape from?

A few hours into the evening, Gil became paranoid and had to have his gun taken away as a precaution. Nothing would bring the house down like an accidental shooting, so John suggested that we all relinquish possession of our firearms.

"Alright," I agreed, my high wearing off as the alcohol took affect. "John has a point! Guns are checked at the door when we come in here for recreation. This area is now deemed our R & R room." I finished by knocking my empty beer bottle on the window ledge- very Judge Joel of me.

"But Joel," Earl complained, "this is our best spot in the house for standing guard, what good is it..."

I cut him off.

"Earl, it's only when we're having fun, if someone is on duty in here they'll keep their gun. The others will leave theirs at the door." I scratched my face, feeling the itch return. Earl noticed and began to laugh and scratch at his chest. We all joined in. The laughter felt good and warmed us, unreal, but real enough.

*****

The remainder of the night had its ups and downs. After all, this was only the second day of the new world, and my friends still had to get over their losses. Eventually the addition, or 'Skylab' as we'd renamed it in our stupor, began to empty as people staggered off to bed. Our mystery pot had certainly come through in a pinch, I thought as I rolled the last joint of the night and sat against the east wall with Sara, Kevin, Jake and Sonny, the diehards.

"Before we lose our buzz," I said, holding it up in front of everyone, "here's to... our futures..." I lit the joint and passed it around.

Sara was nodding off on my shoulder; I felt sleep encroaching also, so I relaxed and yielded.

Chapter Twelve

My head was heavy when I opened my eyes again, and I felt alone and disoriented. Realizing suddenly how hungry I was, I high-tailed it out of Skylab.

As I hurried through the house, a mental haze messed with my locomotion as well as my equilibrium. I found it increasingly difficult to maneuver. Suddenly I lost my footing, tumbled down the staircase, and landed in the front hall on my back.

Lying there, still as a corpse, I mentally scanned myself for shooting pains or some other sign of injury. Nothing. Slowly, carefully, I got up.

"Joel! Are you alright? Did you just fall down the stairs?" Sara had heard me from Skylab. I gave her the thumbs-up as she bent over the railing.

"Just took the express route down." I caressed my ass.

"I'll do that for you," she grinned saucily. "Come up to bed."

I double-timed it back up the stairs, forgetting food in a flash. Entering my room, I found the girl of my dreams lying in my bed, naked under the covers. She was as high as a kite. The pain had left her, if only for tonight. If only for tonight we were who we were, the kids we really were. That made me smile, to know the world outside was nonexistent to her right now, that it was just me and her in my room during any given evening in the first few days of an endless summer. I walked silently to the bed, undressing along the way. Taking her face in my hands, I kissed her intensely. That night would not be the last of its kind by any means, but I can say that it was one of the most powerful memories I have of her, of us...

After an hour or more of almost animalistic passion, we lay there, slowly falling out of our fantasy and returning to the reality of where we were, of *when* we were. Sara spoke softly into my chest.

"I miss them Joel... you know? I can't believe…" She couldn't continue. I hugged her tightly as she cried against me. "I miss them so much..."

"I know," I said. "I know."

She held me close and said what I'd known after our first encounter, or had hoped I'd known. One thing was sure though, it felt good to hear it.

"I love you, Joel. I really *love you.*" Our eyes met and I broke down.

We embraced until sleep overcame us.

*****

I must have woken up five times that night. My blankets were all over the floor with the exception of the comforter Sara had managed to hold onto. Shit, was it hot. My sheets were soaked, and each time I'd wake it felt like a new river had opened on my forehead. Trying not to rouse Sara, I sat up. Another nightmare troubled me, a new one. God, in how many different ways was my unconscious going to tell me I was 'not in Kansas anymore?'

This time the images defied interpretation. I couldn't seem to pull a meaning from what I remembered. The problem being I just couldn't remember enough to put anything together.

My temples throbbed. I eased them with my fingers, and then rubbed my eyes hard, producing flashes of white light. They in turn sparked a memory of the events leading up to my waking state. Despite the sweltering temperature in the room, I shivered.

Sara watched me. "Someone walk over your grave?" she asked, half asleep.

"What?" I asked.

"You shivered. It's an old saying: when you shiver, it means that somebody just walked over your grave."

"How could anyone have walked on my grave if I'm not dead?"

She had gone back to sleep, so my answer would have to wait until morning. My watch read 6:30 a.m. I glanced out the window, hoping to see the sunlight slowly brightening the sky. A knee-jerk reaction I guess, one I wouldn't give up on too quickly.

*****

nocked at our door minutes later. "Joel, you up yet? Your watch,"

ght," I replied, coughing up smoke from the night before. "I forgot, t in a sec." I maneuvered around Sara, careful not to wake her. I kissed her damp forehead and got dressed.

vas making his rounds when I reached the addition, checking all of indows and doors.

p in, Joel?" Caroline asked, gun at her feet as she sat in a patio chair g the north windows.

lty as charged," I replied. "I'm exhausted: I must have woken up a lred times last night."

bbed a chair and sat down at the east wall while Jake covered the . I pulled the pistol from its holster and popped the clip out, double-ked that it was full, and forced the barrel back to be sure there wasn't llet in the chamber. "Anybody see anything this morning?"

n't seen much," answered Jake. "So much rain, I can't see through it."

ink the rain will keep people inside," added Caroline. "Earl went out a minute to get something out of his truck and-" She stopped as Earl red the room.

e rubber on the wheels is starting to disintegrate – not good!" he orted. "It's brutal, man. At this rate we won't have a vehicle that'll ve from the driveway, and what's worse is we can't do anything to stop

it the gun back into its holster and set it on my lap. "Can we fit them nto the garage?"

eah, I was thinking that. I'll get the boys and start the move before any re damage is done." He threw me a half-assed salute and walked off.

el, hey Joel..." It was Jake. "You got some more of that pot?"

m not giving you any, Jake."

ere, I said it. He wasn't getting any weed unless there was a party going and the majority of us was partaking, never mind while on duty. His n hand began to shake, and the sweat teetering on his eyebrows dripped wn, burning his eyes. I felt sorry for the poor bastard, but was steadfast not letting him slip away.

oel, I-I'm dying here, man. I really need something. I-I smoked and ate l my stash... "

"Good. I don't want to have to worry about you being high and not doing your part."

It was tough love. I knew he understood the concept on some level, a level he'd forgotten. His gun hand shook a little more violently. I approached him.

"Jake, we couldn't do much for you in the past, but maybe now is the time." I knelt in front of him. His head dropped against his chest. "What do you say, Jake?" I took his rifle and put my hand on his forearm.

"It's too hard," he whimpered. "I'm not worth it.... it's too hard." He raised his hands to his face and started to cry.

"You *are* worth it, Jake. Don't say that shit, man. You just lost control. You lost your way. I know we can get you back on track. I know it."

His eyes met mine and compassion crept into my heart. I saw the Jake I grew up with, the friend who had shared his lunch when I had forgotten mine in sixth grade. This wasn't some burnout, this was Jake. This was my buddy Jake, who was a kind and giving soul before an awful accident took all that he was away from him. He'd never been able to talk to his dad like I could with mine, leaving his mom. She was killed along with my dad in the untimely car crash that sent us both into therapy. The therapy did a wealth of good for me, but Jake couldn't get past the pain.

"No! God damn it! I don't want to, I don't care anymore... I don't care." Now he was pulling his hair and sobbing. I held him awkwardly around the shoulders.

"Caroline, go get Connor up here. I don't know what else to do," I begged. She wiped her eyes and hurried out of Skylab.

When Connor arrived, he sized up the situation right away, and produced a joint he'd never lit up the night before. I nodded, and he handed it to me.

"Jake, here - I've got something that'll take the edge off. But know that this is not going to happen again." I gave it to him, hoping he'd decline the offer, but he snatched it eagerly. "Never again, man, if you smoke it's because we're all smoking, never again by yourself."

Through the frantic puffing, he thanked us. "My last one," he said, exhaling. "This'll take me..."

I stand and turn to Connor. "He wants to clean up,"

"Clean up? No more drugs?" He almost laughed out loud. That angered me and he felt it. "Sorry, but you're talking about..."

I butted in. "Yeah, I know who I'm talking about. He's a mess and wants to change all of that."

While we discussed him, Jake consumed the whole joint in under a minute. He leaned back in his chair, and that blank look crept over his face once more like a shadow.

"Hey, that's commendable, Joel. Don't get me wrong, I remember Jake too when he was like us. He'd be a great addition to the group if he was clean. The thing is, this isn't going to be easy what with the end of the world to work through and all."

I look down at him and shake my head. "I know it, but he's reaching out. I feel like we should have done more for him before it got so bad. I should have done more..."

Connor interrupted me gently. "Don't go there again, Joel. We went through that two years ago."

"I'm not. I- I just think he wants help now."

Caroline spoke up. "Joel, I think Connor's right. Don't put it all on your head. Jake hasn't said once that he wants to quit. You told him he wants to and it's my experience you can't force someone to do something they aren't prepared to do."

My back went up when she said that, but in reflecting on the conversation, I had to admit that my dialogue with Jake had been basically one-sided. "Listen, I just think it's worth a chance. He's not this lost cause, there's more to this guy. You never really knew him when he was a regular guy, Caroline. He wasn't like this."

Jake remained in his chair, slouched over in a stoned paradise. Hell, I'd have liked to join him but then that was the difference between us: I knew when I could and when I shouldn't. Jake had lost that particular ability long ago.

"I'll stay and do his shift," offered Connor. "You have his gun?"

I handed Connor the rifle and reclaimed my seat.

An hour later, Kevin came through the door with a determined look on his face. Everyone noticed. He marched to his paintings and grabbed a large pad of paper. Sitting on the floor, he began to draw tenaciously. I hadn't seen him inspired like this since before the weekend. It made me feel good, like a piece of the past just barged in and reminded us who we were. I turned to Caroline to see her reaction. She was smiling and studying Connor's face, as he was the only one close enough to see what Kevin was drawing. Suddenly Connor's face changed radically from that of an amused spectator to scared.

"Who is that supposed to be?" he asked. Kevin looked up at Connor and frowned thoughtfully before continuing to sketch.

"I'm not sure really," he answered. "I've been drawing him since I was a kid, but I haven't for awhile now. I just woke up this morning and felt I had to draw him, to see him again." Kevin handed the pad to Connor. "My mom always said she thought maybe he was my guardian angel. She thought that was why his image would always come to me so clearly." Remembering his mother, Kevin flinched.

Connor studied the picture in his hands, and then lifted his gaze to Kevin. "Then he's mine too."

"You know, some of the others have seen a similar drawing before." Kevin walked over to his pile of art in the far corner and sifted through several sheets and sketch books until he found an example. We were all standing in a semi-circle now surrounding the first drawing. He rejoined the group with three other portraits of the man he called his guardian angel. "I did these within the last four months."

We each took one and compared them to the most recent version. "Freddy saw this one last month and couldn't believe his eyes." He pointed to the one Caroline was holding. "He thought I'd drawn someone he knew. He couldn't place it but he was sure he'd seen this guy or even knew him. That didn't shock or surprise me, but the very next week me and Earl were up here hanging out when he came across the same picture and goes, 'Don't I know this guy?' That's when I got a little freaked out."

I asked Connor why he thought the face was familiar. He answered, "Like I said, I've seen my guardian angel... that's him."

"What do you mean, your *angel*? When?"

"Listen, Joel, it's not a Biblical thing so much as a spiritual one. You know me and my sixth sense. I've seen him, the first time I ever saw him I found a Bible and read the whole thing."

"You never told me that."

"It was a phase, and I forgot about the angel, at least until yesterday." He paused. "I was about to tell you, Joel - when you were sitting on the floor sorting through those boxes, he was standing over you. You called me on it; you knew I was hiding something."

"You saw this guy with me?" I point at the sketch in Caroline's hand. Though I knew he wouldn't lie to me, the idea that Kevin had been drawing the spirit Connor thinks he just saw with me blew my mind. He just nodded, massaging one hand with the other.

"This is starting to scare me." Caroline shuddered as she handed the drawing back to Kevin.

"I draw him," Kevin said, "but I can't say I've ever seen him beyond my mind's eye. I'll bet that if we took this picture around the house, everyone will say he's a familiar face. They just won't be able to place him."

"Alright," I said, "let's test that theory. Post 'em, all the pictures. And we'll see what everyone says."

While Kevin complied, Connor and I resumed our seats.

"You've got to tell me more about this vision, Connor. What else did it do?" I asked.

"Nothing more to tell."

"Well, when did you started seeing it - I mean, him." I had no reason to doubt my friend's vision, or that he had a guardian angel. I knew Connor's sixth sense made him different.

"I can't remember exactly when I first saw him, but I'll guesstimate it at around two years ago, when we were at the lake, with Jill and Ruby!" He snapped his fingers.

"Ruby? Oh God, Connor!" Caroline winced.

"Anyway," he continued, ignoring her, "it was up there. That's weird though, eh? For sure it was at the lake. Nothing spectacular, just a sighting, really. He stood in the darkness just beyond our campfire, then turned and walked into the woods. Jesus, I almost got up and followed him." He stopped to exhale at the rising temperature and mop his brow with the back of his hand. "Since then, I bet I've seen him thirty times, but seeing him with you was different. Usually all he's doing is walking by, staying at a distance, but now I guess he's looking out for all of us. We might all share the same angel."

It suddenly dawned on me that maybe the skunk was his way of approaching me. Maybe he couldn't show himself to me directly, and only Connor could see him because of his gift. It was all pretty out there, but these were unreal times, and it fit.

"It makes some sense though," offered Caroline. "The idea that we all share the same guardian angel, I mean. We are all alive." The tears came as she realized the enormity of what she'd said.

"It's alright to cry, Caroline." I got up and approached her. I knelt and squeezed her hand.

"Why us, though?" She asked the question we'd all had on the tip of our tongues. There was no answering that one.

Chapter Thirteen

Hours later, Sidney, Sonny and Julia came to relieve us in Skylab.

"Alright, kids." I addressed the new blood enthusiastically. "Stay sharp. The rain plays tricks on the eyes and the ears." They huffed and rolled their eyes, guard duty didn't appeal to anyone. Connor and I moved Jake to the living room while Caroline went on to the kitchen to grab some breakfast.

As I entered the kitchen I found John frying up some bacon. Bread was toasting for sandwiches as Sara sliced tomatoes.

"Hi guys," Sara greeted Connor and I, winking at me. "heard your watch was pretty uneventful." A pause. "For the record, and I've already admitted this to Kevin, I know the man in his drawing too. Why? No idea." I found myself drawn to the tomatoes. I watched as Sara's knife cut through their fleshy exterior exposing the meaty center. They were a brilliant red, I couldn't help staring. It was as though I'd forgotten color until just then.

Caroline chimed in. "It's really spooking me, because Gil and Seth also recognized the portrait. I still don't think I've ever seen him, and neither does John."

John turned from the frying pan where, until that moment, all of his attention was focused. "We were, uh, feeling kind of left out of the whole guardian angel thing. Like maybe we didn't belong here with the rest of you. Because, you know, we weren't actually supposed to come on the camping trip."

"Hey, don't think like that!" Connor interrupted. "Sonny and Sidney haven't yet admitted to recognizing the picture. Neither has Julia."

It was funny how this whole idea of a guardian angel had taken off. For a bunch of skeptics who a few days ago had been arguing the existence of religion around a campfire, we had grabbed onto the guardian angel with both fists clenched, as if it were the last thread of reason in an unreasonable world.

We ate in silence at the kitchen table and listened to the rain fall outside. When would it stop? First the ash and now this: a paralyzing rain holding us hostage in this house. Reality hit me again and a wave of paranoia crashed like thunder in my head, or was that real thunder? You're too damn sensitive, Joel, I scolded myself. Take a lesson from Earl. Learn a thing or two about keeping it all down. God, I respected that cool son of a bitch! I didn't think anyone save Connor was holding up as well. My neck craned to see around the corner and into the living room, where we'd laid Jake on one of the reclining chairs, and wondered how he would fare.

"Have you seen Jake today, John?" I ask, ready to recite my recent story.

"No Jake sightings this morning to report." We all laughed, recalling the novelty of a 'Jake sighting' in the past. "Of course there aren't any ditches or park benches in your house so I wouldn't know where to look!" he added. We each chuckled again under our breath.

Speak of the devil and he'll appear. Jake strolled into the kitchen as if on cue. Caught off guard, we went quiet, and I greeted him with a wave. He went to the fridge, pulled out a Coke, and left without a word.

Shit, did that ever make me feel like a first class asshole, especially after the speech I'd given Jake about cleaning up. I could see that we were all feeling the same: ashamed, of ourselves and our thoughtless words.

"Sorry, Joel," John studied the crumbs on his plate.

"Not your fault, John. I'll go talk to him." I pushed my chair back.

I found Jake curled up on the floor in a corner of the family room, shaking. Coming down, I guessed, and too embarrassed to ask for another hit. I knelt and laid a gentle hand on his back. He wasn't responsive, but I couldn't blame him. God, I felt like shit.

Sensing the presence of someone behind us, I looked over my shoulder and saw Connor standing in the hall, staring at the air above us. His gaze was fixed, his expression indecipherable. When I questioned him with a single raised brow, he slowly approached.

"Joel," he whispered, "he's back. He's with you both."

My skin crawled and tears came in force. I buried my face in my arm. A strange feeling of calm replaced the angst and paranoia that had overcome me in the kitchen, knowing we were being watched by a higher power. As a soothing presence engulfed us both, even Jake's shaking stopped.

Kevin approached Connor in the hall and noticed his bizarre stance. He realized right away what was happening.

"You see him, don't you? It's the angel isn't it?"

Connor didn't speak. At this point the girls and John joined the group in the hall and Kevin explained what was happening. Sara crouched next to me and kissed my face. After several minutes, Jake's body relaxed. He sat up and looked at his hands, which had stopped shaking.

"Did you feel that?" he asked. Wonder and bliss settled over his features, drying the tears and restoring color to his hollow cheeks. "It's like I shed my skin."

In a moment of fleeting clarity, I saw a changed man. I touched his arm, wanting to tell him how proud I was, how proud he should be. But words wouldn't come; nothing would, so I just let it go. Sara, smiling, helped me up.

The others surrounded Jake and knelt down beside him, excitedly lifting him to his feet, trying to get a read on what had just happened. Jake was smiling, ear to ear, his chest heaving dramatically as he took in deep, cleansing breaths. His personal struggle was over. I felt that much through touch, while it was happening. I felt the ecstasy of being freed of the addiction that was killing him. There was much more to this angel than met the eye.

*****

Later that day in Skylab, Kevin brought me the pipe, which had been making its rounds behind me. The group had gathered here again to blow off some steam.

"Hell of a party, eh Joel?"

I nodded and pulled deeply on the pipe. He was fidgeting, probably a side effect of the pot. "That was really something we witnessed today," he coughed. "Jake's obviously been hit pretty hard by the scene. How are you doing?"

"I'm fine, man." I tell him through tight lips, holding the smoke captive in my lungs just a little longer.

"Man, I got a few seriously wild paintings to do soon." He changed the subject, realizing that he wouldn't get much more out of me. "I had this dream the other night. It was so surreal... like what's happening all around us, you know? Surreal."

"Dream, huh? Do tell, Kev, what are you dreaming about these days?" Ironically, it was the same question he'd asked of me when searching for new material to create, not long ago.

"It freaked me out when I woke up because I never remember my dreams, besides the reoccurring face." He struggled to remember it now though. "Yeah, it went like this. First I saw a leg, without a foot." A shiver ran through me as I recalled the same dream. He continued, "Next came a wing, a feathered wing and following that was a hand... sickly looking, you know? Sickly. The background was a blue watercolor, really working into the deeper tones of the body parts." Now he was fully reliving the dream, using gestures to demonstrate how the images would glide in front of him. "And some other disturbing things. Body parts, animals… a horn…"

"What do you think it all means?" I asked, wondering if my interpretation of the dream would match his.

"It's pretty self-explanatory if you ask me."

"Let's have it."

"It's all about the struggle of man, good versus evil. The body parts are those of a man, maybe mine, and the wing isn't a bird, but an angel! Makes sense right? The horn isn't that of an animal, but the devil."

It did make sense. But was it too much of a coincidence? Were Kevin and I repressing something we'd actually seen? And now, as people were apt to do, were we attempting to look for reason in the horrors of what we'd witnessed? The whole thing with the angel and Jake's transformation suddenly left a bitter taste in my mouth. Look at us morons, looking for hope in this wasteland. I reached for the pipe again, but misjudged my aim and tumbled off the chair. Kevin laughed and lapsed into stoned bliss. I never did tell him we'd shared the same dream. I needed to accumulate more information before I could put the whole picture together.

At two-thirty in the morning, I decided to call it a night. Sara followed closely behind. When we were alone in my bedroom, she presented me with her family Bible. Trying not to disturb the waterbed, we slid onto the rubber mattress, settling on top of the sheets. I wasn't exactly in the mood for such heavy reading just then; all I wanted was a solid night's sleep. "Want me to read to you?"

Not really. But I said,"Sure."

"Alright then, I'll start with something light." I think she read a chapter or a Psalm or something. Whatever it was, it served as my background music, the words melting together as I slipped into a deep, undisturbed slumber. If people needed hope, let them have it. Who knew how long it would last?

Chapter Fourteen

The days that followed that single shot of hope and enlightenment all passed in a gloomy sameness. There were no wandering vagabonds to feed or repel, and we stayed away from town as the acid rain continued its work on anything made of oil and metal. A short run to the neighboring farmhouses did little for our weakened spirits. If they weren't abandoned, they were inhabited by the dead. People I'd known my whole life.

The big book of Sara's kept me entertained through much of the 'rainy season', as we termed it. I read the whole thing, mainly out of curiosity. The most powerful story was, as Sara and Sidney had said that night at the lake, the book of Revelation. Powerful because it was so absolute about the end of the world and a second coming. The Four Horsemen were prevalent. Nasty imagery too, not exactly difficult to conjure up when I was already faced with an ugly reality. But I imagined that at the time the Bible was written, people would have happily seen the end of the world come so they could go to paradise. It almost made me wish this 'end' would come. Were we in a limbo or something? It was written that when the end of the world came, man would seek death and not find it. We were not there yet, we were still hanging on to life, but perhaps that too was not far off.

The days just seemed to blend into one another. I'd lost count at day seventeen. I hadn't even realized that so many had passed until Gil showed me the calendar he'd fashioned from an old school notebook in the kitchen.

"The army isn't picking us up, are they, Joel?" he asked. I'd been asking myself the same question, but Gil looked so worried that I couldn't bring myself to distress him further.

"I'm not counting them out yet. Listen, Gil, we can't give up on ourselves, not ever." Even if doubts had crept like dark shadows into my head, there was no point in letting on. Some leader that would make.

He didn't reply, just picked the M-16 up off the floor and walked to the sliding glass door. The view should have been serene. It should have encompassed the balcony, back deck, pool and woods beyond. We should have been contemplating a swim or a trip through the forest on the five-wheeler.

"Don't know how much longer I can keep it together." His voice was hollow. "I don't know. The sadness, everyone's sadness… I hear them, their cries in the night, the walls can't contain it. I can't listen to it anymore." He began to jerk as emotion overwhelmed him and the tears came. "It can't go on like this, Joel, I know I can't."

I joined him at the glass door and watched the darkness distort all that I loved, all that we were. It wasn't easy to keep it together when somebody else was losing it, but I felt I had a responsibility to be strong. We stood there for God only knows how long. The sky was as the earth, muddied, wretched and dark. You could suffer a case of vertigo from staring for too long.

Standing there, remembering all that this view once offered- the beautiful vistas in the fall, the lush greens of the summer foliage, the crisp whites of winter snow- I realized that memory was all that remained of this place. In my mind's eye I saw the sun come out and cleanly sweep over the trees and the lawn, the field and the pool; all that I knew were there, but could no longer see through the thick black rain falling hard from a bitter sky, just beyond the glass.

"Did you see it?" Never taking my eyes off the scene, I hoped the vision would return. It was so short lived. Was I shown a possible future? Or did I just fall back into memory to protect myself from the present?

"What? Did you say something, Joel?" Gil's response was slow and hollow. He was only reacting to the sound of my voice, never relinquishing his stare into the abyss.

"Forget it," I answered, knowing what I'd seen was nothing more than a memory.

"There's a hole, you know?" Gil was starting to scare me. I listened as his voice took on a sobering new tone. "A huge hole...and I can't fill it, not here, not now." He stared at himself in the blackened glass as the rain snaked down its smooth surface. "No one can... such a hole, nothing to fill it." He paused, flexing his jaw muscles. "Only pain to feed it."

"Gil, listen, man. We're all going through the same shit here. We just have to stick together. Talk to me or Seth when you're feeling down. Talk to someone. It's only been seventeen days, Gil. We've all got cabin fever. It won't last forever."

"I'll keep that in mind." He turned and headed for the basement stairs. "Thanks, Joel."

When he disappeared from view, I headed for the family room to check the guard schedule. Anything to keep from thinking as much as Gil was.

*****

Day nineteen, or close to it. I was sitting up in Skylab with Sara, Seth, Gil, Freddy and Sidney, watching Kevin create another dark masterpiece. Sonny, Jake and Connor were on duty. Sonny was so stunned at Jake's recovery that he would spend endless minutes just looking at him, studying him. Jake took great pride in his sobriety. He had become someone to respect.

"So, what exactly is it you're painting there, Kev?" Fred asked.

"It seems so twisted." Sara chewed her lower lip. "Your stuff's so dark."

"For me, art thrives on the dark side. The dark pieces are always stronger, don't you find? Like memories. I bet your first memory is a bad one. Mine is. Don't you find you remember those feelings best?" He stepped back from his canvas and felt out the perspective. "Even good feelings turned bad are more memorable than purely good feelings. Say you're at a park and it's a sunny afternoon. You're loving life, sipping at your wine, sprawled out on a blanket. But then it starts to storm and your picnic is ruined. You won't remember the sunny part, only the rain." He brushed a line of paint on the canvas. "It's the way we are. We can't help but be pessimists; we recall the bad over the good. And so art should imitate life and be dark and sad: that way, as an artist I'm appealing to your most powerful memory. You don't know why you like it, but you do." He stopped to drink from his juice box. "But hey, maybe that's just me!"

No. You weren't alone in that, Kevin.

*****

The anniversary of our first full month alone in the world was anything but a celebration. It wasn't because we'd developed cabin fever or resigned ourselves to the probability that the military was not coming. No, something terrible happened that day, an event which would prove devastating to the morale of the group.

The fateful morning started the same as every other. We each got up at different hours, depending on our schedule in the addition. Connor and I were pulling an eight to four shift with John. We met at the kitchen sink, where John was pouring water for tea and coffee.

"Gentlemen, ready for your coffee?" he greeted us.

Connor yawned and coughed. We'd all been inflicted with the same nasty cough as a result of our close confinement. He took the steaming mug John held out. "Thanks, buddy. Just what the doctor ordered."

I also accepted a cup. "Looks like we may have to hit town for some more coffee," I said, peering into the final tin. It was barely half full.

"Don't joke about it." Connor lifted his face from his mug. "All work and no coffee makes Connor …"

"Alright, alright, don't go all Jack Nicholson on our ass," John admonished as he stirred sugar into his tea. "I bet we could find plenty of canned goods still untouched at the Super Store."

"Well, when it becomes necessary to venture back into town we'll go," I stated. "But only if we absolutely have to. A tin of coffee ain't that important."

"It's important," sulked Connor.

John and I laughed, and as usual our laughter was accompanied by deep, chesty coughs. I caught my breath. "It's not worth going into town if the rain ruins the wheels on the Caddy. Who knows when we'll need her." My dad's Cadillac had been safely stored in the garage since before our camping trip and so had not sustained any damage from the rains.

On arriving in Skylab we met Seth, Sonny and Freddy. Their eyes looked red and tired, the result of staring blankly into the darkness for hours.

"Get me up when the rain stops," Seth said as they passed us on the way out.

"Alright, let's get settled, should be an exciting morning!" My sarcasm was duly noted. I couldn't have known or been more embarrassed on realizing just how prophetic those words would turn out to be.

Suddenly Freddy thundered upstairs and burst into our midst, eyes the size of saucers and face a ghastly shade of green. "They're cutting him down right now," he gasped. "It's Gil. He did it, man. He's dead..."

Too shocked to speak, we followed him downstairs to the basement. Seth was on his knees, bent over the motionless vessel that once housed our friend. Gil's tongue protruded through his purple lips, his eyes blood red. The scene came into focus one detail at a time. The noose, which he had fashioned from a belt and attached to a rafter in the ceiling, cut deeply into his neck. The chair he launched himself from lay several feet away. Seth had cut him down with the fishing knife he kept on his person at all times.

Gil didn't want to live, not like this anyway. He'd told me that in not so many words. But I told him to talk to me!

His skin was pale, his expression sickening. I'd never seen a dead person. My dad's body had been cremated, as the accident had destroyed his features beyond repair. But Gil was a complete person, just with all the life drained from his face. I tried to process it. I just spoke to him the day before! CPR wasn't even an option. There would be no bringing Gil back.

Damn it, Gil.

Seth cried, blaming himself over and over again. I knelt beside him. "He did this, Seth... not you. This isn't your fault..."

"He said stuff, you know?" Seth struggled to speak. "He said things, I should have known, I could've..."

He put Gil's head down softly and raised his to the sky. "FUCK YOU!" he screamed. Then, broken, he slumped over the body. I squeezed his shoulder and stood. We left him with Gil to make his peace. Upstairs, we gave the others the grim news, preparing everyone for a funeral.

The girls wept openly. The guys shifted in their seats uncomfortably, cursing under their breath.

"Why did he hang himself, man?" Sidney asked no one in particular. "Why not use his gun? Why did he hang himself?"

"What now?" Sonny asked the question that was on everyone's mind. "What do we do now?"

"Now we wait. We wait for Seth." I turned to leave the kitchen. We could only leave the house unguarded for so long. Turning back, I added. "He'll let us know what he wants done and when."

*****

Seth finally came up from the basement later that afternoon and asked us to help him bury Gil in the back woods, by the small creek where they'd first fished together.

"He'd have wanted to be by the water, where the fish are..."

Seth had prepared his friend's body with almost loving care, wrapping it in cloth from head to toe and placing a fishing rod in its embrace He gave a eulogy, something stirring, powerful and yet I can't recall a single line. I just tried to keep it together, if for no one else then for Gil.

Four of us carried Gil out the basement doors, beyond the pool that was now filthy beyond repair. We almost lost our footing on the slick muck that had once been a beautiful lawn. Our journey to the river was a short one, and once we were sheltered by the trees, the rain didn't seem so bad. Sonny, Freddy, John and I picked up shovels and dug the grave by the river. Then Seth and Kevin lowered the body into the hot earth. A brief moment of silence fell over us until Seth gave the signal to fill in the hole. After Sara led the group in a prayer, we left.

That evening was spent in quiet contemplation as each of us mourned in our own way. Rest in peace, Gil. You will be missed.

Chapter Fifteen

The days that followed Gil's demise were quiet and unsettling for everyone. Nobody talked much. Much as this should already have dawned on us, we suddenly started to realize our own mortality, and that was hard. We were teenagers for Christ's sake; we shouldn't have been worried about mortality. Even when my dad died I didn't think about dying. With Gil it was different. He was our age. He had been young and healthy. And we had been there to witness it. Death of one of our own had now stared us in the face.

We had to get out, or convince ourselves we could, before the gloom and fear made someone else do something stupid. With Kevin's help, I graphed a map of the surrounding area within a ten kilometer radius. The map was then mounted on the east wall of Skylab. The point was not merely to raise our spirits by suggesting a future exodus: it was a necessary step to mark the boundaries of what we'd laid claim to and see what was out there, what was left. With the group gathered in the addition, I laid out a future plan.

"We all want out of this house, right? I know I do. I am proposing that we do it." I pointed at the map. "Earl has had this idea from the very start and I feel that now is the time. We should begin surveying; we need to see what is out there."

Earl took it from there. "I've been measuring the rainfall in a steel bucket for the last seven days and have noticed a considerable difference in the amount that fell the first day in comparison to today. In fact each day since I began the experiment, the water level has been decreasing. I think that soon it'll stop altogether. Then we can get out and scout the terrain."

"This is good news," I announced. "This is what we've been waiting for, real proof." I felt the group's excitement. The morale in the room hit a new high.

"Connor's going to pair up those that want to be in the surveying crews," Earl continued. "We'll likely have to arrange for additional shifts up here. You don't have to be on an outside crew if you don't want to."

Everyone's hand shot up. Connor jotted each person's name down in his notebook, and then organized them into groups of two and three. Meeting adjourned, we each poured a drink from the bar. A guitar came out of retirement, serving as background to our excited chatter.

Seth approached me later that evening with a disturbing piece of literature salvaged from Gil's belongings. "Don't want to bring you down, Joel," he began as he handed me a binder. "I only wanted you to see this, as I guess Gil had intended us all to."

Seeing my puzzled expression, he explained. "It's his suicide letter, you know? It's self righteous garbage, justification, a conversation with himself." He twisted the top off his piss-warm beer, slammed the bottle to his lips and swallowed as much as he could before he was forced to take a breath. "Talking himself into the position I found him in: hanging from the ceiling!"

"Seth, I don't know what it was that Gil could have been thinking in order to have done what he did, and if it says why in here, I'm not going to read it. You have to believe that there wasn't shit we could have done to prevent it, not in these conditions." I closed the journal. "We need to remember how Gil lived, not the way he died." With that said, I returned the book to him and walked away.

*****

The following day witnessed the first of the outdoor expeditions. We'd been fighting the mental strain of the day-to-day lockdown, fading under a black sky that concealed a forgotten sun. This was our chance to get outside and beat back the malaise. That's what killed Gil after all, and I didn't need to read his goddamn suicide note to put it together. Stuff he thought and the things he'd seen were shared experiences amongst the group. What he did about it though, was another story.

The first crew consisted of Earl, Connor, and Sidney. We decided to send them east, to the farm where Sonny and I had found the massive drug warehouse. Their mission: to survey the surrounding area, bring back what remained of the drug stash, and report on the farm's condition.

We'd realized that the hydroponics would be perfect for growing food. The idea came to me when I was rearranging the cold room and found seed packets that never made it to the hardware store: carrots, lettuce, celery, a veritable vegetable garden!

Sonny was the navigator, naturally, Connor was at the wheel and Earl sat in the back of the five-wheeler, gun poised, always prepared, a real survivalist. It felt as though we were sending them to the moon or further. They were dressed in layers, each holding an umbrella to protect them from the driving rain. I wished I could go with them, but there was too much to be done here. John had the flu so I was taking over his guard shift in Skylab.

The hours that followed proved as uneventful as the many hundred hours we'd clocked in the addition. But when John announced their return, we sprang to life, rushing to meet them at the door.

Success! It took them all of two hours to return with garbage bags of the choice weed and more good news. The barn was holding its own. The interior hadn't yet been breached, keeping the operation useable for a new kind of plant.

"The hydroponics looked good." Sonny set his garbage bag on the hall floor. "We'll need some fuel though. Their generator is dry."

"I checked it out," Earl pitched in. "It should work fine. The whole set-up is amazing and it draws from its own well."

"Eden," grinned Sonny. I smiled too, remembering that he'd said the same thing when we first saw the strange interior.

"Wow!" Connor exclaimed as he pushed the filthy hood off his head. "I haven't ever seen anything like it!"

Once they were all inside, Sara secured the door. "How is it out there?" she asked. "How's the rain?"

Earl answered. "Not too terrible. I swear it's starting to really taper off. It still smells like sour milk out there though."

The remainder of the afternoon was spent doing a food count and preparing the seeds to take back to the barn the next day. But that night, in the kitchen, Connor came to me with a growing concern for his girlfriend's state of mind. Apparently she'd been dwelling on Gil's suicide, wondering if he hadn't had the right idea. This shocked Connor, knowing how out of character that comment was for Julia.

"She just said it so matter-of-factly, like it had been on her mind since before Gil did it. Like she'd considered it herself."

I tried to reassure him. "She's just sorting herself out. You telling me you haven't thought about it? I'll tell you something, man, the thought crossed my mind. I'll bet it's crossed everyone's at one time." My mouth was dry, so I poured a glass of water from the tap. I took a sip- and promptly spit it into the sink. "Shit, I think there's something wrong with the well water!"

"Damn!" Connor groaned. "All that rain sinking into the soil had to affect the quality of the water sometime." He turned on the tap and poured a glass. We studied it and noticed a slight tint.

"Looks like city water," I said.

"Probably not much worse for you either." John joined us. "Let me have a taste."

Connor gave John the glass, and he took a sip. "Nope, no worse. That's pretty much what it was like last time I lived there. We're just used to better here in the country."

"You're sure, John?" I asked.

"Hey, if it gets any uglier than that we should worry, but for now I'm telling you it'll do more good than harm in this environment." He opened the fridge and threw some cold meat into his mouth, followed by a soft drink.

The perishables, like cold meat were nearing the end of their course, and soon we'd be left with canned goods and freeze-dried noodles. Until we got the hydroponics garden going, that is.

With John out of earshot, Connor continued where he had left off. "So you don't think I should worry about Julia's..."

"I don't know what to tell you, Connor," I said. "Gil talked some pretty disturbing shit before he did it."

"Then I'll talk to her. Maybe she just needs to talk about it some more."

"I'm sorry, I don't mean to switch off on you, Connor. I wasn't any help to Gil. But yeah, talk to her. It can't hurt. I'm going to bed- see you tomorrow."

"Sure, man. Thanks."

Reaching my bedroom, I slowly opened the door so as not to wake Sara, who'd finished a shift in Skylab not long before. Collapsing on the couch, I looked at Rex, who was backlit by the alarm clock on my desk. I got comfortable and leaned into him.

"What do you say, Rex?" I whispered. "Gil's dead, did I tell you that already? He killed himself, hung himself. Now Julia's considering it. Connor's worried. Me, I just don't want to deal with it again. If Julia does do something stupid I don't know how I'll react. I scare myself. If I say the wrong thing or don't say anything at all, which is worse? Which is going to push someone over the edge? Probably better I say something, anything at all, but I said things to Gil and that didn't help. Man, what do I know?"

Snapping out of the conversation with myself, I directed the same question at Rex. "What do you know?" I smiled. Feeling better, as I usually did when I confronted myself, I joined Sara in bed.

That night the skunk came to me in a dream, although I fell asleep with a clear head. This was the first time that he appeared to me while I wasn't drunk or high. But I was vulnerable in sleep, and that was apparently enough to spark another visit. He came soon after I'd drifted off. I was in the midst of a nightmare of sorts; I remember feeling very exposed, defenseless. I don't remember where or why, but my friends were with me. The moon was in the sky, making me pine for the days when I could sit and stare at the moon and the stars for hours. That moment dissolved into a scene set in a forest, at the lake where we'd spent our last normal weekend. I could only imagine how it looked now. When the skunk appeared and sauntered over to me on his hind legs, I greeted him with a smile, sure now that he was my guardian.

He turned and waved for me to follow. As we walked deeper into the woods he spoke. "You have more to do here. Live for them. Things will change, things will get better." Then he left me.

I ran after him. "Stop! Stop, damn it! I have a question! I need to ask you..."

The image of the woods intensified. I could smell the pine, feel the needles against my face as I pushed through the dense brush. Suddenly the air turned damp and cool, and the forest floor morphed into a thick sticky muck that stopped me in my tracks. "Damn it!" I fumed.

My shouting woke me up. That wasn't so unusual, as I'd roused myself before by talking in my sleep. What stunned me was that I woke up outside, in the woods behind my house. I didn't know where I was at first. I shook my head and made damn sure I was awake. Satisfied that the dream was over and I was definitely outside, I pulled my bare feet out of a patch of deep sludge and began the short walk up the trail back to the house.

I had chased the skunk in my dream, and ended up out here. Why did that happen? He'd said that things would change, things would get better. What did he mean? The answer, I realized as I came out of the woods, was all around me. Actually, it was no longer all around me! The rains had stopped!

I charged toward the house, forgetting that I was visible from Skylab and that if the guard on duty was paying any attention at all, I might be shot. The back sliding door was locked, so I hurried around the north side to the front where, I assumed, I'd made my escape. Sure enough, the front doors were unlocked. On entering the foyer, I slipped on the tile. Regaining my balance, I shuffled through the house, shouting triumphantly.

The group assembled at the front door. When I was sure that the whole house was present, I simply opened the front door and walked out, arms raised and grinning from ear to ear.

Their reaction was priceless. They walked tentatively out of the house, hands extended, feeling for rain. The beautiful reality struck everyone at the same moment. We danced in the front yard like a bunch of lunatics, some of us screaming at the top of our lungs, while others were too spellbound to even speak. Needless to say, no one made it back to bed until the early hours of the morning. Our situation was improving, maybe in response to our bold move in venturing outdoors despite the weather. Take a little and get a little. Now there was hope, hope for something better. Perhaps now, with the burning rain gone, the rivers and soil would find a way to regenerate.

The skunk had led me to salvation when we needed it most. I no longer doubted that he was in fact the spirit of Connor's angel, our angel. I felt awful for Gil, who did not live to savor the moment.

*****

The sky was still ominous, a perpetual midnight, but without the rain, it was easier to bear. I kept checking the phone lines. After all, 'what if', right? But communication with the outside world, such as it was, remained dead.

Mapping and marking of the terrain had been completed and now we only needed to fence off our property. One afternoon Freddy and I stood on the porch, looking at our charts and discussing it. Caroline looked on from the steps, where she had been sitting just for the sake of being outside.

"What will we use as fencing for a job that size?" she asked.

Freddy offered several possibilities. "We have access to good sources of organic fencing like large driftwood pieces and dead trees. We also found some rolls of snow fencing and barbed wire at the barn. Oh, speaking of the barn, Joel: how's the garden growing?"

"Connor's got garden duty." Gesturing toward the sky, I added, "Now we wait for the sun."

Caroline sighed and adjusted her bra, the only top she'd wear in this heat. "The day I have to wear my sunglasses; that'll be the day. Have you given any thought about going north now that we can travel again?"

"Perhaps in a few weeks we'll send a scout party to find out what's happening there, but for now, right here is where we need to be. Shit's getting better, and I think it's worth holding on to for as long as we can."

She stretched and got up. "Yeah, this is home. I'm going inside- see you in a bit."

Freddy looked intrigued. "You really think the sun'll come out?"

"Who are you, Little Orphan Annie?" We laughed. "What do I know? A little skunk told me." I headed toward the garage, leaving Freddy with more questions than answers.

Sonny was unwrapping the Cadillac. "Pretty sweet huh?" I offered as I joined him and ran my hand along its smooth metal surface. "My dad was the last to drive her. Sweet ride, though. I rode shotgun the last time."

"Are we putting her back on the street?"

"Eventually - we need to hit town soon. Connor was there with Kevin early yesterday. They said there were still grocery stores full of food."

"Cool, sign me up for the next tour of duty." He rolled the tarp back over the car.

"Count on it, big man!" I slapped his shoulder, and then noticed movement under the car. Just as I was about to say something, I realized what it was: the skunk, my skunk. Sonny left the garage. Kneeling down, I whispered, "Listen, had I known you were in here, I would have brought you a little something to eat. I'll leave you some food tonight."

"Talking to yourself again?" Connor was back from the barn. "I thought we'd covered that?"

"Jesus, man! Stop sneaking up on me!" I punched him in the arm as he faked a block. "I was just talking to the car." I slapped away his weak attempt at retribution and grinned. "Cars are people too."

"Your dad would appreciate that." It was true: he would. "I've got some good news for us. The first few plants are showing growth."

"What! That's great, man!" Giddy with success, we continued to play-fight until Connor had me in a headlock. Then we went inside, where we found the girls playing cards at the kitchen table with Sidney.

"Where's Jake, Joel?" Sara asked. She looked up from her hand, munching on a saltine cracker.

"I don't know. Where should he be? Is he on duty again?" I studied the schedule posted on the wall.

"No. It's just that he hasn't been around for the last... well, I think the last time I saw him was yesterday!"

"Is he not upstairs?

"No need to worry," declared Jake as he entered the kitchen. "I'm not lost. Not anymore." He smiled strangely at me as he helped himself to a slice of bread and peanut butter from the cupboard.

"Where have you been, Jake?" Julia asked.

"I was meditating in the yard, just beyond the shack. There's a spot there that's got all of the light. I'll have to show you guys. It's beautiful, really. My fortress of solitude. It can be all of ours if you like."

"Light? What light? What's he talking about, Joel?" Julia, still uneasy around Jake despite his recent rejuvenation, turned to me.

"There's no light, Julia, there's nothing outside." I faced Jake again. "In the future, we'd like it if you could just let somebody know when you're going to be out. You had the girls worried."

"My apologies," he said, although he sounded far from contrite. "It won't happen again." He then took his leave.

"Well, that's that, I guess. All's well that ends well," commented Kevin. I followed him out and stopped him in the hallway.

"Say, Kev, are you done those paintings yet?"

"Well, I was sort of working on all of them at the same time so no, they're not done just yet." He leaned in closer. "Just out of curiosity, have you or Connor seen the angel again? It's just that I find it all very inspirational, for my art, and obviously for our future."

I wished I could tell him we had, but the truth was that I hadn't ever really seen anything, and Connor would likely have told me if he'd witnessed the apparition again. I just shrugged.

"Alright. No harm in asking, right?" Kevin seemed so hyper, jittery. Maybe he had been into the pot. Not a terrible idea, really.

*****

The following week proved productive, as we'd successfully grown the seedlings in the hydroponics lab and a trip into town netted more food and supplies. I left a bowl of water and some dog food out in the garage for Stinky. I cherished a strong connection to that skunk, and felt obliged to support him.

Days were still virtually as dark as the nights but there was a different feeling pervading the group now. We were no longer helpless, no longer required to stay indoors and wait for God to fix things. No, now we were able to try and improve our lot on our own steam.

Mom's hardware store was in the town to the west of us, and we all agreed that the time had come to make the journey there and see what we could scavenge.

"So who's coming?" I asked as we gathered at the foot of the driveway.

"I'll come," volunteered Kevin, throwing his semi-automatic over his shoulder.

"Me too, count me in!" Earl, armed to the teeth and resembling more a mercenary than a recent High School graduate, raised his fist.

"Okay, I got Kev and Earl. I have room for one more in the Caddy."

"I'd like to come. Julia and Sonny are on garden duty today so…" But despite his offer, Connor seemed strangely apprehensive about volunteering.

"Alright man, you sure?" Then it hit me: he knew we were going to Mom's store. His brother had worked there, maybe even died there. "It's cool if you want to hang back, Connor."

"No, no, I want to. I have to."

"Say no more- get in."

The drive was longer than I remembered. It never took more than twenty five or thirty minutes, but today, what with pitch darkness and slippery roads, the short trip became a marathon. This road was much more widely travelled than our route home from the lake had been, and we passed dozens of abandoned vehicles and one transport truck that had veered into a ditch. When we reached our destination, we beheld mirror images of the carnage in our own main street. Downed lamp posts, windows blown out, blackened brick, rusted fencing; all signs of a great fire that swallowed much of its resources.

The grocery store here appeared to have been thoroughly looted, as did the army surplus outlet where Connor had acquired so many of his accessories in the past. That was alarming, so caution ruled the day. I cruised along the main drag, passing one sacked shop after another, while Earl and Kevin gripped their guns and scanned the empty sidewalks and alleys. Clumps of filthy clothing concealed the dead, who'd been dragged into the streets from their homes and businesses. Some were charred, burned to discourage an imagined outbreak of some ancient plague. So there it was – proof, proof that there were others who survived the initial weeks of ash and rain. Were they still here? Were they still occupying this looted wasteland, lying in wait to overpower us and take what little we had? Whatever the case, we were prepared.

The storefront came into view on our approach to Third Street. Like the other buildings on the block, it was a smashed, hollowed-out shell. My throat tightened as memories assailed me. Four months ago, Mom and Connor's brother Duncan had requested my assistance with the inventory count. Despite my complaining, I always ended up with clipboard in hand, jotting down the numbers. Shit, I'd have given my left arm to be holding that clipboard right now.

I pulled into the parking lot slowly, rumbling over the downed chain link fence. Earl was the first to enter the premises through the fire entrance, whose battered door swung from one hinge. Kevin remained outside, standing guard while we staked out the interior.

Connor's anxiety bubbled through his otherwise calm exterior. I asked him if he wanted to stay with Kevin.

"No, Duncan's not here." He said it with such certainty that I just took his word for it. "He didn't die here."

"Okay," I said. "Okay, let's get on with it." A slap on the shoulder offered some encouragement. We split up, covering the three aisles at a slow and steady pace.

"Looks as empty as the rest of this ghost town," Earl commented when we regrouped.

"Someone's been here, but they've long since gone," I added.

"Where do we hit first?" Earl looked about the store, although there appeared to be little left that we could use.

"The back room should still have boxes of seeds for the barn garden, and I think we'll find tools and stuff behind the counter."

Earl and I looted the main part of the store, collecting whatever batteries, cables, flashlights, and light bulbs remained. Connor slipped into the back room to gather up the seeds. We were carrying our second load to the car when I realized that Connor was still in the back. Going in, I found him immersed in another of his trance-like states.

"You alright, old man?" I asked.

"Sorry. Yeah. I got stopped in the moment. Another déja-vu."

"No shit. That one lasted forever."

"I didn't let it break. I let it run its natural course." He smiled slightly. "It was... educational."

I started to feel uncomfortable, and looked for an out. "Well, maybe you'll share it with me some time, but right now Earl's doing all of the work and Kevin is starting to freak a little. I think we should get going." I picked up a box of seeds, and Connor followed.

Kevin was getting a bit antsy outside, complaining that there was too much going on for a ghost town. Several shadows moved on account of a cool wind that had picked up from the north, pushing its way through the lifeless trees that lined the perimeter of the lot.

"Are you almost done in there?" he called. "I really think we ought to go."

"Chill out, buddy," Earl chided him gently. "We've got another couple loads to bring out. Stay sharp!"

I approached with my car keys, not trusting Kevin to stay calm for much longer. "Kev, do me favor and start up the Caddy."

"Sure, Joel!" Relieved, Kevin hopped into the driver's side and turned the engine on. Behind the wheel, he visibly relaxed. He sat there, scanning the environment, until we finished loading up. Then he yielded the driver's seat to me and joined Earl in the back.

As we passed a bank on the way home, Earl commented, "Hey, we should rob it."

"What would be the point?" replied Kevin. What indeed?

It was then we first saw the flag, a symbol that would again change the way we lived, the way we viewed our existence in this sad new world. It went up like a rocket in the distance, beyond a blackened gas station. A chant arose, so loudly that we could hear it over the hum of my motor. None of us could make out what they were chanting, but we recognized the flag emblem, and it scared the shit out of us.

Drawing closer, we saw that they'd blocked the road. We stared at each other, breathing heavily, the sweat of fear dotting our faces. Then I slammed my foot down on the pedal and sped past them, scattering them and destroying their piece-of-shit barricade. If this was supposed to be an ambush, then it was a pathetic attempt.

"What the hell was that!?" shouted Kevin.

"I don't know." My eyes were locked on the road ahead. "But I sure as hell wasn't going to stick around to ask."

"Those were people, man!" Earl exclaimed. "People!"

"What do you want to do… go back and introduce ourselves?" I asked. "Didn't you hear them and see that flag? You want to get mixed up with that?"

"No, but…. I don't know... all I know is that those were people! Shit! Just when I was starting to think that we were it! Man, people." He fell silent, but you could see a thousand different scenarios playing themselves out in his mind, his eyes moving back and forth in their sunken sockets.

It took the remainder of the trip for the color to return to my face. I felt a little embarrassed, but damn! That was a shot of adrenaline. Nothing more was said. Our thoughts were our own, each of us experiencing his own brand of possibilities. I wondered if we'd encounter this cult again. The scenarios that played themselves out in my mind weren't good.

Chapter Sixteen

Back at the house, we told the group what had happened, and Kevin drew the flag on the addition wall. Its wheel-shaped emblem was yellow and black, stark color against a cruel, ruinous background.

I wondered what priorities the flag-bearers set above ours, and what rules, if any, they lived by. Could they possibly be friends who mistook us for enemies? Or was it better to simply view them as the enemy and deal with them accordingly? What would we do if they were to show up on the property? Would we let them get that far? So far we believed that violence was a failure to communicate. At least that was my stand. Earl saw things a little differently, but he would follow my lead should things escalate to an actual encounter. Adrenaline had taken over in town, and diplomacy might have been lost on them given the circumstances. But should we believe that they would always be hostile, or should we still assume that people are inherently good and give them the benefit of the doubt? "Give them that and we lose our opportunity. We lose surprise," Earl would say. And he was right. That was reality, but that was cruel wasn't it? Shouldn't they be offered a chance to move on, to live? Maybe they were prepared to kill us that day. Maybe we shouldn't allow them a second chance. They would not have given us one. We could not hesitate for a moment: this was war.

"Joel!" Connor called to me. He was standing next to the generator, situated just beneath the back balcony. I had wandered into the backyard via the walk-out basement. "We've got a problem!"

"What's the problem?" I asked, knowing full well what it must be. When I arrived, he shifted aside, allowing me to view the meter.

"You see that? Fuels not going to last much longer."

"Looks like we'll have to make another trip," I said. "We knew this was coming." Dad had designed the house with a huge underground tank, but in spite of our efforts to conserve the fuel, it was nearly dry. "The generator at the farm is running on empty too, right?"

"Right. That's why I came to check the house supply. We can't really afford to pull any from here though." Connor closed the gate on the generator shed and walked with me down to the garbage pit.

The facts were the facts. We needed fuel or in the next week we'd be completely out. The comfortable lifestyle we'd become accustomed to would disappear. With the generator, battery cells, pump, and septic tank working, this house was a bio-bubble, but without large quantities of fossil fuels it was a dead fish, good for nothing more than keeping the elements out. Oil was no problem, but we hadn't had any use for the furnace. The septic seeped into the soil as well as into the tank and only needed to be pumped once every five years or so. The pump and electricity worked off the generator and the generator worked off gasoline. Therefore we needed fuel.

I'd had the attendant at 'Joe's Gas and Snacks' fill our tank with the black gold before the lake weekend and it had just about run its course. Next I'd have to find a station that hadn't been devastated by the fallout, and where on earth would that be? North, I thought, it would be north.

"We'll have to go north," I decided.

Connor agreed. "There are a couple stations just northeast of us that may have something left to offer. I don't think we ought to go west again for anything."

"I hear that. I don't want us running into those people again unless it's on our terms. We should try Joe's first."

We loaded empty canisters into the Caddy, opened the garage door, and backed out passing the vehicle graveyard that was once my front lawn. Catching Sonny on his way into the house he climbed into the back seat and we were on our way.

The ride into town was uneventful. The quiet of the place was eerie. We pulled into Joe's and managed to fill the Caddy's tank, but feared that we had asked our last favor of 'Joe's Gas and Snacks'.

"I guess there were a few more gallons in here after all. But we are gonna need to head north." Connor struggled with the hose as he replaced the nozzle.

The lights on the Caddy fluttered as we raced across highway thirty three. My heart skipped at the thought that the lights might stop working. The roads were in bad shape here too, full of vehicles and various debris. The asphalt itself seemed to be crumbling. Suddenly a small dark shadow bolted in front of us and I swerved to avoid it. In doing so, I misread the angle of a truck that jutted out onto the road and had to veer so sharply that I lost control of the Caddy. Skidding past the truck, we slammed into a weakened wooden fence. The fencing stood little chance against the Cadillac and splintered into a million pieces as we passed through it. We jerked left, and the car stopped. Connor ended up on my lap, and Sonny could be heard cursing from the back.

"Christ! Sorry guys, you okay?" I asked, shoving Connor off me. "Did you see that truck?"

"Did you?!" Sonny retorted. "Jesus, I should check my shorts!"

Connor looked back at the truck that had sent us flying, and froze. "Guys, look at that - it's a fucking GAS truck."

At the magic 'G' word, we all got out and hurried to the silent vehicle.

"How do we know it's full?" Connor was excited.

Sonny slammed a fist against the hull. The resulting sound was a dull thud, not a clang. "It's full," he confirmed as a smile worked its way across his broad face. "It's full!"

It was an absurd stroke of luck. Gas with wheels: it was ridiculous. We knew it was, but I also knew never to look a gift horse in the mouth, and that's exactly what this was.

"Let's check the cab," I suggested. "Maybe this rig's got some life in her."

Connor circled around to the passenger side while Sonny peered through the driver's window. He tried the door and, finding it unlocked, opened it and disappeared into the cab. Then I heard the door on the passenger side open and something fall out, hitting the ground with a thud. I felt a little sick at the sound.

"It's not what you thought it was." Sonny stuck his head out of the window, smiling. "Just a nasty old duffle bag. Get in, I'm gonna try startin' this thing up!"

I clambered into the cab. Connor and I watched as Sonny turned the key. We heard the familiar click of a vehicle that says 'no more' about a dozen times before the payoff. A few violent thrusts of the stick and stomps on the clutch, and Sonny got it running!

"So you do know trucks!" Eyeing the gears and pedals, I certainly hoped he knew.

"You're the fucking truck whisperer man!" declared Connor, slapping the dashboard.

"Sure, I drove a thousand miles once with my dad back in the day." Sonny was proud; this was his shining moment.

"Yeah, but have you been in the driver's seat before? I think that's the relevant question here." Sonny blew him off and threw it in gear. Off we went with a jerk and a stop, jerk and stop.

"Whoa! Wait a second!" I shouted. "We can't leave the Caddy behind!" I struggled with the door as Sonny slowed the rig to a crawl, and jumped out. Connor stuck his head out the window.

"I'll follow you guys there!" I shouted. Connor offered a thumbs-up as I hustled back to the Cadillac. The Caddy turned over on the first try. What a gem. I navigated it over the shattered fence, through the ditch and back onto route thirty three. Sonny was just a few yards ahead, still a bit jerky on the clutch but we were on our way. Things were looking up. The tanker's cargo meant power for a lot longer than two months. This would be a major morale boost for the house.

*****

"Are you kidding me?!" was Earl's response to the massive tanker.

"I know," I replied. "Can you believe it?"

His head shook back and forth, a smile pulled the thin flesh across his bony features.

Everyone wanted to know how we located such a treasure, and we told them the story.

The celebration went deep into the night as the barbeque was pulled out of retirement and the last of our meat products cooked. We drank our alcohol and smoked our premium marijuana. Our future would be written one day at a time, and one day, someone theorized, our present would resemble our past.

Chapter Seventeen

We woke up the next morning with a start. Sidney's voice rang through the house with news that rocked our foundation, a foundation we'd worked so hard to build.

Our south gate had been compromised. A parade of cars, trucks and motor homes drove slowly through our property, ignoring our barrier. Sidney had spotted them while on duty in Skylab with Sonny and Sara, pulling the four to eight a.m. shift. The entire house now assembled in the addition, peering through the windows.

"Joel, what's our next move?" Earl asked.

"Just everyone sit tight." I paused, conscious of what weight my next few words would carry. "You all have your weapons, yes? Alright then, we wait. If just one of these cars stops, we assume the position, but until then we do nothing." Earl sent me such a disparaging look that I repeated firmly, "We wait."

The next few seconds felt like a lifetime. The silence in the addition was palpable, our heartbeats now audible, the tension building to a crescendo. But the cars did not stop: they passed on, moving off into the distance. We could breathe again.

"Shit, that was unreal." Seth pressed both palms hard against his eyes. Then Kevin spoke up.

"Great gates, Earl. Solid!"

He rolled his eyes. Earl punched him in the shoulder, lightly, as laughter diffused the anxiety that had permeated Skylab. People, regular people, maybe hundreds of them just drove right past us on a mass exodus north, like so many before them. Maybe we should too, I thought. The moment passed, and reality set in. This road hadn't seen that kind of traffic since the highway to the west of us flooded some years back.

"What do you figure: thirty, forty vehicles?" I asked Sidney.

"Maybe more!"

These people were either running from something, or to something. North- where were all these people getting the idea to go north? Or if they were running from a threat, then what could it be, what could frighten a group that large? These were the questions brought up at the group meeting held in the addition immediately following the sighting. Surely the black rain we had encountered upon our return to 'civilization' had reached the north by now, and the pristine conditions of our former campsite had long since vanished. We sat in the dark for some time, discussing the turn of events, popping our heads above the window line once in a while. The reminder that other people were out there, groups of survivors like us, was intoxicating- until you realized that not everyone was following the maxim of live and let live. To know we were not alone was a gift, but a curse as well.

During a break in the conversation, Caroline peered out one of the large windows that overlooked the back yard and forest. Her chest began to heave and her hands pushed unconsciously against the glass.

"People," she whispered. Then again, louder: "People... forest...THERE ARE PEOPLE IN THE FOREST!"

She shrieked.

We sprang off the floor in unison and rushed to the west windows. Squinting into the darkness, we saw several armed figures glide through the woods on approach to the pool. In Skylab, guns slid out of holsters and off shoulders. Windows were opened and barrels thrust through them.

"Earl, get to my parents' room!" I shouted. He'd have a prime shot there, as it had a large picture window overlooking the back yard. "Connor, go downstairs: Sonny, get to the light switch, Kevin, Seth go with him! Sara, come with me." I took her by the arm and led her to my room, where we knelt on the couch that backed against the window overlooking the backyard. The horde was almost upon us.

"Sonny, hit the lights!" I yelled.

The spotlights snapped on and illuminated the whole yard. There they were, stopped like deer in headlights. I counted them quickly. Six...

seven... ten. Looked like around ten or eleven. I slid the window open and began my 'first contact' speech while they were temporarily stunned by the artificial sunlight.

"Identify yourselves!" I yelled.

No answer.

"You're in no position to..."

BANG! A gunshot cut me off. I couldn't tell you who shot first, us or them, but it took roughly two minutes to end the confrontation. I heard Earl shout, "They're trying to shoot out the spotlight." I aimed at random stranger who was firing his rifle wildly at the lights, and fired. He fell, then two of his companions fell. I had the higher ground, and was shrouded in darkness.

When the shooting began Sara shrank away from the window, curling up next to me and hugging my arm. I tried to shake her, as her hold was interfering with my marksmanship, but she held on, terrified. Her rifle came in handy when my cartridge was spent. A shot broke through my window, screaming past my ear: it would have killed Sara had she been actively involved in the shootout.

I saw figures fall one after another. The scene was surreal. I dropped another one myself. Then the firing stopped.

Earl stumbled into my room seconds after the silence. "No more movement," he assured me through steady, even breathes. "I think we won." A thin smile finds his lips.

He sounded as though we'd just finished a paintball game. Admittedly the adrenaline was shooting through my veins too, but my brain was still trying to rationalize what had just taken place. Why hadn't he broken yet? What was his secret? "This isn't a game, Earl! We're not *pretending*!"

His grin sank and his head followed. He knew I was right, or did he?

Sara was still clinging to my arm as the others gathered at my door. "Everyone's okay. No casualties on our end," reported Connor.

I asked the guys to go outside and perform a perimeter search to double-check our status. "Be careful. Check the bodies first. Take whatever weapons they may have. We'll bury them later."

Freddy, Sonny, John, Kevin, and Earl filed out to complete the gruesome deed, Connor, Jake, Seth and Sidney sat with Sara, Caroline and Julia on the couch, trying to control their post-battle trembling. "Cover their backs," I asked Seth and Sid, pointing to our team outside. "We don't know who else may be out there." Then I hurried to throw up in the bathroom.

*****

The scouts came back an hour later. They had collected some nice new guns and ammo, three crossbows, a spear, and a pair of Japanese swords. With bated breath I waited to hear whether the dreaded flag was included in the bounty. Upon receiving a negative response, I exhaled loudly. The idea of a flag-toting clan of murderers being out there upset me to no end. But for now, they weren't here. Our enemies were strangers.

Our next task was to bury the dead.

We decided to simply dump them into the garbage pit out back and cover them with the wet muck from the forest floor. The act was grisly but necessary. On closer inspection we noticed that most of the corpses were covered with red burns and welts. Sara called them radiation burns.

"They're like flash burns. I wouldn't wish these upon anybody. They must have been in constant pain." She studied one man's abrasions, trying to ignore the bullet wound in his chest.

The job done, we returned to the house and washed up in the basement bathroom. As we retired to Skylab, our minds wandered, thinking about the fight, the killing. Kevin, Sara and Seth stood guard at the windows while the rest of us sat in the remaining chairs we'd scavenged from the dining room and opened the floor for some healing deliberation on the subject.

Emotions ran high and tears were shed. Buried in the forest, not a hundred feet away, were the remains of eleven people, people we'd killed. In order to appease our fragile consciences, we would reiterate to each other that we killed in self-defense. Some couldn't seem to bear the weight of their actions and swore never to take up arms again.

"Listen." John took it upon himself to give us a reality check. "It was us or them, man. Joel tried talking them down but no go. We were left with no alternative but to fire back. They asked for it! They signed their lives away by firing at us." With each spoken word John became more determined. "Christ, I think I shot two of them dead myself. You think I feel guilty about that? You think I feel bad about protecting my girlfriend, this house and my friends? Screw that, I'll do it again in a heartbeat, I look forward to it!"

Jake nodded and sipped at his water. Shit changes everyone in some way. Jake, I now believed, had had a helping hand; that was the accepted word around the house. Just to have been present for Jake's transition was enough to believe in a higher power.

The evening saw Sara, Kevin and Seth finish their shift and join what had transformed into another victory party. We'd essentially accepted our decisions, accepted who we were and who we would have to become in order to stay alive. The weed made us laugh. It also made us forget the awfulness of the afternoon.

*****

October delivered a wind so powerful that it blew the tops off the dead birch in the front yard and felled many more trees whose roots had long since lost their hold in the black muck. It was a stronger wind than that of September's, still from the north and getting cooler.

On the first Friday of the month, we celebrated Caroline's birthday. The clan gathered in the addition to enjoy a party that, for once, had nothing to do with victory over the elements or our enemies. Caroline was visibly touched by our efforts to make the day special for her.

"Thanks, you guys," she said, standing at the north end of Skylab while we looked on. "This means a lot to me..." Then her face began to contort, thoughts of her absent family haunting her. John hugged her against his bare chest. Then he turned to us.

"A little music, Maestro…."

Sidney pushed the button on the CD player, and John and Caroline's song came on over the speaker system throughout the addition. We watched them dance to the gentle, haunting melody while candlelight shadowed their movements. It was beautiful. Our new existence had its ugliness, like the darkness, the mud, and the murdering. But it never got so bad that love failed to flourish. I reached for Sara's hand and squeezed it.

I noticed the vacant stares from those in the group that didn't enter into this nightmare with a partner, or had lost their partner soon thereafter. Their loneliness was palpable. My heart went out to them.

The party skyrocketed not too long after the dance. The shifts at the windows were shortened to an hour at a time so that everyone could enjoy the evening. Except for me - I couldn't relax my vigilance.

My spell at guard duty passed quickly enough. After saying goodnight to Sara, who arrived to replace me, I stumbled to bed.

I stood in my room, rubbing my eyes to ease the ache. I fell easily into bed, my body limp with fatigue. But no sooner had I closed my eyes, they were forced open again by an awful vision. A vision so realistic, I knew I had to tell someone immediately. What was happening to me? First the skunk, then the angel and now this, was I turning into Connor?

I knew better than to doubt a vision so real, given the circumstances, so I hurried back into the addition, where everyone was slouched in their couches and armchairs. "We've got to close the gates," I said urgently.

"Right now?" Kevin looked confused.

"Yes, right now! Don't ask why: let's just get it done!"

Four of us moved quickly down the driveway and along the ditch that led to our recently ravaged gates of wood and metal. The majority of our crew remained behind to continue watch in the addition. Moments later, we heard the soft growl of approaching vehicles and high-tailed it back to the house without having accomplished our task. Then their headlights shone mercilessly over our sanctuary, and we were compromised.

Chapter Eighteen

We lunged for cover behind the line of cars along the front lawn.

"How'd you know, Joel?" Connor whispered as we huddled behind his old four-runner. "I mean, you couldn't have seen them."

I raised a finger to my lips as the motorcade approached. Then I glanced at Earl and John, eyes like slivers, muscles tense, anxious to spring into action.

The intruders were riding motorcycles: big, nasty-looking engines. We counted seven of them. They stopped barely ten feet from us, parked, and looked the silent house up and down. Their leather jackets, long hair, and decorated hogs identified them as bikers. One of them made a comment about this being a great new clubhouse; another wondered if any women were inside. My stomach muscles clenched and my trigger finger itched as I imagined our sanctuary - and our girlfriends - being exposed to the desecration of these assholes.

John sprang out first. He shoved his shotgun barrel right into an approaching biker's balls. Connor, Earl, and I appeared over the vehicle hoods, covering them all.

"Walk away, jerk-offs," I ordered. "This place belongs to us. You either walk away from here or we take you down."

John nudged his gun, making his target wince and step back. "Your dick is going to take the bullet train to the curb, asshole!"

The other bikers glanced at each other uncertainly. We were at one of those terrible stalemates, in which both sides had too much to lose by giving in. Then there was a flash of movement - John's man was grabbing for the rifle barrel.

BOOM!!!

The stranger fell heavily onto his back, blood exploding from his crotch. Behind us, the door opened. Seth was there, framed by the interior light, aiming an M-16 at the invaders.

"Get inside, boys!" he shouted to us.

We ran for it. Seth slammed the door shut behind us. Seconds later, bullets thudded into the door, exploding the windows. The sentries in Skylab fired back, mowing the enemy down, while Seth, John, Connor, Earl and I threw ourselves onto the hall floor. After minutes that felt like hours, the gunfire stopped.

"They're scattering," we heard someone yell from the addition. "Joel, they're scattering!"

We ran upstairs and into the addition, taking advantage of the ceasefire. "How many left?" I asked.

"Three - and they just booked outta here." Freddy reloaded his automatic.

Slowly, silently, weapons poised, we went back downstairs. When we opened the bullet-pocked door, the first thing we saw was the silent form of the biker that John had emasculated. The porch light flickered, making the corpse the focus of a horrific light show. Beyond him were three more bodies, slumped on the grass with exploded skulls.

Seth stumbled onto the lawn and began puking. So did Sidney. I took deep, gulping breaths to avoid following their example. That was when Earl took charge. I wasn't complaining.

"Let's take stock of these bodies, and then throw 'em into the pit."

Callous as his words were, they were practical. We didn't need the odor of putrefaction to remind us of our actions. Kevin brought a wheelbarrow from the garage, and we hefted the five bodies in, one after the other. When one guy's brains dribbled over the side Seth puked again. Sidney helped him indoors while Earl walked ahead to the pit. The rest of us flanked the makeshift hearse as Kevin maneuvered it toward the burial site.

"My ....face....hurts."

Kevin dropped the wheelbarrow handles and stumbled backward so quickly that he fell on his ass. "Guys, I've got a live one here!"

We all stared in disbelief. It was one of those surreal moments when you don't know what you're supposed to do. One of the bodies was moving, weakly at first, grasping at the wheelbarrow's metal edges. Then a shape sat up straight, brushing aside the lifeless limbs of his buddies, and stumbled out onto the grass. The man's face was partially shot away and one arm hung like a bloody dish rag, but he was alive.

What should we do? Should we take out our weapons and finish this guy off? No… no, we couldn't. He had survived: he was a survivor just like us.

"Go," Kevin hissed at him. "Go, run! Get out of here!"

The biker staggered toward the field. Just then Earl appeared from the pit, shovel over his shoulder. He took one look at the fleeing figure and yanked out his automatic. Before we could shout, he fired. Three bullets punched through the man's bare back and exited his chest in a red cloud.

"What are you doing, asshole!!" Connor yelled at Earl.

"Shooting this prick before he brought back reinforcements, what the fuck's your problem? Why'd you let him go?"

We couldn't answer. Standing there in the dark silence, a mass grave awaiting this most recent offering, I had a sinking feeling we didn't know what was right anymore.

*****

The next morning, after breakfast, I wandered around the property, ostensibly patrolling it but really trying to remember everything as it had been before the darkness and blood. During my rounds I came upon Jake in his fortress of solitude. Sitting on the ground, gazing into the inky distance, he showed no sign of having noticed me.

"Jake…" I approached him carefully. "Jake, you awake?"

"I knew you were there, Joel," he answered without moving anything but his lips.

I didn't know what to say to that.

Jake rose from the filthy ground in one fluid motion. "I hadn't expected you so soon. What brought you to 'the forbidden zone'?" He waggled his nimble fingers, gently mocking Earl's disdain for places outside our protected bubble.

"Just patrolling. And… remembering."

His face was the picture of empathy. "Yeah, I do that a lot myself."

We fell silent for a few minutes. Then suddenly, I began to laugh. Not giggle. Not chuckle. Hysterical laughter ripped through me at a memory of us here, at the shed. Jake grinned patiently while I doubled over.

"I'm sorry," I choked. "It's just…"

"I think I'm remembering the same memory." He pointed to the broken window and gave up a toothy smile. "What would we be without them?"

That's when Jake left us. A shot cracked behind us, and he lunged in front of me. A bullet tore into Jake's small frame, puncturing his heart. I caught him in my arms and pulled him from the shed doorway. He groaned terribly, blood flowing freely from his chest. I struggled to stop the bleeding, but it was a losing battle. Two more shots sank into the earth next to us.

"It's supposed to be this way," Jake whispered as blood bubbled from his mouth and nostrils.

Tears poured down my cheeks, which seemed to disturb him.

"Don't do that for me, Joel… please…."

His head was on my lap. I crouched over him, crying, pushing down on the wound with my fingers frantically. "It's supposed to be like this," he kept saying.

"What? What are you saying? What are you talking about?" I choked.

"The angel, Joel…. He told me this would happen." Those were Jake's final words. His eyes fluttered, and his spirit departed.

Jake now lay dead on my lap. I gently lowered him to the earth, picked up his machine gun, and peered carefully around the shack doorway to scan the area where the shot had come from. I couldn't see anyone. I had to move, to get to the safety of the house.

"I'll be back, Jake," I whispered into his ear. Then I sprang to my feet and ran. I hadn't run like that since the skunk last challenged me: I was fast and agile, weaving around trees and under fallen branches. Shots were fired again- I could hear some hitting the trees while others whizzed past, searching for me. The adrenaline pushed me to my absolute limit as I drew closer to the hill, closer to home. I almost didn't realize I'd been hit.

The bullet penetrated my right upper leg, making me stumble and fall. Grasping the wound with both hands, I got up again and struggled to the shelter of a large spruce. The shooting finally ceased and I waited there for some time, listening for my assailants' approach. They didn't pursue me, and soon I heard the voices of my friends as they rushed through the woods, calling out my name.

Sonny found me. "What's happening here, Joel? We heard shots." He scanned the surrounding forest. "Where are the shooters?"

"Gone, I think." The pain was pulsating now, interfering with my motor skills. My whole body throbbed. "I'm hit, Sonny. And Jake..."

"Jake? He's out here too?"

"Jake's dead."

Sonny flinched as if struck. He scanned my pale, tear-soaked face. His chin trembled. "Where… where is he?"

"At the shed."

"We've got to get you to the house. I'll come back for Jake when we've got you safe." Sonny hoisted me over his shoulder and headed up the path. Earl and Kevin bolted down the lawn to meet us.

"Guys!" Sonny hollered. "I got Joel!!"

"What happened to him?" Earl asked.

"He's been shot in the leg… and Jake's dead."

"Dead?!" Kevin turned white. "Dead?" he repeated incredulously. Sonny just nodded. Earl said nothing, but he looked just as sick. Gripping their guns and glancing backward, they accompanied us to the house in silence.

Sara met us at the back basement door. "Oh God, what happened to you, Joel? Were you hit?"

"He took one in the leg, Sara." Sonny laid me carefully on the floor. He bunched up a corner of the area rug to create a pillow for my head.

"I'll get the first aid kit!" Sara was on the verge of hysterics. Connor pulled her aside.

"Don't lose it, Sara," I heard him whisper to her. "Not when he's hurt like this. You have to be stronger than that for him. He's going to be okay. He's only hit in the leg."

"That could mean a million things, Connor. People die from leg wounds. If he's been hit in an artery-"

"He's *not* going to die."

"I'm not ready for him to die, I – I'm not prepared for this…" She started to panic again.

"Clear your head, Sara. Think about Joel."

She took a deep breath. "Okay… okay. You get the first aid kit, I'll stay with him. Get the advanced kit, grab some towels, and have someone boil some water."

Connor disappeared up the stairs. The group stood at a concerned yet respectful distance while Sara hovered over me.

"You'll be fine, Joel." She brushed the hair from my forehead while my bloody fingers clasped hers. "Connor's getting the first aid kit. Sonny, pull his pants off."

"Shit, Joel. You'll owe me for this one," Sonny said as he obeyed.

"Jake..." I whispered under my breath. "I'm sorry, Jake…" My eyelids flickered. I felt cold.

Sara stared at Sonny and asked him what I meant. He told her and the others about Jake. The shock of losing another friend incurred gasps and, from some, tears. Sonny refused to give in to grief.

"That's why it's imperative that we all get back to our watch. Earl, I'd put people outside on the ground to listen for whoever did this."

Earl nodded. "Joel would have wanted us to keep the watch."

"Jesus, Earl, don't say 'Joel would have wanted'. He's not dead!" Sara's voice rose in pitch but she otherwise remained calm, wiping the sweat from my brow and smiling reassuringly at me.

Earl temporarily took command. "Anyone who can't be of help here, take your place at a window. Sonny- you, John, and Sid listen for anything out back. Stay on the porch, close to the house." He knelt beside me and laid a reassuring hand on my chest. "You'll be alright, buddy."

The group scattered as Connor resurfaced with the medical kit. Sara loaded a syringe with morphine and jabbed the needle into the meat of my leg with great care and purpose. I winced. She went to work on my leg while Connor hovered nearby, ready to lend a hand if needed.

The morphine took effect immediately. I remembered finding it while scavenging for medical supplies in a downtown clinic where Sara had worked during her co-op with the high school. Thank God she had. The injection deadened the pain, but exhaustion and blood loss finally made me pass out.

Hours later I awoke in my bed, groggy and in pain. I rubbed my eyes slowly but deeply, seeing stars when I opened them. When the lightshow cleared, I saw Sara. She was leaning over me, running her fingers gently down my face.

"I'm still here," I reassured her, smiling goofily. The morphine left me giddy.

"I'm glad." Leaning in, she kissed my forehead. "Your leg should be fine. The bullet didn't break any bones or hit an artery. It passed right through your Vastus Lateralis."

"I thought you said it went through my leg," I pouted. We both laughed. Then Sara's face changed mid-laugh from an expression of exuberant happiness to one of deep pain.

"What is it? What's wrong?"

"The guys picked up Jake this morning." She struggled to continue. "He's been out all night, all by himself. He - he's in the garage... in a bag…" She began to sob. The memory of Jake's death assaulted my senses and I lost it too. We cried awhile, together. They say that a man is never gone until he is forgotten. I would see to it that Jake lived forever.

Chapter Nineteen

I managed to get out of bed in the afternoon and, with the help of a walking stick Kevin had fashioned into a cane for me, maneuver around the second floor fairly easily. Sara refused to let me use the stairs for the time being. She wanted me to stay in bed for a few days, but that was unfathomable to me.

We buried Jake during that once mystical hour when afternoon transformed to evening. Connor and Sonny carried me gently down to the basement, where the shell that had been my childhood buddy was laid out. He was positioned on a tarpaulin as if asleep, the terrible chest wound concealed by a new shirt. Julia, Caroline, and Earl weren't present, being on guard duty, but everyone else was there. Their solemn faces all registered grief as they paid their respects to a friend who'd been suddenly restored to us, only to be taken away just as quickly.

Kevin, Sidney, and Sara took one edge of the tarp while Seth, Freddy and John grasped the other. While the rest of us followed, they carried Jake out through the sliding glass doors of the walk-out basement. We trudged in silence along the path, toward a gravesite that John and Earl had prepared earlier.

As we lowered yet another friend into the ground, Sara said a prayer. The others repeated her words under their breath while Connor and Sonny watched the forest, guns drawn. After filling the hole with earth, we stood there in uncomfortable silence. No one wanted to be the first to leave Jake.

Suddenly gunfire erupted. It was a single shot, but it came from within the house! Knowing that Jake would understand, we abandoned the site and hurried to the house. When we piled through the door, Caroline and Julia met us, pointing at the garage.

"Earl finally did it!" Caroline exclaimed.

My heart sank. The garage! The skunk!

"Earl just went in there to check on a noise he thought he'd heard through the floor," Julia began. Then Earl appeared from the garage. With his broad grin and triumphant expression, he oozed satisfaction.

"What, Earl? What's the good news?" Connor asked.

"You'll never believe who I just got even with." Earl returned his pistols to their holsters. I couldn't speak.

"Who? You saw someone? You shot someone?" Sidney couldn't take it anymore. The suspense was killing them. Not me though. I already knew what had happened.

"My nemesis!" he declared. Of course, he didn't realize the impact it would have on me to learn that he'd finally put down his 'white whale'. "My great and worthy enemy is dead."

He led us to the garage via the office to the main attraction. The lights went on, much like curtains in a theatre might rise, revealing the hidden spectacle. There he was; little Stinky, shot through the neck. I felt sick.

Unaware of my inner turmoil, the crowd showered congratulations on Earl, as they'd all heard the story of his great humiliation. Connor knew immediately that I was floored by the murder: all he had to do was look at me. I hobbled over to him with the assistance of my cane, took him by the arm, and walked him out of the garage.

"Remember when I told you that I talked to the skunk when we were at the lake?" I began to rant. "Remember when we were all messed up on acid and I saw him and had a conversation with him and got sick from it? Well, there he is!" I pointed back toward the garage. "There he is, dead. I knew he was in there the whole time we've been back, Connor! I kept him alive and this is what happens! Jesus, does Earl need more killing?"

"Joel, calm down man." Connor's voice was sympathetic but firm. "He didn't know, man. No one did."

"I know that. But how could I have told them without-"

Connor steadied me as I faltered. Just then Sara came into the office, wondering why I was raising my voice.

"It's nothing." I took her hand.

"Help me get him upstairs, will you, Sara?" Connor asked. "He's had a hell of a day."

They assisted me to my second story bedroom. Connor left after promising me we'd talk again later. Sara thanked him for his help. Then she laid me back on the bed and removed my pants to check my wound.

"It looks good. Clean. I'll change the bandage in the morning."

"You're the best," I told her as my head involuntarily shook. My throat seized as I struggled to speak. "Sara, what's going to happen to us?"

"What do you mean? There's nothing wrong with us."

"Not just you and me. I mean all of us. What's going to become of us?" I wept.

She cradled my head in her arms. Music could be heard through the house – Earl's victory party was in full swing. I choked back hate.

"Pray with me, Joel." Sara gently laid my head on the pillow. "Pray with me." She placed my hands together and wrapped hers around them. Our eyes met. I waited for her to begin.

"It's good to pray, Joel. It's the only way you'll be heard."

"You can hear me. That's all that matters to me."

Sara recited a familiar prayer that my mother and I had said together for several nights after Dad died. It had sustained us until we could sustain ourselves. The prayer had soothing qualities. It was beautiful, like Sara. I let myself relax. When she finished speaking, we dropped off to sleep.

*****

While I slept, I was visited by someone I had, quite frankly, not expected to ever see again. My skunk. Once again he invaded my most intimate and vulnerable state, but I was happy just to see him.

"Hello, Joel." he began. Light shone everywhere as he slowly morphed into a reproduction of Kevin's drawing, of the angel. There were no wings or halo, just the familiar face that oozed compassion and strength.

The dream broke, and the vision left me as I awoke.

Chapter Twenty

My eyes opened. As soon as they adjusted to the darkness, I glanced down at Sara, who was stirring. My sudden jolt back into the world had woken her.

"What was that, Joel?"

"Nothing," I replied. I still couldn't bring myself to tell her about my visions. I didn't want to scare or worry her. Connor - I had to talk to Connor. Pulling away from Sara, I tried getting out of bed on my own. My leg wound throbbed terribly at the movement.

"Shit!" I whispered behind clenched teeth.

"Joel, don't move so fast. I need to change your dressing first!" Sara sat up and grabbed the first aid kit on the nightstand. I laid back and let her work, wincing at the pain that pulsed up my thigh.

"Not much new blood," she pronounced. "Good. Means that it's healing fast."

Lying there, I felt my earlier anger and antagonism dissipate. I still grieved over Jake, but the angel's visit had cushioned the pain of the skunk's loss. I harbored no ill feelings toward Earl for killing him. Not anymore, anyway.

Sara completed her work on my leg. "How is the pain? Are you coping or do you want something for it?"

"I'm holding up against it."

She checked her watch and realized that her shift in Skylab would begin in twenty minutes. "I'm going to take my shower now and get ready for watch."

"Cool. I need to see Connor; if you pass him, can you send him in here?"

"Sure." She kissed me, pulled the comforter over my legs, and departed. I shook four pain killers into my palm and swallowed them down.

Connor came in fifteen minutes later and sat on the couch. He told me he had been in the basement, getting his hair cut by Julia.

"What's on your mind, old man?" he wanted to know.

"That's a nice haircut. I should book an appointment with your girlfriend."

"She'd be happy to do it. Cutting mine and Freddy's seems to have put a smile back on her face. She said it made her feel useful. How's your leg?"

"Fine man, no worries." I struggled out of bed. Connor rose to help me, but I gestured for him to stay put. Grabbing my cane, I stood up and limped to the couch, where I sat next to him. "Look, I just wanted to clear up that incoherent junk I laid on you last night. I'm sorry for putting you in that position. It was unfair to lay it all on you like that."

"Don't give it a second thought. You obviously had a lot of steam to blow off."

"It was all for real, Connor," I explained. "The skunk, all of it. All real."

"I realize that, Joel. You've got your visions; I've got these déja-vus." He tapped his temple. "I believe you, buddy. Maybe if I was any less screwed up than you I wouldn't, but we both know that isn't the case."

"That's the truth. Jesus!" I laughed.

He laughed too. "Man, what a pair of freaks we are."

"Yeah!" I shifted my gimp leg, displacing its weight for a moment's relief.

A feeling of nostalgia washed over me. It was wonderful, but distressing too. We were sitting here, having a carefree conversation that reminded me of the times when we would go to the hill, watch the city spread out before us, and talk.

"Let's go back to the hill," I said suddenly.

"Sure, if you want to." But hesitation hung in his voice. I understood: the view could only be that of devastation. All the same I felt a need to return, to maybe close the book on that life, to accept this one once and for all.

"Good, let's go then." I threw on a shirt and struggled with the pants while Connor rolled a joint for the road. He and Seth helped me down the stairs. I had to relinquish the Caddy's keys to Connor, as I was unable to drive, and soon enough we were off to the spot, just the two of us.

*****

Half an hour later, we were there. After Connor pulled into the same spot that we'd visited four months ago, I stepped out, holding the door for support. Still half-expecting to behold the cityscape, I was staggered by the infinite nothingness that one man's evil deed had placed in its stead. The horizon that would once glow at dusk with the distant city lights was now invisible. Small fires burned out of control in the distance, and white smoke poured from open wounds in the earth. It was an alienating sight that gave closure to a past life.

"No longer the inspiring vision it once was, is it?" Connor joined me. "I have to admit, Joel, that I've been here since, once when I was heading to town for supplies, I took a detour. I screamed bloody murder when I saw all this, but the experience was good for me. It helped me to accept that the old world is really gone."

"I don't blame you. It's something we need to see. I'm surprised I hadn't thought of it earlier."

"It's brutal isn't it? Here you can really take in the whole scope of what's happened, whatever that is… the Apocalypse?" Connor fell silent.

"I haven't got an answer for that, Connor," I admitted. "I do know this though: it's not the end. It's the end of what was but it's not the end of everything."

"How do you know that?"

"Because we're still here. Why would we be here if there was nothing left to accomplish? Why us? Why any of these people? Why? Christ, I'd like to know the answer to that one. Jake died because he thought he was 'supposed to', for my good, for the good of us. He took the bullet for me. But how the hell does it benefit us that I survive? Who am I?"

Connor was stunned. I hadn't told anyone that Jake had thrown himself in front of the bullet clearly meant for me.

We sat in silence for a long time. Then we heard the sound of distant cars approaching - lots of them. We hurried to the crest of the hill and looked down.

Lights seemed to explode on the road below us as a caravan of vehicles journeyed over the horizon. Each one flew a flag- the same one we saw en route from Mom's store that day. This was the same group that had attempted to ambush us. This time there were a lot more of them.

"Shit on that!" Connor tried in vain to count the cars. "Holy shit..."

"Let's get going. The house needs to know about this."

We returned to the Caddy and drove home at breakneck speed, keeping our lights off so as not to alert the motorcade to our presence. Once at the house, we gathered the troops in the front yard and reported the grim news. No one panicked. We were worried, true, but we were resilient. Their greater numbers were a serious concern, but we had weapons, and if they ventured onto our land, they were setting themselves up for a slaughter as far as we were concerned.

"They shouldn't be here for a few hours." I glanced back toward the road. "They were slowing down when we saw them, maybe even setting up camp. We may not see them today - we may not see them at all. Just stay sharp."

Earl and Sonny positioned themselves two kilometers to the south of the house, acting as long range scouts. They took the four-wheeler in case it became necessary to make a quick exit and alert the rest of us to an imminent danger. The rest of the crew stayed in the house, stationed at the windows.

The day passed into night without further sightings. Day and night were still measured in hours. I was beginning to wonder whether it would ever be separated by light and dark again. When Earl and Sonny returned, we all had a nightcap in memory of our lost companion. Jake would be remembered, whether he'd thought himself worthy of that honor or not.

*****

The following morning cast a shadow over our home and lives so far-reaching and so profound that things would never be the same for me.

What we'd anticipated the night before came to fruition. Dozens of cars and RVs, all sporting the flag, rolled through the grounds defiantly and came to a halt, forming a line of vehicles that extended beyond our driveway. The entire house witnessed the event from the addition windows, as Kevin and Sidney had woken everyone with the news.

"Wow." Seth whistled. "This can't be good.... Can it?"

"I'm not sure, Seth," I replied, trying not to let everyone else see that I was on the verge of panicking. "But we don't have the luxury of optimism. Everyone keep their guns at the ready. We still have the high ground."

Watching the flag bearers pour out of their vehicles and onto our property was a discouraging sight. They outnumbered us by at least five to one.

"Joel?" It was Sidney. "Joel, I think we should act now. It'll be our only chance. There are so many of them."

"We don't fire first and ask questions later, Sid. They may be harmless."

"They didn't seem harmless during our last encounter with them." Kevin's nerves were getting the better of him.

"Calm down, Kev." Connor had my back. "Joel's right. They'd waste us anyway you cut it. They've got the numbers."

"I'm going to start with my 'first contact' speech, like always. I don't need another scene like last time. We can't afford to snap on these guys." After checking my weapon, I cupped a palm around my mouth and shouted out the open window, all the while keeping my head low.

"Identify yourselves! You're trespassing. We have the high ground. Identify yourselves!"

"Joel, they're stopping," Earl whispered.

A middle-aged man who was obviously the flag's leader pushed to the front of the crowd and looked up at us. He wore a black robe that was belted at the waist resembling a monk's habit.

"We appear before you in peace." He raised his arms and turned a full circle, showing that he carried no weapons. That was hardly reassuring: the men and women behind him all clutched guns. "Our only purpose is to carry out the removal of our enemies, and I hope, yours."

What the hell was this guy talking about? Which enemies?

"We are on a crusade to uncover and eliminate those who support the Reaper." His smile was jagged and unnaturally long; I later saw that most of it was a facial scar. "We are not here to harm you or pillage your home. All we want is proof that you and your group are not sympathizers who could carry on the devastation that the Reaper started."

A shared confusion passed between each of us as we struggled to understand this group's purpose. I played along. "And what must we do to convince you that we do not support the Reaper's ideas?"

"We must be allowed to interview each member of your party separately. All we want to do is question them. If they are not sympathizers, they will be free to go. However, should they be found guilty, we would be compelled to remove them." He didn't clarify what he meant by remove. He didn't have to.

I loathed this guy on sight. I detected a sanctimonious prick who'd taken advantage of the universal chaos to seize power, dominate weaker minds, and hurt others. "Why would anyone agree with what the Reaper has done? That's ridiculous. What you're on is little more than a witch hunt!"

"This is not a request. I am a tolerant man, so I'll let you take your time to decide what you will do. But at six o'clock this evening I will expect your final answer."

Some members of the flag army returned to their vehicles to wait out our decision while others took up positions around the house. They were carrying out nothing less than an inquisition, a throwback to the brutality of the McCarthy trials. We debated our next move.

"Joel, do you think we'll truly have a chance at defeating those numbers?" Sara questioned the odds. So did I.

"I'm hoping to avoid it altogether," I replied. "If we can appear to be stronger than they are – make them think that we have the numbers - perhaps they'll leave us for weaker pastures."

Freddy looked troubled. "Won't they assume we are 'sympathizers' if we don't go along? Then they'll definitely come at us."

"Shit." Sonny clenched his teeth. "He's right."

"We don't know that," Julia countered. "We can't be sure they'll attack us. I say we wait and see."

"If we wait, we'll lose any upper hand we may still have," Earl argued. "They've already trespassed onto our property and are right now taking up positions in the trees. They're serious about this. This is what gives them purpose. If we wait and let them entrench themselves further, we could – no, make that will -lose everything."

"How would you propose we attack them?" asked John. "They're everywhere. We've already lost what little control we had over this situation."

"Maybe we should just let them ask us their questions," Caroline suggested. "If they're really serious about just wanting Reaper groupies, it won't take them long to know that there aren't any among us."

"Then we'll vote," I decided.

"One thing's for sure- we'll never beat those odds in a battle. No way. There are just too many of them." Connor shook his head. Everyone except Earl nodded somberly. Therefore, the outcome of our vote wasn't a surprise: we would surrender ourselves for questioning. We could only hope that the proceedings would be fair and just.

*****

At six on the dot, the leader called up to us from the front yard. "We require an answer! Will you agree to participate freely in our investigation or do you choose otherwise?"

I opened the front door. "I will talk to you inside!" I said, gesturing. He scanned my face, saw only weariness and sincerity, and stepped past me into the house.

Viewed up close, the flag leader looked more like a visiting missionary than a potential judge, jury, and executioner. He was forty-five at most, and sported a neatly trimmed beard that partially covered a heat burn across his lower face. Although he was now in our domain, and technically at our mercy, he showed no fear or even concern.

"This is a wise decision on your part," he told me as I led him into the kitchen. "You are the leader of this group?"

"Yes, my name is Joel. We are always ready to welcome new friends. I only hope that our efforts are not in vain."

"You have done the right thing, Joel," he assured me with a satisfied smile. Damned if that bastard wasn't getting off on this somehow. He stood stick-straight, thrust his chest out, and wore his robe like it was some kind of royal cape instead of a survival garment. He clearly regarded himself as the Second Coming or better. "My name is Gareth. I am responsible for the formation of this crusade. We are on a mission to seek out Reaper sympathizers and eliminate them."

"So you said. I suppose my word is not enough for you?"

"I'm afraid that won't do, Joel, as it has been my experience that the Reaper's adherents hide in groups such as yours. Like parasites, they seek shelter in the guise of a survivor, but meanwhile they plot to destroy any remaining vestiges of our former civilization."

"This isn't just some paranoid quest that's just as dangerous to the innocent as it is to the guilty?" This guy and his group technically had me by the balls, and we both knew it. I just wanted to make it clear that he was gripping some big ones.

My accusation seemed to amuse him. "Joel, someone always has to pay for the crimes of another. Accomplices and sympathizers are as guilty as the criminal himself, because they can and do carry on where he left off. Any sympathy for the Reaper's ideology is enough to make those who harbor it a danger to me, to you. The impure thoughts have to end so that we can be assured a future."

"That doesn't leave much room for free thought. Fear-mongering is just as deadly to a recovering society, don't you think?"

"You speak well, Joel." Gareth studied me. "You, I can say with certainty, are not a sympathizer. Do you know how I can tell?"

I remained silent. Unperturbed, he continued. "I can tell because contempt for the Reaper flows from your very being. I see it in your eyes. I hear it in your speech. You're pure."

"And I can assure you, the others here are as pure as I am."

Gareth surveyed his surroundings. "I see that you power your home with fossil fuels, and I assume that the large barn facility growing fruits and vegetables is also your work. These are the marks of a thoughtful people, people getting back on their feet regardless of the Reaper's devastation, people moving forward."

They knew about the barn. That was troubling.

"This puts you all in a very favorable light, and tells us a lot about the type of leader you are, Joel." He offered his hand to me, and I took it. "We'll be staying awhile. Feel free to allow your group to mingle with mine. We are good people, and I feel that you and I will be friends. I offer you support in the defense of your home for the duration of our stay. I'll speak with you again tomorrow."

I walked him out. When I closed the door, Connor came out of the family room, where he'd been silently listening in.

"That went well, man. I heard the whole thing."

"That was tense, that's what that was. I'm burned out. I need a drink."

We went up to the addition, where the rest of the group waited. After Connor and I poured ourselves a stiff gin, I filled the rest of them in on how the meeting went.

"It looks as though he's going to want to put each of us under the 'magnifying glass', so to speak. The idea of it doesn't sit well with me, but I seriously doubt he'll find any of us guilty of the crime he's punishing. None of you will come off as a member of the Four Horsemen if you demonstrate hatred for the Reaper when he tests you."

"So, when are we to turn ourselves over to this witch hunt?" Earl wasn't happy. None of us were, but what could we do? This was just another form of surviving. That was how we had to see it.

"Gareth says we can mingle with his company," Connor said. "I heard him tell Joel that."

"Gareth?" Freddy made a face. "The fuck kind of a name is that?"

"Gareth is the leader of the flags," I answered. "Just walk lightly around him; I get the distinct feeling that he's someone who could turn on you at the drop of a dime."

We would have to become comfortable with the deal we had agreed to. I only hoped that it wasn't a deal with the Devil, although somehow, I knew that it was.

"We're to wait for further instructions, so I can't say for sure when the questioning will begin, but like Connor said, he told me to let you guys mingle with his people. So go for it. But while you're 'mingling', try getting information from them. Find out where they're from, and where they're going. Anything you think will be useful to us: numbers, male to female ratio, types of artillery. If this whole inquisition goes south on us I want to be able to hold our own."

With that said, Sonny led the group outside, where Gareth's solders greeted them with open arms. Sara and I watched from Skylab as our two armies began to intermingle with trepidation. The flag bearers seemed normal and friendly enough. Maybe it would be all right after all. A sense of well-being overcame me. Then another shiver coursed through my body.

"Oops, someone just walked over your grave!" Sara rubbed my back gently.

"As long as it isn't Gareth." My smile vanished. So did Sara's. We returned our gaze to the front lawn. "You know, he's prepared to help us defend the house for as long as they stay."

"Sounds like someone that we can trust to be fair and not judge too quickly." Sara was so good, too good. She was too trusting.

"I don't know. There's that glimmer of power in his eyes: they're lit up, like Sonny's when he realizes he's about to get into a fight. You know the one?"

She nodded.

"Power like that can be used one way or the other. Either way he knows he's got it and that leaves us at a disadvantage." I hugged Sara with my right arm, pulling her close.

Our two factions stayed up late into the evening. Although they carried weapons (heck, so did we!) the flag bearers were not as sinister as we'd initially believed. It was actually both energizing and soothing for our group to talk to new people, to share experiences and commiserate over personal tragedies. Sara found common ground with a fifty-something woman who once practiced medicine in the city. They were simply led by a man possessed.

The evening ended at midnight, when Gareth ordered his troops to bed by sounding one of the many horns. Our crew returned to Skylab to discuss the day's events and ponder the future.

Chapter Twenty-One

The weather changed rather dramatically overnight, as the northerly wind had gone from cool to cold. Our heavy coats came in handy once again. The summer was a memory, fall had come and gone, and now winter was upon us. A nuclear winter would be the joke around the house. Jokes kept you sane. Our humor may have become darker since the apocalypse, but at least we could still laugh.

Kevin was playing a favorite CD in the addition as he toiled at another drawing. Goosebumps broke out on my forearms as I listened. The beautiful echo floated throughout the room and reverberated off broken glass, empty bottles, and drywall. Music had become less a luxury and more a necessity to break the gloom since encountering the tanker.

I opened the east windows of Skylab to allow the flag army to enjoy the music as well. One by one they gathered on the front lawn, staring up at me, listening. When I spied Gareth making his way through the crowd, I waved. He gestured for me to come down, so I did.

We met on the front step, which was still bloodstained from our encounter with the biker invaders. Gareth stood on a particularly large stain, seemingly oblivious to the fact.

"Let us begin the process. It's time," he told me. Such a diplomat. "I want your full compliment to meet me at my trailer. There I will tag and place them accordingly, to be questioned when their number is called." His tone was colder, and the crooked smile twitched under his beard. I felt broken then, no longer able to protect my group. Gareth knew it - I knew it.

"I'll let them know."

When he took his leave, I closed the door and called for Connor. He appeared above me, leaning over the railing from the top floor.

"Connor, let the house know that we're being called to the inquisition today!"

"Right now?"

"Right now, my friend. Everyone needs to be processed. I'll get the guys from the basement."

The flag army surrounded our house, protecting it from further threats while we, its residents, were to be put through the wringer. Gareth had kept his promise in that department. I hoped that he would therefore conduct a straightforward question and answer session with my friends. I had to hold on to that. But what would happen if he were to – intentionally or otherwise- find one of them guilty? Sara? What if he declared her to be a sympathizer? Or Connor, or anyone? I couldn't just let them be executed. I wouldn't!

A wave of nausea hit me as I watched my friends be numbered and tagged liked animals. The preliminary processing went quickly. Each member of my proud group was now itemized to Gareth's satisfaction, ready to be called upon. My blood boiled- what right did he have? But before the interrogations could begin, mass excitement broke out.

"We've got movement in the woods!" A frantic voice came on over Gareth's walkie. "Lots of movement…." Gunshots sounded, followed by an ominous static.

The flag troops on front yard detail raced to aid their compatriots in the woods. I ran to Skylab. From my new vantage point, I watched as figures moved through the forest, trying to climb the hill as they dodged trees and bullets. It was like a turkey-shoot out there. Remembering the spotlight, I went back downstairs. But when my hand touched the switch, I stopped.

Those whom I was assisting: were they the real threat or did we have more to fear from the charging horde? Should I let this new enemy overrun the flags? Who was the more dangerous of the two? Neither was an outstanding choice. I made the call to help Gareth's people, as they were actively protecting the house. Then I turned the powerful lamp on our common foe.

The approaching horde was indeed a force of comparable size. I hobbled as quickly as I could to the front yard to rally my own troops, numbered and tagged though they were. To my relief, Gareth was willing to let us help his "perfectly capable army" defend our home.

I gathered my friends in the front foyer. "Girls, you stay in Skylab and pick your shots from there. The rest of us are going into the thick of it. Gareth's people have no idea of how to fight on our terrain."

Sara, Julia, and Caroline went to the addition while the guys followed me to the garage. We exited via the back door and crouched in the bushes, clutching our weapons and watching the two groups exchange fire.

Several of Gareth's men and women were dead or dying on the battlefield. They'd been pushed back at least ten yards by the horde, which was now shielded by the planters. I signaled for my men to flank the enemy through the cornfields to the north and make our approach under cover of the forest.

"Alright," I whispered as we reassembled at the edge of the woods. "Spread out three feet from one another and choose your shots." The rush of adrenaline was invigorating, helping me keep up with the group despite my injury. I waved them down and positioned myself to the extreme left of the line. We were ready.

Climbing over their departed comrades, the invaders cautiously navigated the tortured terrain. They began splitting up, leading the great bulk of what remained of their army in our direction, flanking the flag's men. The spotlight's beam penetrated the trees, giving us a good advantage. Looking at my friends' faces, I saw that the majority were struggling with the idea of an ambush. It may not have been the most sporting thing to do, but this was war. It was us or them.

"Everyone, pick the target to your right. That way we won't be firing at the same person," Earl whispered from the extreme right of the line.

"Fire!" I hissed.

We discharged our weapons, dropping several of them. Then we advanced on their position, careful not to be caught in crossfire with the flag army. While we waited on the enemy, worry for the girls in Skylab gripped me.

"Sonny, Seth, Kevin- go back and see to it that no one gets past the flag's troops. Join the girls!" They nodded and headed back as stealthily as they approached. The rest stayed with me, and waited.

We were nearly trampled when three sets of legs crossed in front of our line. Earl, seeing his opportunity, tackled one around the ankles, taking him down. We ambushed the other two. No shots were fired. John pounded on one man's chest while Earl knelt on his arms. Earl studied the face of his enemy, one hand covering the man's mouth. Then he blinked hard, produced his army knife, and jabbed the blade repeatedly into his target's throat. Targets. We had to see them as such if we were to fight and win.

Connor's fingers were gripping his opponent's tangled hair as he pounded the man's head against the forest floor. When his hands tired, he let fly with his famous right-hand punch, ending the struggle permanently.

Freddy's man got away from him during their tussle in the grass. Sidney caught up with him first and looped a belt around his throat to secure him to a tree. Freddy then lunged up and swung his fist with such ferocity that the man's neck snapped. The body went limp, and Sidney released his hold on the belt.

I watched it all as I covered their backs, witnessing a brutality that none of us would have been capable of before hell rained upon us. We had become soldiers, each of us, not just survivors. As I reviewed the last twenty-four hours, I recoiled at the thought of allowing a monomaniac like Gareth decide whether we should live or die. It was preposterous. Who did he think he was - God's gunslinger? I definitely knew what we weren't: his prisoners. Fuck him, and fuck his inquisition. We would go back and reclaim our freedom.

Connor leaned over the limp torso he'd long since stopped hitting, one hand still wrapped around his foe's throat while the other rested on the man's still chest. Breathing heavily, he rolled off the corpse and lay flat on the forest floor, arms out, legs sprawled. Earl sat with his back braced against a tree, knife in hand, eyes fixed on the gore-coated blade. John kept a watchful eye on the cliff from whence the three men had materialized, frantically shifting this way and that, staring down the barrel of his rifle. Sidney searched the clothing of the man he and Freddy had taken down, looking for anything we could add to our stockpile of weapons and ammunition. Suddenly he let out a strangled cry. "Oh, no! Oh shit, man!"

"What, Sid?" Freddy hurried over, gesturing frantically for him to lower his voice.

"It's a girl, man. It's a little – a little girl! We just killed a little girl, Fred!" He wasn't going to shut up. I knew it and so did everyone else. Soon he would give away our position. The gunshots were loud but he was getting louder, as if he felt it necessary to challenge the noise so that he could be heard over everything. He kept repeating that he'd killed a girl.

"Damn it, Sid! Shut the fuck up!" John hissed. "You're gonna get us all shot!"

"What did I do? What did I do?!" With that, he broke away from us and started running, out of the protection of the forest and into the open field. I started to follow him to drag him down, but Connor stopped me. "Let him go, man. He's got to get away from us."

Before I could respond, machine guns opened up on us. We were being targeted now. Bullets ripped through the trees. Dead branches snapped and fell all around us. We hit the ground.

"Let's fall back," I said. "We'll do better if we get to higher ground."

"Wait, Joel." It was John. "I think I saw where that fire came from."

"You're sure?"

"I'm telling you, it's just one gunner over there." He pointed toward the path. "I can get him!"

"I'll come with you." I crawled next to him, my heart pounding and my leg throbbing. "You guys cover us. We'll take this prick down!"

"Joel, your leg," Connor pointed to my pant leg, where a patch of blood was slowly spreading.

"I'm going with him," I repeated. Connor looked worried but said nothing further.

"We'll lay down a line of fire to the left of you guys," Earl offered.

John and I slid over the small cliff, making our way toward our target. When we were roughly forty feet from the others, we stopped and waited for the gunner to fire again. John put his index finger to his lips and then pointed into the woods, where I presumed he'd detected our enemy's whereabouts. He then formed a gun with his other hand, followed by a quick slash to his throat. The meaning: when he fires on our guys, we will pinpoint his precise location and then rush in, killing him. I nodded back, gripping my pistol with sweaty palms, anxious for the moment to end. Seconds later, the gunner shot again, signing his death warrant.

We hurried up a small hill, following the gunfire, the sound of our approach muffled by the artillery. Upon reaching the top we slid into a natural foxhole, where the enemy had bunkered in. John leaped upon him and stunned him with a solid punch to the head. I collected his weapon and asked John to back off, as I was interested in getting information from our prisoner first. John did so, but not before slapping him across the face to remind him what his current position was in the food chain.

To our surprise, our captive seized John's foot and twisted it violently, throwing him onto his back. My trigger finger squeezed down hard. The resulting splatter was like a fine red mist, covering John and I completely.

The man wheezed as he died, the deep hole in his torso gushing blood. John bit down on his sleeve to stifle his moans; a later examination would confirm that his ankle was broken.

We crawled back to the safety of our friends, gunfire now sparse and distant. On our final approach, I whispered loudly, "It's us. Grab John- he's got a broken ankle."

Earl lifted John over the cliff while Freddy and Connor helped me to the top. We stayed there no longer than the brief time it took for Freddy to immobilize John's ankle by splinting it with sticks and wrapping it with one of the dead men's shirts. I checked my own wound by tearing open my pant leg and examining the blood soaked dressing. It looked worse than it probably was.

The shooting had stopped completely now. "Time to go back," I said. "But not to submit to Gareth's goddamned questions. What do you say? We fight?"

"Damn right!" Earl had never been for surrender. "Why waste all of this adrenaline?"

"Agreed!" John whispered through clenched teeth.

Connor nodded. So did Fred. We were experiencing such powerful adrenaline surges right then that not much would stand in our way. Not a broken ankle, not a damaged leg. We were a ragtag band of brothers, covered in the enemy's blood, armed to the teeth.

And ready.

Chapter Twenty-Two

Arriving at Gareth's mobile home, we listened for voices, but no sound issued from within… or without, for that matter.

"Where is everyone?" Freddy wondered.

"Maybe they've moved into the house. Maybe they've got the others trapped!" Earl's mouth tightened at the thought.

"Alright, let's make our move to the garage," I ordered. "From there we'll go straight up the stairs to Skylab."

We got into the garage without being detected despite our injuries. The trek up to the addition was quiet and measured at first, but gradually became louder as the wooden stairs became creaky near the top. We flinched.

"Joel?!" It was Sara. "Joel, is that you? We're in control of the situation."

"It's me," I answered. We climbed the remaining five stairs and discovered that our team was indeed in control of Gareth's depleted army. He'd taken a major loss, as there were no more than twenty of his followers left, and these survivors were now disarmed and disheartened.

Sara threw herself into my arms. Caroline reacted to John's injured foot by assisting him to a sofa and hugging him, and Julia kissed Connor while tears of relief coursed down her cheeks. When I released her, Sara directed John and Caroline into our bedroom so she could treat his ankle. I approached Gareth and looked him up and down. He and his remaining people were huddled in the north end of Skylab, under heavy guard.

"Is this all of them?" I asked Sonny.

"Every last one of 'em," he assured me. I couldn't help but smile. Then I turned back to Gareth and reclaimed our lives.

"We do not agree to your game plan any longer," I informed him. "We will not be subjected to your questions and we will not be bullied against our will to join your morally bankrupt bullshit ideal!" My voice raised in pitch as each word drilled into Gareth's ego.

"We will not harm you, as justified as we may be in doing so. You promised that you would help us protect this house, and you did." I paused, giving my words time to sink in and make them understand who was in charge now. They were stunned at their loss; frankly, so was I. They'd come with over fifty people comprising their ranks, and now only twenty remained. That was still more than our side had, but they were weaponless and exhausted. "We will let you go, and extend an invitation for any of your people to stay should they wish to. But that doesn't include you, Gareth. You are not to return to this house: you are not welcome here."

Gareth listened quietly, even meekly, at first. But when none of his followers accepted my offer to shelter them, his crooked smile returned and the uncertainty disappeared from his eyes.

"I'll be back," he warned, ignoring the weapons trained on him. "This hostile action your group has taken will not be forgotten. I have little doubt that there is a sympathizer in your ranks. But you can still be saved from my wrath, Joel. I stand by my decision that you are clean of this sin." His finger was now in my face. Sonny and Seth approached, guns ready, but I waved them off, knowing that deep inside Gareth was desperate. He was embarrassed to have lost control.

"I made a deal with the Devil once, Gareth. I did it to avoid a confrontation and play the odds that we'd all come out of this inquisition of yours unscathed. I see you in a different light now. I see you for what you really are: a small man, an angry man, a man possessed. You wouldn't have been happy coming here and questioning us without having fabricated something from nothing and sacrificing one of us to satiate your sick sense of self-worth."

Now my finger pointed sharply at his face. I must have presented a menacing sight. Dried blood caked my face and neck, dirt covered my forearms and knees, and the tear in my pants exposed the old yet newly bloodied wound.

"Shit! I get it, Gareth. These people latched onto you because you promised them something magical. You fed off of their personal tragedies, tragedies we all share. Deep inside you know damn well that most people would love to get the Reaper in a room for five minutes. But when someone crosses you, you declare them a sympathizer and murder them. How many innocents have you murdered? You're grasping at nothing to have purpose. Well, I'll give you a purpose – to stay alive."

My piece said, I staggered back and pointed at the stairs. The dull, passive eyes of Gareth's followers were fixed on him, waiting for him to tell them what to do. They acted as if they hadn't heard a thing I'd said.

Earl added his own parting speech to the group. "A foolish faith in authority is the first enemy of truth." A quote from Einstein, he later told me. Fitting.

Gareth glanced scornfully at Earl before facing me again. "I have every right to come here and order your people to prove their innocence! You have all made a grave mistake in defying us. We are not evil people, but we do represent a necessary evil." He headed for the stairs. "Soon there will be far more than the mere fifty-three members I brought to your home, and you will have no choice then. You will be judged."

The rest of his group fell into line behind him. Sonny whispered to me, "We don't have to just let him go like this, Joel. I'll do the fucking prick right now!"

"We won't see him again. He knows that we're stronger than he is, stronger than he'll ever be. Make sure they leave."

"Damn straight!" Sonny and the others walked the flag bearers downstairs, out of the house, and into their motor homes. With fewer people left to drive, we gained what vehicles they could not pilot, as well as several more weapons and ammunition stores.

I sent Sonny and Connor to follow the flags as far as the next intersection and watch them continue north until they disappeared from view. An hour later they returned and helped clear away the dead. The smell of blood was thick enough to almost see in the fog that had set in. The spotlight remained on as we hurried through the grisly work, but we treated it as such- work- and were becoming rather efficient at ignoring the lumps of flesh we dragged to the pit, save the ones that moved or moaned despite their mortal wounds. When that happened, gunshots broke the darkness with flashes of orange light. I couldn't pull the trigger on these survivors, so that horrible task fell to Earl and John.

Sara dropped down and buried her head between her knees when she heard the shots, hands pressed tightly against her ears. Earl went about the executions coldly, his face expressionless. He assured us he did it to end their suffering, but nonetheless it was a chore I could not bring myself to do. Thank God he was there.

After we threw the last corpse into the pit, I decided to send Connor, Sonny, Seth and Freddy to the barn to ensure that Gareth didn't show up there to steal our food and sabotage our efforts. Earl and Kevin finished up outside, tossing earth over the pile of what had once been people like us.

*****

During our looting of the abandoned RVs, Sidney apologized yet again for his reckless actions on the battlefield. I told him not to sweat it.

"Shit, Sid," I said, ducking one of the many archways in the motor home and narrowly escaping another bump on the head. "Any one of us could have lost it over anything out there. What you have to understand, though, is that she'd have killed you if the opportunity had presented itself. Christ, they weren't here to sell us vacuums. You've got to think like that."

"I know, Joel. But in hindsight I can't stop thinking how you guys could have been discovered because of my-"

"Forget it, Sid. You lost it. End of story. We won in the end, so look at it that way. You keep playing it over and over again in your head and you'll go nuts."

"It was a bizarre scene, that's for damn sure." He put down his Coke, one of a dozen we found in the vehicle's undercarriage storage. "You know, I don't think I told you everything that happened after I bolted."

"Tell me now."

Sid smiled. "It's not a long story." He leaned against the RV's kitchen counter and began.

"So, obviously, my head was in a bad place right? I kept running until I reached the edge of the field. The noise of gunshots was still behind me. When I looked back, I wiped out on an old corn stump or something. There I was, lying face down in the dirt, bawling my eyes out for that woman, or girl or whatever she was. She was all I could think of." He stopped for a minute. I could see that the memory still pained him.

"Anyways, I rolled onto my side and looked into the back yard through the pines, and there they were, the flag army, what was left of them, all huddled behind the planters." He stopped again, studying the cabinet above my head, not looking at it, but rather looking through it, reliving the memory. "Then I saw the strangest thing." Again he stopped.

"What, Sid? What did you see?" I leaned forward.

"I saw myself in action before I actually did anything. I hit my head pretty hard when I fell, so maybe it was a concussion. But somehow I knew I was being guided, shown what I had to do. I saw myself move in on Gareth's people. I saw that they needed to surrender to us. And so I did it. I grabbed the nearest one, and stuck my rifle into his ribs Then Sonny and Seth came out of the basement and saw what I was doing. They raised their guns and ordered the group to drop their weapons. And every one of them was so shocked they did exactly what they were told." Sidney beamed. "It was the angel wasn't it? He guided me."

The story truly lifted my spirits. Back in the house, I made sure that Sidney relayed his experience to everyone else, so that they could hope too. After a day like this one, hope was a commodity we couldn't live without.

Chapter Twenty-Three

Exhilaration. Joy. Glee. During the early hours of the morning after our victory over Gareth, we finally found ourselves able to discern day from night. The sun, that iridescent sphere of warmth, had returned.

While I tore through the house, frantically waking all sleepers, John and Sara remained in Skylab, watching the clouds break apart. As sunlight penetrated the grey blanket and illuminated the landscape, I realized that we'd been living in black and white, like we'd been locked inside one of Kevin's chalk drawings.

We all gathered on the front lawn, awestruck at the combined beauty of color and light. As the soil warmed, steam rose from the earth as if it were exhaling, emitting a great sigh of relief. When the sun completed its climb over the horizon, the cloud that had been holding it captive for months drifted south, exposing a brilliant blue sky.

For the rest of the day, we kept interrupting our tasks to raise our faces and hands to the sun's healing rays. When it finally set, we were just as bewitched by the arrival of the moon and stars. Standing in Skylab, eyes never leaving the night sky, I picked a star….

"Reminds me of a painting." Kevin took a haul off the Sweet Bitch, and then passed her to me. "I don't think I've ever seen such brilliant stars."

"Is it any wonder so many civilizations worshipped them?" Caroline wiped away tears.

It was a cool evening, crisp even, so blankets and pillows were collected from beds, brought outside, and suddenly we were all camping again. We were inspired by the night sky, lost in its vastness, once again able to see beyond our own borders and reclaim our dreams. Gone was the heavy ceiling of despair that had hung over this house for months, that crushing, suffocating ceiling. Seeing those stars made me feel as if I'd been granted a pardon from a life sentence. If I could see the stars, anything was possible.

The sunrise woke us as we slept on the black, sooty lawn. A new day had begun.

*****

After breakfast, which we cooked and consumed outdoors, we held a group meeting in the addition. Earl outlined a new mission that he had proposed to me earlier, in response to the sun's return.

"We need to continue being proactive," he explained. "We need to know what, if anything is up north. Is the military there? Are those bands of people we've seen headed in that direction alive? Have they created a community?"

I stood. "These are important questions to answer. What if there is some semblance of community there? What if the government has taken those people in and sheltered them all this time? It's an information-gathering mission."

"It is a good idea," Sonny conceded. "I volunteer. We need to know."

Earl added, "Those of us that go on this mission will also take the opportunity to catch up with Gareth's group."

"That's right. We should catch up with the flag army and, while keeping a safe distance, observe and later report on any activity. If there are others north of here we don't want Gareth getting his claws into them and recruiting a new army."

"Should we really send some of us away when we just barely defeated the last attack on the house?" Julia wondered. "I mean, we wouldn't have won at all if the flag army hadn't supported us. I think it's not such a good idea."

"I'm not saying that it won't be a dangerous move on our part," I admitted. "Yes, you're absolutely right that without Gareth's help we'd have probably been overwhelmed last time, but this is something we've got to do."

"It's a mistake!" Julia insisted. Her agitation grew. "It's a mistake!"

Before she could say more, Connor took her by the shoulders and walked her out of the addition, whispering into her ear.

Kevin spoke up. "I'm not going to say it's a bad idea, but I'd rather stay here and defend the house."

"Okay," I said. "It's your prerogative Kev. All of you have a choice to make."

"We don't want more than three people for this job," Earl stated. "I'm willing to be one of the goers, and Sonny says he's in. Who else?"

We scanned the group for a hand hovering above the rest, and saw that Freddy's had worked its way up.

"You're sure, Freddy?" When he answered in the affirmative, I turned to Earl. "Get all the gear ready to go today and also get some rest, as you'll leave tonight."

The meeting concluded, and I went outside. Truth be told, it was difficult to be anywhere else. Sitting on a lawn chair, I checked the makeshift connection between our generator and the gas truck.

"Sorry about Julia's outburst during the meeting."

Connor caught me off-guard. I was indulging in a hoot off the pipe and coughed violently.

"Slow down, man, enjoy," he chuckled, slapping my back.

"Shit," I croaked through a tightening esophagus. Once I could speak again without choking I asked, "What was that about Julia?"

"When she freaked out over the plan up there. She's been brooding too much again. I thought the sun would have been enough to stop that - wishful thinking."

I breathed deeply, quieting the tickle in my chest. "Now what's she thinking about? Not suicide again?"

"No, it's not about that any more. It's something else, pretty serious too."

"Do you want to talk about it?"

"She'd kill me if she knew I was telling you, or anybody." Another pause as he deliberated. "Joel, she thinks she's pregnant." His head shook back and forth as though he were fighting with the idea of it.

My response almost knocked him on his ass. "That's amazing, Connor!" I exclaimed. "Shit! She must know that we'll be happy for her! What this could mean: new life, the future of the human race."

"I agree. But she keeps saying that she doesn't want to bring a baby into a world that's less then perfect." Connor was becoming more and more distressed. "I really think she's going over the edge, man, really. You don't know what it's like at night with her now. She's a basket case. I can't talk sense into her."

"What do you want to do? How should we handle this?"

"We can't do anything, Joel. Nothing. I'll have to deal with it until she decides what she wants." Connor started to back up. "Don't concern yourself, man. I just came here to apologize for her." With that said, he left.

Forgetting about the generator connection, I pulled out my sidearm and checked the clip. Full. Then I limped off into the woods, feeling an overwhelming need to walk this out.

Ten minutes into my stroll, I found myself at the creek bed where we'd buried Gil. Stopping, I gazed down at the dirt mound. Gil would have enjoyed this day. Maybe he and I would have stuck a pair of rods in the stream and waited for the fish to return. Then I noticed something odd beside Gil's grave. It appeared as though someone - or something- had begun digging another hole to the right of his.

"That's odd," I muttered. Reaching down, I grabbed the dry earth and watched it crumble from my open palm. "Who's this for?" The hole was no more than a foot deep but it was long, and wide enough for a body. It was creepy, and felt like an omen.

"Stop thinking so much," I told myself. "It could be anything."

Jake's rudimentary grave was next on this grim tour. God, I couldn't have imagined the turn of events that would see two of my friends buried in my own back forty. I lowered myself to the ground, wincing as my injured leg protested. When the throbbing ceased I reached out and patted the earth covering Jake.

"How come you knew so much, Jake?" I wished I could have asked him personally. God, did I wish. "Miss you, buddy." I took a few more moments to smooth over the dirt and left it at that. What else could I say? He was a friend who had played a much larger role in my life than I could have imagined.

I got up carefully and moved eastward to the shack. I had to confront the memory of Jake's death. The sun hit the path intermittently through the ravaged tree-tops, and branches littered the forest floor.

The shed was still standing. I turned the corner, half expecting to see him sitting on his sacred ground. Coincidentally, his spot *was* getting all of the sun. I smiled: he knew so much.

*****

After supper, we all prepared the three voyageurs for their long trip. At least we assumed it would be long. Honestly, we hadn't the slightest clue just how far they'd need to travel before seeing something worth mentioning.

"Without wheels we'll probably make about twenty kilometers a day. That'll put us near Elle Lake by Friday," Fred guessed. Though we had vehicles to spare, we agreed that to send them on foot would not only save gasoline but make their presence less detectible.

"We'll be fine," Sonny said as he pushed his chair back from the kitchen table. "It's all a matter of picking our battles."

"That's ironic coming from you," Earl laughed.

They departed with an air of confidence about them. Watching them recede from view, I only hoped that this angel we had created would watch over them.

Chapter Twenty-Four

Later that evening, Kevin decided to paint a 'Last Supper' that depicted the twelve of us as Jesus and the Apostles in a parody of Da Vinci's classic masterpiece.

"I'm not sure who will represent who yet. It's something I'd planned to do last summer, but with all that happened, I never started it. Anyway, this is the canvas I'll use." He pulled the piece from his portfolio case and set it on his easel.

"Sounds interesting," Sara commented. "Who'll be the Christ figure, I wonder?"

"Good question," I said. "Kev?"

"Well, isn't it obvious?" he grinned.

"You?" she wondered, furrowing her brow.

"Me? No! I think it'll be the angel. I can't come up with anyone else who's that close to God, except Joel."

I was embarrassed and laughed it off. Sara did not.

"You know, that's the most twisted thing," she was not kidding. "You honestly picture Joel as the Christ?"

"Don't get all hot and bothered, Sara. I said it was going to be the angel, not Joel. It's just a painting, for fuck sakes!"

"Alright, that's enough of that." I attempted to end the conversation before it escalated into an argument.

"Look at you, Joel." Her voice cracked. "You like it, don't you? You like that your friends think of you like that."

"Easy!" Irritation crept into my voice. "Go easy, Sara, you know I haven't let any of this go to my head."

"Be sure that it doesn't." With that said, she took her leave. Deeper within the house, a door slammed.

"She's got to let up on the whole religion thing, man." Kev, still flustered, lit a cigarette, one of thousands he and Earl had pilfered early on. "We don't know what it is we're dealing with."

"I used to think that too." I gazed out the window while I spoke. "But this angel thing, it's got me reeling."

Without even thinking, I picked up the pipe from the bar and lit a toke for myself. Kev watched in amazement, wondering whether I'd changed the rules about getting messed up on duty.

Before he had a chance to say anything though, Sara returned for the twelve to four shift and saw the state I was in. She assisted me to my room. As she tucked me under the covers I smiled, overwhelmed by my love for her. I'd hit a high with her at the lowest point in my life, in all of our lives. I only wished that the others had what Sara and I possessed.

*****

During my pot-induced slumber, I had a dream. I was walking the grounds outside the house. I had the distinct impression that I'd been walking for years and would continue to do so. Was I in purgatory? The wind picked up from the north, blowing my hair about my face. Looking down at my feet, I saw the trench my pacing had created.

"You are not set upon this path to walk alone, Joel." The voice came from inside my head. Was it my own?

"This burden is not yours alone," the voice explained. I suddenly realized I was talking with my angel. "Do not let an ego overwhelm your good sense." I couldn't stop walking the trench as I listened to the angel's words.

"The others know peace now. Keep your good sense about you, Joel. It won't be long."

I was still walking, but now I wept as well. "To what end? We've lost three friends to your precious path. Fuck you! You ask too much!"

I woke up staring at the ceiling, muscles rigid and fluttering. I was angry. Angry with this insane vision giving me hope. Angry with Sara for instilling some sense of religious fanaticism in me. Angry with myself for the pedestal I'd put myself on. Did I think I was on my way to sainthood? I was turning my dreams into some sort of hope for the future. My spasms stopped abruptly. Putting things in perspective I reminded myself it was just a dream. I kissed Sara who was now draped over me, and fell back into a restless slumber.

*****

It turned out that Julia was as worried for Connor as he had been for her the day before. Sitting in the backyard with me, she expressed concern over what she called Connor's late night disappearances. I glanced discreetly at her belly, careful not to give anything away.

"What do you mean by disappearances, Julia? What's he doing, going for a piss?"

"For three hours?"

"Three hours? Have you ever thought to follow him?"

"I always decide against it. It isn't every night, maybe two or three a week. But we're going on week three."

"And you're sure he isn't getting up early for his four to eight?"

"Yes, and there's something else. When he returns, he gets back into bed with his knees and hands covered in dirt."

"Dirt?" I was stumped. "Maybe you'd better ask Connor what he's up to."

"I was kind of hoping that you'd do that for me, Joel. I mean, we're having a hard time right now. Our relationship ... please, will you ask him for me?"

"Sure, I'll find a way to ask him." I offered a reassuring smile, which she returned with one of gratitude. I watched her rise and leave, her hands gently brushing across her abdomen.

Chapter Twenty-Five

The Caddy pulled into the garage early that afternoon. Connor, Sidney, and Seth had gone on a scavenging expedition to a town fifty kilometers to the east. There they siphoned a small amount of gasoline from the pumps and found something almost as exciting - chocolate bars! Lately our attempts at salvaging any useful goods from the surrounding towns had been anything but prosperous, so they acted like they'd found the Holy Grail.

"We've got chocolate bars by the dozen!" Connor beamed, lifting a garbage bag full of assorted sweets above his head. The last sweet fix I had was a spoonful of white sugar, so I salivated. "Found 'em in a gas station vending machine."

"How were they not ruined?" Sara wondered.

"Hey, I'm not saying they resemble their former selves, but they still taste like chocolate! Here!" Pulling out three misshapen bars, he bit into one and tossed the others to us.

"Was there any resistance?" I asked.

"Nothing," Seth confirmed as he hauled another bag of treats from the trunk.

"Wow, everyone's going to be so happy to see these," Sara exclaimed.

"I hope so, 'cause we had to roll that vending machine over to get at them." Sidney explained that the machine had collapsed on its face, shattering the glass but concealing the contents from would-be scavengers. "Got some chips and nuts out of it too. You wouldn't believe how heavy one of those things is. No wonder people died when those things fell on them!"

I gestured to Connor, indicating that I needed to speak to him alone. While Sara and the guys inventoried our new stash of party snacks, Connor and I went into the backyard, out of earshot.

"What have you been doing at nights?" I asked him.

"What?" He recoiled, and then frowned, as though I'd just overstepped my bounds.

I persisted. "Is it you back there? You digging up that earth next to Gil's grave?" I stared at him, hard. "Is it, man?"

Connor glared. Then he lowered his head and approached the picnic table, where he slowly sat down. I followed.

"What's wrong with me, man? There must be something wrong with me..." His jaw muscles flexed.

"Is it like a sleepwalking thing?"

"Yeah, yeah, I think it's something like that. Or maybe I'm going crazy." He ran both hands through his hair and bit his lip.

"Don't say shit like that. You're not."

"Joel, I can't explain what's happening to me. It's like I'm under the control of someone else. That doesn't make any sense, I know, but I don't know how else to describe it."

"Like you're outside looking in?"

"No, like I'm actually someone else, walking a path that they'd once walked. Like when I let the déja-vu run its course. Maybe that's it. Maybe it's nothing to worry about."

"Are you kidding? You could get shot walking around in the woods in the middle of the night! Then we'd have to bury you in the grave you dug yourself. That's messed up!"

"Maybe I was digging a grave for someone else." He looked sick at the thought. "Maybe it's for the baby... for Julia's baby."

He caught me off guard with that one. "The baby?"

"Yeah, maybe this means that the baby won't make it to term and be a miscarriage."

God, it was a horrible thing to hear coming out of his mouth but a better scenario than him dropping dead.

Slapping his shoulder, I stood up. "Come on, let's get back. We'll figure out what's going on somehow." Together we resurfaced from our hidden position under the balcony and walked out into the sun.

During lunch, Connor drank more than he usually did. I didn't stop him: he was dealing with a lot. I limited myself to the tainted tap water, which was now bearable thanks to some flavor crystals that Sara had found in the dry storage, but lit a joint to accompany my sickly sweet drink. We wondered how Earl, Sonny, and Fred were making out. Julia stated again that she thought the expedition was a bad idea. Connor looked up from his third glass of straight gin and blurted, "Why do you have to be so negative? Don't tell me it's PMS: you're pregnant, remember?"

Everyone gasped. I fought the urge to strangle my best friend. All eyes fell on Julia. Her quivering chin sank and she blinked in slow motion, as though trying to erase the last thirty seconds. Then she slowly laid down her sandwich, stood up, and left the kitchen.

I pushed down on Connor's shoulder as he started to rise. My touch was hard: he got the message. Sara also gestured for him to stay put.

"Let me, Connor." She wasn't asking permission. She pushed her chair away from the table and followed her best friend.

Silence hung over the kitchen. Then Kevin asked, "When did this happen?"

Both Connor and I shot him a look. He shut up and feigned interest in his beef jerky.

"She'll be fine, Connor," John added. "Caroline missed her period once too, man, it doesn't always mean they're pregnant."

"Julia hasn't had hers for two months," Connor replied dully. "She is going to hate me for saying anything. She's going to hate me."

"She's not going to hate you, man," I insisted. My anger had dissipated and I started to feel sorry for him. "It had to come up eventually."

"Yeah, really, Connor what was she going to do, claim to have found a baby somewhere?"

Kevin's special brand of sarcasm wasn't helping. Connor didn't react though. He just stood up and went to the basement. I left him with his thoughts and stepped onto the patio with Kev and John. Kev lit a cigarette as we planted ourselves on some lawn chairs. John slipped a joint from his pocket and lit it using Kev's smoke. When he offered it to me I took a deep toke. It had been a hell of a day.

*****

Later that night, when Kevin and I shared guard duty with Sara, she told us Julia's wrenching story. It was one of self-pity, a loathsome emotion we were all familiar with, as well as survivor's guilt, another deeply traumatic sensation everyone had to deal with. But unlike us, Julia chased all of those painful and self-destructive emotions and nourished an enormous sense of self-hate over allowing something like a pregnancy to happen at all. She was adamant that she couldn't let a baby be born into a damaged world like this.

"The way she was explaining herself - trying to justify her reasoning –was frightening," Sara went on. "I think I might have talked her out of an abortion. I mean, I could try to perform it for her but it'd be dangerous. Besides, I told her that a baby would be a beautiful addition to our group, a representative of hope. Anyway, I think I gave her something to sleep on tonight. Connor will take it from there. I just can't believe she didn't come to me with this information as soon as she knew."

"Sounds like maybe you've gotten her off on the right foot again," Kevin offered.

"Thanks," Sara said. "I hope so."

When twelve o'clock rolled around, Caroline and John came in to relieve us. Sidney was behind them, looking too tired for someone about to begin the night shift.

"Ready for eight hours of this?" I asked, rubbing my eyes.

"I figure it can't be much worse than the four to eighter," John replied. "Just knowing that the sun's going to rise is enough to keep me up."

"Amen to that," stated Sidney, taking his place at the north window.

"Enjoy..." Kevin, Sara and I took our leave, never guessing what the morning would bring.

Chapter Twenty-Six

"Joel!" My eyes flickered open. I could hear the distressed voice of my best friend. "Joel..."

He began to shake me. Sara woke up too, and was the first to see the look of helplessness and horror in Connor's red-rimmed eyes.

"Oh no," she whimpered, knowing instinctively that it had something to do with Julia. Her chin trembled and tears streamed down her cheeks. When Connor nodded at her, confirming the worst, Sara jumped out of bed and charged out of our room.

"What is it? What's happened?" I sat up. Sara could be heard crying frantically in the spare bedroom, Connor and Julia's room. Peering closely at the hunched figure of my best friend, I saw with alarm that blood covered the front of his shirt.

"It's Julia." Connor couldn't speak further. When he began to sway, I scrambled out of bed, ignoring the pain in my leg, and caught him. I could see Sara across the hall through my open door, kneeling beside Julia's bed, holding her lifeless white hand. Jesus, there was blood everywhere!

I helped Connor onto my bed. He stayed there, gripping the blankets and pulling them over his head. Then I ran across the hall and dropped next to Sara.

Julia was dead, and had been for hours from the look of her. The stench of blood was overpowering. My eyes fell to her hands, where I saw deep, vicious cuts in her wrists. The morning sun permeated the room, enhancing the contrast of red on white, red on everything.

Sara remained kneeling beside the bed, weeping into Connor's pillow as I massaged her shoulders. Glancing back into my room, I saw Connor sitting on my bed, swaying back and forth and pulling at his hair. He'd never be the same either. Just when you think you've mastered your situation, fate throws you a curve ball. We'd come so far, I thought we were actually getting a grip on this. I would never overestimate myself or my friends again.

*****

Sara stayed with Connor in our room while Kevin and I wrapped Julia in a soft yellow sheet. It was now painfully obvious as to who would fill the plot Connor had so diligently - albeit unconsciously - dug over so many sleepless nights. We would lower Julia's small and delicate vessel into the plot beside Gil.

During the brief funeral service, only the Lord's Prayer was recited. Words, even prayers, were powerless to soften the grief and melancholy. Connor never spoke. His chin rarely left his chest as he stared at the grave and accepted handshakes or hugs without offering any eye contact. I showed my support by sitting with him constantly, being there should he wish to open up after the funeral. Which he did.

We were seated at the edge of the backyard, overlooking the woods, the newly erected grave marker in plain view.

"How bad could it have been?" he whispered. I said nothing, just listened. "Having a baby... how bad could it have been?" He lifted his head to look at me, eyes beseeching me for an answer.

"Connor…." I started to speak, but stopped. I turned away, closing my eyes against the orange glow fading on the horizon. Nothing I could say would make any difference.

"Go back to the house, Joel," he said softly. "I want to be alone for awhile."

*****

When night fell, I sat in one of the RVs out front, trying to piece together all that had happened, to find a pattern or purpose. I smoked a bowl, or two or three. When I was ready to reenter the world, I wandered into the house. It was late and my direction was utterly aimless. I ended up in the basement, where I came across Kevin's gallery of the bizarre. He had moved many of his paintings here from the addition to make room during the occupation.

"What are you doing, Joel?" asked Kevin. I jumped slightly as he materialized from the darkness like an apparition. My nerves were shot.

"Nothing, man. Can't sleep," I stated. Eyes traveling over his art, I asked, "Aren't you working anymore on this one?"

I pointed to the multi-canvas piece that captured one of my earlier dreams, one Kevin had shared. It was titled 'Body Parts', and featured a torso, wing, arm, horn and other pieces of anatomy.

"I'll be honest with you, Joel; I can't seem to find any inspiration in much of anything these days. The one thing that inspired me the most has let me down. I want to see the angel! I want to talk to him, I want more than what he's willing to give me." He scratched his face vigorously, suggesting that he'd been into something.

"Yeah, but careful what you wish for, Kev."

I was thirsty, so I went to the bar at the south end of the basement. Picking up a glass and blowing it free of dust and cobwebs, I poured the rust-colored water. "Seriously, Kev, you should be proud of the role you've played in this. He gave you that face to draw, the one we all recognized. That face built the theory we exist around. That's real."

"Like I said before, Joel: real to you, real to Connor and Jake, well not Jake anymore... but, how is he real to me? Real means more than just a dream. Christ, since when did dreams or visions define reality?" Kevin sat at one of the stools.

"Don't forget Sid's story," I reminded him. "Remember, he'd been shown a vision just before he approached Gareth. That was a gift. That's real."

"I suppose." He paused. "Or plain old adrenaline." Kev moved back toward his painter's box and fumbled with a baggie. "You feel like getting high?"

I was. But yes, I did.

*****

Thankfully we slept like the dead or we may well have fallen to our deaths. After smoking enough pot to buzz an army, Kev and I climbed atop the roof, directly above the addition, and stretched out. We were discovered by Sidney and Seth, who'd been looking for us all morning and checked that spot as a last resort.

"I gotta ask... why?" Seth exchanged amused glances with Sid after I opened my eyes. "You two look like shit."

"Why are we on the roof?" I wondered aloud, temporarily forgetting. The sun's rays felt like lasers boring into my eyes. Sidney took pity on me and handed me his sunglasses.

"That's what we want to know," Sid smirked.

Kevin awoke then. When he saw where he was, he pressed his body against the shingles: Kevin was petrified of heights. "Shit! How did you get me up here, Joel?"

Needless to say, we had a hell of a time getting him off the roof. A hit off the Sweet Bitch settled his nerves enough for him to crawl to the antenna secured to the side of the house, which was the only way up, and down.

Kevin and I apologized profusely for causing any alarm. We were all on edge after Julia's death, and what Kev and I did was our way of blowing off some steam. Regardless, we felt terrible that we were the cause of such a fierce search effort, especially in light of current events.

Connor was melancholy, but he assured us that he was managing and didn't need our constant smothering. I would respect that. When I invited him to join Sidney and I on a patrol of the property, he nodded.

It was a grey afternoon, and when we came upon the fresh earth that covered our Julia, grey somehow seemed appropriate. Sid and I hung back as Connor knelt before the mound. Resting his hands upon the lifted soil as if he were touching her again, he moved from its center to the outer edges, dragging his fingers slowly across where I imagined her waist was. He placed his forehead against the earth. After a moment he stood, wiping away the trace dirt on his brow.

As we were about to continue our walk, I spotted something that froze the blood in my veins.

Another grave had been started.

Grabbing Connor's arm, I pointed it out. Sid, who was a few paces ahead, turned around, but I motioned for him to stay put. "Did you do this, Connor?" I whispered, praying that he'd deny it.

"I found dirt in my fingernails this morning." He looked like he was about to throw up.

"Go to the shed, Sid," I called. "See if we caught anything in that trap Earl left there and report back to the house.

"Sure thing, Joel." Sid was confused, but knew better than to question. He checked his weapon and hustled the rest of the way.

I tried to reassure Connor. "Maybe it's just a routine now, and doesn't mean anything."

He shook his head violently. "No, that isn't it, Joel! Haven't you seen enough to know? Haven't you experienced enough? It's for real." He paused, and then turned to look me directly in the eye. "And this one's for me." He grasped the trunk of a tree as if he were about to fall.

He slid down the trunk of the tree, breaking into tears. The thought of losing him crushed me, making me collapse near him. I was so tired, so drained. Crawling over to my friend, I too sought support from the tree's failing strength, but in doing so, sent the weak trunk crashing to earth, taking us both with it. The shock on my face actually made Connor laugh despite his misery. I followed suit. Surrendering control over our overtaxed emotions, we sprawled on the ground and howled until the tears returned. We were still at it when Sidney rejoined us.

"What is it, guys? What's happened?"

"Sorry, Sid," I got up. Connor, sitting cross-legged in the dirt, wiped his eyes.

"What's going on?" He was genuinely concerned. "Were you guys laughing, or crying?"

"What's the difference?" I helped Connor to his feet and threw an arm around each of them. "Did we catch anything?"

"No, not yet."

As we headed back to the house, I sent a silent appeal to the angel: please, let Connor be wrong.

*****

A week later, I cornered Connor to have it out over Julia's death once and for all. He was still refusing to talk about it, and I worried that his cool veneer could explode at any moment. I approached him as he sat at the bar in the basement with guitar in hand, bent over and holding it as if it were a child.

"Connor, let's have a talk."

He swung around on his stool and placed the guitar at his feet. "What's on your mind, old man?"

I pulled up a stool next to him and sat. "You, that's what. Are you really okay or do I need to sic Sara on you?"

He had to smile at that. "I'm alright, Joel. Seriously."

"How can you say that? I mean, she was your girlfriend, you must miss her." Either he was lying or he was a lot colder than I could have imagined.

"I'm still shattered that she took her own life. No one deserves to be that unhappy. But the fact is, Joel, I never loved her like you love Sara." He smiled sadly. "There was potential at first, sure, but over time she became so depressed and moody that I just lost interest. I would have left her for sure if we were back in the old world."

"But you didn't think you should in this one."

"Right. I mean, Jesus, what if she cut herself after I had split from her? Then it would have been my fault. But I stuck it out and gave her plenty of reasons to live. The baby was number one. Shit, I could have been a father, Joel. Truth be told, that's the thing that's messing me up the most."

"Really? Never saw you as the type."

"Me neither," He looked up at me, an uncomfortable smile played on his face.

I stood again and picked up his guitar. "Play me something loud- all this easy listening you've been pumping out isn't doing anyone any good."

He grinned and took the guitar from me. I squeezed his shoulder as I left through the back sliding doors.

Chapter Twenty-Seven

Eight days after they'd set off in search of what lay to the north, Earl, Sonny and Fred returned to the house with much to tell. When they learned of Julia's death, there was a moment of silence, followed by condolences. Then, while we all grouped in Skylab, they told us what they'd seen.

"Beyond our position, there isn't much in the way of people. Not living, anyway," Earl said.

Fred spoke next, shuddering as he did so. "It was like a mass grave, but no one had taken the time to bury the bodies."

"The military.... We think they did it." Earl said solemnly. "At least, that was the conclusion we came to. There were too many of them to explain it any other way."

"It stunk..." Sonny stared out the north window. "I mean, it was worse than the pit out back. This was awful."

"How many?" I asked.

"Aw fuck, Joel. A lot man." Earl took a seat. "So that was the first thing we encountered: the killing fields. That was two days into the journey. We decided not to go any further. Who knows if we'd suffer the same fate. Whoever did that was cold, man, and powerful, obviously."

"A good idea. Probably saved your asses," Seth said.

"Yeah, so we decided to veer off to the east and who do we see? None other then Gareth and his flag cronies." Earl waited for a reaction, which he quickly got. Everyone looked alarmed. Satisfied, he continued. "Not that we actually ran into them, but we did come across them camping out in a clearing. So we set up just a few yards outside their encampment, close enough to watch them but far enough away to go unnoticed."

"That's fantastic!" I exclaimed. "Then you managed to get more information on them?"

"Better than that!" Freddy said. "I mean, we camped out at that spot for three days."

"They're no better off," Earl went on. "Still no larger than the twenty or so we sent packing, but they seemed to know more about what's going on up north than we did. Let me tell you something, the bodies up there stretch the length of a football field, along an open area that was once a farmer's field. No one else could have wiped out that many people. It could only have been the military."

"What do you think the military had up there?" asked Sidney.

"Whatever it was we'll never know, trust me on that one. No one in Gareth's group seemed to have any idea either." Sonny was dead serious. His attention did not waver from his view out the north window. I could tell he was harboring ugly memories of what he'd seen.

"Anyways, they didn't look good at all. Pale, malnourished! Heard them talking about ripping us off at the barn but nothing ever came of it."

Sonny grunted. "Wouldn't have let it."

"So they looked pretty tired, then?" I asked.

"They're finished, Joel. Even Gareth isn't talking much."

"And some of them are becoming disillusioned with their 'leader'," Freddy said. "More than one of them questioned the way he handled us. In fact, two of them actually went as far as to question his motives. I think what you said to them on their way out brought that on."

"Perfect!"

"So these two 'mutineers' got to talking one night, and there we were in the ditch just beyond the fray, taking it all in." Earl spoke slowly now, reliving the experience. "We think it was a husband and wife team. We listened as they conspired but we didn't interfere with the natural course of things. Then, when the dissenters approached the group, we crawled forward, shadowing them, hoping to witness a full-on rebellion."

"So what happened?!" Sidney was on the edge of his seat. Truth be told, we were all hanging on Earl's next word.

"When they spoke out, they were both shot in the head. Swift justice. Gareth's rule is not open for challenge."

"Where did they get the guns?" Sara wondered. She winced, and I couldn't blame her. It was an ugly story.

"They likely had a few stashed in one of the vehicles we let them leave with. It was a shock to us too. We hadn't seen them with any firepower until that moment. We backed off and that's when we started home."

"Good work, guys." That was a considerable amount of information for an eight-day trip. Connor brought each of them a drink of gin and flat pop that we'd been saving in the cold room for just such an occasion.

Their safe return prompted us to indulge too. Connor got drunk again, but who could blame him. I lit the pipe. Earl, Freddy and Sonny split up and answered additional questions. Seth perched on the arm of my easy chair and I passed the Sweet Bitch to him.

"Hey Seth, what's your take on déja-vu?"

"Déja – who?" he answered. When I started to explain, he stopped me. "No, no, I was just messin' with ya, Joel. Actually, I've had a theory about it for awhile, based on something my eighth grade teacher said. It made sense then and it makes sense now."

"What is it?" I was intrigued.

"He said déja-vu is the universe's way of telling a person that they're on the right track. That if you feel like you're reliving something, then whatever it is you're doing is the right thing."

I pondered his words. Before I could ask another question, Seth noticed that his glass was empty and went off for a refill. That was fine with me, actually. I was exhausted from the day, and after a couple more hauls off the pipe, I was ready to give my brain a rest.

Chapter Twenty-Eight

Sara spent much of her free time in the barn now, helping tend and harvest the plants. It made her feel useful, she said. I was on my way to visit her when I heard Seth yelling something from the house. Changing course, I hurried back inside.

"What's up, Seth?"

"We've got three travelers at the end of the driveway." He pushed the curtains back so that I could see.

They seemed harmless. There were no obvious signs of weapons. If they had any, they were well concealed. I decided to dispense with my usual 'first contact' speech, and allowed them to approach the house. We watched as they rang the doorbell, a courtesy that was almost comical, with hands that were raw and scabbing over. Our bell didn't work anymore, but they had no way of knowing that. They stood there patiently, hunched over and wearing little more than rags. Doubting that they posed any kind of threat, I nodded to Seth and unlocked the door. John and Kevin stood at the top of the stairs, weapons ready in case my judgment was off.

I swung the door open, pistol in hand. Seth stood beside me, gun at the ready. Our show of force seemed to frighten the arrivals. Raising their hands, they took a step back. All three were unkempt and obviously had not seen the inside of a shower since the last missile had landed some seven months ago. They had clearly not been blessed with a roof over their heads, so I decided to hear them out and help if possible. I watched as Seth's expression softened with pity.

"Can we help you?" I asked.

"Sorry." A heavily bearded man who was sunburned where his hair had fallen out stepped forward. "Didn't mean to overstep, ringing your doorbell like that. We're just so thirsty, and the water is toxic everywhere."

"Water is all you want?" I asked them. They nodded meekly, so I waved them in and motioned Seth to get them some from the tap.

"We really appreciate this." The bearded one spoke again. The others just bobbed their heads. Sweet Jesus, they stank of every kind of stink imaginable, but the smell of death was the most troubling.

When Seth brought the water, they drank it down eagerly. "Thank you so much," the spokesman said gratefully, handing back the glasses.

"Set them up with one of the four gallon jugs from the tap, Seth." I felt charitable. "You don't need to leave here thirsty. Where are you heading?"

"We've heard others talk about a place to the north. A safe haven. Is this that place?"

I hated to disillusion them, but I had to. "No. But I don't recommend you keep going north. We've just had a group return from an expedition in that direction, and what they witnessed is not a safe haven. It's a killing field."

He flinched at my news. His upper lip quivered and lifted, revealing a blackened tongue and teeth. I felt as though I'd just driven the final nail in his coffin.

Then suddenly the man's eyes widened and gleamed. The water jug Seth gave them fell to the floor, distracting us for the split second they needed to pull guns from their layered rags.

John's trigger finger came to life, sending a bullet into the shoulder of one of them. Blood splattered across the front door, and everyone scattered. The three strangers, one dripping blood, ducked behind the wall that separated the dining room from the front hall. I swung into the kitchen while Seth took the living room. Connor came through the kitchen's sliding doors on all fours.

"What's going on?"

"We've got three unknowns in the dining room with weapons," I replied. "John wounded one."

"Just three of them?"

"Yeah." I checked the clip in my pistol and replaced it, satisfied that I had enough bullets. Keeping flush with the kitchen cupboard, I twisted around the corner to see what I could.

Upstairs, John could be heard ordering Sidney to keep Caroline in the addition while Kevin slid on his belly down the carpeted stairs, then pressed himself against the hall tile, and trained his gun on the dining room entrance.

My heart pounded madly as I waited for something to happen. I could see Kevin sprawled on the hall floor, barrel raised to meet the enemy. Beads of sweat trickled down his forehead but he fought the urge to wipe them away. John, despite his broken ankle, slid down the staircase as well, ending up beside Kevin, who motioned for him to be silent. He looked from Kevin to me and nodded sharply.

Fifteen minutes had passed, and we couldn't hear a sound. Everyone was silent, including the intruders. We kept watching the entrances to the dining room while Caroline and Sid remained in Skylab, waiting. But at some point, Caroline couldn't take the pressure any longer. Dodging Sidney's grasp, she hurried down the hall, looking for John. Seeing him downstairs, lying on his stomach beside Kevin, she whispered frantically, "John? Are you alright?"

John didn't dare answer or wave her off, which would require him to release his grip on his firearm. Distraught at his failure to respond, she began to descend the stairs, each step advising the enemy that someone was advancing on their position. Finally John jumped up without a sound and limped to the stairs, grabbing Caroline's leg and pulling her down against the steps.

Suddenly the three intruders left their cover and bolted for the front door. One turned and fired. John was caught in the back by a bullet and slumped onto the stairs, blood pumping from the wound. Kevin opened up from the floor and hit the shooter in the chest and face, dropping him like a rag doll. The other two retreated back to the dining room.

Kevin continued firing at the wall separating the two rooms, hoping that his blind aim might cut them down. When his ammunition ran out, he scrambled over to John, who was lying across a hysterical Caroline's lap. He hauled John's limp form up the remaining steps to the second floor, while Caroline trailed behind.

Connor and I opened up on the wall where the intruders sought refuge. Seth joined in. We could hear the windows smashing as our bullets made it through. Encouraged, we expended the last of our artillery. During the silence that followed, I crept forward on all fours and peered cautiously into the dining room. The last two intruders were dead, huddled together in a mangled pile of punctured flesh and shattered bone.

Our victory complete, we ran upstairs. Caroline was holding John's head in her lap as she rocked back and forth, crying. Kevin had been applying pressure to the entry wound on his back, but it didn't help. The bullet must have been hollowed at the tip, it exploded in his chest on impact. Wiping the blood from his hands on his t-shirt, Kevin said hollowly, "He's gone."

Seth, Connor and I each lowered our heads in turn. Sidney was now at the top of the stairs, leaning over the railing. Sonny, Fred, and Earl, who'd been out in the woods when the shooting commenced, burst through the front door, arriving too late to do anything. Luckily Sara hadn't returned yet from the barn.

The fight was over. And then there were ten.

Chapter Twenty-Nine

John was dead now, shot through the back. Jesus, his blood was thick and dark. As we gathered in the front hall, where Kevin and Seth eventually laid out John's body, a strange buzzing sound filled my head. The room spun slowly as I seemed to leave my body, floating overhead, watching each of my friends react.

Had Connor dug his latest hole for John? Maybe he wasn't predicting his own death at all. Maybe he just knew on some unconscious level that we'd require another grave. We fill one and he goes right to work preparing another. Who would be next?

Caroline was inconsolable. Sara returned and tried desperately to comfort her, but Caroline had a hard time buying the whole God concept. She was wrought with guilt, blaming herself for John's death. No one could argue the point, but to keep her from blowing her own head off we had to sell her on the idea that shit just happens.

*****

A few nights later, I sat on the ledge outside my bedroom window, smoking a joint and trying to forget. This had become a nightly habit for me, but tonight it wasn't working, so I turned to climb back through the window.

Then my bedroom door opened. Shrinking back and out of view, I watched as Connor came into the room, followed closely by Sara, who closed the door gently behind her so as not to make a sound. The two sat on the bed, my bed, with their backs to me, unaware of my intrusion on their conversation. What were they doing? I suddenly felt utterly betrayed by both of them.

I listened as they whispered back and forth. What the hell was going on here? Since when were Connor and Sara close? Come to think of it, hadn't I seen them together a few times lately? But suddenly they were secreting themselves away in my bedroom. For what purpose? Were they becoming involved? Were they planning on overthrowing me… my authority? IA picture forms in my mind of Sara rolling her eyes at all the times I'd tried to act like a leader. I clutched at my chest as if to silence my quickening heartbeat. The pounding became ridiculous, almost audible. Before I could listen to any more of their conversation, I slid away from the window, worried that my labored breathing might give me away.

I made my way to the antenna at the south corner of the house, where I could climb to the ground. The blood roared in my ears as I kept recalling the sight of Connor's arm reaching around Sara's shoulders, comforting her.

"Who goes there?" someone called from the addition: Freddy, I think.

"It's me!" I shouted back at him. "It's Joel." I was sweating now and uncomfortable in my own skin.

"Sorry, Joel!" he responded. The echo of his voice rang in my ears as I lost consciousness and fell.

*****

I awoke in my bed hours later. Earl was seated on my couch, playing with Rex. No one else was in the room. Outside, it was dark.

"They're plotting against me," I whispered to him.

"Say again?"

"They're plotting against me." I struggled to sit up. "They were talking about me."

Returning my T-Rex to his place on my desk, Earl tried to make sense of what I'd said. "What? Who? When?"

"Just today, right here, in my room."

"Joel, who is plotting against you?" Earl looked seriously concerned.

"Forget it." I sank back onto the pillows.

Earl still looked worried.

"I was just rambling."

"Okay, well, since you're up and apparently better, I've got to head out to Skylab for my shift at the window. You gonna be okay? Sara checked you over, said you got a couple of nasty bruises but no broken bones."

I winced at her name. "Sure, go ahead."

"Yell if you need anything." With that, Earl left the room, closing the door behind him.

I replayed what I'd heard of the conversation between Sara and Connor over and over in my mind. Each time I closed my eyes, the dialogue recommenced and I listened again, teeth grinding behind quivering lips.

"He's an addict, Connor," Sara exclaimed. "He's changing, changing into someone that honestly scares me."

I was an addict? Really?

"Sara, I know he's been dipping into the bag a lot more than the rest of us but he's got the most riding on his shoulders."

Atta boy Connor, let her know. Make her understand. "I can't say that I would react any differently," he admitted.

"Oh bullshit, Connor. We let Joel get away with it because of who he is. We turned a blind eye, me because I'm in this relationship with him and you and the rest because you respect him." Jesus, she wasn't pulling any punches. Christ! This was what the person who loved me thought of me?

"Alright, Sara, alright. You're right. I was aware of the problem and I was hoping it would work itself out but you're right, he's slipping away. We're losing him to the drug."

Connor changed his tune pretty easily. Why? He thought I was a junkie too? That's bullshit! He was looking to get on her good side, but why? What was his real objective? Did he miss Julia so much that he'd stab his best friend in the back to score with my girlfriend?

"I can't do it anymore, Connor. I can't let him fall into that life. And if he's intent on doing this I can't be with him anymore." She was crying now, crocodile tears. She can't love me. No one could say those things about someone they really loved. Connor wrapped his arm around her shoulders and she leaned into him. What was happening here? What was he doing?

"I'll talk to him. I need to talk to him anyway."

"What will you say?" Silence. "No, I can't let you confront him, I have to tell him."

Tell me? Tell me what? That you think I've turned into some fucking junkie, that you prefer Connor over me? Fuck you! Fuck the both of you!

"Fuck that!" I shouted, not really giving a shit who might hear me.

Opening my eyes I saw no one. Only Rex sitting on the desk where Earl had left him.

"So what? Huh, Rex?" I addressed my confidant from across the room. "So I'm a junkie now. So I'm not good enough, so I'm human!" My throat tightened. "Why couldn't we have just died with the rest of them? Huh? Screw a second chance!" I swallowed hard.

Rex had little to offer me as I ranted on. Finally I stopped myself. My eyes closed as I fell back onto my pillows. As hate replaced sadness and loathing evolved from hate, I realized that I was hopelessly alone. Cupping my hands over my face, I cried. Or did I laugh? Like I had said, who could make the distinction anymore?

Lighting a bowl, I pulled the drug into my lungs, held my breath and passed out.

*****

When I regained consciousness, Sara was sitting on the bed, gazing down on me. Seeing that I was awake, she said, "I like you best like this."

"Like what?" I asked. "On my back or asleep?"

"Calm. At peace." Smiling sadly, she ran her fingers through my hair. "You're such a good man and I do love you, Joel."

Tears. She was going to break the news to me, perhaps an ultimatum. I knew she wasn't going to stay with me.

"I think it's time I changed my plan here." I squeezed her hand a little harder than I meant to as I removed it from my head. "I've got some thinking to do. Until I've figured this out maybe we'd better sleep in separate rooms."

There, I said it for her. For some reason wanted to make it easy for her.

"Joel, I..."

"Just go." I said, cutting her off. "I'm not the same person I was and that may never change. I'm on a path that I can't alter and I think it's time I just accepted it. You'll have to do the same." I let go of her hand. She slowly released her grip on mine. After wiping her face, she got up and left, closing the door behind her.

Alone once again, I felt sad and angry with myself for having let her go so easily. But I could not forget what I had seen and heard. They had disrespected my authority. They sought comfort in each other's arms, abandoning me! I got up, went to my desk, and packed a pipe to settle my nerves. After smoking the bowl, I crawled back into bed and covered myself with the tattered comforter. Soon I was asleep. The only place I was really comfortable any more.

Chapter Thirty

The following morning I was in Skylab with Connor and Freddy for the 8:00 a.m. shift. We watched the sun creep over the horizon, igniting the sky. Then I asked Freddy to bring me some more ammunition. I needed him out of the room: before coming on shift, I'd hidden the bullet boxes for my sidearm, ensuring that he would be searching awhile.

After he left, I faced Connor. "I sent him out on purpose. I want to talk to you."

"What's up?"

"Connor," I said slowly, deliberately. "Did you and Sara have a little talk about me yesterday?"

"Yesterday?" He stared at me. Damn it, he even looked confused.

"Yesterday," I reiterated. My face was solemn, and in a flash, so was his. He knew now that I had either heard everything or been tipped off somehow.

"Yes. We did." His eyes never left mine. "Nothing bad about you. Just some general concerns, because we both care."

"Spending a lot of time together lately, aren't you?"

The questions were becoming accusations: I wasn't holding back.

"What? What?" That was all he could say. He'd been caught. There, I'd caught him now, now I knew. I felt dizzy.

"I told Sara last night that I wasn't going to be with her any more, that she was a free woman." My adrenaline was surging.

For someone who was sleeping with my girlfriend, he seemed pretty upset. "That's the fucking stupidest thing that's ever come out of your mouth, man!"

"Hey, since I'm a junkie, maybe she belongs with someone better."

"Where are you getting all of this?! What the fuck is wrong with you?!" he shouted.

Wrong with me? Was he kidding?

"Don't yell at me, don't you fucking yell at me! This is your fault! You did this to me! You want her? She's yours!" I strode over to him. He did not flinch, although the anger and bewilderment never left his expression.

My anger spilled out of me as I yelled my accusations into his face.

He continued to deny it. Sara came running into the addition with Fred and Sonny. Seth and Sidney soon followed, attracted by the yelling. As I panned each of their faces, I saw shock and horror.

"Stop it! Stop it! Stop it!" Sara cried, rushing past Fred and Sonny to get between Connor and me. "Why are you fighting?"

She looked terrible. Her skin was white, and dark circles marked her puffy, red-rimmed eyes. Behind her, the guys looked like they'd just been kicked in the bag. They'd never seen us at each other's throats like this before.

"This is between me and him. I don't want any of you here!" I shouted.

"It's okay, Sonny," Connor said. "Just go."

"Why are you fighting?!" Sara insisted.

"It's nobody's business, Sara!" I snapped.

"We'll be done in a minute," Connor told Sonny, who refused to budge.

"You're a real piece of work, Connor!" I could hold back no longer. The blood roared in my ears. "I'll give 'em something to talk about!"

My fist slammed into his face, knocking him to the floor. I moved to boot him in the ribs, but the other guys intervened, ending the one-sided battle as quickly as it had begun.

Connor let Sonny and Fred help him to his feet and lead him out. He muttered something under his breath as he touched his jaw gingerly. To the others he added, "Don't let him near the drugs."

Sid and Seth released me when Connor cleared the room. Sara asked them to leave us and they did, albeit reluctantly.

"What's wrong with you, Joel?" she wept. "What would possess you? Your best friend?" She was sitting on the floor with her hands supporting her head. I stayed on the floor as well, shaking uncontrollably.

"I know all about you two. I heard your conversation yesterday." My tone was covered in a layer of frost so palpable the whole room actually seemed to cool. My heart was pounding violently, and my breathing became ragged as the adrenalin pushed through my veins.

"What the hell does that mean? What? What about us?" She had managed to look angry and innocent at the same time, no easy feat.

"Don't do that, Sara. Don't treat me like an idiot. Give me that at least."

"Joel, I..." Her voice broke. "Joel, these things are IN YOUR HEAD."

"You're saying I dreamed up that conversation? 'Cause if that's what you're suggesting, then you'd better rethink your next words or this conversation is over."

"Stop it! Just stop it, alright?" She banged her fist on the plywood flooring. "We did have a conversation about you yesterday. But not to drag you through the mud. You've been giving us reason to worry about you. I'm allowed to talk to Connor, aren't I?"

"You've been talking a lot lately, Sara." I was losing what little composure I had left. "You two have been doing a lot of talking lately."

"Did you ever stop to think about why that could be?" she shouted at me. "Did you ever think that maybe if you didn't bury your emotions and your thoughts in that goddamn pipe daily, two or three times a day, that maybe we could talk like we used to?"

"The drugs are keeping me together right now, alright?!" I yelled back. "They're helping me cope!"

"The drugs are killing you, Joel!"

"They keep me sane!"

"They're making you insane! The pot is making you paranoid! The more you use it the worse you get! You don't see it but we do!" She wiped her eyes. "It's making you crazy, Joel. And I don't want that for you. I don't."

"But you'll fuck Connor in the meantime, is that it?! Is it?! Well, fuck you and your bullshit half-assed concern because I'll be fine! I'm better off on my own."

I scrambled to my feet and left Sara there on the floor, weeping. Storming blindly downstairs and out the door, I jumped onto one of the Harleys we'd collected. For a fleeting second I felt like an asshole for leaving her in such a state of misery, but righteous indignation soon took over. I'd been betrayed. I'd lost face with everyone, been humiliated, embarrassed, betrayed! How could she do that to me! How could I face any of them again?

I had no idea where I was going. But I would soon find out. And it would mean the end of everything.

Chapter Thirty-One

Passing the abandoned north gate, which had been dismantled months ago in order to tighten our defenses and shorten our supply lines, I resolved to keep going until something or someone made me stop.

The wind in my face felt fresh and real, which I relished: real was so hard to come by anymore. I was sure that Connor and Sara, the two people whom I'd trusted the most, had betrayed me. Their treachery disillusioned me, made me question everything.

I checked my pockets for a spare bag of reality. The bike swerved from left to right as my concentration shifted, but I steadied her out. Good- I found a half-quarter. Pulling over, I parked the motorcycle and sat on the road divider. The Sweet Bitch was tucked into another pocket, so I eagerly packed the bowl and lit it.

I inhaled several times before exhaling, holding the smoke captive in my lungs, shaking my head to speed up the process. My heart was broken, my life was over, love had left me. In a strange way it made me love Sara more, want to love her more, show her how much I appreciated her, but the thought of her and Connor… Bitch! Prick! Fuck!

Bang! I was hit. My mouth fell open, my eyes closed, and my head pitched back. The painful thoughts were still there, but distant now. I could focus only on what was taking place in the here and now. I waited until I felt steadier, then mounted the bike and resumed my journey.

Continuing north, I passed the place where we'd seen the farmer's cattle break loose while the forest beyond his home burned, when things were in their infancy, when shit could've gone either way. As I rode by, I turned to look at the blackened farm buildings, taking in the full extent of my neighbor's misfortune. Or was it their good fortune? Nothing good had come of us making it this far.

Turning right, I headed east with no purpose in mind but to keep moving. Thoughts came and went with little effort or accompanying emotion. The smile remained on my face, the bike motored on.

The wind was artificial. It was me pushing through the atmosphere, not the atmosphere pushing at me. We, as humans, were always pushing. We pushed the limits of everything. We pushed our environment, pushed each other. We were a race of bullies. On the flip side, we pushed through adversity. We pushed through hardships and impossible scenarios. We didn't necessarily come out on top but we did try, didn't we?

As green signs whizzed past me, announcing town names and their former population totals, I recalled that Elle Lake would soon appear to my left. As I took the bend, the bike seemed to know where it was going, so I let it. How could I detour from my destiny? Whatever I did, destiny would find me.

Squeezing my eyes shut, I tested my theory. I tested my destiny. The sensation was incredible. It was as though I were invincible. Then, ten seconds later, I veered off and crashed through the dead saplings and thick, dead brush that lined the ditch. Caught in the face by a low-hanging branch, I was thrown from my seat and landed solidly on my tailbone while the bike slammed into a stump and flipped over.

Slumped there, watching the bike's front wheel spin, I felt dizzy and collapsed onto the dusty earth. Looking up, I saw the blackened trees stretch toward the sun, wishing for a second chance. Then I closed my eyes and blacked out.

*****

When I regained consciousness I was still lying on my back, arms at my sides. Slowly, carefully, I sat up. I could hear something.

It was unmistakable. I could hear people in the woods below. People! I found my pistol, lowered myself onto my stomach, and aimed in the direction of their voices. Then, suddenly, they stopped. I listened carefully, but heard nothing further.

Had they only been in my head? Strange, they had seemed real enough. I waited what seemed like an eternity before letting my guard down. Then I rose, picked up my bike, and pushed through the brush that covered the sloping hill. Suddenly a small encampment materialized in front of me, appearing so suddenly that I froze. Was it real? Or an illusion??

A voice rang out. A horribly familiar voice. "Joel!"

Gareth.

My fingers gripped the motorcycle handlebars so tightly that my knuckles cracked in protest. My pistol was holstered inside my coat, but I'd have been cut down before I could go for it.

Several of the flag people materialized from the woods around me, closing in. Gareth was approaching from the direction of the camp, his smile cruel.

"Wait!" I said. His pace slowed, and I thought fast.

"I- I've come here to see you." The words were out of my mouth before I could really process what I was saying.

Gareth lit up. He looked at his followers as if to say, I told you so. Then he approached, his manner more relaxed.

"Knew you would," he said, almost gleefully. "Knew you would…" Smiling through that filthy beard, he reached me and slapped my shoulders in a manner not unfriendly. I remained glued to the bike, afraid that any movement on my part might spark a violent reaction from the others.

"Give our guest some room, people!" Gareth shouted, noticing my discomfort. The group fell away. I dropped the bike and let him lead me toward the camp.

"Just give me their name, Joel," he said. "The one you are here to present to us. Did you bring them?"

"Their name?" I repeated, trying not to sound confused. Any indecision would turn the situation violent. I felt it.

"Yes, Joel. A sympathizer: you found one in your midst. I can tell. A traitor to your cause." He began shaking his head again. "I was tipped off by a divine vision, a vision that you would visit us and present us with this gift."

The group studied me. Nothing can describe the extreme angst I experienced standing there. Thought escaped me, my head went empty. Please, I did not want this to be my destiny. After all I'd been through, I wasn't going to find my end at the hands of Gareth and his religious rejects.

"Tell me then, tell us, who has wronged you?" Gareth breathed through his mouth, wheezing, the wiry hairs surrounding his lips pushing out with each exhalation. The group seemed to sway back and forth as they too waited with bated breath for my answer.

Two people had wronged me but only one name came to mind. I hated him, I was sure I hated him. I couldn't let it end here. I wasn't ready to die. Not like this. So I spoke the name.

Gareth smiled like a jackal.

My heart sank and I flinched. What had I done? What did it matter? I had offered Gareth a lamb and saved my own neck. My mind began to race. I was offering a friend to certain death. But if he were out of the picture it would solve many more problems for me than it would create! I could never hurt him like that myself... No, my part had to be such that no one could suspect me. I couldn't let the others know this was my doing.

"It is done." Gareth savored this phrase as he would a good meal. "It is done!" This time he shouted, raising his arms triumphantly to the excited crowd around us.

They began to mass-chant the name of my former friend, my traitorous, conniving, back-stabbing friend. I looked slowly around the circle, knees shaking, while they praised me as the latest inspiration driving the flag army toward a new hope. Bile rose in my throat. I pushed my way through the tightly packed circle, staggered into a bush, and vomited.

Gareth followed me. When I stopped heaving, he laid a reassuring hand on my back. "Joel, we have you to thank for our renewed strength."

"Then you let me do this my way," I replied, breathing through my nose until the nausea subsided. "I'll set this up for you, but I don't want any credit for your continued success, you understand me, Gareth?"

One more brutal convulsion followed my demand, painful and deliberate. The muscles in my back ached and my throat burned.

"There will be no mention of you, Joel," he promised. "No one will know that you had any part in this. Come, you will spend the night with us. We will discuss a plan of action over dinner." He spoke as if he intended to discuss plans for a surprise party or something.

After drinking some water that they offered from a surprisingly clean cup, I took out my pipe and lit up without bothering to ask for permission, needing to escape into oblivion. Gareth said nothing, just watching me with unholy glee warming his features. Something stood behind him, something dark. Was it a shadow? No, it left me cold. Escaping worked. I remained there on my knees for some time.

*****

Later that evening I sat with Gareth and his followers in front of a fire that roasted a small animal carcass. The smell was all-encompassing, triggering a powerful memory.

It was a memory referenced from our camping trip, one of many I would now have to forget: meat cooking over an open flame, my friends surrounding me, my Sara next to me. A single tear tracked the contours of my cheek and I brushed it away angrily. It was my destiny to carry out this plan of Gareth's. Sara and Connor were dead to me, and I was already alone. I couldn't be sad, I was certain. The word destiny repeated itself over and over in my head, lulling me into a trance. It was all I had left to believe in.

Gareth watched as I tilted my head back, closed my eyes, and breathed deeply, enjoying the heady cooking scent permeating the air.

"They're all over these parts," he said, gesturing toward the carcass, which had been removed from the flame and laid on a platter. Snapping away a few meaty ribs, he handed them to me. I didn't need to be asked twice: shit, I hadn't eaten a piece of fresh meat in months. Biting down on the charbroiled flesh was rejuvenating. I felt like a person again. Like a man.

"Good, yes?" Gareth looked amused as he watched me tear into the meat so eagerly, grease covered my lips and chin.

"It's good," I confirmed.

"We don't waste a single organ: even the tongue and eyes are eaten. It is the perfect balance. We use everything we catch. We use the animal completely."

When the meal was over and some members began cleaning up, Gareth took me aside so that the real business could be attended to. The first thing he wanted to know was what my friend looked like.

"I'll point him out to you," I replied.

"How can we be sure the others will not retaliate? Could you take him to a secluded spot?"

I shook my head. "I wasn't exactly on good terms with anyone when I left. If I took him away with me and returned without him, they'd suspect I'd had a part in it. No, they'll have to witness his death."

"They'll have to be unarmed."

"That's not going to happen. They're too used to carrying guns everywhere."

“Then we’re at an impasse, and that is unfortunate.” Irritation hardened his tones. “I won’t march into your stronghold without a guarantee that my people will come to no harm. I offer you the same guarantee.”

“I'll make it happen, there'll be a way. I just have to figure out how I'll get them all outside, but I need more than your word that you'll only take him, and hurt no one else.” I meant it. My destiny was coming to fruition; but I would not allow any harm to come to the others.

“You have my word, Joel. That is all I can give.” He rose. “We leave tomorrow.”

After bidding me goodnight, he disappeared into his trailer. I walked back to my bike. Leaning against the motorcycle and methodically licking free the dried, sappy fat of dinner from my fingers, I told myself, I could kill them all right now. I could. I could take my spare canister of gasoline, pour it all over their camp, and throw it into the fire.

But I couldn’t, much as I wanted to. I needed them now. I needed them to complete my destiny.

Strangely, I slept soundly.

Chapter Thirty-Two

The ride back to the house was like a bad dream. It was happening. It was really happening.

After camp was broken and the RVs rolled out, I started my bike and assumed the lead position. Gareth raised a hand to me as I passed, not looking at me directly. His eyes were for the road only, the road ahead. I had to hand it to the son of a bitch- he was intense and driven. Even during that fateful moment when we reclaimed our freedom, he had not for an instant played the victim. He could sense a destiny playing itself out, maybe he had always known. Maybe that was why he never lost his edge. He could accept his destiny where I had failed to do so.

Pulling ahead of the pack by half a mile gave me enough time to stop a moment and light the pipe. Shaking my head violently, I looked back to see whether the caravan had caught up. When they drew close, I pulled back onto the road, tires spitting the loose gravel behind me.

When we were roughly two kilometers from the house, I stopped and dismounted. Gareth got out of his RV and approached.

"This is as far as I want your trucks," I told him. "The rest of the distance we'll cover on foot."

Gareth agreed. He turned to his followers and gave them the signal to exit the vehicles.

"When we get there I want you to sit tight in the back woods until you see me appear by the pool." I scratched my face and rubbed the end of my nose. I was having trouble hiding the fact that I was anything but straight right now, but I did my damndest. "When I'm at the pool, it means that in about five minutes I'll have everyone out front and ready."

"Understood." He turned to address his group. "Everyone hear that? When Joel reveals himself we will slowly move in, flanking either side of the house, closing in on his position at the front." Turning back to me, he added, "Will we be certain not to run into any resistance?"

I assured him that my friends would not fire unless fired upon. "They are trained to follow my orders. If I order their guns down, then they'll do it."

"Be sure that you do, Joel. I'm not looking for a bloodbath: I want the sympathizer."

With those chilling words, we began our approach. After positioning the flags safely beyond our defenses, I left Gareth with a final order. "Do not mess this up. You have one chance at this. We can't afford any screw ups."

He nodded.

The walk back to the house took me past the graves of Jake, Julia and Gil. Beside their sites was an ominous, yawning hole, the latest fruit of Connor's dark obsession. I stopped and knelt at its edge.

What a thing, I thought. "What a thing to do, Connor, what a burden to carry. You've gone and dug your own hole." I rose and kicked loose dirt into the abyss. "You knew the whole time, didn't you? You knew. You fuckin' knew. So why didn't you do something to stop it? Why did you let it go this far?"

All that answered me was an indifferent silence. I turned away and continued toward the house.

Sonny, who was on duty in Skylab, saw me approach. He alerted the others, who met me in the kitchen as I entered through the second floor sliding doors.

"Joel!" Sara cried. She rushed toward me, but the scowl on my face stopped her cold. "Where have you been?"

"Just clearing my head." I avoided eye contact. "I'm back now though." A pause. I had to do this. "Where's Connor? I need to see him."

Sara looked pleased at the question. "He's been pretty eager to see you too, Joel."

"So where is he?" I asked again.

"He's in his room." Seth spoke up. "Good to see you. We were getting worried."

"Thanks." I went up the stairs, heart pounding. I was going to confront him, to see him, to accept that I was fulfilling a destiny that was bigger than both of us. Reaching his door, I hesitated for a moment. Across the hall, I could see Rex lying on my bed, looking at me.

"What!?" I whispered at him. "Shut up!" This was not the time for him to start talking. Then quickly, abruptly, I knocked on Connor's door.

"Come in." Connor sounded despondent.

I opened the door. He was sitting on his bed, elbows resting on his knees and eyes on the floor. When he looked up and saw me, his eyes didn't brighten. "Hey," he said.

"Hey." I forced myself to smile. "I've got to ask you to come out front with me, you and the others. It's important."

"I had a déjà-vu last night," he started.

Shit!

"It involves you, Joel. And me."

"I don't want to hear anymore." I told him, shaking my head, blinking madly.

"Well, you're going to." His tone was lifeless. "So you'll want to take a seat, old man, and listen to my dying declaration."

My whole body went numb. He knew. I sank into an old rocking chair.

"Your paranoid delusions are just that. But they're also your reality. The déjà-vu has shown me everything. What has happened, what is about to happen, and what will happen when we're both gone. I saw it all." He stopped. "We are players, Joel and destiny will be realized no matter what choices we make. Though the choices we make are our own, destiny is not something that can be so easily derailed."

Tears collected in my eyes. I willed them back.

"I know that what you think you saw is as real as this conversation. I get that." He paused. "So now it's up to you, Joel. Do you listen to the voices in your head?"

"Aren't I supposed to?" I interrupted.

"Or do you look to common sense?" He continued unfazed. "I can't judge you either way. I just have to trust you'll make the right decision… for you."

"I..." I couldn't speak.

"So, let's go outside."

We stepped slowly into the hallway, Connor leading the way with purpose in his every step. This was it. I could stop it. But he wouldn't let me. He felt the march of destiny forcing each forward step as I did. I moved through the scene as if being carried forward by a current stronger than myself. I couldn't. I just couldn't stop now. The fear was overwhelming. Fear for Connor. Fear for the life that was to follow. On descending the staircase, I saw that the bulk of our clan had come to meet us in the front hall.

As I approached the back of the house, I heard Connor explain that we would be convening on the front lawn for a meeting. I stopped in front of the back door, and held the handle for several moments. The metal felt warm in my hand. My muscles twitched. Turn the knob. Do it. Turn the knob. My stomach churned. I willed myself to remember the hurt and hatred I felt towards my friend. I let it linger on an image of Connor and Sara, together on my bed. I was ridding myself of an enemy now. I couldn't trust him. I made myself feel certain I could never trust him again. I turned the knob.

I made my way to the pool, knowing I was visible to Gareth's troops. In five minutes Connor would be at their mercy. There was now no way for me to stop this. I had made my choice.

Everyone came outside. I approached the group, who eyed me expectantly. I stood next to Connor, making sure that Gareth's people would not take out the wrong 'sympathizer', and studied the surrounding trees, knowing that Gareth would emerge when I gave the sign. My friends' guns were either holstered or slung over their shoulders, unprepared for the act that would momentarily play itself out in front of them.

We were surrounded almost immediately after I laid a hand on Connor's shoulder. My friends froze, unable to comprehend what was happening. I envied them their ignorance. The flags relieved them of their firearms. Then they grabbed Connor by the arms, pulling him aside. Enraged, Sonny slammed a powerful fist into the face of one of Connor's captors. The man dropped to his knees, groaning and bleeding. His comrades aimed their weapons at Sonny's head.

"Stop!" Connor cried. "Don't react, Sonny. Please. I don't want anyone to die here."

"It wouldn't be wise to continue your course of action, Sonny." Gareth appeared next to Connor, staring at him as he addressed us. "Connor knows what he's done, being a secret supporter of the Reaper's ideals."

Gareth now faced to the group. My friends regarded him with fear and hatred.

"Connor is a classic sympathizer. He cannot be changed, only destroyed!" He strutted through the circle, relishing this moment.

Sara whimpered. Her feelings were betraying her: proof that she favored Connor now. Caroline was shaking and crying. Sidney comforted her. Earl's eyes met mine as he realized what was about to happen; I could tell that he was trying desperately to keep from charging the nearest flag member. I shook my head and he relaxed, acknowledging that we would not stand a chance.

Forcing Connor to his knees, Gareth waved in his depleted forces, keeping a hard line on our movements. Connor was looking at me. Tears fell to the dusty earth as his head bent forward. Helpless to change what had come to pass, I honestly couldn't feel anything anymore. In that split second, the same split second it took for Gareth to end my friend's life, I did not exist.

Then suddenly, as if the gunshot blast had awoken all of my senses, the paranoia, hate, and jealousy left me. There was Connor, face in the dirt, blood trickling from a hole in the back of his head, silent, dead. I could no longer stand. I lost use of my legs and sank onto the ruinous earth beneath me just as Connor had. I was not the first to fall, I was not the last. We were all experiencing the same nightmare.

Chapter Thirty-Three

Their bloody deed accomplished, the army left, weapons trained on us as they returned to their vehicles.

Caroline screamed after them. "Murdering bastards!"

"I'll get you! Every fucking one of you!" Sonny yelled through his shock.

I let them vent their pain and rage as I crawled to Connor. He was warm. I gathered him in my arms and cradled him against my chest. The exit wound on his forehead oozed blood over his blackened eyes and bruised face. I closed his eyes and rocked back and forth, letting the blood cover my chest and stain me with my guilt. Connor was dead. What had I done?

My friends gathered around, watching silently as I struggled with my grief. Unable and unwilling to release him, staggered by the magnitude of the act, I focused on how I had brought it about. Throwing my head back, I cried out. The sound of my anguish sent some reeling backwards, my pain echoing off the house. It was a sound that would reverberate in my head for the rest of my life.

The others left me alone with my grief, understanding only that I had lost my best friend. I remained on the front lawn for hours, cradling him. I kept talking to him, like it was old times and this nightmare had been erased. I stayed with him until the body was cold and ridged and the others, unaware of my role in this catastrophe, urged me to come inside.

I picked Connor up, his stiffening limbs made it difficult as I positioned him across my shoulders. I wanted him buried, I wanted him comfortable, and I wanted to do it myself, as a last favor to him. But when I took my first step in the direction of the graveyard, my legs gave out and I collapsed. Slowly, I rolled his heavy frame off of me as the others hurried over to assist me.

Sonny, Earl, Kevin and I carried Connor to the site. The rest followed. Sara didn't bother to pray this time, but instead looked on in stony silence. I helped lay him into the grave that he had made for himself, and covered him with the soil as carefully as I might have tucked him into bed in days gone by.

The ceremony over, I walked slowly from the graveyard into the woods, hoping that I could also leave behind the feelings of guilt and betrayal, buried forever with Connor in the fetid earth. The group gave me the space that I needed and returned to the house in a solemn, devastated procession.

Passing the shed and its attendant memories, I continued to the outer perimeter of our property and crawled over the rusted fencing. The daylight was fading but the sky above remained undaunted by the scattered clouds to the north. Finding a spot next to a dry riverbed, I sat and picked at the dead foliage around me.

In the silence of the woods, I recalled the biblical story of Judas and the betrayal. Stunned, I realized we were one in the same. The revulsion I felt for that traitor in reading the biblical story of denial, I now felt for myself. "What made you do it, Judas?" I wondered. "Was it the silver? I doubt it. Was it your destiny? Did a little angel make you do it?"

I laughed, nausea billowing in my stomach, as I poked at the dry earth with a lifeless twig. The burden that I now bore, that had overwhelmed me at Connor's death, surged in me once again. I'd done a terrible thing. If someone or something had told me to do this, it wasn't God or a guardian angel. It was my own ego poisoning me all along. I had listened and this is where it had gotten me. Bobbing back and forth on my haunches, I could not control the deep regret. The feeling was so overpowering that my vision blurred and my strength left me. I crashed onto my back, hands covering my face.

I could hear my pain echo around me as the corrupted forest became my father confessor. The world seemed cold as my suffering intensified with each passing moment. Opening my eyes to the cruel environment, I quieted the sounds of an unequalled pain radiating up from deep within me. The few wavering clouds that had drifted in from the north had now accumulated overhead, growing in size, reaching from one end of my peripheral to the other.

My side ached, so I jabbed one hand under my ribs to ease the cramp. Breathing deeply in an effort to soften the pain, I watched the clouds overtake the sun. A foreboding shadow now labored its way across the forest, shielding me from the judgment I felt weighing down upon me. What was taking place here? What was developing up there? Then, suddenly, a drop fell from the sky. A drop! It hit my face, followed by others.

"Rain..." It was almost too much for me to bear. "Rain."

Connor would never see this now. Connor could have seen this had he still been alive. I wept for things that would never be, things that could never be. The rain came in force now, beating down on the tortured soil. Running back toward the shack, I stumbled over the fencing. Picking myself up, I made it to the building and pushed through the door, landing hard on the ground.

The rain stung, but was it only because it was falling so hard, so suddenly, or was it acid rain that had come back to finish us off? My mind raced. I poked my head out the door of my childhood clubhouse, hand cautiously extended. It did not burn. I cupped my hands and drank. It was good.

"Rain," I repeated aloud. A smile broke the frown. I could feel it on my face, genuine. Things would be better now, things would grow…

Wham! Pain exploded on my forehead. I had hit myself, eliminating the warm glow I had felt for that split second. I was in no position to relish this rain or the hope that it might offer. I had no right!

"Fuck!" I shouted.

Wham! Again I hit myself, my nose spraying blood from the right nostril. Who was this hitting me? Who *was* I? I couldn't allow myself another moment's pleasure and if I was to become some sort of masochist then so be it. I kept hitting myself, each blow harder than the last, picking out new spots on my face that hadn't yet felt the sting of my guilt.

When satisfied that I had hurt myself enough, I sat down on the dirty armchair, a flurry of dust exploding out of its worn cushions. Blood drooled from the corner of my mouth. My teeth had cut the inside of my cheek. I rubbed my jaw and nose, concentrating on the pain. The rain continued to hammer down on the roof above me.

I couldn't go on like this. Judas had played out the destiny promised him. I too would have to complete the course that I was fated to follow.

*****

I entered the house through the kitchen door. A heavy silence dominated throughout. My friends sat on the balcony overlooking the backyard, watching my approach, watching the rain. Without a word to them, I went upstairs to my room.

Sidney called to me from the front hall.

"Joel! The rain, Joel, it's good...."

I didn't answer him. I couldn't, as the lump had returned to my throat. I rounded the banister and made my way up to my room. The thought of what I now had to do to make things right weighed heavy on my mind, stirring up several new emotions. In my room, where I made my final preparations, smoking from the Sweet Bitch was a matter of extreme urgency.

What a joke I was, what a victim! How could I ever look at myself in the mirror again. I couldn't live with myself. My path was clear - I would end my existence myself if the gods couldn't see their way clear to do it for me. Fuck the angel and his grand plan, fuck 'em! The circle broke here, no more, Joel, no more!

Epilogue

Only now, in my most crucial hour, do I feel that I should let my friends know what had transpired to bring me to this end.

With paper and pen in hand, I sit at my desk. It's roughly seven forty five in the evening. My pen begins to move across the paper, composing the letter that will explain everything. Tears resurface at the realization of how much I have changed, how far a cry I am from the Joel who existed before the Reaper struck.

But maybe if someone comes in, sees what I'm doing, and stops me, then maybe I won't do it. No, wait. No, I have to do this. I won't be able to live with what I've done. I don't deserve to!

Someone knocks softly on my door.

"Go away!" I answer, rising to my feet and falling heavily onto my couch. After a moment's pause, I hear footsteps receding.

I begin to slowly knock my head against the couch's wooden frame. The repetition is therapeutic. With each blow, I cement the idea of taking my own life. "There is nothing left of this one. Finish him." I hear, or say, either way, I agree.

"Not yet!" I cry. "Not yet!" I must sound like a madman to the people I can now hear gathering outside my door. Picking up my fallen chair, I return to my desk and resume writing.

I hear them in the hall, whispering their concerns. I don't care. I can't look after these people anymore. My job was only to survive, never to lead them. That was their idea. I was never meant to be a leader. It had gone to my head. I had led them into misery and death. What did they have to hope for, besides the rain?

I drop my pen and walk to my window. Sliding it open, I squeeze out of my room and lower myself down the antenna to the wet ground. Stealing into the trees, I escape the scouting eyes in Skylab.

Without a course plotted, moving only to evade the conversation outside my door, I fall over an exposed root that the rains have washed free of its earthen prison and land hard in the muck. My face pressed against the slippery forest floor, I begin to scratch at the ground. Digging my fingers deep into the earth, I shovel out a great deal of the dirt, piling it next to me. My speed accelerates as the wet soil on my skin sends a rush through my body. Sitting upright, I summon my strength in an effort to pull up more of the dirt, faster. The rainfall creates a small stream that tracks down the hill, washing over my efforts.

A small puddle of water collects in the hole I've made thus far, softening the harder dirt so that I may continue my work. Looking to my right in the darkness, I see Jake's gravesite a few yards away, then Gil's, Julia's and Connor's. Mine is not as deep as the others- not yet, but soon. I redouble my efforts, tackling rocks and roots, cutting my hands and pulling back two fingernails. I ignore the pain.

Finally the job is finished. My heart pounds while my fingers bleed. Looking to the sky, I let the rain fall on my face, cleaning the filth from my hands and arms.

"I'm going now!" I yell to the heavens, as if they cared. I'd carried out their little plan. "Are you there!?" Where's my divine intervention now? My face is flushed and my eyes burn. I feel like my head is going to explode. Don't fight it. Let it go.

Bowing my head, I surrender and resign myself to the knife. Standing and walking back toward the house, I feel strangely calm. My heart rate slows dramatically, my breathing levels out while a feeling of acceptance overtakes me. This is my destiny, to do this thing.

The trip up the antenna seems speedy, the walk across the overhang effortless. Climbing through the window into my room, I accidentally step on Rex, crushing him. I offer an apology. He accepts it.

Searching my shelves, I find the Bowie knife I'd purchased some years ago and a partially full bottle of painkillers that Sara had given me for the leg injury. What else though? What else would I need? Water, a bath perhaps, yes... yes, something to bleed into, not like Julia, not all over the bed.

After carrying everything to the bathroom, I place the knife and pills on the counter and peer up at the Mickey Mouse clock above the toilet. It reads eight-thirty. As I lock the bathroom door behind me, a strange feeling overcomes me. It is as though I've been here before, like a déja-vu. The thought sickens me. My stomach muscles contract violently, forcing up bile, burning my throat. I swallow it down.

"You're not me!" I speak to the mirror now. Spit hangs from my lips as I salivate rabidly. I am so far gone, so far removed, I can see that now. Shaking, I grip the granite counter top. "Stop staring at me!" I shout, throwing my fist into the reflection. Funny, I don't even cut myself.

When the mirror shatters, I snap out of my trance and begin picking up the pieces from the counter and floor. My sanity has left me. I sweep the mess into the garbage pail and pick up a spray cleaner and rag from a basket next to the toilet. In the periphery, I hear a knocking on the bathroom door and ignore it.

During the time it takes me to clean the bathroom, I recall a moment of my childhood. In the tub, with mother watching, smiling. Long before the unimagined pain. But of course moments like that are never to be experienced again. It is over. Once again I feel at peace with the situation, accepting again what I must do, knowing that it is all I have left.

By ten-thirty my work in the bathroom is through. I direct my attention to the cold porcelain tub and kneel beside it. When I suddenly shiver, a final thought enters my mind. "Who has walked over my grave?"

The moment gone, I turn the cool water on, still staggering my time.

"Death brings an honest response."

I hear it clearly. Is it the angel? Turning slowly, I expect to see him standing at the door, prepared to talk me out of my decision.

"Death brings an honest response."

There it is again! No angel though. Raising my hands to my ears, I momentarily block all outside noise.

Pouring a glass of water from the sink, I shovel the painkillers into my mouth. Halfway there! I take the knife from the counter and spend a moment with it. Getting undressed, I step into the tub. The water is cold but I immerse myself, dunking my head below its surface. I come up for a breath, pulling my hair back. My lips begin to quiver as I think of the people I am leaving behind, even Mom, who may be dead already. For her sake I find myself wanting that for her.

I feel alone, frightened, guilty. I sit there in the tub long after I've gotten in, thinking, pondering, exploring. Looking toward the clock, I see that the time is five minutes to twelve. My lips stop quivering as I bite down on them.

The rain has ceased for now, but I know that as sure as the sun will shine tomorrow, the rain will follow it and life will be restored. Life will return. For those who deserve it, and can manage the strength to continue.

I look at my wrist and then at the knife in my other hand. The knife is so sharp that my flesh would offer no resistance to one quick slash. That's all that it'll take, I tell myself. One quick motion, just one cut: then, release.

Pressing the blade against the softest and most tender area of my wrist is easy. The steel is as cold as the water and I feel nothing as I immerse my arm. They say it is painless. I wait for some signal that I may commence with the execution. Of course there is no gun to sound or flag to fall. I am waiting only for myself to be ready to truly end the life that has plagued me so much in such a short time. It should be easier than this, I should not hesitate...

Suddenly it happens. I pull the blade down my forearm, tearing my flesh indiscriminately. It is not painless. My hand goes numb but the gash throbs horribly. I breathe deeply. I watch my lifeblood color the water, lightly at first and then darker with each passing second.

"My God..." I catch myself muttering. "My God..."

The scent of blood seeps out of the water, stinging my nose, as I squirm uncontrollably. My first thought is of Sara, to yell out to her but I stifle any attempt by covering my mouth with my one good hand. When calm, I lift my right arm out of the water. I can't help it. Curiosity has gotten the better of me.

The sight is overwhelming. My whole forearm is gashed so deeply that I can see tendons. I watch as blood spurts aimlessly from my wrist. I grasp at the wound, covering it. The feeling of blood escaping through my fingers is grotesque.

I've done it. There's no turning back now. Even if I wanted to, I'd be too faint to drag my near-corpse out of the tub. I feel the color drain from my face. I am thirsty but fight the urge to dip my tongue into the ever reddening water. Was I crazy to end it like this?

As I lie here in a shallow watery grave, cold as death, I feel something through the dense haze of pills, something approaching euphoria. My death is an exit from a tormented existence. What I've done here is a mercy killing.

All that matters now is that I know peace. My head fills up with the idea of it. I giggle, this time losing all control. It comes in force now, without reason or purpose. Perhaps the purpose is all too clear. It's funny that I should leave this earth in such a state of peace, of joy. It's a wonderful feeling; the regret is forgotten. I relish a joy I have been denied too long.

And so my life, such as it was, flows through my muddled head, on the edge of reality much like my pending death. Like a high I can't come down from; I wouldn't want to. The giggling stops as abruptly as it began. My head slips under the cold sheet of red water. My sight blurs, and sound is now reduced to a faint and sparse heartbeat underwater. It's so unreal.

The world is fluid. There is a knocking under water; and a tiny voice that accompanies it, calling my name. Joel. A murky image. Am I being lifted?

The last feeling I remember took me by surprise: it was the feeling of wrapping my arms around a tree. It was a little like love.

REBIRTH

The second book in The Judas Syndrome series

Michael E. Poeltl

To the past

May you be remembered.

Power can be taken, but not given. The process of the taking is empowerment in itself.

Gloria Steinem - Journalist

Sara Speaks….

I can't find my son. Anxiety overwhelms me. My heart pounds as I rush through the compound, in my panic it seems more like a maze than the place I'd called home the past eight years. *Where is my son?* The night comes alive as search lights expose the darkness between buildings, igniting the tight spaces a boy of eight might find himself. A sinister thought enters my head: *My mortal enemy currently shares this space with us*. A renewed sense of urgency overcomes me, my pace quickens.

*****

Your Father would have so loved you. You were a blessing when you were born; you were a mystery when you were conceived and a terrible struggle while I carried you seven months in my belly. Seven months: it's not really long enough, but you seemed to time your arrival eerily close to the date of another's departure.

This place is like a concentration camp you'd see on TV, when there was TV. Something from a Second World War movie. Did we live through the Third World War? Hard to say. Color is absent here: the walls are a battleship grey, the floors a polished concrete. Not ideal surroundings for a baby to grow up in, but at least you grew up.

When we arrived you were very small and still at my breast.

Somehow we had escaped a plague that ravaged much of the surviving world.

Children are very important; so many died from this plague that took the very young and very old. Most adults over sixty years old and those under the age of twelve died soon after the Apocalypse, choked to death by fall-out, while those who survived were left to suffer this final indignity some months later. A plague, a flu of some design. I have worked closely with the doctors here, and they have not been able to succinctly label the disease that had methodically killed off so many.

The base was designed to train special ops and special forces in the war against terror. It has only a skeleton crew assigned to it, though it was expecting an influx of 1000 soldiers and their families the month following the end of life as we knew it. The base is well protected, with steel walls reaching heights of 20 feet in places, outfitted with watch towers, a stockade, family housing, a mess hall, hospital and the central training and parade grounds. It even has a greenhouse.

The parade grounds are framed with civilian vehicles, RV's, camper vans, cars and trucks of all shapes and sizes. They belong to those who fled the devastation to the south and came north. I recall the many motorcades we witnessed traveling north, right past Joel's house, where we had hidden out. We were fourteen friends, caught in something as unfathomable as the end of the world. Teenagers, whose families had all been wiped out by one violent act against humanity. I remember talking to people as they stopped at the house. They said they were going on a *feeling*, going north.

The Sergeant told me that barely a year after the majority of civilians had arrived, the plague had hit the base, and hundreds were quarantined. Almost all of them died, eventually. The base lost many of their own to the mysterious plague as well. The army doctors worked day and night to suppress the disease, to stop it in its tracks. In doing so, the hospital lost over 75% of its staff.

Finally the plague had run its course. No more were dying, no more were feeling feverish or showing red spots on their necks and torsos. Those who had survived, roughly half including both the base personnel and civilians, would carry on, burn their dead and start again.

*****

I remember asking about the water planes my friends and I had seen putting out forest fires as we drove back to town, returning from our camping trip the day after the Reaper had followed through on his promise.

"They flew out of Kingston Air force base," explained the captain. She removed her hat as she spoke. Her short blonde hair fell around her high cheek bones. She was an attractive woman, but she'd suffered an unimaginable loss, and the lines in her face mapped that story. "It's two days' drive west of us. They were retrofitted to do that job, those planes. They would load up on water at Elle Lake, and run water dumps all over the area. Now, you said you were a good two hour drive south of here, Sara?"

"Yes, about that." I replied.

"I'd say the planes would have penetrated just south of that, and then west." She confirmed.

"We saw three or four at a time."

"Yes, you would have. They employed thirty odd. They ran day and night for about 48 hours following the attack, and then, nothing."

"Nothing?" My voice cracked.

"We lost contact with them." The captain's tone was thoughtful.

"What happened to them?" I asked.

"Fatigue. The pilots wanted to keep flying. Keep up the momentum. Best we could tell, two of the bigger planes slammed into each other and then into the control tower while attempting to land and fuel up. They wiped out everyone, and with them any chance for the other pilots to continue their work."

"That's so awful."

"We sent a patrol to investigate, and this was their conclusion." Her eyes met mine.

"No wonder you never came for us." My friends and I had held onto hope of a rescue for weeks after the sighting, believing that they had seen us, and that they would come for us. But they never did.

"Even if we were made aware of your existence, it's unlikely we would have come for you. We were undermanned ourselves and had been ordered to stay put."

"Makes sense I guess." But I wondered what my life would have been like had they come for us. Would Joel still be with me? Perhaps we would have succumbed like the others to the plague, like the captain's husband and daughters had.

*****

The world wasn't always like this, and perhaps one day it will be better. The military houses us now. They have graciously put us up here in the hope that you will survive, have children of your own and rebuild. That may sound like a lot to put on a child not yet eight years old, but know that you are very special, and not just in the way only a mother can know.

You would have had it so good in *life*. That's what we called it *before* the Reaper dropped the bombs: *life*. We were all someone else, kids barely out of high school. The *Grimm Reaper* as the media had coined him, was a mad man. A man, an organization, a country, no one really knew. The threat seemed almost laughable. But he wasn't laughing. He had demands that were never met, he had crazy ideals that required religions and governments to disappear. The things he asked were impossibilities. So he showed us just how serious he was. The initial blasts killed our families. My friends and I had been spared, having taken a camping trip that weekend, *the weekend*. And when we returned, our worlds were changed forever. We, fourteen of us at first and within seven months only eight, managed to stay alive, at my boyfriend's house in the country. We felt privileged, chosen to survive, to rebuild.

More than nine years ago my life was very different. Was I lucky to have experienced life in all its normalcy, in all its abundance? I think so, I still have my memories. Though sometimes my memories seem like little more than movies, something from someone's imagination.

The people here, the soldiers, they believe that much of the planet has fared better than our little corner. To believe is a powerful thing. It can keep you from despair, it can offer you salvation. *Belief* is sometimes all you have, your faith. I lost it once…

Part One
Chapter One

You think you know someone. Really know them. You think they're in control of their thoughts, themselves. You give them the benefit of the doubt, believe that they will make the right choices that they'll make you proud. Do they sense that? And when you're trusting someone to lead you in the right direction… are those who lead more susceptible to the expectations of those who would follow? We're not all cut out to lead. Some don't choose to lead. It is thrust upon them and when the burden proves too much to bear, they wish it away like a dead limb, weighing heavier each day the wish is not granted.

I've often asked myself, in Joel's defense, how might I have performed under the same circumstances? Would I cloak myself in a drug induced haze, would I become paranoid with power? Would I finally kill myself, knowing so many would suffer for my actions?

Is it any different than what the Reaper had done? To paraphrase Joel's note, scribbled on stationary from his mother's hardware store, found in his room, *our* room, on his childhood desk; *"I know now that a single action can put in motion a series of repercussions. Should that action be positive, the repercussions are rewarding, but when that action is negative, so too are the events to follow. A single action can change you forever. Sometimes, if the deed is large enough, if the intent evil enough, the results can be disastrous."*

I heard it in my head as though he were speaking to me, whispering in my ear, and I wept. What irony is this? What sadness this implies, such a good man, tormented and turned. Could this happen to me? Time will tell. I will tell. And only then will I know.

*****

The rains had returned. Connor was dead. Joel was holed up in his bedroom, and those of us remaining felt more victimized now than when the Reaper had unleashed his evil upon the world. The rain, a blessing to us, to the whole world, would take a backseat to our internal demons. Incapable of rejoicing in this miracle, we waited on Joel to emerge from his self-induced confinement.

"He's in there," I whispered to Earl as I paced just outside Joel's bedroom door. "He's quiet though. I'm really worried, Earl." I picked at the skin peeling from my fingertips, the nails having been chewed to the quick long ago.

"Sara, let him be. Jesus, we're barely an hour into Connor's funeral. Imagine what's going on in his head." Earl could have been right; maybe he was just decompressing. But the look on his face, after what Gareth had done, after Connor had been shot… it was almost as devastating a sight as the execution itself.

I decided to knock on the door, lightly, so that he knew I was there. Earl shook his head in disapproval, but remained silent.

"Go away!" Joel shouted. I jumped. Such pain in his voice, such … regret. Earl threw his hands up and backed away from the door. "I'd let him be for a while, Sara. He's obviously got to work through this on his own."

"No one should have to work through this on their own, Earl. I'm worried about him." My eyes flew back to the door as we heard first a thumping sound coming from within, then a murmur and another shout. "Not yet!" Joel repeated. My skin crawled and goose bumps overtook me.

Earl gently placed a hand on my shoulder and rubbed. I felt more anxious at his touch than comforted. I removed his hand and wiped away a tear. He smiled narrowly at me. I'd never been able to read Earl. He was never my type: intelligent yes, but his intensity had always frightened me. His mind was like a runaway train.

"I have to get back to Sonny; just thought I'd see what's what up here." He turned to leave, but I stopped him.

"Earl, you're not planning anything are you?" The idea that we might now go to war with the flags was not something I could stomach. Not so soon after losing Connor. Couldn't we just bury our dead and mourn for a time? Earl shrugged and smirked as though there were little else to do. "Earl…." I trailed off as he went down the hall and into Skylab.

The flags (so-called because of the ominous flag they carried, declaring themselves an autonomous nation of survivors) had been a cruel interruption into an otherwise solid foundation built on the ashes of the past. We had survived a nuclear holocaust. We had built a life for ourselves, and then the flags showed up. Led by Gareth, a man possessed by the idea of weeding secret Reaper sympathizers from surviving groups like our own and executing them to further his twisted purpose, the flags posed a threat unlike anything we'd imagined. His group consisted of nearly sixty upon his arrival at our door, but after a third party attacked our house from the devastated woods, he was left with little more than twenty. We retook control of our home and our lives by ousting the flags, ordering them away, and relieving them of their weapons and morale, or so we thought.

But they had returned, executing Connor in front of us after they'd caught us unaware. A sympathizer, they called him - Connor, before they shot him in the head. A sympathizer to the Reaper's ideals, as if anyone would claim such madness after the hell the *Grimm Reaper* had unleashed on us all.

Left alone to contemplate further what scheme Earl and Sonny were planning, my eyes fell again to Joel's bedroom door. I pushed my hands against the frame and slowly lowered my head until my forehead gently rested against the door. My cheek made contact with the cool wood. Eyes closed, I listened for movement, a sound, something that would let me in. What horrors was he experiencing in there? "Let me in," I whispered to the door.

A moment later, Caroline came up the stairs and took my hand. I resisted, hesitant to leave my vigil at the door. Her eyes were red and swollen. The sight of her made me break down. Caroline followed in turn. I pulled her close, and we hugged. And we cried.

*****

Caroline finally released herself from our embrace and rubbed her eyes hard. "What, what do you think he's doing in there Sara?" she asked.

"I wish I knew. I wish he'd let me in." My arms crossed defensively as I looked back at the door.

"Is Joel going to be alright, you think?"

"I don't know, Caroline." I couldn't hide my own inability to read him anymore. God, we had grown so far apart in such a short time. It felt like a microsecond. From *'I love you'* to a break up, separate rooms and a blow out that sent him off to who knows where, in search of who knows what! "I don't have those answers."

"Should we get back to the others?"

Reluctantly, I agreed. Sucking in a deep breath, I pushed my fingers through her long, somewhat greasy blonde hair, as though tidying her up for an interview. When I reached the ends I carefully patted them down on her shoulders. "Okay, let's go see what they're doing." Holding hands, we walked down the hall and into the addition, where the rest of the house now gathered.

We walked into a fierce speech, told in unwavering absolutes. Phrases like *'we must'*, and *'how could we'* and *'how dare they'*. It was an impressive rant, not unlike many of the one-sided conversations he'd mastered in the past. No one could put together an argument like Earl, and in this, he was making his stand.

"This is not how this is going to end!" He pushed on, while a captive audience of our peers stood in silence. "This isn't an *ending*. This is a new *beginning*. Gareth and his flags cannot be allowed to just walk off into the sunset."

"What are you proposing, Earl?" I blurted out, angry he'd gone and done exactly what I had feared. The room held a distinct sense of immediacy. It permeated the air and made it hard to breathe.

"I propose we *fight,* Sara!" He glared at me, the devil in his eyes.

"Why would you want to pull us all back into this now, after having lost so much!" I studied the group, panning the room while their eyes betrayed them. A perfect moment to rally the troops perhaps - to offer them a solution. On the other hand, an excellent opportunity for someone to take control, to give the group a reason, purpose. Did Earl know what he was doing? Did he see what he was becoming?

"Whoa, Earl," Caroline broke in. She was shaken and it resonated in her voice. "What are we talking about here? Running after the flags? Hunting them down? Two wrongs don't make a right." She was pleading to the group now. "Right? I don't want to fight anymore. How could any of you want to *fight* anymore?"

"What else is there to do?" Sonny phrased it as more of a statement than a question.

"Rebuild," I said. "Rebuild, regroup. Jesus, anything but get into another fight!"

"What if they come back?" added Kevin. I wasn't surprised. I didn't much like Kevin. His allegiance would fall to anyone that took the initiative to lead. He was weak.

"Listen to me, Joel is still here, *okay*? He's still our leader, by vote! It's his call whether we send people to track down the flags, not yours." I pointed at Earl.

"I'm allowed to have an opinion aren't I, Sara? It may not be the same country anymore, but as far as we're concerned, it's still free." He glared at me.

I readdressed the group. "All I'm saying is not to get caught up in Earl's hype. We don't need to throw away our lives. Connor wouldn't want to be a*venged*."

"Says you!" Earl may have respected Joel's leadership, but he would not concede the point. "Connor was a good man and a good soldier. And he went to the grave for all of us! All he needed to do was say the word and we'd have all died that day in defiance. But he knew that, and he died *for* us!" He sat down on a stool by the west windows, exhausted. "And it's eating me up inside…" His words were not falling on deaf ears. Freddy, Sonny and Kevin approached Earl and stood next to him.

Seth and Sidney did not move, positioned at the east wall, guns dangling from their uncertain grips. I approached Seth and knelt beside him. We exchanged looks. He was no more ready to go to war with the flags than I was. I recognized indecision in Sidney's face. Admittedly, a small part of me cherished the idea of going to war with the flags. I was still reeling from the events that lead to Connor's death.

I turned to watch as Kevin stood and stared out the west windows. The forest still resembled something from a children's Halloween picture book. Stripped bare of their leaves, the trees stood as dark silhouettes against a grey-black background. It had been raining on and off since Joel had returned from the woods, after having left us at Connor's graveside.

It was approaching 8:30 pm when I heard a door shut. Joel was moving. I rushed out of Skylab and across the hall. His bedroom door was open and the bathroom door now closed. I pressed my ear up against the door and listened. In my peripheral vision I could see the group gathered by the addition entrance.

There was a murmuring inside the bathroom, followed by a hard thump. Something broke. I jumped back. Looking for encouragement from the others, I slowly approached the bathroom door again. They were frozen in place, unable or perhaps unwilling to move.

I pressed my ear to the door and heard Joel inside rustling around. I knocked lightly and tried to speak but nothing made it past the lump in my throat. He was ignoring me. How long would this continue? How long could I let it continue? Seth was behind me, gently pulling me away from the door. I held up a restraining hand.

"I'll be all right," I smiled, although I felt like I was in a dream at that moment. My head swam with emotions and memories, making me dizzy. "I need to be alone right now." Seth nodded and released his delicate grip. I walked into Joel's bedroom and sat on the bed. A low rumble of thunder rolled through the clouds overhead.

I wanted to pray, but felt there was no longer anyone listening. My faith had been shaken by the return of the flags, and the devastation they left in their wake. I couldn't bring myself to pray at Connor's funeral. Should I have felt I'd let him down by foregoing a prayer? Will his soul not rest now? Crossing my heart I bowed my head in prayer. "Amen," I muttered aloud after completing my appeal.

As I panned the room, I felt alienated and lonely. The foreign feeling I got from this place, where I first told Joel I loved him, where we shared so much of ourselves, hurt me deeply.

I stood and walked towards his desk, where three pages of stationary rested. The top page had been filled top to bottom with Joel's handwriting. He'd never had a very attractive script. But this scrawl was especially hectic. This writing was done in haste, by a hand that wanted to write as much as possible as fast as possible and move on.

I sat down to read.

Chapter Two

Blank Page, Blank Mind, Blank Brain, Blank man. Blink and Blank man disappears, blink and Blank man disappears. Blink, and nobody cares. Blink blinky, blink blinky, blink Bitch! If I could, I'd blink, if only I could blink. I'd be Blinky, blinking. Blank man would disappear.

I frowned as I struggled to understand. Was *he* Blank man? No, he wished he were Blank man. Or was it Blinky he wished he was? Was Blank man the angel? He wanted Blank man to disappear. He wanted to erase something, a memory, an action… a person.

I read on.

"I know now that a single action can put in motion a series of repercussions. Should that action be positive, the repercussions are rewarding, but when that action is negative, so too are the events to follow. A single action can change you forever. Sometimes, if the deed is large enough, if the intent evil enough, the results can be disastrous."

This verse was well thought out and easily understood, but I was still confused. What *action* was he referring to? Was this written to express his view on what the Reaper had unleashed on humanity, or was this something more personal?

"What did you do, Joel?" I whispered, my hands covering my mouth as tears flowed down my cheeks. I looked back at the poem. Was Blank man Connor? Could he really have thought Connor and I had been…? Of course he could. He was capable of believing anything. He had confronted Connor on the subject before hitting him. The memory of that moment would never leave me. "Please, no. Please tell me you didn't,

Joel." But the more I thought it through, the more likely it was that he had somehow orchestrated the execution of his best friend, and if he did, how could I ever love him again?

I read and reread the poem. I broke it down line by line on the stationary while writing my insights down on another sheet of paper.

Blank Page, Blank Mind, Blank Brain, Blank man. What was he trying to say here? He saw a blank page, nothing yet written, he had a blank mind again repeated in blank brain, suggesting he himself either couldn't remember something or didn't want to remember. Finally he mentioned Blank man. This character could be one of three people I decided. The angel, Connor, or himself. I read on.

Blink and Blank man disappears, blink and Blank man disappears. With an action he was able to block out the Blank man, making him disappear. Should this have been taken literally? If so, perhaps the Blank man was Connor. But it also might better describe Joel separating himself from something.

Blink, and nobody cares. Blink blinky, blink blinky, blink Bitch! No one cares... He felt no one would care if Blank man went away, no one would notice, or that the Blank man is worthless. He became repetitive now. He was hell-bent on snuffing out the Blank man. He became frustrated. He couldn't do it. His inner turmoil was surfacing.

If I could, I'd blink, if only I could blink. I'd be Blinky, blinking. He knew he needed to do this thing, to erase the Blank man, but felt powerless to do so. He would go to extremes to make Blank man disappear.

Blank man would disappear. He needed Blank man to disappear.

I summarized everything I'd been writing down. The conclusion was more revealing, and upsetting than I could have imagined.

Blank man *was* Joel. He was deeply disturbed. He felt worthless. He'd done something that he couldn't forgive himself for. He needed to stop the Blank man. He needed to stop himself. The question was, could he? Could he change? No, nothing in this spoke of change. He wanted to disappear...

The writing started with *Blank page*, he wanted to start again.

I suddenly noticed how silent it was. Had water been running in the bathroom? I looked automatically at my watch. 10:30pm. I'd been toiling over the poem for nearly two hours. I placed my hands at my lower back and stretched, tilting my head back, rolling my neck.

"What is he doing in there?" I wondered aloud.

A muffled cry rang through the bathroom wall as Joel thrashed in the tub. Alarmed, I jumped up from the desk and ran into the hall. I pressed my ear against the bathroom door but all was again silent. "Joel," I said tentatively. "Joel?" I knocked again. Nothing.

Sidney rounded the corner out of the addition. I waved him over.

"Something's wrong, Sid. He's not answering. Something's wrong."

"Joel?" he yelled. I looked at him with my best pained expression.

"Please Sid, kick it in." I pleaded. Sidney nodded and kicked the bathroom door in.

Chapter Three

Nothing could have prepared us for the scene inside. I pushed past Sidney and stopped cold when I spotted the bright red water in the tub. I lived a thousand different scenarios in that moment. As the seconds passed the picture became more and more surreal.

"No." I muttered. "No, no, no, no, no, no, no, no." My head shook from side to side, my face tightened and my throat went dry. "NO!" I shouted. I screamed. "NO! JOEL! NO!" I fell hard on my knees to the tiled floor and thrust my arms into the cold water. Pulling Joel free of the icy wetness, I gasped as I saw the life drain from his face.

"Jesus Christ!" Sid cried from behind me. "What the fuck!" I looked up at him and suppressed my own urge to lose it. I needed to be smart here. I needed to save Joel.

"Sid," I said. He didn't respond. "SID!" I shouted. His eyes focused on mine.

"Yeah?"

"Help me move Joel to the floor."

He snapped into action and grabbed Joel's feet. We struggled to move the dead weight over the side and onto the floor. Blood trickled from his forearm, soaking the floor mat.

"Sid, take off your belt." He reacted without as much as a pause. "Now wrap it around his forearm, above the wound, and pull it as tight as you can." Oh God, the wound. What had he used, a skill saw? I checked his pulse. The heartbeat was barely there, but there was hope. Had he been submerged for long? I listened at his nose for breath. How much blood had he lost? How would we ever replace it? How was I going to close this wound? He'd cut things I was sure I couldn't mend. We would have to resort to amputation.

"Sara?" I could hear the panic in Sid's voice. "Sara, is he alive?"

"Yes." I could barely think now. I tried to remember the minuscule training I'd been given at the clinic and my stints at the hospital during my co-op.

"Will he be okay?" His eyebrows threaded together over his frightened stare.

That depended on the amount of time he had to bleed out, I thought. "Joel can't have been like this for long. I only just heard the bath water shut off." The makeshift tourniquet was doing its job: the blood had stopped flowing from Joel's forearm. Sid held his ground, hovering over Joel's pale body, applying pressure to the arm with his right knee while pulling up on the belt.

"So, what now, what do we do now?"

I was working on that. What next? Shit I'd never done this. I'd never even *seen* this done. Would he slip into a coma? It depended on the blood loss.

"Talk to him, Sid. Slap his face, try to wake him up." I got to my feet and realized just how weak I had become. I found support on the counter and collected myself. "Stay with him while I get my books."

When I charged out of the bathroom, I nearly ran into the others. They were speechless. Watching. I moved past them frantically on my way to the bedroom. I dug around the couch until I found my medical textbooks under a pile of papers.

"Can we help?" Seth hovered in the doorway. "Can I help?"

"Boil some water and find me some clean linens." Flipping through the pages, I came to a section on amputation. Scanning the technical illustrations and brief explanations, I gave him another order. "Find something metal, wide but thin, maybe 6 inches square. We'll need a saw, a couple of gloves, alcohol and fire as well." Just scanning the steps to a successful modern day amputation told me I had no chance. I would have to amputate like a field surgeon in the Civil War.

Seth ran out into the hall and communicated my orders to the others. I was scared to death. Maybe one of the boys - possibly Earl- could do the cutting while I supervised. "It needs to be able to cut through bone," I shouted out to them. "The saw." My hand rose to my mouth, shaking uncontrollably. "Be strong," I whispered to myself. "He needs you."

Back in the bathroom, Sid had worked some color back into Joel's face with all the slapping. "Nothing," he reported. "Nothing's happening, Sara. Shouldn't he have woken up by now?"

"It's just as well, Sid. We're taking the arm off below the elbow." A look of horror struck him. My chin began to tremble but I forced myself to stay coherent. "It's the only way we can save him. The damage is too severe. I don't have the tools or the training to fix that." I pointed at the ruined arm. The soft flesh I so prized, the flesh of the arm I would rest my head upon while we drifted off to sleep. The skin I would put my lips to and swear was softer. And now, I was going to remove it.

The group returned with the requested items, Seth leading the way. "Where would you like everything?" he asked.

"Let's just do it here, on the floor," I answered. They placed everything on the counter. I poured the boiling water on Joel's arm and open wound. If ever he would wake up, surely that would have caused it. The alcohol was next. Then I sterilized the saw: a small saw with a thin cutting surface.

"It's a bone saw," said Earl. "For hunting."

"That should work."

I positioned the saw and closed my eyes. One quick push should make it through the muscle, I thought. Then four or five hard pulls through the bone and then more muscle. Less than ten strokes should do it. I felt sick at the thought. Could I have ever been a surgeon? "Fuck it," I said, as I wiped my forehead with my forearm and mouthed a prayer.

Chapter Four

"Sid," I ordered, "hold his arm down at the bicep and don't let it shift around as I cut." Earl circled round me, took Joel's hand and pushed down hard. With Sid at my left and Earl at my right, I wiped the sweat from my eyes and pushed the blade into Joel's lean muscled forearm.

"Jesus," whispered someone above us.

I dared not stall for long. I continued the grisly work on Joel's arm and upon hitting the bone, slowed considerably. I struggled for a moment. The blade warped as I realized it was stuck in the bone. I pulled at it roughly, wishing desperately for the job to be done. A scraping sound made everyone wince.

Suddenly Joel's eyelids sprang back, and his eyes bulged out of their sockets. His back arched violently and a scream burst from his mouth. He looked down at his arm, the saw in my hand and his friends gathered around, their faces white as ghosts at this unexpected turn. He wailed once more. Then his eyes rolled to the back of his head and he slipped into a comatose state.

I was frozen in place, too shocked and sickened to move.

"Let me, Sara." Earl took the saw from me. His right hand still holding down Joel's, he used his left to free the blade and continue the cut. In four short tugs he had separated Joel's forearm from the rest of his body.

Earl looked to me for further instructions. "Uh, heat the plate," I remembered, feeling my composure return. The metal plate was set up on the sink and a fire lit beneath it. Joel's severed hand twitched on the floor and I moved away from it, pulling myself up to the counter. "When its red hot, use the gloves to carry it over to the open wound and press it against his arm." When Freddy complied I turned my head and shook.

"It's really smoking, Sara." The stench of burnt flesh had permeated the room. Sid and Earl were literally waving the smoke away from their faces as Freddy continued to push the plate to Joel's stump.

"Dump some of the alcohol on it and remove the metal." Skin pulled away along with the plate as Fred removed it, but it was working. "More alcohol and heat the plate again."

We repeated the process a few more times until the flesh and muscle and bone were charred at the stump. "Apply the antibiotic cream and wrap it in the linens." It was my final order of the day. I was exhausted, and nauseated. The heat of so many bodies in that small bathroom, and the smell sent me into the hall and then into Joel's bedroom, where I gave myself permission to go to pieces.

"Would you like us to place him on the bed, Sara?" asked Caroline, leaning in through the doorway.

I looked up from Joel's desk, tears streaming down my cheeks. Caroline knelt down beside me.

"Look at my hands, Caroline." I said, shaking. "We... *I* just took off Joel's *arm.*" My hands were stained red, leaving gory marks on everything I touched.

Caroline gently pulled me up from the desk chair. "Let's get you cleaned up."

We walked down to the bathroom on the main floor, passing the scene as our friends cleaned up the mess on the second floor. I caught a glimpse of Earl through the haze of smoke and bodies, gripping Joel's disembodied hand in his. He was hitting Kevin with it, as though it were a prop. I hadn't the energy to confront him, but what an asshole! I stared them both up and down- Kevin and Earl. They must have felt the burn of my gaze as their eyes met mine. "Assholes," I mouthed. Earl quickly put the hand in a bag and sent Kevin to the yard with it.

I never understood Earl. I always felt as though he hadn't given himself the opportunity to vent, to *feel* after everything went to shit, after the Reaper. But upon witnessing that spectacle, playing with Joel's hand as though it were a toy, I think I understood him better. It wasn't that he hadn't allowed himself to feel. It was that he *couldn't* feel. He talked a good game, he made others feel, but he himself, I don't think he had the capacity. What did they call that in *life?* A psychopath?

*****

That evening no one slept. If they weren't in the addition, located over the 3 car garage (on guard duty), they were in the bedroom with Joel and I. I tended to him at his bedside. Earl remained in the addition, in Skylab, hopefully embarrassed over his actions in the bathroom. His thoughtlessness, his blatant disregard for my feelings and those of the others… to play with a severed limb, a limb that used to belong to your friend… It was beyond comprehension, and beyond contempt.

"Earl *is* an asshole," Caroline agreed after I'd told her what I'd seen.

"I wanted to jam it down his throat, see if he thought *that* was funny." I gazed at Joel as he slept under the covers. I held his right hand in mine and leaned in close to listen to his breathing. It was erratic. "He's going to become a real problem if Joel doesn't wake up…"

"Earl?"

"Yeah."

Our conversation ended with the arrival of Sonny. Sonny was one of Joel's biggest supporters, figuratively and literally. Sonny, though he had lost a fair bit of weight over the past few months (like the rest of us) still carried a substantial frame, big-boned and muscular.

"Hey, Sara, Caroline."

"Hey, Sonny," I answered. Caroline smiled and nodded.

"Can I talk to you, Sara?" He eyed Caroline. "Outside?"

I looked at Caroline and passed Joel's hand to her. "Can you stay with him awhile?"

"No problem." Caroline took my place at the bedside. I followed Sonny down the staircase and out the front door.

"How are you holding up?" I asked him, hands in my pockets. The night sky was clouding over; a breeze hit us from the south, warm for January.

Sonny took a seat on the concrete porch. I stepped around the dark discoloration that stained its center as I had a hundred times before. A bloody reminder of past victories.

"I'm confused, Sara," the big guy admitted. "What happened here today, the flags, Connor, and now Joel…. I thought we had it all figured out. I thought we were winning this thing."

I sat down next to him and wrapped an arm over his bulging shoulders. "I'm at a loss too," I conceded. "I can't understand how, if we have a guardian angel watching over us, how he would let something like this happen."

"Exactly, right. What the fuck? Worst fucking guardian angel ever." He snickered, despite himself. I smiled, shaking my head.

"What happened up there?" I knew what he was talking about. "Joel isn't the type, is he?"

"I didn't think so, Sonny." I pulled my hair off my face and tied it in a ponytail. "I'm not convinced he did this *himself*."

Sonny looked at me, confused.

"What I mean is, I don't think he did this freely. I think the drugs, the pressure, and the flags might have had a hand in this." I didn't dare tell him my deepest fear. That Joel couldn't live with himself, that Joel may have deliberately caused Connor's death.

"That adds up. I mean, none of us know what he's been dealing with. Then the *flags* show up and off Connor." His fists tightened into balls. "Glad I got my shot in." Sonny had reacted first when the flags moved in on us, crushing a man's nose with his fist and knocking him unconscious. Connor then pleaded with us not to react. It was as though he knew his fate and didn't want us to suffer similarly.

"Listen, Sonny, don't let Earl talk you guys into something you don't want to do."

"Sara, the *only* thing I want to do right now is wipe them out. All of them. Make them eat that fuck'n flag."

I guess I knew that was coming. I left it alone and went to go back inside.

"He didn't tell you anything, eh?" Sonny raised his voice as I opened the front door. "Joel?"

I froze a moment, not sure how to answer that question.

"You saw what happened, Sonny," I started. "He accused Connor and I of having an affair, then went berserk, hit Connor, and left. You know about as much about where he went and what he was thinking as I do. What are you asking?"

"I'm not sure."

"If you don't have the balls to ask it, then don't *think* it."

He must have known I would defend Joel. I knew what he was asking, it was a terrible thought to entertain, but the motive was there. So was the *letter.*

I moved inside and shut the door behind me.

*****

On my way to Joel's room that same evening, I caught Freddy and Kevin mid-conversation in the hallway. Satisfied they hadn't heard me, I eavesdropped.

"Why wouldn't we follow Earl?" That was Kevin. "Earl knows what he's doing, shit, he *counseled* Joel half the time."

"I'm not against it Kev, I'm not. If I have to make the choice I'll stand behind Earl. Sara's the only other person here to rally behind and I'm not getting behind a girl, Joel's girlfriend or not."

I winced and choked down indignation at Fred's insult. What was worse was that they had already written Joel off. I bowed my head, fiddling with the cup in my hands, fighting to keep my mouth shut.

"That's what I mean, Fred. Sara will have Seth and Caroline on her side for sure, and I'm guessing Sid. I think he and Caroline are sleeping together."

"I'm pretty sure Sonny is behind Earl. He wants revenge on those prick *flags* as much as me."

"Then the house is split. 4/4. How will we have a leader?" Kevin sounded perplexed.

"Well, whatever happens, we're stronger than they are. They couldn't do much to stop us from *taking* control."

Jesus, Earl had his hooks in Fred. I almost dropped the glass in my hand.

"Probably not," agreed Kevin. "Two girls, a *queer* and Sidney."

"Queer?"

"Yeah, pretty sure Seth is *gay*."

"Really?"

"I don't know, probably."

"Whatever. Listen, we'd better get back up to Skylab. You got the movies?"

"Yup. Earl will like these," I could hear the DVD's shake in their boxes as Kevin rattled them. "Lots of blood and guts!"

I listened as they left. It was a terrifying conversation to have overheard. Fred and Kevin had just pledged their allegiance to Earl, calling four friends nothing more than an inconvenience.

Chapter Five

Joel died the following day, making my nightmare complete. We buried him in the backyard, next to Connor. We were experiencing one of the most profoundly distressing periods in our short lives. This was comparable with losing our families in the initial blasts. This was what I'd remembered being lost felt like as a child. Panicked. I had lost my best friend, the man I'd loved - the knowledge that I would never have that back was suffocating me. I couldn't bring myself to be at the funeral. *I wasn't with him.* This was a final regret. I wasn't at his side when he'd passed on. Had he asked for me? Had he spoken at all? I hadn't asked Caroline. She had been with him. All I could feel was grief mixed with envy. She'd seen his final moments. I should never have agreed to sleep. I had exhausted myself with him all night. And so I had missed his final breath.

*****

In the very early hours of the morning, before Joel left me, I had laid with him in bed, under the covers, remembering something I'd said to him once. It was the night before the big fight with Connor. He had been exhausted (high no doubt) but he was lying in bed, looking contented. It was a look of calm.

"I like you best like this," I'd said to him.

"On my back or asleep?"

"Calm. At peace"

He had that look now. No expression passed over his face as I listened to his shallow breathing.

I laid there beside him, stroking his dirty blonde hair, keeping it out of his eyes at first, and then just repeating the motion. I could imagine we were still living the summer months before everything went to hell. We were new, our relationship was in its infancy, but we'd shared so much in such a short time that we could just lay there and not speak. He would indulge me, let me stroke his hair, kiss his shoulder. This usually followed a passionate and impressively lengthy session of lovemaking. I'd only been with one other boy before Joel and that was anything but impressive. Not that I had much experience to draw from, but a girl knows what a girl wants.

At three in the morning Joel spoke once more. It wasn't profound, at least, not at the time. It seemed almost sad that this was what he'd said with his last opportunity to communicate to me. "Go North," he whispered, catching me completely off guard.

"Wha-what?" I whispered back. He did not reply. "Joel…" I sat up, took his head in both my hands and leaned into him. "Joel?" Tears welled up in my eyes and fell on his face. "Say that again," I pleaded. "Say it again, Joel." I lifted his eyelids and stared into his eyes, though they had rolled up into the back of his head. I shook him. "Please… Joel, say that again. Say something, anything. Please!" Realizing he was not going to speak again, I set his head onto the pillow and cried for hours.

*****

The first few days after Joel's passing were numbing. Upon hearing the news from Caroline and falling to my knees, my mind went a mile a minute. I stared at the floor, my unblinking eyes darting back and forth. A hand on my back, meant to comfort me, felt like nothing. I stood and called Caroline a liar. I couldn't grasp that he wasn't coming back, that one evening Joel wouldn't just wake up and turn to me and smile. I wasn't prepared for this. Though I had tried to be logical, understanding that the blood loss, the time spent underwater, and his comatose state did not bode well for his chances, I had convinced myself that his survival was a real possibility.

I charged to the bedroom and stopped short of the door. I stared at Joel on the bed, studying his torso, watching for his chest to rise and fall. They might have been wrong, they might not have checked everything, they weren't doctors. What did they know? I moved to the bed. Had they checked his pulse? Had they listened for his breathing? As the questions ran through my head I pressed my finger to his jugular, and my ear to his mouth, desperate for any sign.

"I tried CPR too, Sara," Seth had followed me as far as the door. I shot a look at him and he stepped back, his eyes falling to the floor.

"Do you even *know* CPR?" I asked spitefully. His hand went up limply and I started the life saving technique, straddling Joel, pushing violently down on his chest, desperate to restart his heart. 1, 2, 3, 4, 5, "Breathe!" I shouted at him. His face was white. I tilted his head, pinched his nose and sealed my mouth around his. I blew hard and long into his lungs, encouraged by the rise in his chest. I repeated the process time and again until after a half hour I was pulled off him, physically exhausted and emotionally crushed.

For days after his burial I replayed his voice in my head, remembering only the good, only the special moments. I couldn't bring myself to think a single negative thought about him. Instead I ran through all the scenarios that would never be. I'd lost everything. He was my every day, in my every thought. How could I survive this place without him? Who would I read to at night? Who would I sleep next to? Who would I share my most intimate thoughts with? The lost opportunities endlessly played out in my mind. I was utterly heart-sick and spent many of the days to follow alone in his room, our room, bed-ridden.

Caroline would visit often and was really the only person I would let in. I let her into my head and into my heart. We'd relive shared memories of Joel and occasionally I would find myself laughing out loud with her as the stories became more ridiculous.

"He was an incredible person," I said, and in saying that aloud, talking about him in past tense, I realized he was gone for good, physically at least. Caroline embraced me as the corners of my smile pulled downward. Caroline was a really good person, someone I wished I'd known better in *life*. She brought me back from the brink, and for that I will be eternally grateful.

I'd decided she would be the first to hear my news, something that would change everything. I had suspected it for months, and I had no way of being entirely certain yet. But sometimes you just know. And I knew.

"I'm pregnant, Caroline," I told her as we sat on the back balcony, taking in a rare afternoon of clear blue skies.

Her mouth opened but no sound came. An expression of fear seemed to pass over her pretty face, a darkness that didn't disappear for some time. Finally, after digesting what I'd told her, and all of its implications, she responded.

"Are you certain? I mean, could you be wrong?" A fair question: it wasn't like we had any pregnancy tests on hand. I hadn't had a period in about two months, but it was more than that. My body felt different -heavier. I felt already a yearning for it. To see this child I could feel growing inside me. I couldn't have been more than 10 weeks along. But already I felt like a mother.

"Yes, I'm sure."

"That's wonderful news, Sara." She smiled, attempting true happiness, despite the circumstances. "Joel's?"

"Yes, of course." I took the defensive. "You didn't believe anything Joel had accused me of with Connor did you?"

"You'd never said either way." She lowered her head. I took her chin in my hand and brought her eyes to mine. "It's Joel's. My God, of course it's Joel's." I shuddered, realizing I was the only one of us alive who could confirm or deny this. "Is that what the others think? Do they think I cheated on Joel with Connor?"

"No, I – I don't know Sara. I shouldn't have asked that. I'm sorry."

"I just don't want there to be any confusion when I tell everyone." I already felt protective of my unborn child.

"Are you sick? What do they call it? Morning sickness?"

"Not really. Not everyone gets that though."

"I guess not." I could tell she wasn't convinced of my state.

"Caroline," I said, smiling. "I'm *pregnant*."

Caroline finally smiled convincingly. The darkness disappeared. "It's great news, Sara."

"Thanks. I'm really scared, but excited too." I stood and paced a moment. Turning to her I felt tears resurfacing. "It feels like an incredible amount of responsibility. And this isn't exactly the best time or place to have a baby."

Caroline stood too and placed her hands on my shoulders, calming my nerves. "People have been having babies in worse places than this. I'll help of course, I'll do whatever you need doing. And you're a med student, or would have been…"

Had the world not taken a turn for the worse, I would have been at one of the finest universities in the country, pre-med. I had been given the opportunity in my final year of high school to co-op with the local hospital where I had witnessed two live births. I just shook my head and hugged her hard. She hugged me back.

Sharing the news had settled me into my new existence. Though I would miss Joel every time I laid my head down to sleep, in every room I entered and every time I looked in the shattered bathroom mirror, I would recover in the knowledge that he would live on in his child. And I would love this child more than I could ever have loved him. I would need to, to make up for the cruelty of bringing a new life into this uncertainty.

While I was making ready for a new life, Earl was making ready for a war.

Chapter Six

A week passed before I shared with Caroline, Sid and Seth what had happened before Joel had died. What he had whispered, impossible as it seemed, in his dying breaths.

"North? Earl and the guys said *not* to go north," reminded Sidney. After we'd successfully beaten back the flag army, Earl, Sonny and Fred had followed them north to be sure they had travelled far enough, that they would no longer pose a threat to our continued survival. In the time since the bombs fell, several caravans of survivors had passed our fortress. Some we had the opportunity to speak with. All were headed north towards something unknown that was beckoning them on. Their fate became clear when Earl explained what his crew had seen. Two days' march from our position was a vast, mass grave that stretched on for miles. Burnt out vehicles and bodies strewn across the asphalt. They recommended that we not cross that path, that we stay put.

"I don't know why he said it, but that's what he said." I lowered my voice as we had gathered in the kitchen. I drank a glass of the semi transparent water, the well compromised by months of fall-out and radioactive rain early on in the Apocalypse.

"Listen, I'm not sure that's a good idea, going north… what they described was pretty graphic." Seth had a point, but all we had to go on were the words of Earl, Sonny and Freddy, none of whom I held in very high regard anymore.

"There's something I didn't tell you about what he'd said."

"There's more?"

"Not more, just, I don't know, something…"

"Well what, Sara? What is it?" Caroline was frowning.

"It felt like, I don't know, like someone else was speaking through him."

"Like the angel?" Seth interrupted.

"Yes, I mean I wouldn't know what that was like, but there was something about the voice, or the tone or something that just didn't say *Joel* to me." I made a face as I always did after a glass of the dirty water. "What do you guys think? Should we try it?"

"We're still living pretty well here. I don't know if I want to lose that." Seth was right; it might be the dumbest thing we've done, leaving the safety of Joel's house. "Let's see how things work out here over the next little while, then make the decision."

"I'm not excited to leave either; we don't know what's out there," I admitted.

"Should we confront Earl about it?" Caroline stood and opened the fridge, mindlessly panning its limited contents.

"I think we should feel out how things go, like Seth said. Keep this little bit of information to ourselves and make a more educated decision on what to do next."

Sid summed up our situation with three words. "Then we wait."

Chapter Seven

Earl had counted the guns and ammunition and placed them in the addition, save the ones he had hidden around the house. Freddy and Sonny hung on his every word now, while Kevin sat at his right side mimicking Earl's arrogance.

As I approached the four of them in the addition, which had acted as our watch tower for the past nine months – with a clear view of the east, west and north – I heard them discussing their plans once more. It was February and my birthday had just passed, like so many others, unnoticed and unannounced.

"We're still in good shape: the ammunition collected from that last attack really set us up…." Earl was caught off-guard by my entry. I sensed his lingering embarrassment over the hand incident, but it lasted just a moment. He turned to greet me. "Sara, how are you?" False concern. I flinched at the thought of his arms on me – *comforting* me.

"I'm coping," I said. "What's all this?" I waved at the arsenal in front of me.

"Inventory," Sonny offered. He had been sheepish around me since our last conversation. He shouldn't have asked what he did about Joel, and he knew it.

"What brings you by, Sara?" Kevin was at his post at the east windows.

"I want to know what you four are planning. It affects us all."

"Of course it does," Earl broke in, "and it's in all our best interest to support our plan. We can't sit here hoping the flags won't come back."

"So you're going then? *All of you?* Abandoning us here to fulfill some hateful revenge plan?"

"If you could just see it for what it really is, Sara," Kevin jumped in. "This is an important step in securing our futures."

"Is that what Earl's told you?" I glared at him.

"It's what we believe, Sara." Freddy spoke up. "I don't know how you're not getting behind this? You lost Connor *and* Joel."

"*We* lost Connor and Joel." I corrected him. "We all lost a good friend in Connor, and I lost everything when Joel died, and I'm *not* behind this. What does that tell you?"

"You have different ideas of what should be done," answered Earl. "We believe this is what Joel would have wanted."

"Oh, bullshit! Don't drag Joel's name into this. This is what *you* want Earl." I looked accusingly at the other three. "And you've all bought into it."

"It's been decided, Sara. We're going, with or without your blessing." Kevin. What a little prick. I flushed and turned to leave, but thought better of it.

"You do this, and you're separating the house. Seth, Sid, Caroline and I are against it. For the record."

"To each their own," Earl replied.

"I'm pregnant." I don't know why I chose that moment to tell them.

"What?" Freddy was stunned. The other three froze in place. If I could have willed them to remain in that state, we would have all been better for it.

"I'm two months along now, at least." I crossed my arms in front of me.

"Jesus, Sara." The repercussions of this revelation were working their way through Sonny's head.

"That's not good." Kevin's response. Earl slapped Kevin's arm dismissively.

"Joel's?" Earl asked the burning question, licking his thin lips.

"Yes, Jesus Christ, Connor and I weren't…" I felt it was a hopeless argument and just shook my head hard.

"Okay, all the more reason to remove the threat of the flags." Earl faking respect for his fallen leader, and friend, used my news to further his agenda.

"You'll do what you'll do; I just needed to tell you." With that, I left the addition and they returned to their task at hand.

"We leave tomorrow," I heard Earl shout over my shoulder. Part of me hoped they wouldn't return.

Chapter Eight

As we watched them leave, I thought it odd that Caroline hadn't joined us in the front hall to see them off. Seth and Sid shook hands with the four and wished them all the best. No hard feelings.

"We'll watch the house," Sid assured them.

"I know you will, Sid." Earl smiled, his teeth now yellow from the cigarettes. In that moment I wondered how many more they must have. I remembered how Kevin had made finding cigarettes in town a priority.

They left in the Caddy: Joel's father's Cadillac. So many of the vehicles we'd acquired over the months had stopped working, blamed on the weather and lack of maintenance. The caddy had remained in the garage, protected from the elements, and lovingly maintained by Sonny.

"Good riddance," I said aloud.

"Don't say that, Sara." Sid wrapped his arm around me. His touch was soothing. I felt warm and safe but unthreatened, which was the polar opposite to how Earl's touch made me feel. Caroline had told me that he and she had found comfort in each other's arms over the course of the last few weeks, long after John's shooting death in our front hall. She had blamed herself for that, and I knew she'd taken the death of her high school sweetheart terribly.

"I don't know if I mean it or not." I was angry at Earl's ability to just keep going despite everything. I was equally angry at the other three for willingly following Earl so blindly.

"I'm not defending their plan; I think it's flawed. But Earl leads with aggression. You know, he's a 'best defense is a strong offence' type." Sidney had summed Earl up tidily with those words.

"Yeah, I guess I always knew that about him." I turned and put an arm around both Sid and Seth as we walked to the kitchen. "Where is Caroline?"

"I don't know. I woke up alone this morning." Sid admitted.

I was taken aback. "What? Why? Where would she be?"

"Honestly, I thought maybe she'd spent the night with you, talking about your baby, making plans. You know how she likes to make plans." Caroline was gifted at putting things in perspective. She had helped us organize our resources and because of her efforts some of our food and toiletries had outlived their expiry dates.

"Nope, she left my room about midnight last night." We had been talking about the baby, and she had stayed with me until I'd mentioned the time.

"She didn't say where she was heading after that?"

"I didn't ask. I assumed she would have made her way to your room." Sid and Caroline had bunked up in Julia and Connor's old room, across the hall from mine.

"Seth, have you seen Caroline this morning?" Sid pulled away from me while Seth also maneuvered out of my reach.

"I haven't," he said. We all stopped there at the foot of the stairs and looked dumbly at one another. Where was Caroline?

Chapter Nine

We each took a floor to look for Caroline, Sid took the top level, Seth the main floor and I looked in the basement, each of us calling out her name. It was a very large house. Joel's parents had done very well for themselves and built this colossal home in the country. It was an excellent refuge for our original group of fourteen, but full of empty spaces now that we were so few.

Searching the basement I moved through the rooms quickly at first and then slowed down, taking my time, opening closets, although I didn't know why she would be hiding. This was maddening. This was very out of character for Caroline, making it all the more distressing.

After losing hope of finding her in the basement, I opened the door to the cold room where we kept what was left of our canned goods and vegetables from the barn garden. There I found her seated in the fetal position, hugging her knees into her chest, rocking slowly.

"Caroline!" She looked up and I saw a misery in her eyes that stunned me. "What - what's wrong?" My heart sank. The cold room was freezing and smelled of potatoes and dirt.

I approached her quickly, startling her. She pulled away, shivering. I did my best not to touch her; I didn't want to make her worse.

"Oh Caroline, it's freezing in here," I rubbed my arms and looked around. The room was dark: the light from the open doorway made me realize I would have only been a silhouette to her.

"It's Sara, honey. Why are you in here?"

She burst into tears and crawled toward me on all fours. I took her up into my arms and rubbed her back softly. "What's happened?"

She tried to speak, stumbling over her words. She wanted to say so much at once. I hugged her harder, my knees digging into the concrete floor.

"Don't speak, Caroline. Let me take you to Sid."

"No!" She half whispered into my ear. I pulled her back and looked in her eyes. What I saw left me cold.

"What? Why? Tell me what's happened."

"No, not Sid, please, he can *never* know."

"What is it, Caroline? What can he never know?" My skin crawled in anticipation.

"Please, swear to me, you'll never tell him. Never, never." Her face contorted into a twisted, pained look that stayed with me a long time afterward.

"I – I swear," I heard myself say.

Just then Seth and Sid came in. Caroline looked horrified.

"Caroline!" Sid exclaimed. "What are you doing in here?"

"I'm taking her to the shower," I said as I pulled her to her feet. "She's not hurt, Sid, she just needs me right now."

"What's wrong with her?" His voice cracked.

"She's fine Sid, she's uh, had an episode."

"Episode?" He looked confused. I hated lying. I was just trying to protect my friend. Had Sid done something? I couldn't believe that, but why was she so insistent he not know? I was desperate to find out.

"She has them once in a while. Let me through and we'll fill you guys in when we're ready."

"But she's okay? Caroline? You're okay?" He reached for her and she pulled away, using me as a shield.

"She'll be fine, Sid. Seth, you guys just hold down the fort while we work through this."

"What kind of episode are we talking about?" He sounded honestly worried for her. It hurt me to have to avoid his questions; I was making everything up as I went along.

"She's, uh, got a disorder. Just let us through, Sid!" I became more forceful as Caroline's nails clawed into my arm. He and Seth moved aside to let us pass. I smiled and raced with Caroline to the basement bathroom, where I locked the door behind us.

The bathroom had seen better days: it was outfitted with a sauna/shower where I set her down on the cedar bench. Though the sauna hadn't been used since the bombs dropped, it still smelled strongly of damp cedar.

I knelt down in front of Caroline and placed my hands on her cheeks. "What's happened, Caroline? Tell me please."

She sat there shaking as the memories took hold. Though I knew from her state that she had seen or experienced something traumatic, I was not prepared for what she would tell me.

Chapter Ten

Caroline was beside herself. I sat next to her and held her hand. Her grip was crushing. I let her cry until I felt there was an opportunity to ask again.

"What *happened*, Caroline?"

"You don't know," she uttered. "You *can't* know."

"Don't you want to tell me?"

She took in a deep breath and exhaled.

"It was awful…." she said, convulsing at the memories. "I – I don't know *how* to tell you."

"Just take your time, Caroline. I'm here for as long as you need me to be."

She was staring at the tiled floor, her head shaking back and forth. I took a deep breath next, anticipating the news. What could have happened? Had she left the house and seen something so disturbing? Had she had a run-in with someone? The questions were percolating one after another in my mind.

"Promise me you won't tell Sid," she repeated through gasping breaths.

"I promised, Caroline. You know I wouldn't." I wiped her hair from her forehead gently.

She looked up at me and put on a brave face. "Those bastards...." She broke down again, her head shaking from side to side. *Those bastards?* Who was she referring to? Surely not...

"*Earl*." The name was like a curse coming from her lips.

"What did he *do,* Caroline?" I was beginning to feel sick to my stomach. This wasn't the baby inside me, it was in anticipation of what she would say next.

"He's an evil bastard," she spat out.

"What did he *do*?" A lull in her explanation gave me a chance to breathe again.

"He *raped* me! Okay?! He fucking *raped* me!" she said bluntly, her eyes fixed on me.

I squeezed her hand hard. "Jesus, *what*?"

"*Him*, then Kevin, then - then that *Fred…*" She stopped suddenly, rhyming off the names I would hate forever after. I said nothing more, I only listened. "*Earl* first, cornering me in the kitchen after – after I left your room last night… *was* it last night?" She looked away again trying to focus.

The sauna was the best place in the house to have this secret conversation as it had a heavy wooden door, and the bathroom door itself was shut and locked. If she wanted secrecy, this place would offer it.

"He said he wanted to *kiss* me. He said he'd been *lonely*." She released my hand and placed both hands on her knees, perhaps unconsciously forcing them together. "I told him I wasn't interested. I told him no…" I could see the memories play out on her face, and she frowned deeply. "Please don't tell Sid. Please…" She wept involuntarily and caught her breath. "I'm so *ashamed*."

"*No*," I said automatically. "*No,* Caroline. This is *not* your fault, don't you do that."

"What if I had let him kiss me?" She questioned.

"Goddamn it, Caroline." I was livid. Not with her, but with her thought process. "You are the *victim*."

"He said he was lonely. He said they were *all* so lonely." Jesus Christ, *all of them*, animals! "I – I hate them now." She had every right. I should *kill* them for her, I thought.

Caroline continued to relive the memory. "He took my wrists and pulled me into him, into those yellow teeth… and I *fought* him, I *did*, Sara!" It was crushing to hear the details.

"Then I felt a sharp pain in my stomach." Her hand moved to her midsection.

"I *know,* Caroline." I massaged her shoulder. "And Sid will know that too."

"No! Please don't tell him, Sara." I wanted to so he would take matters into his own hands and kill that fuck. All of them. But I'd promised.

"Okay, Caroline, I won't. If that's really what you want, I will keep my promise." It ate me up inside, but maybe she'd change her mind in time.

"He dragged me to the basement by the neck, I – I couldn't scream or speak." She was stone-faced now. "I tried to wiggle free, but he was too strong. When we reached the bottom of the stairs I knew I was in trouble. He kept dragging me across the floor and I went limp. I thought maybe my dead weight would make it harder but he kept going. Then he threw me on the couch and I said I would scream and he hit me in my face." A hand moved slowly to her temple where I guessed Earl had punched her.

"Jesus Christ, Caroline. I'm so sorry." I stroked her hair. I wanted to make it better for her. I thought briefly how this could have been me.

Tears burned my eyes and I rubbed them out. I felt I needed to be strong for her. She continued her story saying that Kevin and Fred had followed. The attack had clearly been planned in advance. Tears rolled down both of our cheeks. Had they only spared me because of my pregnancy? What if I hadn't revealed this the day before? A full-body shiver went through me. How had it come to this?

"But they were drunk; I could smell the gin on their breath, in my ear. Maybe if they weren't drinking…"

"Jesus, Caroline." I managed through my hoarse throat. "Don't give them anything. They did it, that's enough. Don't give them *anything.*"

"I don't know how long I laid there. I don't even know how I ended up in the cold room. I just knew I couldn't face any of them."

"Where was Sonny during all this?" I asked, propping myself up.

"Never heard his voice."

"Sons of bitches." I growled through clenched teeth. I vowed I would kill them then and there. The how and the when would eventually present themselves.

Chapter Eleven

The night Earl, Fred, Kevin and Sonny left to chase the flags, I found myself in the addition with Seth, trying to keep busy while we kept watch - as we had countless times before. It was a chore, one which I'd always dreaded. The boredom of sitting alone and staring out the windows, often into an abyss of blackness, was numbing. When the clouds dominated the skies and there were no stars, moon or even a faint flicker of light in the distance to focus on, your shift, in what we had nicknamed Skylab, seemed doubly painful. Of course, with the absence of light, seeing the enemy was made all the more easy, as they would carry either a torch or a flashlight, something to light their way in the darkness.

This night did not produce an enemy, thankfully. Nor was the sky as black as it once was. Clouds moved slowly, offering us a glimpse of a star or even the moon. It was waxing Gibbous that night. Gibbous, a term I had learned recently, in one of Joel's childhood books. Having read virtually every book in the house, I had turned to purely educational reading, and then finally to educational children's books. I liked to think of the moon waxing rather than waning; the idea it would reveal itself gave me hope. Watching it wane made me feel as though it would disappear again, as it did in the beginning, and maybe forever this time.

While poking around in Earl's things - he and the other three had taken to sleeping in the addition - I came across a booklet under a pillow, a journal of sorts. It was one of Kevin's sketch books, with a black textured cover and about 200 bright white pages. Many of these pages had been filled with a very steady hand. The penmanship was impressive. It was Earl's handwriting; I recognized it immediately from his maps and charts and timetables which he'd posted around the house.

After thumbing through the pages I closed the book, my interest falling back to the cover which had been carved with a knife. The carving formed words, and the words alarmed me for several reasons.

MY STRUGGLE

The title itself told a story. But knowing Earl, and relating the title to a history lesson on the Discovery Channel a few years back, MY STRUGGLE became profoundly more disturbing when translated into German; *Mein Kampf.* Hitler's autobiography, and political ideology which propelled him into his role in infamy. Knowing Earl, he knew exactly how this title translated, and to whom he would be comparing himself. How would I live with someone I hated, someone I wanted dead? I opened the journal again and read, suddenly feeling Seth's eyes upon me.

"Are you sure you should be reading that, Sara?" he questioned timidly.

"What's the harm? They won't be back for days."

"What did Caroline say to you today when you found her?" he asked, changing the subject.

"She's fine, Seth," I lied. In fact, I wondered if she'd ever be fine again. "She had an episode." I was sticking with that answer. People seemed to stop asking when you said the word 'episode'.

"Okay." He let it go and I started flipping pages, hoping to gain some advantage over Earl by reading his secret thoughts.

"I was impressed more than anything with the way Gareth carried himself. The total control he had over his membership inspired me." He referred to the leader of the flags, who had hoped to grill each of us in an attempt to weed out supposed 'sympathizers' to the Reaper's ideals. Gareth was a small man, and he ruled with fear. Joel saw that.

I read on. *"Gareth was well spoken, superior in his demeanor. People need to be led. People need to feel safe. Gareth offered those things. Two things to rule: offer safety and offer leadership."* He was taking notes the whole time!

"Leadership is often thrust upon an individual. Joel was voted our leader, and Joel cracked under the pressure. What is better is to take leadership, there is power in that and people respect power." I felt a pang of anxiety. He was building himself up to lead us all, and he would *take* control. As I read on, I found more passages that related to leadership; entire pages filled with plans to lead an army of his own, schematics of battles we'd fought. He took nothing for granted. He learned from everything and he documented it. I'd said before that Earl was too intelligent to have such a scary side. The very idea of Earl in control made me sick with fear.

Flipping through more of the text I stopped again at a section entitled; ***Sexual cleansing - the immediacy of procreation.*** *"The purpose of life is to procreate and evolve. In a world where humanity has likely lost most of its populace, procreation is key to the survival of the species. What does not encourage procreation cannot be allowed to consume resources. A sexual cleansing is necessary. The homosexuals need be exposed and exterminated, so as not to consume that which will feed humanity's future."*

"So, whose journal is it? Kevin's?" Seth sounded despondent. My heart went out to him. I knew he was gay, I'd always known, and reading Earl's grand plan, I wondered if he knew it too.

"No, Earl's," I replied and cleared my throat. Should I show him? I felt I had to protect him.

"So, what's he saying? Kill the flags - good. Hate your neighbor – good. No more ammo – bad. Something along those lines?"

I laughed and smiled at him, then shook my head.

"He's fucked, Seth, and I'm afraid we're in trouble. He's talking about taking control, leading us all."

Seth didn't like the sound of that. "Earl can go fuck himself. The guy's a pussy with a gun. I'd never follow him."

"But what if he used the others to back him up? We're two women and two men. He's got four men."

"Well, I can't see those guys actually forcing us to do something. I mean Jesus, we're all friends here right?"

I thought of what they'd done to Caroline and almost used it as an example but stopped myself.

"I think they're all under his spell and are capable of anything. The most we can hope for now is that the flags get to them before they get to the flags." And I meant it. They would be doing us a favor if they killed Earl. I feared for our futures and for the future of my baby if he returned.

Chapter Twelve

Earl, Sonny, Fred and Kevin returned to the house a week later. My heart sank at the sight of them. One, two, three, four, I counted as they moved through the front door, no worse for wear as far as I could tell. Sonny went straight to the kitchen, passing me without a word.

"What happened?" I asked, struggling to contain my hatred.

"We got them," Fred said on his way to the basement. I became nervous: they were all behaving strangely.

"Well, is something wrong?" I asked.

"Nothing to concern yourself with." Kevin marched past me, following Sonny into the kitchen.

"You fucking pussies!" Earl cried from the front hall. I jumped out of my skin. I flushed at the sight of him.

"Rest easy, Sara." Mistaking my rage for fear, he approached me. "We got *all* of 'em!" While he spoke, he flapped a piece of *something* between his fingers. He also wore a colored cape draped over his shoulders.

"Oh my God." As he got closer I could see what he held. It was *skin*, flesh! I backed off automatically. *"What have you done!"*

"This is my *prize*!" he shouted. "All of ours! Think of it as *our* flag, courtesy of *the* flags!" Then he removed the cape from around his shoulders, threw it over the railing of the staircase and went to the kitchen. I was frozen in terror at what I was seeing.

*****

That night, I couldn't sleep. The mental image of human flesh draped across the railing just one floor beneath me was too horrifying for words. I could only imagine what my subconscious would conjure up if I allowed myself to sleep. I had seen so much death by this point, nothing should have shocked me. But this blatant desecration incurred a new level of horror. Finally, when I could toss and turn no more, I got up and wandered outside, escaping through the bedroom window, crossing the rooftop and navigating down the TV antenna to where Sonny was standing on the back patio.

Chapter Thirteen

"Talk to me, Sonny." I begged him. "Whose skin *is* that?"

"It's Gareth's," he replied. "*Jesus*, Sara..." His head lowered and his eyes closed.

"I don't think I want to know any more."

"We killed them all. We killed most of them in their sleep. But when the guns went off a few of them woke up, and we shot them down." He paused. "Maybe to them it was all a dream, you know? Doesn't everyone hope they'll just die in their sleep?"

"Yeah," I said, mesmerized by the monotone of his voice.

"We shot them like cattle. One, two, three… they fell like sacks of potatoes, blood everywhere." Judging from his tone, Sonny had realized revenge wasn't all it was cracked up to be.

"I wish you hadn't gone, Sonny."

He turned then and looked at me wearily. "Yeah. Me too, Sara."

He continued to describe how Freddy had located Gareth during the early part of the melee and secured him to a tree with rope, letting him watch his army be gunned down in front of him. Earl swaggered over to Gareth when the last of his followers were dead, and before cutting his throat, said; "Ever seen an animal *skinned*, Gareth? Know how many animals *I've* skinned? Enough to know how to skin a man." Then the knife came out and Earl slid it across Gareth's throat slowly, a shallow cut. Thick red blood ran slowly down his neck and chest, collecting on his robe. The cut was not deep enough to kill, only to torture. Gareth's mouth opened as if to protest and Earl jabbed the knife down on his tongue cutting through his jaw. He left it there for a time and circled his victim, sizing him up.

Finally, after facing the leader of the flag army once more, Earl pulled his sidearm and shot Gareth in the head, just as Connor had been executed. Freddy then untied Gareth and Earl went to work on the corpse.

"*Jesus*, Sonny," I choked. "That's horrifying."

"Yeah, pretty fucking sick."

"What are we going to do about him?" He knew who I meant: Earl.

"I don't know anymore." He was distraught. "I'm not taking sides. I'm leaving."

He said he wanted to resume his long-abandoned search for Tom, a friend who we'd lost during those first crucial hours after the bombs had dropped. Tom was a gawky looking kid, his eyes too big for his face, his teeth misshapen and his self-esteem non-existent. Sonny was looking for purpose again, some semblance of reason to go on. I pleaded with him to stay, to watch over me and the baby.

"Sonny, I - I'm so sorry things between us got so messed up. But you see now, you *see* what Earl is. He's sick!"

"I see that. I guess I always knew that, Sara. But after Connor, and Joel…." He trailed off. "After the flags and everything went to shit, after all we'd accomplished here. I just needed someone to tell me it was alright to take revenge."

I placed a hand on his shoulder. "Sonny, I'm scared for us. I *need* you to stay." I wiped away a tear with my other hand.

Sonny gently removed my hand. "Sara, I'm *not* staying. I *can't*."

"I'm begging you, Sonny." I began to cry. "He'll kill us all, eventually. He'll write a reason in his journal and then he'll carry it out." Sonny's heavy hand touched my head gently.

"There's nothing for me here, Sara."

I couldn't argue that there was nothing here, but what was there *beyond* here? Part of him had died when Connor and Joel died, the other part perished during that trip he had taken with Earl to exact revenge. We were all dying inside. How much more could any of us take? I resigned myself to his departure.

"Come with me." He suggested.

"Where would we go?" I asked.

"East. Tom had family on the east coast. And then we could find a boat. And then…"

"And then?"

"Then we'll sail it." He turned to look at the house and breathed deeply. Looking back at me his gaze lingered. "You're not coming, are you, Sara?" He smiled sadly then.

A journey like that was not something I could manage while pregnant. Open to the elements, food and shelter uncertain from day to day. "I'll miss you, Sonny."

"Don't," he said, before he turned and entered the house for the last time. I would never see Sonny again.

Chapter Fourteen

Caroline had not recovered from the attack, and her deep depression left Sid with little to work with.

"I don't know what's going on, Sara. Caroline won't so much as let me touch her. Has she said anything to you?" Sid sat with me on the edge of my bed, where I huddled and fought back pregnancy-related nausea.

"The episode." I kept up the lie. "She's still shaken from her *episode* last week. She'd never experienced anything like that before and she's afraid it could happen again." I was becoming an excellent liar. Not something I was particularly proud of, but necessary to keep a promise to a friend.

"I can't seem to reason with her and it's scaring me you know? I feel like Connor must have felt when Julia was so depressed." Our friend Julia, a former resident of this home and my very best friend, had cut her own wrists months ago to avoid bringing a child into this world. This memory haunted me more than ever, having now become pregnant myself and experiencing the same sad thoughts.

"Sidney, give her some time. I'll continue to talk with her, you just be her rock until she can open up to you again."

"I guess. I miss her though."

"I know you do. I miss the old Caroline too. Be patient, okay?"

"I will. Thanks, Sara." Sid left me to my thoughts. I was sitting up in bed, caressing my ever expanding stomach. What would my baby look like, I wondered. God I hoped it would be healthy. Who knew what the last few months could do to a fetus. I put those thoughts out of my mind and decided he would be a he, and that he would look like Joel. Ten fingers, ten toes, bald, and terribly handsome. I smiled and realized I was looking forward to meeting him. But what would I call him? I had no names picked. Should I call him Joel after his father? No, I decided that would be too painful. Maybe I'd name him after my own father, Leif. That was a strong name, and he would need all the strength he could get.

Just then Kevin appeared at my door. "Sara," he said flatly, "Earl would like your ear."

"Then tell Earl to come see me. I'm not jumping every time he calls."

"I'll let him know."

I wasn't looking forward to facing Earl one on one. We were used to arguing with each other now over just about everything, but in front of everyone, never just the two of us. I felt an urge to get up and call Sid back into the room when Earl's frame blocked the doorway.

Chapter Fifteen

"Earl." I greeted him uncomfortably. His hands were hanging from the top of the door frame and his feet jammed up against either side of the opening as if to fill the space completely.

"Sara. Can we talk about this baby of yours?"

"I see no reason to discuss that with you," I shot back.

"No reason? I'm the one protecting this house; you have every reason to discuss this with me."

"We're *all*, all of us protecting this house, Earl. Not just you!"

"Sara. Who's in charge here? Who in your mind is leading this group now?"

"Not you."

"Oh, no? Then who? Who lives in Skylab, keeping watch day and night?"

"That's your choice to live there. The rest of us are doing our part too."

"Let's not just agree to disagree this time, Sara. I need you to acknowledge my leadership so we can move forward." He motioned toward me, trying to intimidate me. I wasn't scared of Earl, though maybe I should have been after what he did to Caroline and Gareth. But, for some reason, Earl was still just Earl to me, my boyfriend's sycophant.

"You won't get that out of me, Earl."

"Why do you hate me so much, Sara? Why, after all I've managed to accomplish here, why do you *hate* me so much?" His voice lowered to a menacing hiss.

"Are you kidding, Earl? You know *exactly* why I hate you. You, Kevin and Fred." His eyes narrowed as he understood.

"So, you know." He stood upright and his hands shot down to his sides. "Get over yourself, you little bitch! She wanted it! And that's between her and me."

My eyes widened and he knew he'd said the wrong thing to the wrong person. He took a step back as I got to my feet. I slammed my open palms against his chest and shoved him out the door. "You just pray I don't tell Sid and Seth. Caroline asked me to promise. But I'm rethinking the whole thing now."

"Careful, Sara. You be careful what you say to who." His finger was in my face. I slapped it away. "I'm the leader of this group now," he hissed through clenched teeth. "You get comfortable with it. Disrespect me again and I'll show you what it is to go against me."

I slammed the door and paced. I could hear the addition door slam also. I fanned my face and sat on the bed, breathing deeply and exhaling slowly. We had to remove Earl altogether. But how?

Chapter Sixteen

We spent the ensuing months tending the barn garden, collecting seeds from the plants and replanting them. This garden had been nothing less than a miraculous discovery during the early days after the Reaper had struck. In the midst of all of the chaos, we discovered a barn facility, untouched by the fall out, complete with hydroponics equipment and a lifetime of marijuana. What had been someone's (perhaps the government's, based on the size and level of operation) enterprise had become our lifesaver. We had replaced the marijuana with vegetable seeds we'd scavenged from hardware and department stores, and began using the barn garden as a source for fresh vegetables and fruit. The barn had a similar setup to Joel's house, boasting a private well to feed the crop and a generator that ran on the same fuel we used at the house. Without the hydroponic garden we would surely have suffered a bout of scurvy or worse, seeing how the last of our canned fruits and veggies had been consumed within the first year. At just a few minutes' drive from the house on the ATV, the barn was a welcome change of pace from the stresses at home.

When I wasn't in the barn garden, helping out, sorting seeds or checking hoses I'd spend time alone, usually in the bathroom adjacent to Joel's room, staring into the shattered mirror as my hand gently caressed my baby bump.

More often than not I would cry. Not because my pregnancy upset me, or that my hormones were getting the better of me, but because I missed Joel, my baby's father. That the baby would grow up without a dad made me anxious. Then again, if he *had* survived, what irreparable damage would he have suffered and how would his pain translate to his child?

Jesus, I was studying myself in the very mirror he'd smashed the night he chose to take his own life.

The bump had grown slowly in the last couple of months. With these limited resources, I didn't have the privilege of eating whatever I craved. Had that been the case, I was sure I would have been bigger by now. Still, I tried to eat as well and as often as I could and the size of my belly had proven that my attempts at proper nutrition were at least growing something in there.

Nothing made me happier than feeling my baby move. It was a constant source of relief for me. In our present circumstances, with no vitamins and barely any meat products save the recent stash of jerky Earl had found in an abandoned trailer, my diet consisted of berries, lettuce, and canned beans for the most part. Feeling the baby move inside me was an experience I often enjoyed alone. I would think of Joel then as well. Imagining his hand on my belly, with mine guiding his to the kicks and punches.

Six months into my pregnancy (or so was my best guess), I was really showing. My lower back ached even when I sat down. Caroline remembered her stepsister lying on her side with a pillow between her legs when she was pregnant years before. I gave it a shot, and it did help some in relieving the constant pressure.

"Thanks, Caroline."

"Anything I can do to help!" Mercifully, Caroline had come around a couple of months ago. We had a real breakthrough session that put a smile back on her face and love back into her heart. Sid was thankful. He had endured a lot those past months and with little to no explanation as to why. He was an excellent boyfriend.

Seth, to his great shame, had slipped on something in the kitchen and bruised his tailbone on the tile. He was mostly couch-ridden, seated on a collection of pillows to keep him from resting directly on his bruise. We watched movie after movie on DVD together, me pregnant and him an invalid. I loved Seth, and he loved spending time with me. I would say that our time together those days meant more to me than he could ever imagine.

Unfortunately, despite the good times spent with Caroline, Sid and Seth, things had remained as tense as ever with Earl. I was wondering how much more of him I could bear, and carefully weighing my options.

He and his group remained in Skylab, caressing their guns and counting their bullets. They'd moved a TV and DVD player up to the addition as well. We'd split the movies, seeing each other only in passing or to swap one film for another.

I knew eventually I'd need to make a move. But for now, I let my body do its work. The life growing inside me was all that mattered. I almost couldn't believe it was a real human being alive inside me. I longed for an ultrasound, if only to prove to myself that it was really happening, although the occasional kick to my ribs or organs assured me it was. Still, without an image or face, I already felt the inherent need to protect my child, this little person was a part of me. So I waited. And I grew.

*****

I was getting a little stir-crazy at what I'd decided was nearing the seventh month of my pregnancy. My belly seemed to have dropped dramatically in the past week and I'd felt a greater stress on my hips. I was honestly *waddling* around the house, legs bowing as though to clear a path should the baby decide at any moment to drop out of me.

"We're heading to the garden, Sara. You good here with Seth?" Sidney and Caroline were dressing for the strangely cool weather in the front hall.

"Actually, mind if I come along?"

"Not at all. Is Seth good here on his own?"

"I can't see why not." I stepped into the family room. "Seth, mind if I go to the barn with these two? I need an escape for a couple of hours."

"You're going to miss the movie!" he shouted from his plush throne. I smiled at him. "Go on." He waved me away. "We've both seen it like, 10 times in the past year. I'm good."

"Thanks, Seth. We won't be long, honest, and then we'll watch it again, okay?" I laid a hand on his shoulder and he reached up with his, before I followed the other two out of the house. I hopped on the ATV and we pushed out across the field towards the barn.

The bumpy ride over the hardened dirt wasn't exactly a good idea, but Sid took it slow. The sun would set in a couple of hours so we'd try to get in and out within a reasonable time, so not to have to navigate the dark.

Once inside we pushed on with our chores but all the while I was feeling guilty for having left Seth on his own, in that house, with Earl, Kevin and Fred there to bully him. Suddenly, and for whatever reason that passage from Earl's notebook popped into my head, and reminded me why I might be feeling uneasy over leaving him on his own.

Chapter Seventeen

The trip back through the field on the ATV left me terribly anxious. I was convinced something awful was unfolding back at the house. At my insistence we pulled up to the front door and rushed inside.

"Seth!" I called as we poured into the front hall. "Seth, are you in here?" No answer. Then an ache struck my abdomen, travelling from one side to the other and back again. I fell to my knees from the pain, Sid and Caroline on either side of me.

"Is it the baby, Sara?" asked Sid as he helped me up.

"Of course it's the baby," Caroline said as she held my other arm. "It could come any time now."

"Do you want to lay down, Sara?" Sid was practically dragging me to the living room.

"Sure." I felt too weak to argue. "Can you please look for Seth?"

"Sure, Sara, Sid will look for him and I'll stay with you," Caroline soothed while Sid left the room.

"If they've done anything to Seth…." I screeched through the pain.

"I'm sure he's fine." Caroline helped me recline on the couch. "Is this a contraction, do you think?"

"Maybe." I doubled over again and grasped my belly. "Oh, shit, Caroline it hurts like hell."

"I think you might be having that baby."

"Get me upstairs."

Caroline slowly assisted me up the stairs to Joel's room.

"I want Seth! Where is Seth!" It sounded pathetic, but I couldn't help myself. Pain and anxiety were tearing me apart.

"Don't panic, Sara."

"Get me boiled water and towels, Caroline, and scissors and something to clamp off the umbilical." These were some of the things I'd trained myself to ask for when the big moment arrived.

Sidney appeared a second later. "The entire house is empty, I-" he stopped himself. "Shit, are you having that baby?" He looked scared to death. Was it the current situation or something else? Again the pain struck. Such pressure. All other thoughts and concerns flew from my mind. I concentrated on the pressure and my breathing. I couldn't believe it was going to happen. I knew from experience these things usually took much longer to progress, especially with a first child, and I was worried at the close proximity of the contractions to one another. Maybe something was wrong. But this baby wanted out, immediately.

"She's having her baby," Caroline hissed excitedly as she rushed past him with the pot of water and towels in hand. We had decided earlier that we wouldn't tell the others when the birth was taking place. I didn't want any of them involved, so we'd made this pact to do it alone. I looked again for Seth, the only other person I wanted to see right now, but there was no sign of him. Just Sidney standing awkwardly in the hall, the blood draining from his face.

"Jesus, *really*, Sara? Isn't this early?" he wondered aloud.

"I think so, but then, what do I know?" I moaned. The pain was just bearable. I knew it would become increasingly worse as the night went on, and from the way the first contractions felt, I wasn't looking forward to the big ones!

"Wow, Sara…" Caroline was so happy for me, for us, it made me weepy. My hormones had been all over the place the last week as well. Perhaps I should have known this would happen sooner rather than later. Where was Seth? He'd been my rock through so much of my pregnancy. I summoned the memory of his kind smile and voice repeating, *"It'll be okay. Everything will be fine"*.

The labor went on for most of the night. Caroline read anxiously through the same pages of a medical textbook I'd perused countless times the past few months. Sid was in and out of the bedroom repeatedly throughout the night to check on whether anyone had resurfaced. Each time he reported the same news. No one. The rest of the house was empty.

"Check my dilation again, Caroline" I begged as the pain worsened. She lifted the blankets and placed her gloved finger inside me. I knew this was hard for her, but I think she appreciated just how much harder it was for me.

"I don't know, Sara, it feels somewhere between a cheerio and the hole of a bagel, maybe seven centimeters? Three more and you're good to go." Her head shot back to the closed door where Sid stood guard. "What was that?" she whispered to him.

"I'll check it out. Try to be quiet."

We'd all heard it. A door had slammed; maybe the front door. Sidney closed the bedroom door behind him. We listened as he descended the stairs to the front hall. Caroline looked back at me.

"I'm sure it's nothing," she said. "You're doing *great,* Sara. I bet you'll have this baby out in a couple of hours."

It had been six hours already, and honestly, I didn't know how much longer I could keep this up without screaming. The pain of the contractions had increased enormously, and I dreaded the actual pushing. I had almost asked Caroline to light me the pipe, Joel's pot pipe, to take the edge off, but never did. Women had been delivering babies for ages before pain relievers became the delivery room standard. I could do it, but I would have to be strong, stronger than I'd ever been before.

Another violent burning sensation forced my back to arch as I let out a pained cry. Jesus, would it ever let up? Caroline tried to sooth me.

"Is there anything more I can do to help? Do you want a couple of aspirin?"

"Thins the blood," I said automatically. I'd already reviewed all of my options in pain management and none that we had on hand offered any relief for childbirth. The pot would be my best choice, but I didn't want to bring my baby into the world *high.* Since Joel's descent into madness or depression or both, I'd been very careful to stay away from the stuff too.

Sid reappeared a moment later. "I don't see anyone, anywhere." He looked alarmed as well as confused.

"Let's not worry about them. We've got a long night ahead of us," Caroline urged.

"I don't think I can do this," I cried through heavy breaths. "It's too painful."

"You *can* do this, Sara, you *are* doing it, and we'll be right here every step of the way." I caught a look of passing panic in her eyes, but that was quickly replaced with a steely stare that evoked a quiet confidence. I was in good hands, but wished I could be on both sides of the action.

"Sid, take Sara's hand," she ordered in a whisper. Sid rounded the bed and sat next to me. I grabbed at his right hand and squeezed down hard as another contraction overtook me.

The evening turned into night and still, no baby. At roughly midnight the pushing began. "I have to push!" I pleaded. "I have to!"

"You're fully dilated, Sara." Caroline smiled triumphantly and removed her finger once more. "PUSH!" she urged. "PUSH!"

I brought my legs up to my chest, pulling them against my sides with both arms, my muscles straining as I pushed with all my might. Sid was standing next to me, silently patting my forehead with the same wet towel I'd been sucking on to stay hydrated while Caroline coached me. I forgot my earlier resolve to keep the procedure secret, and openly cursed, shouted, ranted and hated the whole experience. My sheets were absolutely soaked in sweat, I was dehydrated and beginning to worry after the first hour whether this baby was going to require a C-section. I put that thought out of my mind, as no one here could perform that with any level of success. Any attempt would definitely kill me, and likely the baby. Not that either of my friends could have brought themselves to cut me open. This was going to happen the old fashioned way, no ifs, ands or buts about it.

Suddenly Caroline declared that she could see the head. A wave of relief overtook me, offering a reprieve from the painful work. That my baby wasn't facing the other way gave me cause for thanks.

"Lots of hair," she noted, sweat glistening on her face as she looked up at me from her position between my legs. "Could be a girl!" But I knew it was a boy.

From the moment she announced the appearance of his head, it was just a few more minutes of pushing before my baby was born.

It was two hours to the minute, five months to the day that Joel had left me. A bittersweet birthday, that his son should be born on the day his father passed away into the dark, forever.

The baby cried as Caroline struggled to cut the cord and clean him off. Thank God he was healthy. If he'd required any medical assistance he might not have made it past his first day.

"Seven months." Sid recalled the brief length of my pregnancy, looking incredulously at the new life in my arms. "Lucky number." We all smiled. In fact, I couldn't will the smile off my face. I stared at the tiny baby in my arms with a love that could not be spoken. A little me. A little *Joel.*

The placenta came out moments after. It was a bizarre thing to behold, resembling a giant organ, with delicate, dark veins running through it. Caroline pulled it gently with the umbilical cord. This part too was painful, but after the relief of finally having the baby out of me, I pushed bravely through my tears of happiness.

I was lucky: no tearing. He was small enough at just seven months not to have done any collateral damage to his mother.

I spent the rest of the day in bed, recuperating, drinking fluids, tended to by Caroline. The baby, Leif, as I'd named him, after my father, rested comfortably beside me. Lucky again to have a healthy baby boy that even at one or two months premature had no trouble breathing. I wondered that something so small and helpless could be alive. But there he was. His eyes opened briefly and although I knew he could only make out shapes at this age, it was as though we made eye contact. He knew, and I knew, we were both in this together. I had brought a new life into this crazy world, one that depended on me for its very survival. And survival was top-of-mind for all of us. With that in mind, I set my sights on feeding him. With no formula for him, I knew it was breast milk or bust. I brought his tiny head to my left breast, expecting him to latch on immediately. Instead, he turned his face away and began to cry.

Each time I put him to my breast, his tiny mouth was unable to navigate my nipple.

"This isn't working," I said to Caroline, frustrated. "He's not getting *anything* to eat." I was becoming frantic.

"We'll get there, Sara. He's going to have to take it eventually."

My mind suddenly wandered to thoughts of Seth. "Has Sid located anyone yet? Seth?"

"No. It's really weird, right? None of them."

"Why would Seth go off with those animals?"

"I don't know." A shared fear mounted between us as we came to the same conclusion. I shook my head and pulled my baby a little closer to my face.

"Sid will find him, Sara. Just concentrate on Leif." She got up from her seated position on the bed beside me and left the room, closing the door softly. With Leif nestled firmly in my arms, I fell asleep, exhausted, but deeply in love.

*****

Sid was out of breath and soaked to the bone. Caroline was trailing as they entered my bedroom. He had found Seth and confirmed the return of the others to Skylab.

"I'm so sorry, Sara." He pushed the hair out of my face, kneeling at my bedside. His hands were hot, but wet. Instantly I knew what had happened. Seth was dead. I would never see him again. Another bloody senseless tragedy. Just as one little life was beginning another had ended. What had I done? Why had I brought a child into this madness? I closed my eyes and wept openly. Caroline lifted the baby out of my arms and handed him to Sid. She crawled in next to me and hugged me until my convulsive, breathless weeping exhausted us both and sleep overcame us. But just as I was about to drift off, I tried Leif once again at my breast. He took it in his tiny mouth, and sucked for dear life. It was do or die for all of us now. Perhaps he sensed this too.

Chapter Eighteen

The next morning Sidney shakily related the gruesome discovery of Seth. After searching fruitlessly within the house he had decided to try the forest behind the backyard, toward the shed. Grave markers of friends long since dead gave him an eerie feeling of dread as he continued past them. It was dark, but the moon was occasionally granted an audience as the dense groupings of clouds moved swiftly by. As Sidney approached the outer reaches of our property, he heard a strange sound. Though the wind had picked up considerably, he hadn't noticed the trees bending in any noticeable fashion. The sound became louder the closer he moved toward the shed. It resembled the sound you might experience if you were sitting on a tire swing, gently moving yourself back and forth on your heels as the rope stretched and pulled against a large branch of a tree. At least, that's how Sidney described it. For a long moment Sid stood listening, his semi-automatic poised, but the sound just kept on, lethargic in its repetition. He continued, slowly, cautiously on the path he had started.

The clouds backed off, bathing the forest in light just as Sid realized what was producing the eerie sound. As we hadn't seen rain in over a week, a sudden breeze picked up dust from the forest floor, filling Sid's eyes with the grit. He raised his arms to protect his face from the stinging needles and debris caught up in the abrupt wind storm. But as quickly as it had come, it left. Sid wiped his eyes with both hands, his weapon slung over his shoulder, his eyes tearing up, blindly walking along the beaten path. Having walked the path a hundred times, both in *life* and in our post-Apocalyptic present, he knew every step and could navigate the way safely, blindfolded, on a bet. But something startled him as he bumped into a foreign object impeding his progress to the shed.

He immediately backed off, opening his blurry eyes, blinking away the remaining grit, rifle pulled out in front of him.

As his vision began to return he realized the object was suspended in space, hanging from one of the larger trees in the middle of the path. The object was not a fallen branch. It was Seth, rope attached to his neck.

Sidney spun around, blinking madly, searching the darkness for those responsible. Were they watching him? Was he next?

There was little doubt in his mind as to who had done this. But why? Seth would never have done this to himself.

With the wind came the rains, hard and falling fast. It would last only a few minutes, but long enough to turn the hardened soil into a mucky mess, exacerbating Sidney's desperate effort to ascend the hill and protect his friends.

Chapter Nineteen

The following day I made up my mind. They *needed* to die. They had murdered Seth. They could not be allowed to hurt us, or especially my baby. Sid checked on Skylab and confirmed our three enemies were now sitting quietly, drinking what remained of the alcohol and smoking what little weed was left. We went to work immediately. They were too proficient with their weapons, and I was afraid if a gun fight ensued we'd lose. So, I'd decided to torch the house that night. First we'd pack our gear, food and water and lay it out behind the pool for easy retrieval. How it had come to this I couldn't say. These strangers had been my friends. We had relied on one another during the most difficult time in our lives. But something had happened to them. Something had snapped in their brains. Like undomesticated animals, they had allowed their instinctual selves to take over in survival-mode. Perhaps the same thing was happening to me. Like a lioness protecting her cubs, I would stop at nothing to see no more harm came to those I loved, those I had left. They had to die.

"Where will we go?" Sid asked.

"North," I said confidently. "That's the plan. That's where I'm going, with Leif."

"*We're* going wherever *you're* going, Sara." Caroline confirmed, and it was done. We would go north, as Joel had instructed in his unconscious state, on his death bed.

After the provisions were bagged and stashed under cover of darkness, we barricaded both the house and the garage doors, locking them in. They were blissfully unaware of our intentions as we carried out my orders, using old food tins to pour fuel from the tanker around the perimeter of the house. I even dumped a can on the Caddy and whispered an apology to Joel's absent father. We then moved inside the house and carefully spilled the fuel up and down the central staircase. Sid had suggested this: *the more that ignites immediately the less chance they have of making it out.* With that logic in mind, I continued to pour the contents of the tanker throughout the house. I wanted to be doubly sure they didn't make it out.

As I entered the kitchen I heard a door swing open on the second floor, and froze. I heard laughing and then Kevin complained about a smell.

"Why does it smell like *lighter fluid* or gasoline or something up here?"

Jesus, this wasn't going to work. I thought they had smoked themselves to sleep.

"Close the fucking door," I heard Fred shout at him.

"No really, there's a *smell* out here."

"Then go see what it is." That was Earl. I was still standing stock-still in the kitchen, afraid my plan was now in tatters. If Kevin came down the stairs he'd surely notice they were wet, and put it together.

"What *is* that?" He was at the top of the stairs now and coming down. "What the *fuck*..." Shit. This was it, he was going to report back to the others and-

"Kevin." It was Sid. Oh, thank God. Sid was coming up from the basement.

"Sid, you *smell* that?"

"Yeah, man. Come here, I want to show you something."

"You know what this is? Should I get Earl?" They met in the front hall.

"Do you need to bother Earl?" Sid played him perfectly.

Kevin glanced up the curving stairs and shrugged his narrow shoulders. "Guess not."

"Are the others up in Skylab?"

"Yeah, man. What's the *deal,* Sid?" Kevin lifted his bare foot and wiped away the fuel. "Is this what I *think* it is?"

That was the last thing that ever came out of Kevin's mouth. I watched from the kitchen as Sid wrapped an arm around his neck blocking his airway. Kevin was immediately incapacitated. No longer in control of his own body, his face distorted and began to turn purple as he struggled against the grip. Sidney started to shake him violently, lifting his whole body up into the air and crashing him down on the tile until Kevin stopped struggling. The look on Sid's face was one of desperation. His lips parted and his own face reddened. As Sid's hold forced Kevin to the floor, still squeezing, I saw in him a sense of relief as a final jerk gave way to a sickening snap.

He quickly got to his feet and dragged the lifeless Kevin to the basement. I stood frozen, still in the entranceway to the kitchen when Sid reemerged.

"We need to get this done *now*, Sara," he explained in no uncertain terms. "We need to finish this."

A sense of urgency propelled me into action. My baby, safe with Caroline and waiting for us at the back sliding doors, remained a secret to the others. Since their return to the house, they had sequestered themselves in Skylab. Thoughts of Seth, and of their callous brutality, spurred me on. I was weak from the delivery, but strong enough to finish what I'd started.

As Sid and I met in the walk-out basement, we tossed what remained in our gas cans on the carpet that adorned the floor next to the fireplace.

"This is it," he said.

"This is it," I repeated, and lit the match.

Caroline handed my baby to me and the three of us stood back to watch the basement catch fire. The flames roared in my ears as they licked the ceiling, the heat intolerable within seconds.

"You go to safety now, Sara. You too, Caroline." Sidney's face had taken on a orange glow as he watched the fire dance through the house. "I'll watch that they don't get out."

Caroline looked worried, her forehead creased while her lips parted.

"No," I spoke up over the increasingly deafening sound of the flames. "I'll hide out in the field and wait for you both."

Caroline smiled and touched the baby's head.

"We'll be right behind you, Sara."

"I know. Be safe, and see you soon." I turned and ran as fast as I could with Leif clenched tightly to my body and didn't stop running until the sound of the fire was just out of earshot. I threw down my heavy back pack and cradled Leif in his makeshift swaddle which hung around my shoulder and midriff, securing him to my chest.

I gasped for air a moment and sat down hard on the field floor. Then I watched as the fire began to crawl up the exterior walls and consume the roof. How could anyone escape something like that? Yet I watched. Just to be sure.

Chapter Twenty

My baby at my breast, I stared as the house I'd called home for over a year burned with a brightness that blotted out the moon and stars. Where were Sid and Caroline? They were all I had left. They shouldn't have stayed behind. There I was all alone, but they had been positioned right next to the exit, so surely nothing could have gone wrong. The house burned like a beacon in the night beyond the muddy expanse of the cornfields, framed by the blackened forest to the southwest and the dirt road coming to a T along the east.

Gun shots! I knelt and shielded Leif with my body. I wasn't so far away that a stray bullet couldn't find me. The shots rang in my ears as they became more frequent. I hadn't considered a shoot out.

"Please, let them get away," I whispered to the night, wishing for Caroline and Sidney to find me. I couldn't do this alone.

An explosion burst from the back of the house. I could feel the heat of it, even at this distance. The ground vibrated under my knees. The gas tank. I could almost taste it. The smell forced my free hand up to cover my mouth and nose.

I could barely make out a silhouette moving toward me and my baby. Were they running? I took a chance and screamed over the roar of the explosions. "Caroline?!" No answer. "Sid?" Still no answer. Next I cursed myself for having called out at all. If this wasn't either Caroline or Sidney, I had just given myself up to the enemy. Remembering Joel's pistol in my bag, I retrieved it. I made myself as small as I could in the dirt, careful not to make a sound. My child was strangely quiet under his sheet. Panicked by Leif's stillness, I unwrapped his head and kissed his warm cheek. He buried his face into my hand. Where was the silhouette? I'd lost them. Oh

Jesus, I thought to myself. I held my breath and listened. Perhaps I'd imagined it?

The roar of the fire increased as it consumed more and more of the house, drowning out any footsteps in the field. But still, I waited, and watched.

I waited there, in that spot and watched the flames burn themselves out, all the while hoping to see Caroline and Sidney. But as the dawn approached, I knew I had lost them as well. I was now completely alone.

Chapter Twenty-One

My baby slept in his wrap tight to my chest, waking up three times through the night to eat, then drifting back to sleep, oblivious to the horror I had just witnessed. He wasn't feeding effectively yet, but this night, at least, he slept a little. I did not sleep. I panned the landscape for movement. Nothing. No one. A steady line of smoke twisted up into the ever brightening morning sky from a central point in the rubble. I heard a snapping from inside the house, then a crunching that went on and on. A wall collapsed in on itself and took the majority of the house along with it. The crash was deafening.

As I bent to stretch my lower back, my eyes locked on last night's silhouette. He was lying on the ground face down, not twelve feet from where I'd spent the night.

"Jesus," I said aloud. Which one was it? Earl? Freddy? Too tall to be Earl.

"Freddy!" I exclaimed, sure it was Fred. He did not respond. Shrapnel protruded from his back. He must have staggered out of the inferno, having escaped the flames through a second floor window, then been taken down by debris from the explosion. A large piece of metal was pointing towards the sky. His hair was crusty, scorched. His pants had stuck to his legs at the back. I wasn't sure his face would be recognizable but I turned it towards me to confirm his identity. It was Fred, his expression forever etched with a look of agony.

"*Earl.*" I spoke with contempt. I hated what he'd become. The way he'd taken the reins the past few months, the way he'd talked his way into the broken hearts and minds of our friends. After Joel, Earl had seized his opportunity. Unfortunately many of my friends, *our* friends, had fallen under his spell. The idea of revenge was a powerful tool. Earl knew it, and he used it to his advantage.

Now I found myself without a home, without a friend. Alone.

The baby rustled and began to whimper. I lifted my shirt. He screamed as I tried to nurse him. Why was it this hard? Sometimes getting him to nurse was mentally exhausting. I didn't have the tools they showed in the text books: the breast pump, the bottles. I hated to think of my baby as a burden. He was everything to me. But the lack of sleep and the endless torturous sessions at my breast were almost enough to make me shut down.

I was utterly exhausted. My eyes caught the sunrise moving behind the smoke, rising from the wreckage. The smoke blurred the colors, making the morning seem more sultry.

I was afraid to approach the smoldering rubble to look for Sid and Caroline. How could I do this on my own? But I had to. As my mind raced, I cautiously approached the remains of the house.

That's when I spotted them lying on their backs behind the pool, on the decline that led into the woods. They were motionless. To my horror I confirmed my friend's fate.

"Caroline! Sid!" I choked. I caressed Caroline's face and hugged her lifeless body against mine with one arm, Leif in the other, shaking all the while. But there was no wishing them back. I laid her back down, next to Sid. I kissed their heads and closed their eyes. I took their hands and interlocked their fingers. When I stood to look at them one last time I broke down and cried recklessly. The baby cried with me and I made no effort to sooth him.

They'd been shot point blank. Was it Fred, in one last evil act before he collapsed in the field with a piece of hot shrapnel in his back? Maybe Earl escaped and found them, exacting his revenge. I spun around, eyeing the woods and the rubble. Imagine, if it was all for nothing? The possibility tortured me. If Fred had nearly gotten away, why not Earl?

I took a deep breath, removed the water bottles and bags of food from Caroline and Sid's supplies, whispered *I'm so sorry,* and returned to the field. My mind spun with pent-up shock and grief. Nothing made sense anymore. All I knew for sure was that Sonny was headed east, and I had to go north with precious few items packed away in my backpack and a baby slung around my torso.

Chapter Twenty-Two

North. It was the one direction we had dared not explore too deeply. When Earl, Sonny, and Fred had returned from their expedition, they had horrible accounts of what we would find if we ventured in this direction. It was a killing field. Vehicles scattered across the highway for miles. Bodies on top of bodies, as if they'd died climbing over one another.

Why was I going north? South wasn't an option: it was flattened by the initial blast and fires still raged along the horizon. East we'd already covered for miles and the west was just more of the same: burned out townships barely capable of sustaining life. The north was unexplored beyond the word of three friends, friends that had become enemies.

I was still very scared, but I had been given hope. I had been in contact, to some degree, with our angel. That same angel Connor had seen and Joel had spoken to, that had guided Jake's last act and who had showed Sidney his path in overtaking the flags. This angel of ours had actively addressed many of us over the course of the last year, but never me. I couldn't understand how a guardian angel could let it get so bad for us. It seemed a desperate attempt to feel some sort of optimism. So transparent.

I was convinced that this angel concept had driven Joel mad. That and his addiction to the marijuana we'd pilfered that first week from the barn garden. Over time the stress of leadership, the angst he felt over the angel's plans concerning his destiny, and the constant smoking overwhelmed him. Then, when Connor was executed in front of us by Gareth, Joel had snapped completely, and to some degree I had blamed this angel of his for having ever causing Joel such hopelessness and despair. But when he finally spoke to me, I listened. It was an out. And so, I marched north.

Before I had ventured far, I felt something guiding me. Maybe it was just intuition. Or maybe Joel's angel was finally giving me some kind of hope to move forward on. Never before had I needed hope more. Even upon discovering the death of my entire family. Even upon learning that the world as we knew it had ceased to exist. Now, alone, with a baby strapped to my chest, I needed hope more than ever. So I listened. And something told me Joel was right. I should go north.

I continued, through my fatigue and fear. Travelling on foot with a new baby was going to prove difficult. If he wasn't crying, he was attempting to sleep or feed. The rumors I'd heard that breastfeeding was a cruel endeavor - something I'd picked up during a stint in the maternity ward during my final month of co-op – were true. But Leif had no other option, so we persevered. Sometimes it felt endless. He would cry for an hour, feed for ten minutes, then an hour later start all over again.

Leif had not 'attached' to my breasts like I had expected. Every other animal on the planet seemed to effortlessly attach to their respective mother's nipples, but human babies required weeks of practice and a team of nurses. What if *this* was the beginning of the end? What if nobody's babies would suckle anymore without these expansive support structures? I don't think Leif had had a satisfying feeding since he'd been born. Mostly he would fall asleep exhausted, never full. But looking at his face, so tiny, so helpless, gave me strength. I would live for him. I would do whatever I had to, to protect him.

*****

The days relinquished their light to the evenings as the sun was selfishly swallowed by the horizon. A gathering of storm clouds overhead. That night I settled down in a field as I had the night before, a single tree whose canopy of leaves had disappeared long ago offering little cover.

As I took a closer survey of our surroundings I saw a light flickering in the distance to the east. "Is that a house?" I wondered aloud.

It looked like candle light. But how far away was it? My perception of distance had all but left me. The monotonous flatness of the landscape and the colors, still mostly variations of grey, removed much of my ability to actually decipher one mile from ten. With so much of the forests burned to the ground and the old cattle and corn fields empty, the openness of everything left a person feeling very vulnerable. Turning back, I watched the clouds mirror the rest of the landscape – shades of grey. Up from down seemed a difficult separation.

I decided to move toward the light. A rusted cattle fence once employed to keep the cows and sheep from entering the adjacent corn field stood as a barrier between us and that light. I ran my hand across the brittle wire, careful not to take a sliver. The fence stood five feet high, just four or five inches shorter than me.

"We have to climb it, Leif," I told him. Our only other option was to follow the fence south until we hit the road again, but there was no time before the darkness made it impossible to navigate. I rubbed his back, his body wrapped closely to mine.

Who might that light belong to? What if it were a group of men? What if they hadn't seen a woman in months? I had my pistol, Joel's gun. And I had a few rounds of ammunition to go with it. I'd shied away from killing in the past, but I resolved myself to do whatever I had to do to protect my baby.

I threw my jacket on top of the fence. Climbing up was easy enough - it was navigating my legs over the top that proved difficult. The fence began to wiggle violently under my weight as my right leg shifted to the other side. "Shit, shit, shit…"

The top wire snapped as I attempted to lift my left leg. I tumbled to the wet earth with a thud, narrowly avoiding crushing Leif. He began to wail. Picking myself up, I pulled him out of his swaddle and kissed his cheeks, bouncing him for a time in my arms until he settled. He was hungry; so was I.

Suddenly there was a voice above me.

"Come child." It was a woman's voice. How was I caught so off guard? How did this woman know I was here? The crying. Still, where the hell did she come from?

"Quickly, the rains are coming." She took my arm and led me toward the flickering light. I followed, slowly relaxing.

It took all of one minute to reach a veranda in the middle of what might have been a yard in *life*. The remains of a house stood just a few meters away, mostly burned out, uninhabitable. The woman picked up the flickering gas lamp and raised it to my face. This was the light I had seen, the light I'd been drawn to like a moth.

"Come." She bent down and lifted a trapdoor in the center of the veranda. "We'll take you in." The old woman gestured that I walk down a ladder affixed to a dirt wall. With little other option, and a sense that this woman was genuinely trying to help us, I carefully navigated the darkness, feeling my way down each rung until I hit solid ground.

Turning, I saw more gas lamps, leading down a long corridor. Behind me, the old woman handed me her lamp and took the lead. "Follow me."

Chapter Twenty-Three

We were in a large room. This was a bomb shelter of some kind. To my left was a massive basin. Like the fuel tank at Joel's house. The ceiling was some twenty feet overhead and lined with cables and piping. The room itself was quite cozy: a smokeless fire burned in the far corner while rugs and furs seemed to cover the place from floor to ceiling. The lighting was dim, but my eyes rapidly adjusted to take it all in. The air was dry, and smelled of steel and leather.

"What is this place?" I asked.

"This is my home," the woman answered. "*Our* home," she corrected herself, panning an outstretched arm across the wall to my right. Here three other women sat staring at me. Each seemed to be performing some task; one knitting, another chewing at something, while the third rubbed a stone against a hide of some kind.

"Hello," I said meekly. Despite my fatigue and bewilderment, I was impressed. This was a well structured hideout. Had these four women survived all this time underground? "I'm Sara," I continued. "This is Leif." I rubbed my hand in a circular motion on the baby still wrapped across my chest.

The women nodded at me. I turned back to the old lady who brought me to the hideout. She was placing the lamp on a table, which was stacked high with dried, prepackaged fruit. "Have a mango, dear."

I was still wary, having learned most things were not what they seemed. Still, the fruit proved too much to resist. Eating the dried fruit, I felt a surge of energy.

"Your baby," said my hostess. "He is how old?"

"Just two days."

"Just two days," she repeated. She looked past me. "The child is two days old." The others nodded.

"Two days is right," said another one; I could see now that she was chewing the end of a rope. Bizarre.

This back and forth puzzled me, and since my baby was the topic of discussion, I fought down suspicion and worry.

"He is a Gemini." Another of the three women at the wall spoke up. "The messenger God rules his house from Mercury." She set her rock down and stared straight at me. "Instill a sense of *destiny* in Leif, and he will be that which he is meant to be."

The suggestion that Leif had a destiny upset me. Talk of destiny was all Joel ever spoke of in his sleep towards the end. To these women, Leif should only have been a baby. My brow raised and creased. My hostess read my face, but ventured another question.

"Where was Leif born, Sara?"

"Just an eight hour walk from here, to the south."

"It is as it should be then," said the last of the three women at the wall. "As you predicted."

"As Tages predicted," corrected my hostess.

"*He is great,*" the three said in unison.

This was becoming alarming. Was this a cult of sorts? Were they lulling me into a false sense of security so they could take my baby from me? My jaw flexed.

"We ask, Sara, because we need to be sure." The old woman rested a hand on my shoulder.

"Sure of what?"

"We've *seen*," said the woman chewing the rope, her eyes narrowed to slits.

"What is it you think you've *seen*?" I crossed my arms over Leif, shielding him from what I feared might come.

"Tages has shown us."

"Who is *Tages*?"

"Tages is a divine being, with the appearance of a child, but the wisdom of an old man," explained my hostess as she circled round the table. "Tages is the ancient seer from the Etruscan religion."

"The Etruscan religion?" I did not relax my guard.

"It is an ancient religion which foretold everything that would ever come to pass."

"And my *son* is mentioned?"

"In not so many words, yes."

"How can you say that?"

"As we saw this end, we have seen a future end." The old woman at the table picked up a long wooden stick, a staff.

"Your religion predicted this end? *The Reaper*?"

"It predicted the outcome of the Reaper's threats, and is what drove us underground."

"You were prepared."

"We were." The woman chewing the rope appeared at my side suddenly. I jumped.

"Jesus Christ!" I shouted. Leif jolted, cried out. I pulled the sling over my head and set him on the table, all the while frowning at the thin woman. I turned him over and rubbed his back. He began to settle down.

"Tell me what you know," I demanded.

"Your child is guarded," the hostess explained, her head tilting sideways as she inspected him.

She picked him up and pulled him close to her emaciated face. Sunken eyes darted back and forth as she examined Leif. She blew along the silhouette of his head. I grimaced. What must this woman's breath smell of – *eyes of newt and wing of bat?* She studied him with an intensity that made me uncomfortable. Why had I handed my son over to this woman? Admittedly I had felt immediately drawn to her. But I could not be too trusting.

"He is guarded by the *others*. He has an *old* soul."

I shook my head and retrieved him. "What are you saying?"

"Your son's aura is like *fire*." She looked as though she had come out of a daze.

"So, what should that mean to me?"

"That means that he is a person of interest to the *other side*."

The *other side*, *the angel*, the undertones of what she was explaining made me want to scream. I became visibly shaken.

"Your aura spoke to me the moment I saw you," she said quietly. "I know you are confused, frustrated, angry, and so very sad. You have lost much, but no more than everyone else. It is what you have *gained* that is important now."

She understood so much about me, that I lowered my guard slightly. "Then what is it about us? Why has the *other side* shown such an interest in me?"

"Everything is for a reason."

"You wouldn't be so sure if you heard my story."

"Everything," she repeated. "We play off one another." She circled the table. again. "It's like Shakespeare wrote: '*All the world's a stage, And all the men and women merely players; They have their exits and their entrances, And one man in his time plays many parts…* '"

"What is it you believe then? Is it fate, destiny?"

"I *believe*; that is enough."

"Do you believe everything that will ever be has already been determined?" I still had a hard time buying this theory. How could any sort of God or higher power have orchestrated the destruction of all it had created?

"There are many different paths, but ultimately, only one can play itself out. For that, we are *all* responsible."

"So choice - free will, that exists?"

"Yes, of course, this would all be little more than a dress rehearsal otherwise. For every path a script will be followed, but the path is a choice made by us all."

"What choice did we all have in the Reaper's decision?" I asked, challenging the old woman's theories.

"I only speak the wisdom of the Etruscans. That the path is written is how seers have seen. That is how *I* am able to see."

"You see the future?"

"Not in so many words. Destiny reveals itself to me through my practices. The Etruscans believed that among us exists an immutable course of divine will. They were devoted to the question and interpretation of destiny."

"Are you a psychic?"

"No. I admit, I am able to see auras, which is the energy emitted from an individual, but my abilities to read events and chart people's destinies are granted through the ancient practices passed down by the Etruscans."

"*Who* are the Etruscans?"

"An ancient people that were conquered and integrated into the Roman empire over two thousand years ago. They were wise in their ability to read the signs in nature by asking questions to Tages, their profit seer."

"How does it work?"

"You are curious, Sara. That's good; we have much to teach you." She lifted her stick and continued. "I use my staff to draw out an invisible frame to the sky and horizon." Her staff was a twisted branch maybe five feet in length and very thin. "Then I ask a question. The answer is interpreted in nature's reaction. It is a complex science. Perhaps more of an art."

My initial interest in this complete stranger's religion had grown into something more. What if she could tell me what would happen next? What if she could guide me and my son to safety? As crazy as it all sounded, the last year of my life demanded I approach this woman with an open mind.

"How can you be so sure it works?"

"I have seen it work, Sara. I have counseled dozens of people in my life through these means. When the Grimm Reaper was first mentioned in the news I drew my box and I watched the sky. I asked the question; *'What might this threat bring about to the world?'* Within two minutes I had my answer. A raven flew into my magical field, and upon entering it dropped out of the sky. Dead."

My skin crawled; was it the story or the story teller? Either way, this woman both unsettled and reassured me. What if she could help me make sense of this chaos?

"The dead bird was nature's answer…" I trailed off.

"Yes, an obvious interpretation of what would come to pass."

"And so did you try to stop it?"

"As powerful as one person's actions can be, I knew that any warning on my part would fall on deaf ears. The powers that be would not succumb to the Reaper's demands. We *all* knew that. And when five billion people share a common idea, it is impossible to change that path."

"So you holed up in here? Waiting?"

"I did. I waited, I prepared. I told only those I thought could help."

A sense of destiny suddenly overcame me, not for myself so much as for my son.

"I invite you to stay here, until we have your baby healthy and strong. His destiny will be realized to you in time, and in between that time and now there is here. "

The offer to stay was very appealing. I was lucky to have crossed their path, I knew that. She obviously noticed Leif's small size and weakened state. She understood I had been having trouble latching him to my nipple. "Yes," I said. "Yes, I would very much appreciate that. Staying I mean. You're kind to take us in."

"Of course we would, Sara."

"I-I need to feed him. Have you any milk?"

"He's having difficulties at your breast."

"Yes. He'll eventually latch on, but not without a fight, and even then, it's not much."

"We will help you." She opened a cupboard and revealed several tins of powdered baby formula. She turned to see the surprised look on my face. "We have prepared for your arrival."

Chapter Twenty-Four

The women were living in a cold war bomb shelter built by my hostess' father in the Sixties. Her name was Bethany. She was a pale and wrinkled woman who'd spent her whole life in her father's house. When he died twenty years before, she'd taken over the household, and with no brothers or sisters, no husband and a mother incapable of looking after herself, there she remained. Her father had revealed the underground structure to her when she was just a little girl. She had never been allowed to enter the space while he was alive. When she had returned home from his funeral, she finally entered it for the first time. There she found a stash of forty year old food tins and provisions long forgotten since the threat of nuclear war had vanished from conscious awareness.

But after having read the future promised to the world with her magic, she had the bomb shelter retro-fitted. That happened just one year before the end came. The smokeless fireplace, the kitchen, toilets and dry storage, all of it was improved and expanded upon. Bethany had spent her life savings on the project: she was so certain of our end.

The storage of food looked barely touched though the four women had lived in the shelter since before the bombs fell. As I became more at home with the women, I found chores to do to earn my keep. Leif had become quite a bit chubbier after only a week underground. The fact that Beth had a massive supply of baby formula convinced me of her ability to see the future.

"It wasn't so much that I *saw* the future, or that I saw you and little Leif showing up at my door," Beth explained as she shook another bottle of the milk and handed it to me. "I did, however, see the baby."

"How do you mean?" I asked.

"Like I said, I can see a person's aura. Yours is quite beautiful by the way, Sara. Bluish orange." I blushed. "But your son's…." She chuckled ironically. "Your son's aura is a *fire*. You might say I saw his *aura*. One night, as I pondered the concept of the Yin and Yang, I realized that if someone were to plunge the world into despair, another would rise to pull us out. So, I drew my magic frame on the horizon, first to the north, then the west, the east and finally the south asking the same question, '*From where will our savior approach?*' Then a great light shimmered in my magical envelope and I knew – I knew the direction you'd come to find us. I knew it would be an aura I would see. I suspect his father's aura would have been quite something to see as well."

"He was the leader of our group."

"Yes, I imagine he was. He must have been a good boy. You are a good girl, Sara, and Leif will command the respect of men as his father did, with compassion and with love."

"Yes," I trailed off a moment, remembering Joel. "He was a very kind man. It's just…"

"Never mind what has been." She waved her hands wildly. "Leif is here now. He is yours and his father's prodigy. You are his rock. Speak only highly of his father and remember that *you* are his teacher, his guardian, his everything."

Leif pushed his stomach out, arching his back as he sucked at the bottle, moving against my arm. I smiled down at him, my heart filled with a love I hadn't imagined.

"It was Leif's aura I saw." She panned the south-west wall with her outstretched arm. "Coming from the direction you said you'd come from, the same day you said he'd been born. His aura was like a light haze on the horizon, where no such light had occurred prior to putting the question to Tages."

Beth walked to her bed, which was positioned alongside the others. She sat at the edge and removed her shoes. "Tages is great," she said, and laid down to sleep.

"Thank you so much for taking us in." Tears welled up in my eyes.

"You are very welcome dear. You are a messenger of hope, in a time of great sorrow."

Chapter Twenty-Five

Occasionally we would venture outside. Jenny, the woman who read horoscopes, insisted that the baby spend quality time outdoors, when the sun was out. Jenny was a heavier woman; I thought it quite likely she was morbidly obese in *life* the way the skin hung from her neck and arms. Her face was kind, with not many lines for her age, which she said was sixty-seven. She, Leif and I would take walks around the burnt frame that once housed Bethany and her parents.

“It must have been a beautiful home,” I commented.

“It was in Beth’s family for generations. They were farmers. Beth made the decision to burn the house in an effort to keep would-be squatters and groups seeking shelter a comfortable distance away from our hiding place.”

“Smart. And you? Did you live nearby?”

“No, I lived in the city. Beth and I knew each other from the Expo circuit, Beth offering her aura readings and predictions and me with my horoscopes.” She shifted her heavy rifle from one shoulder to the other.

“Do you still read horoscopes?”

“I have read your son’s according to my star charts and am currently putting it together. We can discuss it another time.”

“I’d love that.” Completing our umpteenth circle we headed back into the tunnel as the sun set in the west.

*****

We spent our time listening to music, baking, cleaning, maintaining equipment and appliances, and entertaining Leif. I felt very safe underground. The seals on the shafts that opened up to the rest of the world were military grade. They locked like a submarine, virtually airtight. Air was circulated through grates that could pass as sewer covers to anyone the least bit interested, but they could never open them. It seemed the perfect hiding place from the world at large.

Leif was gaining weight at a surprising rate after two weeks with an unlimited supply of food. The women were very understanding over his quirks and late night feedings. They helped when I asked and offered when I didn't. It was like having four midwives at my service 24/7. I wouldn't have had it this good in *life*. My thoughts often turned to my own parents when I looked at Leif. They would have been so proud, perhaps not that their 19-year old daughter had given birth before entering college, but that they were grandparents. I tried not to think too much about my family. All that accomplished was to make me angry, and sad, and I needed to stay as happy as possible for Leif's sake.

Sally was another of the four women sharing her space with Leif and I. She was around forty years old and very thin, even more so than Beth. I worried for her. She never seemed to be eating, and when I thought I saw her chewing it was on that damn rope of hers.

"It keeps me from overeating," she would tell me.

I would fight her on her logic. "You barely eat as it is, Sally. There's not much left of you."

"Never mind Sally," Beth would say. "She's a vain one! Waiting on her Prince Charming to arrive and take her away from all of this."

"It could happen!" she shouted.

"How many times do you need to shuffle that deck of yours before you believe that it isn't?" Sally was a Tarot card reader and, as I found out, also a friend from the Expo circuit.

"What sort of Expos did you ladies attend exactly?" The question had been on my mind since Jenny had mentioned it.

"Psychic fairs, and things of that nature," Jenny piped in while busily loading the ten disc CD player. "Sally was a whiz with those cards. You should let her read your cards, Sara."

"Actually, Tarot cards scare me. Like Ouija boards. I've always steered clear of them. No offence, Sally."

"None taken. I dislike the Ouija board too. *Evil* contraption!" I noted a sarcastic tone in her voice.

"I think we can all agree the Ouija board is a powerful portal that should only be handled by a professional." Beth had a playful look on her face.

"A *professional*?" I asked. "What do you call a professional Ouija board user?"

"A medium." Carol spoke up from her corner. She rarely spoke at all, never mind to me. She slipped out of her dark corner where she spent most of her time reading and re-reading a giant volume of some kind. She kept a comfortable chair, a side table and lamp that looked as though it were pilfered from a Psychic expo. She was the creepy one of the four.

"The Ouija *is* a portal, and yes, it should only be accessed by a medium. Someone with a higher understanding of what you're letting into the waking world." As she moved past me, her long black hair brushed my face and smelled of olive oil.

"I used one once, with my friends when we were fourteen," I said. "There were four of us: two boys and two girls. My friend said we should pair up, boy-girl because it worked better that way."

"True," Carol confirmed. She sat next to me at the table, running her olive-skinned fingers through her long black hair.

"Yeah, so we did," I continued. "It was crazy what happened. We asked questions about silly things mostly but then my friend, Julia, asked something of the spirit."

"And what did she ask?" Carol stared through me, anticipating my answer.

"Well, I remember its name was Samuel, the *spirit* or whatever it was."

"Spirit. That is your best case scenario."

"I guess." I was pleased that Carol was so interested in my story. "Anyways, Julia asked it to prove its presence to us."

"And did it?"

"Yes. The lights went off a moment after she'd challenged it, and we ran out of the basement screaming."

"Your friend conjured a powerful spirit." She looked reproachfully at me. "And so you never played with it again?"

"No." I felt a chill run through me. "That scared me half to death."

"Breaking the connection like that can sometimes leave the spirit in our plane. I wonder if your friend ever suffered a similar experience in her basement again."

My eyes popped and my head involuntarily cocked back. "She did actually. Many times after that night, whenever she went into the basement the light would turn off. She found an excuse to never go back down there. And she never did."

Carol stood and put on the kettle. "It's not a safe game to play. Spirits can become very resentful when left to linger in our plane, and depending on the spirit, or *demon*, they can become a poltergeist."

"Why do they sell that game to children?"

"I wish they never had. There are countless souls that have been left behind in our world, condemned to isolation as a result of the Ouija. As a medium, I used to cleanse homes of spirits, showing them the light. Many of them manifested from the Ouija."

"That's so sad. If I'd known we were hurting anyone…."

"That's the trouble with the Ouija board: they made it a *game*, and so the majority take it as a sleight-of-hand from a friend when they first experience anything." She pulled her long black hair back into a ponytail and tied it. "It is almost *never* a sleight-of-hand."

Bethany attempted to lighten the mood. "Okay Carol, don't scare the poor girl. She's innocent."

"*Ignorant* is more apt a description, but I understand your point. It's just that I *feel* their sadness, the spirits, when I cleanse a house. Lucky for your friend it was not a demon that answered your call. A demon can follow you for the rest of your life. It can interfere with your life in ways you cannot know."

I went white at that. Julia had never really been the same after the experience: Christ, she'd *killed* herself eventually. What if her spirit was a demon that finally took its vengeance? I shook the thought from my head. No, it was the circumstances that forced her hand, not a *demon*.

"Carol summons spirits even now," Jenny called over from the couch. "She confers with them on things that may come to pass. She is one of the reasons we were prepared for you. In fact, after Bethany came to us with her vision of Leif's impending aura, we all used our crafts to pinpoint the time and place of his arrival."

"A wonderful coincidence that he was born an eight hour walk from here," I teased.

"Well, we could go into coincidences with you, Sara, but I think for right now you've heard enough of spirits, demons, auras and the like." Bethany poured the boiled water into a tea pot and placed it on the table.

"No, I am very interested," I assured them. "I have always been a spiritual person. The Bible is something I'd always held very close to my heart."

"The Bible you say?" Sally moved her tiny frame to the table and took her seat. "There's a book I have not picked up in a long time."

"I had written it off myself a few months ago, after our friend Connor was taken from us. But I've revisited it since. Better to have faith in something than none at all."

"Faith, hope, belief, they are what they are." Sally picked up her cup. "The thing about faith is that it comes from within rather than from without. If you get my meaning."

"That it exists at all at a time like this is enough, I should think," Jenny offered. "That is enough for me, for now."

"We had *faith* Leif would come." Bethany sat too, and poured herself a cup of the hot tea. "You are an example of our faith, in our abilities to *see*." She tipped her cup at me.

Leif began to fuss and cry, so I got up from the table and moved to the couch. The others sat drinking their tea, quietly. "You're a *vision,* Leif," I whispered at him, smiling. I bounced him on my knee until he calmed down.

"Take what we tell you to heart, Sara," Sally called from the table, her back to me. The others turned to look at me and I nodded appreciatively at them. They were a coven of witches. What did they call that? A Wiccan? I knew there was no mistake that I had found my way here. They were too sure of themselves, too confident. I mean, why else would you stock baby formula?

*****

My Tarot card reading commenced the following evening. Sally sat across from me at the kitchen table. Her thin fingers shuffled a deck of cards much larger than what I was used to. She placed them in front of me and asked me to cut them.

"This isn't like poker is it? 'Cut the deck, cut your throat?'" I asked playfully.

"No," she replied.

"Okay." I cut the deck.

She explained that she used a very old Tarot card spread with its roots in 16th-century France. She would place seven cards on the table in a circle, with an eighth in the center representing the planets.

"Does it count that Pluto isn't considered a planet anymore?"

"No."

"Okay, what next?"

"Now ask your question. What would you like to know?"

"I think I should ask about Leif. What will he be like as a man, what is his destiny? Will that work or does it have to be about me?"

"No, it can be about anyone. Is that your question then? What is Leif's destiny?"

"Yes, that's my question."

"Very well." She smiled and began placing the cards in order. "If the card is upside down, the meaning changes. Each card placement represents a planet and the planets rule different aspects of our lives."

"Okay." I was excited to get a sneak peek into Leif's adulthood. Tarot scared me only because my mother had been frightened off by a Tarot reader she'd visited once. She told me the reader had only negative things to say and that he even went as far as to tell her when she would die and how! I swore I'd never do this, but in light of what these women were capable of, I felt at least curious to learn what I could about Leif's future.

Sally flipped the first card. "This is his Earth card. It represents the here and now. He has pulled an inverted *8 of Cups* card. Someone close to him will abandon Leif in a time of great urgency. He will feel betrayed at the moment, but perhaps realize that this person's personal quest was necessary for their own growth, and his."

I frowned.

The second card was the *9 of Cups*, also inverted. "This is the Moon card, relating to those things immediately surrounding or affecting the subject. Leif will find he is either seen as someone who is a false prophet, exuding a false display of power or promise to those that surround him, or he will recognize another as such."

"Ha!" she exclaimed as she turned the next card. "This is the Mars card, representing those issues in adversity to Leif, opposing his position. You see he's pulled the *7 of Wands* card, *courage*. Courage, to seize the day. To act decisively in the face of opposition. He will find himself standing up against injustice, taking an aggressive posture against his foe."

"That sounds like our Leif," called Bethany from the couch. I smiled at her.

"The next card is his Jupiter card, representing achievement, gain and expansion." She carefully turned the card to reveal a frightening sight. The Devil! Sally looked up at me sensing my disappointment.

"This is not a *bad* card, Sara. It may look intimidating, but it has many meanings. And look at that. It too is inverted."

"Okay, so what does this represent?"

"The inverted devil card represents an exercise in self-control. An act of selflessness, to avoid distraction and maintain one's sights on their path ahead. Leif will likely and selflessly throw himself onto the proverbial fire at some stage in his adult life, as he works towards what end he has in sight. This act will propel him into the leadership role he is destined to achieve."

She moved on to the fifth card in the pattern. "The ringed planet Saturn represents judgment and an overall assessment of Leif's position." She flipped it quickly. "Ah!" She looked back at her friends seated on their couch. "An inverted *7 of Cups*."

"This is a good card?"

"This represents a desire reborn. A job completed. An overriding will to fulfill what was started. Essentially, hard work bears great fruits." Her smile faded as she continued reading the card. "Leif will have realized his efforts but lose someone very close to him. You see in the card the undetermined figure walking off with a cup? This person means very much to Leif, but they will have abandoned him, either for their own selfish pursuits or for reasons of a spiritual nature. Regardless, Leif will feel very alone in his victory."

"That's sad."

"Yes, but it's the bigger picture that matters and your son knows this."

She turned the sixth card. "Mercury traditionally gives insight into business and professional matters, business associates or acquaintances. He has pulled the *4 of Cups*. This card offers clarity of thought in its inverted manifestation. Leif will see a clear path ahead, knowing what he wants for himself and humanity. His ability to meditate will have reached its summit."

The seventh card was turned. "Venus," she said. "You know what Venus is all about. Love, relationships. It is right side up." She smiled from ear to ear. "Our Leif will find his bliss in a relationship. He will also find he is surrounded by positive energies and an abundance of generosity. Good friendships and a sharing of good times evolve from his efforts. He is happy, happier than he has ever been."

Tears welled up and I wiped them away. "Sorry," I said, sniffling. "I'm just so happy to hear he'll be alright, that he'll fall in love."

"It could also act as a card of memories - items that have been in a person's life but have vanished. Leif may look to the elements in his childhood to solve problems in later life situations. Perhaps a return to innocence is his bliss. A relationship can be a physical thing, but it can also be spiritual."

"The Sun." The last card pulled, in the center of the circle, represented aspirations, fame and accomplishments. "Leif has pulled the *Justice* card." Sally let out a great sigh of relief. "And it is right side up." She turned again to her friends at the wall and gave a nod. They nodded back at us.

"This is good also?"

"Look at the illustration on the card, Sara. The scales represent perfect equilibrium. The sword represents being able to cut to the heart of a matter quickly and keenly. The scales are also the balance of present and future. This tells us Leif has taken responsibility for his actions, realizing that everything he'd done in the past had shaped him, and everything that he'll do in the future would continue to do so. Leif will have reaped what he had sown. Much of the future depends upon what he's done in the past. Leif will have reached a perfect balance."

I was overwhelmed by all of this information. I wasn't sure what to make of it. That the reading had been mostly positive made me happy. I was beginning to really trust these women and their *feelings*. But just as with the *angel* Joel and some of the others claimed to have seen, part of me would always be skeptical.

"This is a good reading." Carol stood and moved through the room towards where Leif lay nestled on my lap, oblivious to all of the energy being generated in determining his future. "I would like to perform a séance with the boy. There is a great deal of spiritual energy surrounding him. The *others* are busy."

"What would a séance do?" I was nervous about this next step into the unknown. A séance was like the Ouija board to me, a dark, misunderstood magic of sorts, talking to the dead and all that.

"I will be better able to speak with the boy's guides, to know what they know."

"I don't know…"

"It's up to you of course, Sara, but it is in the boy's best interest that I perform a séance. The more we know, the more guidance we can offer you."

"Okay, if you truly believe it's in Leif's best interest, I'll consider it."

"Enough for tonight," Beth interrupted. "We have enough now to meditate on. Give the girl time to decide." With that the women retreated to their cots.

*****

The two days following Leif's Tarot reading gave me plenty to think about. Leif's life plan was beginning to take shape and with it, mine. As I rummaged through the cold room, another fifteen steps below the bunker, Carol approached me.

"Have you made a decision as to whether you'd like for me to speak to Leif's guide?"

"I think so."

"Good, Sara. Good. I have a strong feeling this guide can help you."

"How can you know that?"

"My own guide has warned me against channeling this spirit."

"Then maybe you shouldn't, Carol."

"Perhaps." She tilted her head to the left and looked down timidly. "But it is *because* of my guide's warning that I feel I must try."

"If you're sure."

She smiled and nodded. "I'll prepare for the séance. After dinner, we'll begin."

Chapter Twenty-Six

The bunker was usually quite dark, but the night of the séance only candle light was permitted, making the intimate space feel slightly more claustrophobic. We huddled around the circular kitchen table, hands joined. Leif had been put to bed and could be heard soundly snoring from his bassinette. Of course the women had furnished a portion of the bunker with baby furniture in anticipation of Leif's arrival.

I sat between Carol and Jenny. Their hands were vastly different: Jenny's pudgy and soft, while Carol's were bony and strong, but both were ice cold.

"We will begin by clearing our minds. Then focus on me. I will require your energies if I am to pull this off." Sally took a deep breath, held it for what seemed like ten seconds and slowly released it over another ten seconds. The others followed suit and I too took a deep breath, held it and released.

"Good, I can feel your energies entering my space," she whispered. "Now focus on Leif, focus on his *spirit*."

I thought of my son and smiled; he was snoring so loudly. My chest filled up with love and I almost laughed out loud. Carol's grip tightened and I squeezed back. Suddenly, Carol's head tilted back and her eye lids fluttered violently. I turned to Bethany and mouthed: "Is she alright?"

Beth nodded back.

"Concentrate." Carol pronounced each syllable. "I *see* him. It's a *him*." Her brow furrowed. "He is…. *dark*."

That gave me goose bumps. *He is dark?* I didn't like the sound of that.

"He's here now," she whispered. Her eyes shot open. "He's with Leif."

My head swung around to watch the crib. Nothing.

"I will try to make contact." The room fell silent. Everyone closed their eyes but me. I kept both on Leif.

"He's very powerful," Carol said through clenched teeth. "He's showing me he is in control. Our light does not attract him." She became suddenly rigid. "Speak to me," she pleaded. "Speak to me. Why do you attach yourself to this child?"

Silence.

"Tell me what you know of Leif's path so that we might help guide him." More silence.

"Yes… yes, I am listening…" Without opening her eyes, she began to relate the spirit's message.

"He says everything is as it should be." Her eyebrows met in the middle and her head shook back and forth. "He feels guilt over something. He is *sad.* He carries a deep emotional burden. He won't share what it is with me. He assures me his is a special task and that everything is as it should be."

She broke the circle by freeing hands, and looked at me. "He's a shadow, this spirit. He's like a silhouette. I can't really *see* him; he's blocking me. I can do no more." She took a deep breath. "I wish I could have helped him. He suffers a terrible guilt."

"You did well, Carol." Sally smiled at her.

"You can only help those that want to be helped, Carol," said Jenny. "You know that."

"I know." Carol wiped away a tear.

"So Leif is in good company with this spirit?" My concern was for my son and not the spirit that was apparently haunting him.

"He is a good spirit, Sara, rest easy in knowing that. And *powerful.* Leif is in good company. The spirit's sadness should not affect his goal."

"And this spirit's goal is what? To guide Leif's life toward some future purpose?"

"Exactly. He is your son's spirit guide."

Chapter Twenty-Seven

My time at the bunker with these witches was one of the most educational and spiritual experiences of my short life. Some days we sat to sip tea, play board games, or read one of the hundreds of magazines and books Beth had collected in preparation for this period. But on other occasions, one of them would take me aside to teach me some sort of lesson. In one such case, it was Beth herself.

"Take this pendulum." She handed me a delicate chain necklace with a ring threaded through it. "Hold it like this." Taking my hand, she raised my arm up. When my hand was at eye level, she pulled the chain out of my fist slowly until the ring hung six inches from my fingers. "I'll show you what we're all capable of, not just me. What you see is not all that makes up the world we live in. Energy is all around us. *We* are energy and we *emit* energy. When you feel the body heat of another, do you not believe it comes from them?"

"Yes."

"But you cannot see it, can you?"

"No."

"You cannot see radio waves, or microwaves, but you know they exist because science can measure them. Science cannot measure what a psychic sees or how a healer heals. The only way to believe is to experience."

"Okay. Help me understand."

"We lost many of our abilities to technology. Our gifts were left unexplored. Now, in this new world, we must rely upon our natural gifts, our abilities to *see* and to heal."

"Teach me."

"Quiet your hand, child." She wrapped her wrinkled hands around my clenched fist. I stopped shaking. The pendulum went still. "Now with a thought make the pendulum swing."

"With a thought?"

"Yes. Concentrate on the ring and make it move. It is a powerful practice, a first step in your own realization that within you is a power far greater than anything you might have imagined."

I studied the ring and silently asked it to move. I thought about creating a whirlwind beneath it, twirling it counter-clockwise. It didn't take any time at all for the pendulum to actually move and then quicken. It was spinning around and around and I could barely believe it. Then it slowed to a stop. The smile that had grown on my face out of awe gave away my fascination with what had just occurred.

"Exciting, isn't it?"

I nodded. "But it stopped."

"Because you willed it to stop."

"I didn't."

"You did, by not quite believing what you were doing. You might have thought your fingers or your wrist were twitching just enough to make the pendulum swing, or you simply couldn't accept that what was happening was in fact happening. You lost faith."

"I was *really* doing that with my mind, with a thought?" My hand lowered and I rubbed my shoulder.

"You were. There is more I can show you. Lift your arm again and make the pendulum move back and forth in a straight line rather than in a circle."

I did as she asked. I concentrated again, and mentally saw the ring moving back and forth. Seconds later it actually did. The smile returned to my face.

"Good, good, Sara, you're doing very well. Now imagine the circular motion means *no*, and the back and forth *yes*."

"Okay." I focused on the ring.

"Now ask a question."

"And this will give me my answer?"

"If it is a yes or no question, you will have your answer."

Why not? I was intrigued. "Will my son be blond?"

The pendulum slowed and changed direction. It was whipping around in a circle.

"I guess not!" I grinned at Bethany.

I felt empowered. I kept asking questions and it kept answering. Right or wrong I couldn't say, but I hoped the future would confirm my hope that what I was learning wasn't all a hoax, and there really was something to what these women were teaching me.

Chapter Twenty-Eight

The following day it began to rain violently. Thunder could be heard rumbling and crashing overhead. This made a trip around the perimeter out of the question, so I relaxed on the comfortable couch with a book. Leif was sleeping soundly in his crib. Suddenly, Jenny approached with an excited smile on her face. "I've finished it."

"What, Jenny?"

"Leif's horoscope."

I had completely forgotten Jenny was working on an elaborate explanation of Leif's existence via her star charts.

I sat up, placing the book on the coffee table. "That's great!" I motioned for her to sit next to me. As she sat, the couch groaned in protest beneath her weight.

"I think this will give you a good understanding of who your son is."

"I'm very interested. You know, I used to always read my horoscope." I don't know if I always believed it, but some days it seemed pretty dead-on. Weird.

"Good, then you're familiar with the idea behind the art."

"I think I get it," I nodded, anxious to get started. Truth be told, I knew that people born of the same astrological signs were said to share similar personality traits and even physical traits. But my knowledge of this art was weak at best.

Jenny laid out several pieces of paper in front of me on the table and began.

"So, your son was born June 20th of this year. This puts him under the sign of Gemini in the Zodiac."

"Yep, he's a Gemini."

She nodded. "I mentioned he was ruled by Mercury, the messenger god of Roman mythology. I think it fitting he should be ruled by Mercury. Perhaps his is a message of hope." Jenny was so confident in her proclamations, it almost made me smile. But I contained my amusement. I knew these readings were her life's work.

"Gemini is the third sign of the Zodiac. Gemini, the twins, are a mix of the yin and yang and are *never* boring!" She smiled.

"According to my charts, I can tell you where Leif will fall into the very best and the very worst of the Gemini traits." She placed a chubby finger on top of a pile she stacked in front of me.

"Leif will be very capable of seeing both sides of every story. This will help him as a leader to understand conflict and make educated decisions as to a solution. He will make a very good politician, and I mean good in the sense that he would actually be fair, honorable, well-loved by those who know him." I glanced at my sleeping baby, trying to picture him in this light. He sighed heavily and raised an arm across his face, as if this were all too much for him.

"Leif will be a very social person. He will be interested in developing relationships with people. Again, a wonderful trait for a leader. The Gemini is very intellectually-minded, authentically concerned with gathering information from those around them and rationalizing everything. Leif will be exceptionally intelligent, taking this gift to new heights."

"It's fun being able to visualize Leif as a person!"I was truly enjoying this. It had been so long since I had been able to feel anything akin to hope for the future.

"I'm glad you're taking this to heart, Sara. You've been very eager to understand our crafts and I'm sure your curious nature will help feed Leif's characteristics every bit as much as his birth sign."

She moved the top page to the back and continued with her explanation.

"Because Leif is a Gemini he will be mutable. Mutable people are flexible. They can go with the flow, they are adaptable and dexterous, and they are capable of tackling many things at once. Your son will be very curious, as you are, Sara."

She slipped the next sheet under the pile and moved on.

"Leif is an air element. This addresses his ability to think through a problem by gathering information. This element is a thinking-person's sign.

"Leif will have to be careful not to become detached from his course. A Gemini can become easily bored once they have achieved a goal. If he is aware of this pitfall, he can be mindful to avert it.

"One last thing, Sara. Leif should encourage his ability to find people's weaknesses, especially where it concerns their character. This particular trait I see being a very useful tool in his life."

She neatly organized her stack of papers, pushing them into my hands. Apparently she was finished. The loosening skin on her enormous arms flapped happily as she brushed her hands, indicating the end of our session.

"Thank you. Thanks so much for doing this." I really appreciated all the attention these women paid to my son. If nothing else, they were selling me on his destiny.

Chapter Twenty-Nine

Two months into my stay with my witches, I witnessed a bizarre event that heralded both an ending and a new beginning.

It was early morning. I had been up for a half hour feeding Leif at my breast in my cot. It had been a long hard fight, but over the course of two months we had finally gotten Leif to latch on and now he wanted this attachment all the time.

A sound suddenly emanated from Bethany's bed, like a thick rumble from deep in her throat. It was unusual for anyone to be awake this early, so I turned and wrote it off as Beth clearing her throat. Then I heard a tumble of blankets to the floor. I shifted to get a better view and gasped. Beth was sitting upright in bed, eyes closed, mouthing something. She didn't appear to be awake at all, but a series of words were forming a sentence now, in a low repetitive drone. I strained to understand what she was saying. I leaned closer.

"Go north, go north, go north."

Standing, Leif still attached at my breast, I backed away and collided with the open shelves. Pots and pans fell loudly to the steel floor. This snapped Bethany out of her trance rather violently. She seemed stunned to have woken up in a seated position. The others had awoken too, their eyes turning to Beth, who was confused to say the least.

"What happened?" Carol sat up too.

"It was Beth. She was chanting in her sleep and it frightened me. I'm sorry to have woken you all." Leif was crying from the violent abruption to his feeding and I bounced him back and forth on my hip.

"What was she chanting?" Carol looked at me solemnly.

"I can't be sure. I think… I think she was telling me to go north."

Carol stared into my eyes, looking me up and down. "Sara, it is time."

"Time?" I questioned.

"Time to continue your journey towards Leif's great purpose."

I stared back at her, dumbfounded. I had no desire to leave the comfort of this bunker my son and I called a home. Were they telling me to leave?

"It's time to go," Beth said plaintively, staring at me.

"I-I don't want to *go*," I said indignantly. "I'm not leaving." Tears welled up in my eyes.

"It's not up to us, Sara. Leif's guide has spoken through Beth. It is time to go." Carol stood and walked to one of the closets and pulled out a large black bag that resembled a suitcase with wheels. "You can use this to carry your things, as well as water and food."

"I'm not leaving," I repeated. "No. I can't go out there with an infant." I couldn't believe this was happening.

"You knew this was coming, Sara." Bethany approached me, her hands extended.

"I don't want to leave." I started to cry. I couldn't help it; I was completely overwhelmed.

"This isn't a choice, Sara. We have been given a clear sign to keep you moving north. Trust us. If you delay, the order of things may be irrevocably changed. You cannot take this sign lightly."

"If we could keep you here we would, Sara. Believe that." Jenny's kind eyes fell on mine.

"It is not Leif's destiny to stay any longer," Sally reminded me.

With that, they began moving silently through the bunker, collecting items for my journey. I sat on the bed and wept. This was what life had become. A series of disappointments. All I could do was carry on, but had no idea how. Or where I would end up.

Chapter Thirty

The weather was agreeable. The sun was starting to burn away the clouds in the east, which told me the day would be hot.

"Go north," Beth said with conviction. "Your destiny lies there."

"Thank you for everything." My voice cracked. "We would have been lost without you."

"Your stay here has run its course. We only helped you help yourself." She lowered her staff and opened her arms. I hugged her hard, as I was prone to do with the people I loved, and I could truly say I had grown to love this woman.

"I'll never forget you," I said, pulling away from her.

"I don't ask that you remember me, Sara, only that you remember your destiny. Go now, march Leif towards *his* destiny."

The wind picked up, blowing my hair into my face. As I brushed it out of my eyes Bethany had disappeared, back down the ladder, back down her rabbit hole. I would never forget her, and I would be sure Leif never forgot either.

As I marched away from my former home, I began to walk with renewed purpose. It was almost autumn, one of my favorite times of year. In *life* I would have been bombarded with colors framing the farmer's fields, dancing across the dirt roads, carried through the air on a fall breeze. The air would smell of the encroaching cold, making a day like today- warm and sunny- a real treat for the senses. The fields would be bare save the wheat, bundled in tidy rolls, awaiting transport.

As I remembered autumns past, I inhaled deeply, hoping to reconnect with my youth. I had read somewhere that smell was a powerful memory trigger. If I could be transported, if only for a moment, to a time when life was simpler....

I coughed, waking the baby wrapped tightly to my chest. The air was missing the distinct scent of leaves, of soil, of life. It was dry, and burned my throat. Even now, months after the rains had returned with the sun, and the planet seemed to be returning to some semblance of its former self, it was still a foreign place with little more color than shades of grey. The sun was shining. The sky was a brilliant blue, but when would I see a bud on a tree? When would a blade of grass defy the odds and push through the dead soil? When would life really begin again?

I knelt at the side of the road and released Leif from his wrap. He cried and I missed the old women immediately. Back in our hideaway, they would have swarmed around us and rushed little Leif off to soothe him to sleep. But such loving intrusions were gone now. We were headed for a different place: our destiny.

When finally Leif settled down and slept, it was late morning, and I felt I had a lot of ground to cover. I didn't know what lay ahead. But I knew there was nothing here, not anymore. And to get to somewhere, anywhere, I felt I had a long way to go. I could only hope Leif and I would find a safe place to put our heads before the sun set. Jenny had mentioned a fairground with outbuildings not far from the bunker, within a day's travel, admitting she had spent too many months on the carnival circuit. I only hoped I was heading in the right direction.

*****

Hours later, as the sun dipped below the horizon of naked trees, spreading shadows like a thousand emaciated fingers reaching hundreds of feet across the barren fields, I was exhausted. My feet were already blistered in my worn sneakers, and my back ached from carrying Leif. It was fortunate then that I came across Jenny's fairground. But what remained left no impression of the carnivals of my youth. Instead, I was walking into a nightmare.

A déjà-vu overcame me and I shook it off violently. I hated those things, but took comfort in a comment Seth had made to Joel once. Something about déjà-vu acting as an indicator - a marker for your life, telling you that you're on the right path.

I hugged the gutters and then rushed across the four lane highway to the retaining wall in front of the main entrance. The wall stood about eight feet high and swung around the west side of the park in a long creeping curve that ascended another foot or two at its peak. If I climbed up the wall and scurried along the top, I could hop the fence at some point rather than take my chances by walking right through the front gates. I smiled in satisfaction when I found a portion of the fence that had been pushed in and now rested on the roof of one of the attractions. Was this a former secret entrance for teenagers to sneak into the park undetected, or was this more recent? Carefully, I pushed through, holding my breath as the whole park came into view.

The Fairgrounds looked as though they had hosted a brutal battle. Clothing littered the open expanse, blowing in the breeze. They were anchored by something. The immediate danger struck me as I heard the sound of wind chimes in the distance. Turning toward the sound, I could see the funhouse directly across from me. I got down on my knees, shielding Leif, but realizing that this vantage point also placed *me* in full view of any hostile forces that could still be lurking here. Leif was getting fidgety and I couldn't afford to let him cry out when the safety of this place was so uncertain. I crept back to the fence line, unwrapped Leif, and put him at my breast. The connection I felt with my son as he fed was indescribable, and it calmed me. Still no sign of life. Perhaps I was alone after all. Perhaps whoever had made this their home had already been killed, and their killers vanished. With that thought, I returned to the opening in the fence that had been my entry point, surveying the grounds for a safe-house among the many buildings. I could creep along the right side of one building and crawl across the grounds. I decided to wait a while longer and attempt the trip under full darkness.

As the darkness engulfed Leif and I, I listened. The wind chimes continued to play as the wind picked up, colder than before. I wrapped my arms around Leif, kissing his head. What happened next made my heart skip a beat.

Chapter Thirty-One

Boom! It was the sound of a spotlight turning on, or several. The light fell on the grounds in front of me, highlighting the carnage that had taken place here. Bodies were strewn across the wide expanse of the fairgrounds, frozen in contorted positions between the portable game tents and food stations, all of which were in tatters. I knelt next to the fence and craned my neck around the faux dormer of the haunted house Leif and I were hiding behind. Was this simply a timed event powered by some solar panel, or did it mean something more sinister for us?

Leif was becoming fussy again, upset by the loud noise. I pulled him free of his wrap once more and bounced him on my knee. To my horror he made a face, that face he makes just before he begins to cry. I jabbed my finger in his mouth to silence him, allowing him to suck at it until I managed to pull a breast out of my layered tops, shushing him all the while. He latched to my breast immediately.

"Hungry little monkey, aren't you?" I whispered to him, feeling fortunate that I had this method of calming him if and when the need arose. I often felt pangs of anxiety as I studied his tiny face while he fed. How could I provide for him? Would he survive? The thoughts haunted me mostly at night. Why did I leave the bunker? Destiny, I reminded myself. Leif's destiny is what drove me. I took four deep breaths, exhaling slowly. When Leif was asleep again, I checked his diaper before working him back into his wrap. I had a handful of cloth diapers with me, enough to make it a couple of days before washing became necessary. He was wet, but not wet enough to worry about.

Rolling my neck, I realized just how sore I was all over. As I completed the roll and opened my eyes, what was staring back at me, inches from my face, would have forced a blood curdling scream had I not the presence of mind to stifle it.

A German Shepherd sniffed me up and down, licked its chops and then sat, cocking its head to the side, its expressive eyes on me.

"Hey buddy," I whispered, attempting to smile. I loved dogs and hadn't seen one in a very long time. I was absolutely terrified, but I knew not to show it or the dog might attack. His face was gaunt and his body very skinny. His hair was filthy and knotted. I felt immediately drawn to him. He made a whining sound that broke my heart and pawed at me. I took his paw in my hand and shook it.

"Hi there, puppy." I felt as though I were the one doing the tricks for him. "What's your name?" I whispered, and he again whined.

"You're hungry too, huh?" I reached for my bag and unzipped it. Blindly feeling around I pulled out a package of crackers. "Would you like some of these?" He licked his chops. "Okay," I continued. "Can you lie down?" He did. I gave him four of the saltines. I also pulled a bottle of water and after taking a sip myself poured a portion into a Styrofoam bowl I found on the ground near us. The dog lapped up the water eagerly and I gave him four more crackers.

"You're a good boy, aren't you?" I crooned, patting his head softly. He was in need of companionship as much as food and water, I thought. He licked my hand. I patted him again and rubbed under his chin and neck. He rolled onto his side and then to his back, his paws up in the air.

"Oh, you want a tummy rub too?" I scratched at his belly. He made a squealing sound and leaped up. I pulled away quickly when I realized what I had scratched. It was a gash, an open wound. "Oh no!" I was instantly sad. "Let me see, puppy." I crawled towards him but he backed off licking his nose as he went. "Honey, I want to help, let me see." The dog let out a weak growl, then thought better of it and licked his lips, his head moving from side to side. I didn't want to push my luck, so I backed off. I couldn't be stupid about it: I had Leif on my chest and this was essentially a wild animal now. "If you're sure," I conceded.

He lay down a few feet from me, licked his gruesome wound, and slept. I was concerned that if someone was living in this place they might stumble upon us up here. I ached to get across the grounds to the safety of shelter. But the light: the light left me at an impasse. I curled up on the cold, hard ground with the sack under my head and Leif tight to my body. If it was good enough for our host, the German Shepherd, it would have to be good enough for us.

*****

I awoke with a start. The sun was up. I wasn't surprised that I had let my guard down. Thankfully, I had slept flat on my back, Leif safely strapped to my chest. I sat up and pulled him from the wrap.

"Morning sunshine," I said as he rubbed his eyes and coughed tiny, cute little baby coughs. I muted them against my shirt. "Are you ready to eat something?" I kissed his face about a hundred times and then felt his bum and confirmed a messy morning task ahead.

After changing and feeding Leif, I was ready to assess my situation. The fact that no harm had befallen us all night and the flood lights had extinguished themselves made me confident enough to scout around. Remembering the dog still at my side, I knelt to greet him and patted his head lightly so as not to alarm him. When there was no response I patted a little harder, a sick feeling in my stomach. I put his face in my hands and lifted his snout. I leaned in and put my cheek against his cold, dry nose, trying to detect breath. My bottom lip curled down as a frown formed reflexively on my face. "Oh, no," I squeaked. "Oh, no." My eyes instantly filled with tears. I was surrounded by death. But somehow the loss of an innocent dog, one that had just been alive hours ago, seemed too much.

As I sat next to him, I ran a hand across his bony side, glad that he didn't die alone, starving and thirsty. A tear rolled down my cheek and landed on Leif, who smiled up at me. Why had I brought my helpless son into this heartless world? His smile though, it was irresistible. I was forced to smile back. I would protect him.

*****

Walking along the perimeter of the park, I felt uneasy, like I was being watched. I stopped and slowly sank to the ground, making myself very small. Maybe I should get out of here, continue north. The air was still and no sounds beyond my own breathing were audible. I could say it was *too quiet*, but unless I was walking, Leif was crying, it was raining or the wind was howling, sound was at a minimum these days.

I stood up to better assess the situation. Nothing. Nothing had moved, nothing had disappeared overnight. The fair was as dead as the corpses strewn across its grounds. With a renewed sense of resolve, I made my way carefully across the grounds and into the Fun House, as if something were drawing me there. My heart bursting in anticipation and my head down, I pulled the luggage behind me and passed through the door. Once inside I leaned against a wall and slid slowly down its rough surface.

The walls were all very close, like a labyrinth, and all the mirrors long since smashed or stolen. Just as I was about to move further into the dilapidated building, a crackling sound erupted above me.

"WELCOME, TO CARNIVAL!" A man's voice blared over the loud speaker. I froze.

"WELCOME, TO CARNIVAL!" It repeated. Okay, this could just be a recording, timed to come on just as the lights had.

"YOU SHOULD TRY THE HOTDOGS." Okay, I could breathe again. It *was* a recording. The voice was animated, ridiculous actually. It sounded like a cartoon.

"THEY'RE MADE WITH 100% REAL MEAT. JUST LIKE YOU." *Shit!*

"PLEASE, STEP OUT OF THE FUN HOUSE AND INTRODUCE YOURSELF."

I stood stock still. Panic rose like bile in my throat. There was nowhere to go. I was trapped.

"NO PROBLEM, WE'LL COME TO YOU." *We'll?* There was more than one? Instinct told me to once again make myself very small. I fell to the floor, covering Leif. I realized I was kneeling on something that cut sharply into my knee. My hand instinctively grabbed for it. It was a latch, recessed into the thick plywood. I pulled at it and yanked up hard, pulling a trapdoor loose. I peered blindly into the dark abyss. Seeing a ladder, I climbed down as fast as I could, securing the trapdoor above me.

Trembling, I pulled a flashlight from my pocket and panned it around the tiny space. No more than six feet high and maybe another eight feet long by six feet wide: little more than the dimensions of a grave.

As I was checking the sleeping Leif with my light, I heard the front door snap off its hinges and fall hard many feet from the entrance. I killed the flashlight and buried Leif's head into my neck, covering his ears. I shook uncontrollably as I pressed my back into the dirt corner of the secret room.

"It *was* a girl right?" The man had a heavy voice, thick with thirst. "I would like to see a *girl* again."

"It was a *girl*, Thor," said another, smaller voice. Thor, I thought. Maybe he was the Strong Man in the carnival? I pictured the upturned mustache, the bald head and the heart tattoo on his shoulder.

"Let's split up," suggested the small voice. "We can cover more ground that way."

"Okay." They stomped off in different directions.

Neither of their voices resembled that of the man on the loudspeaker. That meant at least three men lived in the fairgrounds. Neither were immediately above me at this moment but I knew they might only be gone for seconds. If they knew about this room, surely they would have checked here first. Was I safe for the moment?

With that, the footsteps came crashing back and stopped just above me. "We *have* to find her."

Dust poured through the spaces between the plywood slabs as he jostled around. I waved a hand above me to keep the dirt from Leif.

They couldn't capture us, I reasoned desperately. Leif had a great purpose to fulfill and these starving savages could not alter that course.

"I don't see her *anywhere*." The small voice reentered the Fun House as well. Suddenly there was a loud crash above me. One of them had fallen. Had they tripped on the latch?

"What's this?" I heard agitation.

"It's a *bag*!" shouted Thor. I could hear the zipper being ripped open and a great sigh coming from both men. "Holy shit! It's full of food and water."

They laughed together for a time as I silently cried for Leif and I. We would be utterly destitute without it. We couldn't go far without water at the very least. Then I remembered. I wasn't completely helpless - I had a gun hidden in my waistband. It was never far from my body.

"Wait!" ordered the small voice. "Let's eat what we want now and then take the rest back to split with the Master."

"I think we ought to just take it all back. But let's hurry: I'm starving."

"What about the girl?"

"She's gone," thundered the big voice.

"We don't know that. We shouldn't leave here without her."

"We didn't *find* her, so she *must* be gone, must have snuck out."

They seemed to be leaving the Fun House, dragging my sack behind them.

"Listen! We haven't looked *long* enough. If we go back now with just the bag he'll be pissed." The little voice was spiked with fear.

"Fine, but I'm eating something while we wait."

"That's all I'm saying."

I crept silently up the ladder and raised the trapdoor. I could see that my interpretation of what they would look like was not far off the mark. The Strong Man was not so much muscle as just plain huge, but the other man was all of three feet tall. They stood on the veranda. A semi-transparent yellow corrugated plastic roof let the light pour in, while the wooden side walls offered them the privacy they seemed to require. Their *Master* must be watching them from above.

I crawled out of the secret room and got to my feet, setting the door down carefully. I raised the gun, white-knuckled, and pointed it at the Strong Man. I hated the idea of killing anyone like this, in cold blood, but letting our precious bag of food go was not an option.

"What's this?" complained the Strong Man. "Fucking *baby* food?" He held the tin up to the little man. The midget, bearded and dressed in something that resembled a young girl's summer dress with a belt around the middle, looked longingly at the tin.

"A *baby*!" he exclaimed. "Now, that would be a treat!" The tall man grinned evilly, saliva dripping from his toothless mouth, his tongue extending out in a sickening thrashing action.

I shot him first, having decided that he was more of a threat to me than the little man. I hit him in the shoulder and he cried out, dropping the tin. He turned toward me, his eyes squinting against the darkness. What he saw next would be a bright orange flash as I pulled the trigger again and hit him square in the chest. His chest heaved up and down twice as he fell backwards, letting out a final cry as he hit the ground with a thunderous thud, dust rushing out from under him.

My gun was trained on the little man next. His hands were up and eyes wide.

"Listen-" he began. I fired several times, approaching with each squeeze of the trigger. His tiny body convulsed as the bullets pierced his torso. He fell onto his back, arms out, bleeding. The parched wooden porch sponged up the blood thirstily as it exited his lifeless shell.

I had made a lot of noise, so I instantly gathered up Leif and then the bag and ran for it. How many bullets did I have left? How many did a pistol like this hold? I knew it had a magazine, and I knew I had two more just like it full of bullets. But I had no idea how many bullets one held. How many had fired off? Five? Six? Once I had Leif back at my chest I zipped up the bag and peeked beyond the wall.

Chapter Thirty-Two

I had proven that I could kill out of necessity. I looked down at the two Carnies in disgust. The blood bubbled from the Strong Man's chest as air escaped his lungs. I was a much better shot than I had given myself credit for. I had no sympathy for people who saw no other recourse than to eat other people. Sure, the thought had crossed my mind. What if we ran out of food? But the idea for me was unimaginable. I would starve to death first.

I peered again around the corner of the veranda, praying that I wasn't being watched, praying that the *Master* hadn't heard the shots. Not wanting to face him with only one or two bullets left in my gun, I reached into the side pocket of my bag and pulled out a fresh magazine. Releasing the old magazine, I placed it in the luggage pocket and jammed the new one up into the handle of the gun. I pulled back on the barrel until I heard the click. I was ready.

"WELCOME TO CARNIVAL," the loud speaker proclaimed again. I jumped at the voice.

"YOU HAVE BESTED THE *STRONG MAN* AND *SIDEKICK*," he continued. I felt a heat rise across my neck, cheeks and temples.

"ALLOW ME TO INTRODUCE MYSELF. I AM THE RING MASTER. YOU'VE GUESSED BY NOW THAT ALL THE ANIMALS ARE GONE, CONSUMED MANY MONTHS AGO.

THE CLOWNS WERE NEXT, AND THEN THE BUSKERS AND SO ON."

"IT WAS THE *FREAKS* THAT SURVIVED, UNDER MY GUIDANCE. AND NOW, TO BE BESTED BY A LITTLE GIRL WITH A GUN… *SHAME ON US*."

This guy was long gone, a long time ago. The patients were running the asylum, so to speak. I pictured him surrounded by human remains somewhere in a little room that overlooked the fairgrounds.

I set down my bag and was deliberating on what to do next when the speakers crackled on again.

"I WOULD VERY MUCH LIKE TO MEET YOU."

It was an invitation to dinner, no doubt. Where Leif and I would be the main course.

"I WILL BE DOWN MOMENTARILY." Then the speakers went dead. Again, silence. I had to act, or take cover. I panicked a moment, unsure of how to face this enemy. He was clearly nuts. He had probably been so since the moment he swallowed human flesh for the first time. I wondered which direction he might be coming from. It was impossible to tell. The speakers carried throughout the park. I looked toward the front gates. No one. Then I looked toward the back of the park, where an amphitheatre, five stories tall, acted as the focal point. Rows of seating overlooked a central dirt pad where, I guessed, the Ring Master ran his Circus.

Suddenly, a violent breeze had picked up the dirt, swirling it in the air. The roar of an engine echoed off the seating, the amphitheatre magnifying the sound. It was deafening.

If his intention was to scare the living shit out of me, mission accomplished. It sounded like he was riding some hellish creation with seven mufflers, eight wheels and an open engine. I was stuck in place, my nails digging into the wooden wall. I couldn't take my eyes off the spectacle. He tore down the grounds toward me, running over the corpses, crashing through the dilapidated food stations and games tents.

I pulled myself away from the vision, backing off into the Fun House. I thought about hiding underground once more, but the idea of being trapped there with no escape plan save shooting my way out frightened me just as much as facing him head on.

The vehicle rushed past me, spewing dust onto the veranda. It was obnoxiously loud. He began circling the Fun House entrance in quick successive right turns. On closer inspection of the vehicle, I could see it was some kind of motorcycle with two massive wheels in the back and one in the front, connected to the bike by a long chrome leg. The man's appearance was blurred by the amount of dust and dirt he was kicking up. Likely a tactic he was using to flush me out. Instead, I decided to take aim.

Leif was crying at my chest, still attached via the sling I'd made over two months before. I curled both hands around my pistol and fired recklessly into the circle of flying debris. I counted my shots until the barrel stopped firing. The motorcycle continued to circle outside the front entrance.

I pulled out another clip, palmed it up inside the handle and took aim, but the cycle's circling ceased, the engine whirring at a lower decibel. I stepped cautiously onto the veranda, the smoke and dirt clearing. I squinted my eyes. Was anyone left on the bike? Had I managed to shoot him off? As surreal as the circumstances had become, I flashed back to a childhood memory of the carnival. I'd spent my allowance for that week firing a water rifle at moving targets for most of the afternoon, desperate to win the pink, stuffed pony. Had I won the proverbial pony here?

The smoke had cleared and the bike continued to hum without its rider. Side-stepping to check the far side of the bike for a body, I carefully rounded the back, gun still drawn. *Jesus, Sara! Don't go any further.* The voice in my head was right: why didn't I stop? I had a screaming baby strapped to my chest. But the curiosity and adrenaline had gotten the better of me, and I couldn't seem to stop myself. Leif was wailing – the deafening gunshots had probably hurt his ears, hopefully not irrevocably, but I dared not set him down. I ignored his pleas to be coddled. I needed to end this twisted chapter in my trip.

"I will blow your head off!" I blindly threatened the Ring Master over Leif's frightened cries.

As the far side of the bike came into view I saw the man, curled over on his side, arms crossed over his stomach, rocking back and forth. He wore leather chaps over faded jeans and cowboy boots whose soles had long since fallen off. His torso was bare save a cape he had tied around his neck. It was his face though which captured my interest. Nothing should have surprised me anymore. But this did.

He wore a red rubber clown's nose torn down the center. His eyebrows were gone. Deep scars split his cheeks, travelling from the corner of each eye down to his jaw. His head was covered in a ridiculous orange fuzzy wig. He looked up at me, and as he did blood rushed out of his mouth, mixing with the dusty earth. He tried to say something through a painted smile.

I shot him in the chest without hesitation. Blood splattered across the ground as his heart exploded from the impact. His head fell hard and fast, his eyes staring into the abyss. Whatever he had to say to me I didn't want to hear. I lowered my arm and spun around, careful not to leave myself vulnerable to another attack.

Then the immensity of what had happened hit me like a ton of bricks. My face hurt as it contorted and I screamed out, stomping my feet. Leif was stunned momentarily into silence, and then cried harder than before. I knew I had to get away. I couldn't be in this place any longer. The motor bike was still running and I thought it looked simpler than a regular motorcycle to operate. I looked the machine up and down. I had ridden dirt bikes before, and this couldn't be much different. I grabbed my bag, tied it down to the wide back rack and climbed on. Leif continued to protest, but getting us free of the carnival was my priority.

I pushed down on the clutch, revved the handle and toed at the gears. I popped the clutch when I had decided I was in first and jerked forward. I was moving! I pushed the clutch again and toed at the gears to second and rallied through the grounds on approach to the front gates. Slamming through the maintenance gate, I made a hard right following my original path, heading north. Whatever lay to the north, it couldn't be worse than this.

Chapter Thirty-Three

I drove the entire day, stopping in spurts to feed Leif and myself. The freedom I experienced riding in the open air was exhilarating. The wind in my face and hair, billowing against my jacket and long pants offered a welcome reprieve from the world at large. I was able to reconnect briefly with a younger me, who used to ride my father's dirt bike in the field adjacent to our house. Leif was lulled to sleep by the motion each time we got back on the road. I kept my speed to a minimum in order to conserve gas, never actually turning it off as we stopped, for fear of it never starting again. I worried about the level of noise the bike created but convinced myself that it would accelerate our path to Leif's destiny. Who knew how long I had until I got to where I was going.

That's the thing about destiny. It seems to know where you're headed, even if you don't. So I assumed we were heading to something, somewhere, north. The devastated landscape was little more than an endless graveyard of rotting forests, still ponds and fields of radioactive dirt. As I moved past them, the forward motion in my peripheral blurred the scenery into torn grey curtains. If others had headed north on this highway, they had done so long ago. There was no sign of life on the road.

*****

After roughly eight hours on the deserted highway I hit a wall. I was exhausted, my eyes burned, and my arms ached from navigating the bike around countless obstacles. Even my back throbbed from the angle I was forced to sit at. I followed the first off-ramp I came to, located a rest stop, and pulled in. Hesitantly I pushed the red stop button on the bike's dash. If it started again, great, but if it didn't I guessed I could chalk that up to destiny. All I knew was that I couldn't ride it anymore. As I stepped off the bike all the blood seemed to rush back into my thighs, igniting a pain so severe it felt as though I had run the whole way. I rubbed my legs and arched my torso, palms pushing against my lower back. Leif remained comfortably in his wrap strapped to my chest, sleeping.

It wasn't a truck stop or anything elaborate, but it met our needs and I was thankful for it. A rest stop this far north normally had a well that could be manually pumped for clean water. This stop was also small enough to be overlooked by most. Though it may offer water, it would offer little else, I noted. Even the information building had been vandalized beyond recognition for the contents of its vending machines.

All I needed was water, and some semblance of shelter.

As I inspected my new surroundings I slipped the pistol out of my waistband. Though the odds seemed remote that I should run into another hostile survivor in this isolated place, the idea of it still spooked me. What looked like birch trees stood along the perimeter of the rest stop, their tops missing. Nothing green remained. A wind had picked up from the south and I flinched as it rattled the dead branches and carried debris down the highway. I cursed its timing.

I crept up to a sign at the end of the parking lot that read *Historic Site, 1814. Site of the James Spring Reservoir, established to aid troops in the war of blah blah blah…* I wondered if future generations would plant signs like these in the hot spots of the world created by the Reaper's evil deed. What I was hoping for with the sign was some indication that a well was near. I spun around and sighed. I had already drained a half dozen bottles of water and needed to replenish them. I had to keep my fluids up. Leif's dependency on my breast milk made this a tantamount necessity.

Suddenly, a new sound, and I froze. Branches again, snapping, but not in the way the wind would push the tree tops and snap them. This snapping was consistent and *deliberate.* The forest was alive with the sound. Someone or something was walking through the woods. I strained my eyes against the encroaching twilight but saw nothing. Then a loud crunch came from behind the ravaged information building.

Whatever it was must not have seen us yet. It definitely came from behind the building. I ran back to my bike on the balls of my feet and mounted it once more. I made myself small, leaning over the gas tank, kneeling on the seat, my gun trained on the far side of the building. Amazingly, Leif was still sleeping. I waited for the sound's creator to emerge.

After several tense seconds, the head of a deer poked around the corner of the ruined building. I was struck by its huge, sad eyes. Its tongue licked at its nose as it stepped out into the parking lot. I remained still, not wanting to scare her. My gun followed her as she moved across the lot and left. The poor thing was emaciated and moved painfully slowly. What had she been living on all this time? Bark? As much as I loved animals, I was no vegetarian and a slab of venison cooking over an open fire flashed in my mind. My mouth automatically watered. I could kill this deer if it was truly life or death. But I had food, I didn't need to kill for anything yet. The bigger question would be how would I skin it and cut it up? Then a vision of Earl *skinning* Gareth forced the thought from my mind. I continued to follow the doe with my eyes as it moved into the woods. I watched as she nosed at a short stump. As she did, the right side of the narrow stump gave way and lifted. She did this several times before I realized what was happening. It was no stump- it was a water pump!

I dismounted the bike once more and slowly approached the doe. The sound of liquid hitting the ground was music to my ears. The pump was producing water! I let the deer drink what water had collected in the cement basin and watched it go. Then I ran to the pump, lifted the arm and pushed down. I did this until the water gushed out of the spout. I leaned down, cupped my hands together until they were full of water. Then I drank deeply. It was good. I ran back to the bike, collected my bottles from the bag, and refilled them.

*****

That night Leif and I settled into the information building. I ate a meal of crackers, canned carrots and canned pineapple, drinking all the water I could stomach. I was so happy to have found a water source, I decided to stay near it as long as no one discovered us.

For about three days after arriving at the rest stop I awoke to the deer at the pump, its squeaking handle bringing me out of a restless sleep. I would trudge to the well, Leif in tow, and fill my bottles to capacity. Our days were spent sleeping, eating, and occasionally playing. Leif was able to respond to my smiles now. His toothless grin could entertain me for hours on end. I would sing to him and tell him I loved him. Thank God this little person had come into my life.

On the fourth day, I started to realize what I was doing. Was it unhealthy to be so attached to the pump, to the water? Was it counter-productive? Who knew if I'd ever find a water source like that again? Afraid to relinquish this link to life, I chewed at my fingernails absent-mindedly, spitting the gnarled nails out and examining the finger tips. Was this a problem? Could I make myself leave? My other hand worked a length of my dark, greasy hair around my index finger as I pondered my dilemma.

This couldn't be Leif's destiny, to grow up here. What sort of destiny would that be? Yet I was so reluctant to get back on the motorcycle and leave the pump that it made me shake to think about it. If I left I was leaving for good. If I left and we never found water again then what? If I stayed and ran out of food the water would only keep us alive for a few days more. So, what would be my catalyst? What would make me leave?

I felt a deep connection with Joel in that moment, understanding what he must have struggled with during those last few weeks. Making life or death decisions on behalf of others was excruciating.

"A little help," I pleaded aloud in a whisper, looking up at the grey sky above. The low-lying clouds moved quickly overhead. "Storm," I said. September storms, they were a force. Joel had loved a storm in *life*. I had learned to love them too. But alone, vulnerable and with a newborn, a storm meant hardships never before imagined. A rain drop hit my nose and I ran inside, Leif in my arms. There were no doors left on the building to close behind me, and if the rain fell in any direction other than straight down we would be soaked in seconds. The structure was little more than a booth and had lost all of its windows to looters a long time ago. The rain began, falling hard on the metal roof. It fell in sheets within a minute. A wind blew into the building, spraying the rain all over me. I sucked in a breath unconsciously and turned my back on it, trying to keep Leif dry.

"Shit," I whispered as a chill ran through me. As warm as the morning was, the rain felt wintery cool against my face and hands. Leif began to cry, the shock of the icy rain on his skin a rude awakening.

The wind picked up in intensity, blowing more of the rain into the building. I might as well have been standing in the middle of the parking lot for all the shelter I was getting. I shifted, moving back and forth in the tiny building, hoping for more shelter, but none was to be found. I was dripping wet in minutes. The roar of the rain pounding on the roof was deafening, and a crash of thunder exploded overhead, Leif screamed into my ear. I was freezing, shaking uncontrollably, praying for the storm to pass.

All at once, as quickly as it had taken me from bone dry to soaking wet, the rain stopped and a glimmer of sun pierced the cloud. Now, I knew something about northern storms in September and I knew that this was merely a taste of what was to come. I knew of no other possible shelter in the area. This building was it. Even the tiny washroom which I'd huddled into had no door left to shut. My blankets were soaked. If this kept up all day I'd have a very uncomfortable night. Perhaps this ought to have been my catalyst. Maybe I could outrun the storm on the bike?

Leif had been crying since the initial spray of windswept rain had woken him. I think I was crying too. I bounced him while I paced back and forth, considering my options. Was leaving too rash a decision?

"Fine." I stopped myself and held Leif under his arms, lifting him to my face. He stared at me with sad eyes. "I'm going to ask you a question, and then give you two possible answers. If you make a noise after I offer the answer then we will follow that path. Understand?"

"Leif," I said in a low tone. "What do you think we should do? Stay?" I waited for the crying to begin, but he remained silent.

"Go?"

He whimpered immediately.

I wasn't going to question Leif's destiny; if he was meant to stay that was not the answer I got. I picked up my wrap and fitted him inside, slung it over my shoulder, grabbed my bag, and secured it to the bike.

My water supply was full save a couple of bottles, but if I was going to beat the storm north I had to move. Looking to the pump, I smiled, blew it a kiss and pushed the ignition button on the bike. It rumbled to life. My heart soared and we navigated back onto the highway, continuing north.

Chapter Thirty-Four

I had managed to keep far enough ahead of the growing storm clouds to pull over and change out of my wet clothes. The artificial wind in my face caused my teeth to chatter and my skin to tighten. It was a chilling experience, like being tossed into a lake in early spring. I noticed Leif could use a change as well and pulled over. I dug through the contents of the giant bag secured to the bike's back rack, pulling out a new onesie and a full set of pajamas. I had become masterfully quick at the process of changing the baby. He was usually happy to accommodate me too. He appreciated the luxury of a clean diaper and fresh clothes.

Once we were both dry and dressed, I climbed back onto the three-wheeler and pushed on, looking over my shoulder constantly. My anxiety increased as the clouds advanced behind us.

I squinted against the speed-induced wind as an alarming thought struck. What if I were to come across the mass grave Earl, Sonny and Freddy claimed to have stumbled upon months before? I would see it long before I came to it. The roads now were straight and flat, the hills on the horizon always a distant marker. I couldn't even be sure whether I was on the same highway. All I knew for sure was my direction: north. The compass on the bike offered that small reassurance.

*****

Three hours into my journey, the storm clouds a distant memory and the sky above me only blue, the bike's fuel light began to blink wildly. Ten minutes later I was pushing the bike into a ditch.

My bag resting on its wheels, the handle extended and my baby strapped to my torso, I once again felt terribly vulnerable as I grasped the bag and moved forward on unsteady legs. I walked roughly three more hours before coming to a deep valley. The angle of decline was extreme but I continued onward, digging my heels into the asphalt. My bag kept clipping at my ankles so I pulled it out in front of me, its weight pulling me off center. *'Don't fall, don't fall, don't fall…'* I repeated aloud. It took an enormous amount of concentration to finally arrive safely at the bottom of the valley. But it was at the base that I felt the most insecure. Looking down at my feet, I saw that I was standing in a small stream. The water was still, the banks had flooded from what must have been a torrential downpour similar to that which chased me from my well. A ripple hit my ankle, approaching from my right. Then a second later, another. My heart lodged in my throat. There was absolutely no wind in the valley. It could be another animal, I surmised, perhaps a frog, or small fish that had survived in this muck? But my gut told me it was something else, *someone* else.

Not wanting to look up and confirm my fear, I kept my eyes on the water. The ripples became more frequent, followed by the sound of legs dragging in knee-high water. I reached into my waistband slowly, fingers wrapping around the handle of the pistol and gingerly pulling it free. I looked to my right, straining to see what the fates had thrown at me this time. The sound suddenly increased in volume and speed. I turned to face the noise with my pistol raised and ready.

Two men mere moments from tackling me stopped dead in their tracks, their arms raised over their heads automatically. One was much older than the other. He looked eighty-five but probably was no more than sixty. The other man, who appeared to be in his early twenties gestured wildly in surrender, backing away. The old man produced a long knife from his sleeve and turned it in his fingers.

"Now, now, pretty lady. All we want is what you have." He inched closer. The young man eyed him.

"What I have is my own," I retorted. "You come any closer and I'll shoot you!"

"Now, now," he continued as he slowly stepped up onto the road. "You don't want to shoot me. You're a nice little girl." At that I cocked the hammer and again he froze in place.

"I've killed men before." I cleared my throat so as not to seem so terrified. "I've killed before and I will kill you where you stand." Trying not to let my hands shake, I thrust the gun further in front of me.

His head cocked and his brows rose. "Oh, I don't believe that." His mouth widened to a smile under his unkempt beard. "I doubt there are even any bullets in your gun. Mine hasn't seen a bullet in over a year."

"I'm not kidding. I *will* shoot you!" I shouted. My voice was shaky. Had I changed the magazine after I took down the clown? All this time I'd just assumed the gun had been loaded. My heart pounded angrily in my chest, my face flushed, my eyes narrowed to slivers.

"I think you're mistaken," he said, resuming his approach.

"Only one way to find out," I said with what confidence I could muster. The man's eyes widened and he lunged towards me, arm shooting up to bring the knife down. I fired twice. To my attacker's amazement, he fell backwards as each bullet caught him in his midsection. He landed with a splash in the knee-high water beside the road and sank to its filthy bottom. I trained the gun on his young friend next.

"Dad!" He yelped before running to pull him out of his watery grave. He looked wildly up at me. "You killed him!"

"What did you think I would do?" I shouted back, shaking. "I have a *baby*!" It was a horrible thing - a son watching his father die - but I was someone's mother now. *Leif's* mother. And I would not let anyone harm him.

"You bitch!" His voice gave out and he sank to his knees beside his father's shallow grave. It had occurred to me that I ought to shoot him too, so he would not follow me and attack us in the night.

"You stay," I told him as I grabbed the handle of my bag and moved backwards. "You just stay where you are and you'll be fine." He didn't respond for a time. I was half way up the other side of the valley highway before he realized I'd gone.

"You!" he screamed as he spotted me. My gun, returned to my waistband for the trip up, slipped through my loose pants and tumbled down the hill as I struggled to retrieve it. Knowing that my only chance was to outrun him, I dropped my bag and raced the rest of the way up the steep hill, Leif crying at my chest. Looking back, I saw to my horror that he was tearing up the hill after me, with *my* gun in hand. Reaching the top of the valley, I ran headfirst into the waiting arms of a stranger.

Chapter Thirty-Five

I heard my gun go off before I was immediately hustled into the back of a parked truck. I remember telling the men that I had a baby, and needed help. They understood that all too well, shooting down my assailant as he appeared at the crest of the hill. He was cut down by the gun mounted to the roof of a jeep. The man whose body I had plowed into jumped into the back of the truck with me. He, like his companions, wore a face mask and combat fatigues. I guessed that this was the military. This was the rescue we'd all hoped for in the beginning. I felt I'd come full circle. There were six of them in total.

"Let me see your neck and your torso," ordered the hollow voice behind the mask.

"My torso?" I wondered whether I was really safe after all.

"We need to inspect you. Are you feverish? How's your eyesight?"

"I-I'm fine," I stammered. "My eyesight is fine. What do you need to see on my torso?" It was difficult shouting back and forth with the baby crying.

"Precautions. We check all unknowns for the plague before they are admitted."

"Admitted to what?"

"The base. Now remove your shirt."

"I have a baby strapped to my chest. Could you please relax?" I slowly pulled Leif out of his worn sling and placed him lovingly down on the metallic truck bed. I then pulled off my top layers, my bra catching on the last of them and a sliver of my white breast popping out. My elbow instinctively snapped into a defensive position, covering the nipple.

"You look fine," he concluded, sensing my embarrassment. "I mean, free of spots. The plague." He struggled with his words.

My brows raised. *Never seen a nipple before?* "Okay, now what?"

"Let me see your baby." He reached out. I picked Leif up and reluctantly handed him over to the soldier. An intense anxiety overcame me. I gathered up my tops and held them in a bunch in front of me.

After undressing him, he gave Leif a thorough visual inspection. "How old?"

"About two months." I answered.

"Little small for two months, isn't he?"

"He was a month or two premature."

He handed Leif back to me and I dressed him quickly.

"What now?" I asked again.

He lowered his mask. "Now we can take you to the base." He gave us a broad and reassuring smile. I couldn't help noticing that he was incredibly handsome. "I'm Sergeant Jones, by the way."

"I'm Sara, and this is Leif." I felt suddenly hot and ran my hands over my rib cage feeling uncomfortably aware of my state of undress.

"Good to meet you both," he grinned, his eyes wandering a moment to my chest, and then to the baby. "I'll see to it you are well cared for upon our return." He stepped down from the truck bed.

"I guess I should thank you for saving my life," I smiled back. He turned and nodded, then tapped the side of the truck and it roared to life.

"I'll follow you back."

Part Two
Chapter Thirty-Six

The base was a modern marvel. It used wind and solar power for virtually all of its energy needs. There were fifteen windmills jutting up into the sky some sixty feet from a central point along with hundreds of solar panels attached to the roofs of the common buildings.

In a way, the base was an upgrade to what we had had at Joel's house. There, we had run power off the generator that ran on fuel and had our own well, but that was it. Joel's cold storage, though essential to our survival, was a miniature version of what the base had hidden beneath the floors of the kitchen: massive freezers and clean rooms that were stocked with dried meat, fruit, vegetables, canned and boxed goods. Enough to last two hundred people for fifty years, they told me. When I arrived at the base, there were only eighty-six people.

One of my favorite things about the base was the animals. I had missed animals, hugging them, playing with them. The base had a large metal barn that housed some twenty cattle, fourteen goats, probably fifty chickens and a couple of pigs. But when the pigs refused to mate, they instead became pets. *One day we'll just eat them,* the Sergeant said once, but his children loved the pigs and he could never put them on a plate in front of them.

The base also drew its water from underground wells. The water was then treated with ultraviolet light, charcoal filters and a variety of other filters before it ever made it to our mouths. They had a brilliant grey water recycling system as well. Rain water was collected and used for the toilets and for washing. It was literally a Shangri-la in the midst of a terrible desert.

The walls, which reached a height of twenty feet in places, were outfitted with watch towers. There was also a stockade, family housing, a mess hall, hospital and the central training and parade grounds. This base even included a greenhouse.

Our daily lives consisted of keeping the base running smoothly. Everyone's unique skills were put to good use, and I had been employed in many capacities, the last three years dedicating all of my time to the hospital.

Eight years had passed since I first drove through the gates in the back of that truck, my heart in my throat. This was where my son grew up. It was more a home to me than anything I'd known since the Reaper struck and the *only* home Leif had ever known. Though the grey on grey treatment to the buildings interiors was bleak, and the military precision as to how things were run felt a little claustrophobic at times, the alternative to living here was not an alternative at all.

We had been given a shower, disinfected, administered shot after shot and issued five sets of clothes each, all within our first hour inside the base. Leif had been doted over by the women here, many of the nurses becoming my close friends within the first month, the doctor a source of great comfort.

I counted my blessings and lived each day grateful for the abundance of food, water, and people. I hadn't realized just how much I missed meeting new people.

Leif attended a school daily and grew up happy, oblivious to the world I had grown up in. It was just as well, as this world was still a mess. There were still no leaves on the trees, no grass in the fields. No nothing. My hope for a future was waning for Leif, but I remained outwardly positive.

I watched him run into our bunkroom and jump up onto his bed. He reminded me so much of his father. The way he smiled at me. His eyes were the same, and I imagined that when he got older, he would have Joel's lean muscular physique. But there was something about my son that went beyond physical features in their similarities. An eerie recognition. Often a cloud of anxiety overtook me when he stared at me. He'd lie on his bed and stare across the room at me while I read.

"What is it, baby?" I would ask, looking up from my book.

"Nothing, Mom," was his reply. It was as though he was trying to work out some great mystery in his head. He looked so thoughtful. Sometimes he didn't even realize I was staring back.

“Mom,” he asked once, “was I born here?”

“Nope, not here.”

“Then where, then?”

“Why do you want to know, sweetheart?”

“Some of the other kids were telling each other where they were born and I said I was born here because that’s where they were saying they were born.”

I sat up and spun around to face him. Our cots were just three feet apart and separated by a night table. The lights in the building flickered. “You were born just a couple of days drive south of here.”

“Can we go see?”

“Not without an escort.”

“Oh, so it’s dangerous?”

“Probably.”

“Will I ever be allowed to go there?”

“Why do you need to?”

“I was talking to Blank Man. He said I would go there one day. I just wondered if we could go tomorrow.”

My heart always sank at the name, *Blank Man.* Leif claimed he was a figure that would visit him, a man who occasionally gave him advice and helped him with his school work.

“*Blank Man* huh?” It had been eight years since my witches had identified his presence, saying he was attached to my son.

“I know you don’t like him, Mom. He told me that too.”

“He doesn’t think I like him? Why is that?”

“Because you don’t,” he said matter-of-factly and tucked himself under the covers.

“I never *said* that.”

“You never had to.” He rolled over and coughed. “Goodnight, Mom.”

“Goodnight, Leif.” He was so intuitive. Or was that *Blank Man* whispering into his ear? I took a deep breath and closed my textbook, its cover filled with illustrations of combat injuries.

The idea that Joel’s angel, *our* angel, was one and the same as this *Blank Man* my son spoke of still sent a shiver through me. It’s visits were becoming more and more frequent, and all I could do was hope that something positive developed.

Chapter Thirty-Seven

I walked to the mess hall at 7:00 am to pick up my food and water ration, my mind running through the conversation I'd had with my son the night before. From the mess hall I went to the post-op where three men were recovering from wounds acquired during a raid that left some of the base's solar panels damaged.

"Hi Sarge," I greeted Sergeant Jeffery Jones, who was recovering from shrapnel wounds. The same man who had saved our lives eight years ago. "How's that knock you took on the head feel today?"

"I'm fine, Sara." He was a tough one. All the men and women here were the toughest people I'd ever met. Tough, but also smart.

"Glad to hear it. But don't try sneaking out of here just yet. The doctor wants to check that gash this morning."

"Yes, sir!" he replied with a wink and a smile. I liked him. If he weren't married, I would have scooped him up years ago. He'd be forty-four the following month but didn't look a day over thirty. He and I had our routine: flirt, flirt back. My face flushed a little every time, and I knew he liked that. He was exceptionally handsome, and just my type. The more I got to know him, the more I liked him. I feared I was beginning to lose the ability to just flirt.

"Thirty-five stitches and no local." I read his update. "Who are you trying to impress!" I smiled as I replaced his chart and moved to the next bed where a drifter, picked up west of here a month ago, laid on his side, his left leg badly mangled. "And how are you faring, Brad?"

"Been better." His smile was pained. "Maybe I should have let them leave me to my own devices." The army sent patrols out in search of drifters within a ten mile radius every week while hunting local terrorists. Of course Brad chose to join our group: left to your own devices meant left to die, eventually.

"Stay off that leg," I smiled. The patients seemed to take to my bedside manner. Perhaps in *life* I would have made a good doctor. Having studied with the local hospital in my last year of high school, I was grateful for what real life experience I'd gained.

That seemed like a lifetime ago.

"Sara," whispered Jeffrey from his cot. "How's Don doing?"

Don was the third patient in the far bunk. He'd been shot in the chest and lost a lot of blood. We pulled plasma from every available resident as often as we could, but lately we'd been going through it fast.

"He's still in a coma. Dr. Bren doesn't think he'll snap out of it any time soon either." I looked at Don, and bit at my lower lip. "He won't keep him on support much longer."

"Understood." Don and Jeffrey were good friends. Don had been shot over a week earlier on a patrol. It had been a mad frenzy when they brought him in. I hated to see the Sergeant so crestfallen. But understanding our limited resources was something we all had to come to terms with, in every aspect of our lives.

"He may yet pull through." Why did I say that? It was in my nature to comfort others. I knew Don had no chance.

"Thanks for saying that, Sara. You know, guys like Don are important now, more than ever," he began. "If good people don't survive, then our very humanity dies."

That was profound. I repeated those words in my head.

"Sorry, I shouldn't have said that."

"No, that was a beautiful statement."

"Still, I …" His head pushed back into his pillow and he closed his eyes.

"You never know, Jeff." I placed a hand on his forearm and squeezed. He smiled up at me, eyes still shut.

I left the recovery room and headed for the operating room, where I would sterilize the tools and wash down the floors. En route I slowed and stopped in the hall. I felt weak, my eyelids fluttering frantically. Then I was suddenly overcome by emotion, tears streaming down my cheeks. Upon wiping them from my face, the tears flowed freely, as though I'd just poked a hole in my own defenses. I cried silently to myself in the empty hall for a few moments before regaining my composure and carrying on. It was what I had learned to do. Just carry on.

Chapter Thirty-Eight

After a modest dinner with my son in the mess hall, we watched a movie in the nursery with the other moms and their children. The kids sat up front while the women talked in low whispers behind them. I almost always sat with Adrienne, Sergeant Jones' wife. She had managed to create a school, and teach all grades single-handedly, while overseeing the nursery, and helping the one chef train an army of cooks. She was a woman of boundless energy, and I respected her immensely. But on top of that, she had won the Sergeant's love and affection, and I think that meant more to me than all of her successes. She was a smart and modest woman. She wondered how, after hearing my story, I could hold anyone's achievements above my own. She made me feel accomplished, as did her husband. Though she held no rank, and Jeffrey was only a Sergeant, they were the power couple on the base. That was unquestioned.

After the movie, we all returned to our bunks. Lights out was 10 pm to allow the batteries to charge over night. Once there I felt a gnawing urge to question Leif on his apparitions. So while I got him ready for bed, I did.

"What does the *Blank Man* look like, Leif?"

"He's tall and shiny around the edges."

"What about his face, honey?" I pressed.

"I don't know." He fidgeted with his shoes.

"Well, does he look like anyone we know? Does he look like Sergeant Jones? Or maybe he looks a little like the Chaplain?"

"Is his hair dark, light, does he have hair? Is his nose long or short? Is he…"

"He said he'd have a face when I gave him one," he interrupted, looking up at me. "That's why I call him Blank Man." Leif returned his attention to his shoes.

That description rattled me. I unfolded his pajama top and pulled it over his head. *"He's dark,"* is how Carol had described him.

"Why is he here, Leif? Does he want something from you?" It seemed as good a time as any to get into it. I knew he was watching us, but as yet, no reason had presented itself as to why beyond the shroud of destiny.

"I don't know, Mom. It's just Blank Man."

"He hasn't given you any reason why he's here?"

"No."

"Leif." I adopted a more authoritative tone. "I'm asking these questions because I love you. Can you *really* not tell me why the *Blank Man* is here?"

"No. It's a secret, Mom, and I don't want to break a promise."

"A secret," I repeated. That made the hairs on the back of my neck stand on end. A sudden urge to protect him overwhelmed me.

"Leif, do you *love* me?"

"Yes."

"Then you shouldn't keep secrets from me should you?"

"But Blank Man said…"

"Forget what *Blank Man* said. If you love me you won't keep secrets from me."

"Okay." He shot a look behind me and to my left. I quickly turned. Our door was shut, the corner was dark. Turning back to Leif, I asked, "Is he here now? *Blank Man*?"

"Yes."

"Is he speaking to you?"

"Yes."

Jesus. My skin crawled.

"Listen to me, Leif. I'm your mother. No one can tell you what to do but me. You trust me right?"

"Yes, Mom." His eyes were still trained on the corner of the room behind me.

"Then tell *Blank Man* he should go, and leave us alone." I was testing the spirit's resolve. Pushing him to explain his intentions.

"I can't, Mom."

"Why, Leif?"

"Because, Mom." He looked in my eyes. My forehead creased, my eyebrows raised in expectation.

"Just *because*?"

"He says he wants to tell you himself."

"Ask him honey. Ask him to tell me then."

Leif's eyes shot back to the corner by the door.

"He's gone."

"Shit!"

"Mom!"

"Sorry, come here." Leif stood and walked towards me. I motioned for a hug and didn't let go for a very long time.

Chapter Thirty-Nine

Days later the base was under siege again.

"What's happened?" I asked as I approached the heavy chain link gate that separated us from the outside world. The siren wailed throughout the parade grounds, signaling to the hospital staff that casualties were on their way.

"Looks like they finally did what needed doing," Doctor Bren, jogging beside me, shouted victoriously.

"What was that?" I shouted back, slowing as we made the gate.

"A run-in with those terrorists. They're on their way back with a couple of car loads." Terrorists, that's what they called the marauding bands of misfits that continuously tested our defenses.

"We have casualties?" The question seemed redundant. The fact that we were called to the gate meant someone was hurt.

"Not ours, I hear." Just then the covered truck transporting the prisoners could be seen approaching. But they weren't slowing to allow the gate keeper a chance to properly unchain and open the gates. They were *accelerating*!

"Fall back!" someone called from the tower, and the hospital staff scattered. I landed to the right of the gates and climbed part way up the metal ladder on approach to the tower. As I climbed I watched in horror as the truck slammed through the gates, running down three of our medical staff in cold blood. It came to a sudden halt in the middle of our compound.

Doctor Bren was at the foot of the ladder. He drew his weapon and shot three times into the cab of the truck, sending each shot expertly into the body and head of the driver. I watched as the man slumped over the wheel. A moment of deathly silence followed. The doctor stood with his firearm raised, feet parted while his free arm held the rail of the ladder I was hugging.

Suddenly, men in tattered clothing leaped out of the back of the truck and raced for cover. The doctor ran for cover himself, firing at the men as he waved his medical staff to safety. At this point the tower guards fired down on the intruders. Men exploded on the ground as the rounds connected. Snapping out of my horror-induced daze and realizing just how vulnerable I was, I began climbing the ladder again, shouting over the hum of the machine guns to the tower guard.

Moments later, I saw two more trucks on the horizon moving toward us in a blaze of dust. Was this more of the same? Then I heard the radio crack on in the tower. "Have they made contact with the base yet?" It was Sergeant Jones' voice.

"They have. What the fuck happened out there, Sergeant?!" That was the Captain's voice now.

"They managed to hijack one of our trucks, but we've got their leader with us now and are in hot pursuit." Jeff's voice sounded confident through the static.

"Not hot enough, Sergeant! They've already managed to breach our gate and raise hell. I need your team back here now!"

Within moments Jeffrey's hummer burst into the compound, slamming into the west wall and crushing one of the terrorists into oblivion. I watched as the Sergeant opened his door and jumped out of the vehicle. I prayed he would be okay. Then I stared at the rear window of the hummer. There sat the leader of the terrorist cell. Impossibly, he seemed strangely familiar.

The melee was in full swing when the second hummer cruised into the base to aid in its defense. Four men jumped out of the vehicle and split up in pairs, keeping low to the ground. I couldn't say exactly how many terrorists there were to begin with, but I knew for certain that four of them were very, very dead.

In a flash of terror I saw a man approaching Jeffrey from behind and to the right, narrowly hidden by his parked Hummer. I anxiously tapped out instructions to the gunner in the tower with me, pointing to the target. The gunner nodded, aimed, and fired. The would-be attacker was thrown up against the wall, his left arm torn from his body. Jeffery, oblivious to the near-disaster, shot controlled rounds into another of the invaders making his way into one of the out-buildings. The man slumped quietly to the ground, hand still tightly clenching a door handle.

"Perimeter check!" shouted Jeffrey when all went quiet. The five soldiers stood slowly and crept around the compound for several minutes. Jeffery ordered one of them to secure the covered truck and the rest to drag the dead to a central point on the parade grounds. Our dead were tenderly lifted onto stretchers and raced inside. When we got the "all clear" I descended the ladder on shaky legs. Crossing the compound to enter the hospital, I noticed Jeffrey moving the prisoner out of the Hummer. *"Oh my God…"* I whispered to myself. I *did* recognize him. A quarter of his face burned away, years since I'd laid eyes on him, I could hear his voice in my ear. *Earl.*

Chapter Forty

The military trial was set for Friday. We buried our dead and burned the invaders' bodies, salvaging what could be useful to the base.

I still reeled from the idea that Earl was in such close proximity. Four days after the attack, I wondered whether I ought to visit him, if for no other reason than to gloat. I imagined what I would say to him, the things I would accuse him of at his trial. He hadn't seen me, of that I was sure, or he would have asked for me by now. I had so many questions for him. How did he escape the fire? Was he responsible for Sidney and Caroline's deaths? Did he get that nasty burn because of me? I hoped so.

Sitting in the daycare with Leif and five other children, my mind wandered. I went back to the day we lit the house on fire. Sidney and Caroline were at my side, Leif was just a brand new baby swaddled and hugging my stomach. I could smell the fuel and feel the cold metal cans in my hand as I poured the flammable liquid along the perimeter of the house.

"Mom." Leif was calling me.

"Yes, honey?"

"What's wrong with Sherri?" Sherri was a six year old girl whom he would play with occasionally. Today she was sitting alone in a corner with a doll in her arms.

"Sherri's dad died in the accident," I explained in a whisper. He had been killed when the terrorists burst through the gate. We hadn't been able to save any of the medical personnel that were run down.

"You mean when we were attacked?" Kids seemed to get to the truth no matter how hard you tried to sugarcoat it. Too many 'accidents' claiming too many lives.

"Yes, honey. Sherri needs your help. She needs you to be extra nice to her and to help her through this hard time, okay?"

"Okay, but Blank Man is actually helping her right now."

Jesus, *Blank Man.* The name always upset me. I believed it was because of the letter Joel had left – his suicide letter which mentioned a *Blank Man* more than once in almost every stanza of his poem.

"*Blank Man* is here?"

"Yup. He's helping explain to her what happened."

"What's he saying to her, Leif?" I leaned into him and looked at the corner where Sherri sat moving the arms of her doll up and down, nodding her head.

"He's just explaining where her dad is now." Leif sat abruptly on the carpeted floor and picked up a toy.

"And where is *that,* Leif. Heaven?" A surge of excitement overcame me. I felt I was on the verge of learning the mysteries of life after death. Where do we go when we die?

"That's not what I meant, Mom. I meant he's telling her where he is in life."

"What does *that* mean?"

"He's in a *baby* now."

Reincarnation. Okay, I'd bite.

"His spirit is in a new body?" I asked.

"I guess so. I guess that's what that means." He knew more than he was telling me.

A question arose in my head like thunder and I asked it without the benefit of forethought. "Did the *Blank Man* tell you if you were someone else before you were you?"

"I was. So were you, so were *all* of us!' Leif became very animated, almost angry.

"Okay, honey. If that's what you believe..."

"That's the *truth,* Mom! We come and we go and we come and we go, it's kind of stupid when you think about it. Why keep coming back for? It's like going to school all your life!"

That was pretty profound for an eight year-old. If this was true, then the Hindus and the Buddhists had it right. We keep coming back to learn more and more and when we achieve enlightenment we stop coming back. I'd read an interesting book on the subject while at the bunker, with my witches. This begged the question I had been struggling with a very long time.

"Did he tell you *who* you were before you were you?" I asked again.

"Uh-huh." He moved a toy wagon up his left leg and down his right.

I asked because I'd been harboring a theory of my own that the witches hadn't even touched on. Though it was confirmed his was an *old* soul, *whose* soul was the real question. Leif's right forearm bore a distinctive mark, a birthmark that ran full around the circumference of it. It was a faint line that had actually gotten quite a bit darker in the past eight years. It was just below the elbow.

"He said I was *Joel*."

Chapter Forty-One

He was Joel, his *father*. Those words would haunt my every waking hour for many days to come. The idea that Joel had lived on in his own son floored me. Yes, I had been playing with the idea, having read in some occult book that occasionally a past life will represent itself in the body of a new life through markings. Old scars, old wounds that carried their energy across the - whatever it had to carry it across- dimensions? Joel's arm had been removed at exactly the point Leif's markings were appearing. The coincidence was too uncanny to even absorb.

Never mind the fact that the spirit, or angel, or whatever you wanted to call it was still with us, with him, still guiding him in some fashion. I sincerely worried for my son's life, for his future. Joel's angel had not missed a beat. He'd let Joel die, and then he reconnected. I needed answers.

"Sara." It was Sergeant Jones calling me from just beyond the entrance to the day care.

"Yes?" I answered blankly.

"Could I see you a moment?"

"Sure."

In the hallway he took me by the arm softly and positioned himself between me and the door. "Jimmy told me what happened up in the tower. I just wanted to thank you."

"Oh yeah, of course." I struggled to snap out of my most recent revelation.

"No, really. I couldn't bear the thought of my wife and kids without a father and a husband in all of this. Thank God for small miracles."

"I – I couldn't imagine this place without *you*." I felt the familiar heat building up in my face and chest.

"Thanks, Sara, really. I was lucky to have had you up there."

"I'm glad I could help." My voice cracked. His face was only inches away from mine. I could feel his breath on my lips. My eyelids fluttered, independent of my will.

"My guardian angel." He smiled widely.

I would have felt uncomfortable in the moment if I hadn't liked him so much. I half expected him to kiss me. God, I wished he had. But I knew my place, and accepted his heartfelt thanks. Though this back and forth had gone on for years with Sergeant Jones, I still found it difficult to navigate. In *life* a man, or boy as it were, would profess his lust for me within the first ten minutes of meeting me. I knew I carried off a certain look that others found attractive. With the Sergeant, though, and his situation, he couldn't, or wouldn't tell me that in so many words. So, the game played on.

"Let's hope that's the last of the raids," I added when I felt I had control over my voice again.

"I'm sure there are more to this terror cell then the ten we stumbled upon." He turned and looked down the narrow hallway. "I'd like to get to them before they come looking for our prisoner."

"You believe you've captured their leader?" I switched gears and began fishing for information on Earl.

"Yes, he's admitted as much. About all he *will* admit though. He's in the stockade now. We've been questioning him for days. He's a tough one to crack." He seemed frustrated.

"I could talk to him." I didn't think. I just spoke. "I mean, have you tried that approach, with a woman?"

"No." He shook his head. "You would be willing to talk to that animal?" His brow furrowed and eyes narrowed. The mole above his left eyebrow hid within the deep creases of his forehead.

"What do you need to know?"

"Well, whether there are more for one - where they might be hiding out. Their numbers, things like that."

"I could give it a shot."

"If you're sure, I'll set it up."

"I'm sure. Whatever I can do. This place saved my life and my son's life. There isn't *anything* I wouldn't do to help." It was true, but at the same time I found myself excited at the prospect of seeing Earl in captivity.

"You're a good soldier, Sara."

"Thanks." I blushed. My knees wobbled slightly and I discreetly held onto the door frame to steady myself. I was often embarrassed by my inability to control my reaction to his presence.

"I'll contact you in the morning and let you know. If you'd like I can be there, in the room while you interview him."

"Maybe. I'll think about it."

He left me there with a smile and a nod. Back to his wife and kids. I was sure I'd given myself away this time. Shake it off, Sara I told myself, and walked back into the day care.

Chapter Forty-Two

Sergeant Jones set it up. I was to come face-to-face with Earl. I would confront him alone. No need for the Sergeant to know I'd ever had anything to do with this asshole. Our interrogation was scheduled for the morning. After a restless night in my bunk where I ran through all of the things I'd say, I felt I was ready. The Sergeant picked me up at my room after I left Leif at day care.

"You're still good with this?" he asked as we walked the halls.

"I am." How would he react to seeing me? Although eight years had passed, I hadn't really changed.

We walked across the compound and entered the stockade where Earl was sitting on a cot in a cell. I took great pleasure in seeing him caged.

"Prisoner!" shouted Jeffrey. "It's time!"

Earl did not acknowledge us. The Sergeant looked at me and whispered into my ear. His hot breath tickled the flesh of my neck. "Would you like me to remain here?"

"No. If he hasn't told you anything yet, he won't talk for me if you're here."

"Be careful. He's very unstable."

"I'll be fine. He's in a cage. He can't hurt me."I whispered back.

"Very well. There's a pad and pen here if you feel the need to write anything down. Remember what we're looking for: numbers, location, strengths, weaknesses."

"I've got it, thanks." With that he left me in the small room. It smelled of sweat and blood. The room itself was little more than a closet. I sat down on the wooden chair and picked up the pen and pad.

Earl shifted in his cell; he was visibly uncomfortable. He had put up quite a fight when they took him, and no doubt his swollen cheek and closed eye were the result. It was especially strange to see him, someone from my past, like this. He was a grown man, no longer the untamable teenager. With so many of my friends from the past gone, I often wondered what they would look like when I studied my reflection. Now here was Earl, eight years older. The others would remain forever young in my memory. Joel, Caroline, the whole group. I was thankful for having had the opportunity to grow as a person, to grow up at all.

"Hello, Earl," I said. This got his attention. No one had been able to get a word out of him, let alone his name. He squinted at me.

"You *know* me? You know my *name*?"

"Look at me, and tell me you don't know me." I would enjoy this moment.

He looked up and then sideways, his face permanently etched with the reminder of the fire he'd survived. The fire I'd set. His left eye swollen shut from a more recent injury.

"*You*," he growled.

"Surprised?" I asked, with every bit of pride I could muster, sitting up straight.

"Sara," he said, his voice trailing. "How the *fuck* did you manage to get yourself to this place?"

"Ha! I could ask the same of you. I never would have guessed you've been the one sneaking around like an animal, causing us so much grief." I leaned closer to the bars. He leaped, salivating, but was restrained by a chain that held his wrists and ankles to the far wall. He let out a shriek, jerking back to the cot. My heart jumped out of my mouth despite my earlier confidence.

"Murderer!" he shouted. "You *bitch*! You fucking *murdering* bitch!"

The door to the building opened a crack and I waved the guard off.

I'd made peace with myself over what I'd done. I'd never regretted it, and I never would. Earl and his cronies, Fred and Kevin, had raped Caroline and executed Seth.

"Does it still hurt?" I asked him, tracing my fingers along the side of my face. The burn was a horrible scar to look at. "Has it hurt all these years? God I hope so."

"You fucking bitch…" That was all he could muster. I was almost happier knowing that he had survived all this time, suffering daily for his cruelty. "You *fucking* bitch…." He was quieting down now.

"You don't need to tell me anything, Earl. I don't give a shit about your ragtag little band of terrorists."

"Is that what they call us? Terrorists?" He seemed offended, shifting around on his cot, rattling his chains.

"Of course. You could have approached the base and asked for salvation, but you, the pig-headed, arrogant prick that you are, thought you could have it all."

"You don't know what you're talking about."

"I know *you,* Earl. That's all I need to know."

"You know *shit.*" Drool ran from a split in his lip, touching his knee before it left his mouth. "What do you know? I've been a leader. I've managed to build an *Empire*!"

"You've managed to find yourself *here*. Like the criminal you are." Leaning in again, I whispered, "You know you'll die here, don't you?"

"I am the leader of *many*. I have many people answering to me."

"You have *shit*. What did you do? Hide in the woods? That's not leadership. That's being an animal. Hiding from civilization, taking what you need from others. You're no better than a dumb animal. You're the emperor of nothing!" I forced a laugh to further taunt him.

"What do you know? I have an *army* waiting for me."

"Hiding naked in the trees no doubt, waiting for their *emperor* to return with some scraps." I could see he had become increasingly agitated by my comments. Perhaps I would get information from him after all.

"We are not animals! We have it better than we did with *Joel*. We live in a castle!" He stared at me through the iron bars, his one good eye trained on me. "A *castle*!"

I had learned the local geography during my eight years here. There was only one place I knew that was ever called a castle. It was the Castle Peaks, the rough survey of rock that jutted up into the horizon some three hundred feet. When the sun set in the west, the resulting silhouette would form the illusion of a castle on a ridge.

I stood up and smiled. "The Castle Peaks, Earl?" His face collapsed and any color that might have been present faded to white. "Is *that* where we should go?" I studied his reaction.

"I don't know where that is," he said automatically, crossing his arms in front of him. "I don't know where that is."

"I think you *do,* Earl. I think that's where your little hideout is and I think I'll let the Sergeant know so he can take the soldiers there and bomb the living *shit* out of it." I knew the Sergeant would approach those frightened and demoralized people with a solution rather than firepower, but for this purpose, I needed Earl to believe they would use force. "You've just become your own worst enemy. And now, not only will *you* die a wretched soulless piece of garbage, all your little accomplices will too."

Earl studied his hands, clenching his fists. Snapping sounds echoed off the bars from his knuckles. He would repeat this over and over. "You know," he began very solemnly, "Seth *begged* for his life. Before I had Kevin gag him. He kicked and kicked in his noose until he strangled to death. I thought it fitting. Just like his buddy, Gil. And then there were Caroline and Sid, I came upon them in the backyard, having escaped your little Barbeque."

He was trying to hurt me now. A last ditch effort to come out on top. But I had always wondered who had murdered Caroline and Sid, and so, morbidly I listened.

"Caroline was coughing from the smoke while Sid tried to wave it away from her face. I watched them kneel down, behind the pool house and realized the fire was no accident, that you three had planned it. They were outfitted with heavy bags full of provisions and hauling the four gallon containers of water. I waited for you to show up so I could take you all down at once. But when you didn't, I decided to ask them myself where I could find you."

My eyes burned as I listened, remembering the night, the explosion, my friends.

"I was able to catch them by surprise. Caroline stuttered something and Sid was so confused. '*Surprise!*' I said and shot the pistol out of his hand. Then I turned the gun on Caroline and asked where you were. '*Where is she? Where is that bitch*?' I asked. Sid tried to jump me but I put him down with one shot. Then Caroline jabbed her knife into my foot and I shot her." He laughed callously. "That foot never really healed right." He showed it to me, lifting the heavy chains.

"You're *garbage*, Earl." My chin trembled, my face soaked in tears. I wiped them away with both palms, sucking in a deep breath.

"Maybe," he allowed, lowering his foot. "But I am a survivor, like you. I took what I could carry from them, and made my way to the barn garden where I camped out for months, hoping one day you would show up, so I could finish you off."

"But I didn't," I said defiantly.

"No, you didn't." He seemed almost respectful with that statement. "And what happened to that baby of yours?"

"Never mind my baby."

"Come on, we're just catching up here."

"Fuck you, Earl." I stood.

"So, you'll tell your Sergeant about my hideout and then what?"

"*You'll* hang."

"I suppose I will." His head bobbed up and down. Something about him had changed over the course of our conversation. He seemed somehow more relaxed, more in control of himself. I wanted him panicked, afraid of his fate.

"You'll hang as an example. But no one will come to your funeral. Your body will be burned to ashes. No one will avenge your death, no one will care. You will not be martyred. You will only cease to exist." I walked to the door and knocked for the guard. "You go to hell, Earl, and you *stay* there."

Chapter Forty-Three

The operation went off without a hitch. The soldiers stormed the hideout of Castle Peak. A few men were shot in the assault. But when they entered the rocky cavern, they found a community of women and children.

"They were frightened, but glad to see us all the same," Sergeant Jones remarked as we sat in the mess hall the night of the raid, chewing on a stick of meat that had been dried and stored in one of the underground lockers years before. "They're in the hospital now, with their children."

"I heard. I'm supposed to help tomorrow with the dental exams. That's incredible. How many were there?"

"Eight women, ranging in age from seventeen to forty-five, but we'll gather that information along with their names, where they originated and how long they'd lived at Castle Peak."

"And the children?" I felt awful for the children. I thought of Leif living under Earl's rule, in that place, and it made me sad.

"Some seventeen kids, from newborns right up to six years old. They were living like animals, their clothes rags. And the dysentery. *Jesus*. They were dehydrated as well. I think that's what pushed Earl to make this last stand against us." He paused to drink from his cup. "It's a good thing you did in there. You got exactly what we needed from him. You're a good soldier."

I loved it when he called me that. "I'm here to serve," I said, sending him a weak salute.

"It's incredible that you knew him too. That you *lived* in that house with him and your friends. That's *unbelievable*." He meant it too; it *was* pretty unbelievable, after eight years, that Earl had taken the same direction I had, at least physically. Of course, our lives could not have ended up more differently.

"There's lots more to that story I haven't told you, but now that he's here, I'd like to volunteer more information. More crimes he committed against my friends, which he's never answered for."

"He'll hang for what he's done regardless. But if it will bring you peace, we'll hear it at his trial."

We rose and left to go our separate ways, him to his wife and kids, and I to the daycare to pick up Leif. The children were practicing a play for the coming holidays. It was nice to celebrate the holidays again. All that time at Joel's house, we'd celebrated just one birthday. God, it seemed like several lifetimes ago. Funny, that thought brought back what Leif had said about reincarnation. What if hanging Earl wasn't the end of Earl?

"Sara!" It was Jess, a girl from the daycare staff. She was waving at me from across the compound while running in my direction. "Sara!!"

"Yes, Jess? What's up?"

"It's Leif, Sara."

My heart stopped. "What about Leif?" I felt a distinctive pain in my chest and my left arm began to tingle. If anything happened to Leif, *I would not survive*, I knew this.

"He's missing."

Chapter Forty-Four

Where was my son?! The *Blank Man* was to blame for this. Or the angel, or whatever it was. That omnipotent presence which had embedded itself into my life like a tick, preaching destiny to my boyfriend, and now, to his son. What if Leif's destiny had him running away from here, from me? Panic rising, I gathered myself up and ran towards the daycare, Jess hot on my heals. I was trying to rationalize where Leif could be. Could he have wandered off on his own? It wasn't like him, and this certainty was causing my anxiety to grow exponentially.

I stopped Jess at the door to the day care to catch my breath and turned her to face me. Her eyes were red and teary.

"Don't blame yourself, Jess. He's somewhere. We'll find him." I didn't want her burdened by guilt. I needed her to be sharp, to remember everything. She nodded and smiled.

"I need you to tell me exactly what he was doing and where he was situated in the room the last time you saw him." She nodded again and we moved into the daycare. It was empty now. The rehearsal had ended and the group disbanded. I scanned the room for Leif's favorite toys.

Jess pointed toward a corner next to a toy chest. "That's the last place I saw him. He was sitting on the chest and playing with a toy, talking to it."

"Okay, good. Do you remember what time that was?"

"It must have been just after seven, Sara. We had finished a snack for break, so it must have been 7:15."

I walked to the corner and picked up a doll. It was a soldier doll, twelve inches tall. I studied it for a moment. "And you checked my room, and the washrooms?" I asked her.

"I checked everywhere I could think to check before I found you."

"We need to announce this to the base." I said. "I'm going to call the Sergeant." I picked up the intercom and dialed Sergeant Jones's room number. When he answered I quickly told him what I knew.

"I'll send an announcement to the base. We can mobilize a search party right away. Sara, it'll be okay, we'll find him tonight. He's probably just hiding somewhere."

"Thanks. Thank you." I was becoming frantic, I could sense it. My resolve was starting to crack.

"Sara, meet me at the hospital. We'll start there."

I hung up and went to my room for a final check. I was hoping I'd see him sitting on his bed, waiting for me to take him for a bath or change into his pajamas. He was not there.

"CODE AMBER. SEARCH PARTIES FORM IN THE COMPOUND. REPEAT CODE AMBER." The base had several codes for search parties, and several search parties designated to each code. In the case of a "*code amber*", everyone was involved.

Chapter Forty-Five

What felt like hours took no more than twenty minutes. The search groups were designated to specific sites. My group searched the perimeter in case Leif had found a way out. My eyes focused on every inch of ground as we followed the fence line, looking for something he may have dropped, some escape route he may have invented. All I saw was dirt, dry and dusty.

Finally, the soldier in charge of our crew heard a crackling sound on his walkie-talkie. I rushed forward to hear the news, full of dread. "We've found him."

"Roger that."

I waited.

"He's in the stockade." The stockade? "We will reunite him with his mother at the hospital." With that I set off running.

He had been found by one of the soldiers in what should have been a locked stockade, sitting opposite Earl. They told me he was unharmed. Although he had not a scratch on him, I knew Earl, and I knew he had more than one way to hurt a person. They had not been able to get an answer out of Leif as to how he had ended up there.

After we were reunited, Leif and I went to the showers where I washed and dried him and took him to bed. I was silent the whole time. He knew he had done something very wrong. I was fighting back tears of joy, but also anger. Why had he gone to see Earl?

In our room I asked these questions after tucking him in.

"It was Blank Man. He showed me where to go, where the key was hidden and…"

"You do everything the *Blank Man* says?"

"Mostly." He shrugged, as though the question were somehow silly.

"What have I told you about the *Blank Man*? Haven't I made myself clear? You do what *I* say, and tell me everything *he* says."

"He's not trying to hurt us, Mom."

"Oh, really? Having you break into the stockade and then hold a conversation with a dangerous prisoner isn't trying to hurt you?"

"He is in *jail,* Mom. He couldn't hurt me." His head pushed further into his pillow as he became more uncomfortable with the conversation. "He said he knew Daddy."

Goddamn that Earl. "How does he know who *you* are?" I asked. "Did you tell him I was your mother?"

"That's the first thing he asked when I got there."

"So you told him."

"Uh huh."

"What else did you tell him?"

"I don't know. I didn't really do much talking."

"What did *he* talk about?" I felt a sudden chill and rubbed my arms as I sat at Leif's bedside.

"He said you were all friends."

"I was *never* Earl's friend, Leif. We all lived together before you were born, but I was never his *friend.*"

"He said you were. He said he saw Daddy in me. That I had his eyes and his nose."

"That's true: your daddy was a very handsome man. And so are you. And you're smart too."

"Like you, Mom?"

"Sure Leif, like me."

"That's what he said, that you were a very smart lady." A compliment from Earl. That seemed unlikely, but Leif had no reason to lie to me.

"I still don't understand why the *Blank Man* sent you to see *him.*"

"He said I should know my enemy." My spine tingled.

"Did your *Blank Man* tell you why *Earl* was your enemy?"

"No, he just said *I should know my enemy* and then took me to the jail."

"Well, you don't have to worry about Earl becoming your enemy. In a few days he won't be able to hurt anyone ever again."

"That's not what Blank Man told me."

"Go to sleep, Leif. Sweet dreams, and remember, I love you."

"I love you too, Mom."

Leif fell into a deep sleep while I remained wide awake, wishing away the *Blank Man.* I watched his chest rise and fall, grateful he'd been returned to me unharmed. But the crazy circumstances that had taken him from me in the first place baffled me. Could I really believe in *Blank Man*? Was this spirit trying to harm my son? Were my witches wrong? Just as these thoughts circled through my head, I saw him. A shadowy figure materialized at the end of Leif's bed.

Chapter Forty-Six

I knew it was him. There was no face, just a form. And as quickly as it appeared, it vanished. Still I knew this was it. The same apparition that had caused so much heartache for myself and my friends so long ago. And now was controlling my son, guiding him right into the arms of my enemy. *"Know your enemy"* it had told Leif, but Earl was *my* enemy, not Leif's. Besides, Earl would be hanged in just a few short days. Then I remembered the words that had been passed on to me through Leif. *"We all come back."* A shiver overtook me at the memory. To think Earl might reemerge as some unsuspecting mother's newborn made my blood run cold.

Something more began to work its way into my head as the thought evolved. What if I was interpreting this the wrong way? What if he escaped from his cell? What if he reestablished an army and came back? I couldn't imagine that in his weakened condition he would have any hope of breaking free. So why did this thought continue to haunt me?

Checking once more to confirm that my son was asleep, I left the room, locking the door behind me. I found myself walking in the direction of the hospital. What if the women and children we'd taken in actually felt some twisted affection towards their captor? What if one or all of them decided to free Earl? Jesus, that was a concern. My pace picked up, and I began running across the compound towards the hospital. The clouds were gathering overhead, grey and black. It would rain very soon.

When I reached the hospital I threw open the doors and they crashed against the walls. The refugees were startled, as were the doctor and nurses. I scanned the large room and performed a head count.

"Sorry," I apologized. "Is everyone here?"

"What do you mean, Sara?" The doctor approached me from his desk.

"The refugees," I answered. "Are they all accounted for?"

"Yes, I believe so. Sonja, could we have a headcount please?" Sonja nodded.

"What's this about, Sara?" He looked concerned. I rubbed at my arms. It was a cool night, and with the promise of rain I felt a chill rise in me.

"Just a hunch, Doctor."

"Everyone is accounted for," called Sonja. A wave of relief. I would have to talk to the Sergeant about my concern. "All but one," Sonja finished. My heart fell.

Shit. It would only take one. "Shit." I said.

"Sara, what's going on?" The doctor stood, placing his clipboard on his desk.

"Just a hunch," I repeated on my way out.

As I began moving toward the soldiers' barracks I stopped and turned to face the jail. What if I could stop it from happening? I decided to visit the jail first.

I entered the building, which was deserted this time of night. The one bulb that remained lit in the hallway provided barely enough light. But I could see all I needed to. The door was ajar. My heart stopped. My right hand swung up to soothe a searing pain, rubbing it away. The light above the door flickered, yellow. I looked out to see the windmills turning frantically against the wind. The scene seemed apocalyptic. If Earl was loose in the base, we were in real trouble.

Chapter Forty-Seven

Earl was gone. He'd been freed by one of the refugees. I explained this to the Sergeant, wrapped in a heavy blanket, my son at my side. "I'm certain of it." I continued. "They're missing one of the women from the hospital, a woman without a child. She's likely so brainwashed that she's gone and broken him out."

"We've got the perimeter under full guard now, Sara. If he's still inside the base, we'll flush him out." He walked to the window, staring out blankly. "This is our *fault.* We should have had a guard on him. And the refugees, they seemed so relieved to have been rescued."

"Don't blame yourself, Jeff," I didn't like seeing him like this. "Honestly, I'm afraid this is all my fault."

"*Your* fault, how so?"

"He gave it up too easily. The information about their hideout. He also knew we would bring the women and children back. He knew we might kill off the rest of the men in a shootout, but the women and children… he knew we'd bring them back."

"You think he gave up his camp just on the chance that one of them would free him?"

"Knowing Earl, yes." My head dropped, and Leif gently rubbed my back. "He is very clever, and the fact that he has no conscience makes choices like that easy for him. He played the odds and he played me, and it looks as though he's won."

"He hasn't won the war, Sara. He's only won a battle."

"Still, he's loose now." I looked at Leif, whose little forehead was wrinkled, his eyes big and sad.

*****

In our room I put Leif back to bed. It was very late, and he needed to sleep. I changed and got into my own cot. Turning on my side, my back to Leif, I started to cry. Why does this *Blank Man* not *do* something? What's the purpose of a higher intelligence if all they're capable of doing is guiding a person in the wrong direction? Why let someone like Earl continue to plague us? Part of the grand plan? Fuck the grand plan!

I felt a hand on my exposed shoulder and an arm wrap itself around me. "Don't be sad, Mommy." Leif crawled under my covers and settled behind me, hugging me. My hand reached up to touch his. "Everything will be okay." I wondered if he actually knew that, or if he was just comforting me in the moment.

"Thank you, Leif. I love you."

"I love you too. Please don't be sad." His logic, that I could stop being sad just because he wanted me to struck me as profound. I turned and lay on my back. He was right. There was nothing I could do except love my son, no matter what happened. I kissed his forehead. Leif adjusted and we fell asleep.

*****

I awoke with a start. My eyes flew to the clock over Leif's bed. 3:33 am. I shifted, slowly sitting up so as not to wake Leif. I sat on the edge of the cot and rubbed my eyes. Whenever I woke up prematurely like this, there was not much chance I was going to get back to sleep. This was when my mind would relive the horrors of my past. Images I couldn't escape ran over and over again in my head. The scenarios I'd lived through would haunt me, and tonight was no different. Feeling sick, I stood up, paced a moment and then lay down on Leif's bed. I breathed in deeply for four seconds, held for seven, then released over eight and repeated. Sometimes this rhythmic breathing left me dizzy, but almost always left me feeling better.

I sat up and crossed my legs. Eyes still closed, I straightened my back and pushed my chest out, rolling my neck. Opening my eyes I was confronted once again by an image I had fought so hard against believing. Sitting not two feet in front of me, cross-legged as best as I could tell, was *Blank Man.* He was very dark, a silhouette. I froze.

A sound very weak rose in my head. Someone was speaking at a distance. It became clearer the longer I stared back at the Blank Man. It was *him.* He was trying to communicate with me. His head cocked to the left and suddenly the words became very clear.

"Ask your questions." He was soft-spoken, and I had to strain to hear, but inherently I understood. I felt the hairs on my arms rise with goose bumps. This was my chance, I thought. This was the opportunity I'd been waiting for.

"Ask your questions," he repeated. What *were* my questions? I drew a blank. Oh shit, I was going to blow this. He must have sensed my anxiety. He placed a hand on my knee. It felt like nothing. Not cold, not warm, not there. The act calmed me though, and I was able to remember the questions I had wanted to ask.

First I asked a question I'd wanted answered when Leif first brought up the Blank Man. "Are you Joel's angel? *Our* angel?"

"Yes," he answered. His voice was soft. I guessed I'd always known that, but was relieved to know I was right.

The next question was broader and I hoped I'd get a more detailed answer. This was something I wanted Joel to ask his angel for me but never got around to putting it to him. "Why us? Why now? How is it *we* are the generation that has to live through the end of the world?"

The Blank Man's head cocked to the right. "*We?* You say that as though you are separating yourself from those that have come before you. *We* all come back. *You* have lived before, as your son has lived through Joel. You have lived through another, and another and another. You are experiencing this time as you experienced the Black Plague, the Second World War, the Inquisition. You have lived before as surely as you will live again to experience again and again. You are here now because you are an important means to this end. Leif is here now because he *is* that end."

Reincarnation. He was talking about reincarnation. *We all come back* was what he'd told Leif when he explained to him that he was Joel, his *father*. "Why would Joel die and be replaced by Leif? Couldn't Joel have done what Leif is destined to do?"

"Joel had lost what ability he had left in him to lead. His addiction had taken over."

"Did Joel have anything to do with Connor's death?" I realized I wasn't speaking but rather only thinking my questions now. "No, don't answer that," I said out loud. I was better off not knowing, I'd decided.

"What is Leif destined to do?"

"This is yet unclear."

"Unclear? How could it be unclear? Isn't destiny clarity by definition?"

"This is why we have such an interest in Leif, and why we held such interest in Joel. Destiny is not absolute. It is driven by fate."

"What's the difference?"

"Consider fate as an outside entity acting through a person, while destiny is brought about by the person themself. Both march towards a predetermined end, but how they get there can affect that end."

"Are you that outside entity?"

"I am only a guide."

Questions started jumping into my head. I felt an urgency to ask them all before he disappeared. "Why allow Earl to escape? Why has he not yet been punished for all he's done?"

"Earl too has a part to play, and fate has seen fit to allow this course to unveil itself in time."

"I don't understand. Who's running this show?"

"Show?"

"Yes. Life. What is it all for?"

"Life is a *lesson.* When it is learned, only then will you understand what it was all for."

"So, who's right? Christians? Buddhists? Islam...."

"Religion is a beginning. It was meant to be the teacher."

"But we messed that up didn't we?"

"Religion became a means to rule rather than teach."

"Why are you telling me all of this now?"

"Leif is a special boy. Protect him, keep him safe and I will guide him as best as I can."

"Better than you led Joel?"

"Joel had his own ideas. He fought me and he fought his destiny. I could not alter his path towards self destruction. He was filled with anger in the end, guilt, hate, frustration. It would be difficult to say whether he could have recovered enough to become leader in what must come to pass. With Leif, we start anew, and you can help. We can work together in this."

With that, Blank Man disintegrated before my eyes, black spots dancing on my eyeballs. I lay back and covered my mouth with my hands, staring up at the ceiling. "Holy shit."

Chapter Forty-Eight

Earl and his woman friend were never found. During the days that followed his escape, the soldiers hunted the surrounding area and placed men at the Castle Rock in case he returned, but he was never seen again. The Sergeant and I questioned the refugees from Earl's camp. Where might they have gone? What might they do next? They were all very forthcoming but for the most part none of them could answer our questions with any certainty. One interesting fact came from a conversation with the oldest of the women, Sybil, who had three young children from three different men. She said that Earl himself had not fathered any of the children.

"He blamed me, but when you force yourself on so many women and still, no children, you need to take a closer look at yourself."

"He's always thought of himself as the Alpha male." I responded. I had a flashback to the time I stumbled upon his journal. He spoke of destroying the homosexuals, and those unable (or unwilling) to have children. He saw repopulating the planet as every person's duty. Yet here he had proven he could not have children of his own.

The woman who had freed Earl had been young, and probably quite taken with her leader. Just seventeen, Mary blindly followed him in everything. Earl would have thought he'd have his best chance to conceive with the youngest of them, and so kept Mary in his own tent. His control over her had led to his escape, and so the most I could hope, is that we never saw him again.

*****

I took Leif to the greenhouse the day following my encounter with Blank Man. Leif had taken an interest in nature, and studied one plant in particular. He would go daily to watch this plant develop from a seedling to a towering tree. With each new development his amazement never ceased to amuse me. But on this day, I brought him there hoping we could talk. The greenhouse was humid inside, no matter what the season. The smell of pine permeated the place, washing away the distinctively chemical smell of the outdoors. Next to the barn animals, this place most inspired him. We walked through the aisles, pine needles and dried leaves from the fruit trees that lined the concrete floor pad crunching underfoot.

The army Chaplain, and our full time botanist, was a tall man of African descent. He wore army issue glasses, a buzz cut and always dressed with his collar exposed, making him readily recognizable as a man of the cloth. We'd shared a few brief conversations over the course of my occupancy at the base.

The saplings had taken off during the last six years, and upon entering the greenhouse one was reminded of the indigenous forests that once populated the local landscape. The man-made ponds that acted as fisheries bred trout, bass and also feeder fish like minnows. The idea was that the Chaplain and his team would tag the fish and place them in Elle Lake, which was a mere stone's throw from the base. This process was repeated time and again in a netted area roughly ten thousand square feet along the lake's southern shores. This area was under heavy guard to prevent poaching. The objective was to have the fish repopulate the lifeless lake. The experiment worked, as the fish adjusted quickly to the lake water, feeding off the abundant fly population that bred along the shores in the dead fish the Chaplain's team had placed for that very reason.

We found the Chaplain at one of the fish ponds, where Leif snatched up a shell from the rock wall.

"What are these?" I asked, pulling it from Leif's hand.

"Zebra mussels," the Chaplain replied. "They multiply like rabbits and eat all the toxins out of a fresh water lake. They number in the thousands in Elle Lake now, feeding along the lake bed, scooping up all the nasty goo that has collected there, suffocating the soil." He knelt down beside Leif as he explained the process, his palms clapping together as he demonstrated the mussels at work. Leif got a kick out of it.

"Sounds cool." Leif was truly fascinated.

"I'm excited about it," he agreed and stood up, patting Leif lightly on his head. "We're also considering planting a few of the hardier pines next month beyond the family housing buildings and maybe even the apple trees."

"Wow," I mused. "You were *really* prepared for the worst weren't you?" I shook my head in awe of the planning that would have gone into this place. Hundreds of indigenous seeds stored, hundreds of plants in seedling form, fish eggs, animals to breed, birds of a dozen different varieties, a bee hive. There wasn't much they'd missed. This base was like Noah's ark.

"It's a testament to man's understanding of his environment. Of course, if the earth rejects our efforts, it was all for not."

"Are you nervous about the planting?"

"Yes, of course, but I am also very encouraged. I believe life will find its footing again." He pointed down to where an ant hill had formed in a crack in the cement. "Look at that. Have you ever seen an ant, Leif?" he asked kneeling down again with my son for a closer look, careful not to disturb the colony.

"I've seen pictures," Leif said, bright-eyed. "Look at them all, Mom. Look."

I knelt down beside him. "Aren't they amazing, Leif? Did you know they can lift 10 times their own body weight?"

"Ten times! Wow." He was mesmerized by their movements. Each step taken with a clear purpose of survival.

"I've been feeding them since I first discovered the colony," he admitted, smiling ear to ear. "This is just another example of life reclaiming what it had temporarily lost. God's creatures. Resilient, aren't we?"

I smiled tight-lipped up at him and stood. "You must have a pretty interesting opinion on what's happened, Chaplain."

"Must I?"

"Mustn't you? Isn't *this* the end time? Haven't we been living through the Apocalypse these past nine years?"

"As a man of God, I can say with conviction that the end of the age was prophesized. And an ending of sorts did occur."

"And what about Jesus?"

"What about Him?" He moved to the raised pond and shook a can of fish food over the water.

"Well, I guess what I mean is, where *is* He?"

"You're referring to the Second Coming." His tone became tighter, like he'd been asked the question a thousand times. I moved closer to him while Leif remained behind, fascinated by the six legged insects.

"That's the *big* one, isn't it? *Where is He?"* He placed the fish food down, picked up a towel, wiped his hands and turned to face me. "Why hasn't He come to rebuild His kingdom? When will the thousand years of peace begin?"

"Exactly."

"I'll tell you what I've told those that attend my sermons. That I can only quote the Bible, Sara, I do not presume to understand God's plan, only to have faith in His divine will."

"No offence, Chaplain, but, isn't that a bit of a cop-out?" I flicked at the water abruptly with my fingers, frightening the dozens of fish into the far corner.

"Faith is a paradoxical thing isn't it, Sara? You suffer an experience, or a vision, or a miracle, however you'd like to categorize it, and you find faith. Look at me. I was a botanist for many years before I was called into the service of the Lord. I studied plants, right down to the atomic level, and do you know what I found?"

"No."

"God, Sara. I found God in those perfect, intelligently designed life forms. And imagine, if I could find God in a plant, God must be everywhere, in everything. I was blessed with new vision, to see God in *all* things. But just because *my* faith was secured, doesn't make it make sense to someone else. We all must experience our own epiphany."

I shifted my weight from one leg to the other. "I understand faith. I do. But Revelations spoke of this time, did it not? *Isn't* this the end?"

His bottom lip curled. "I guess not." He walked past me toward the vegetable garden and I followed, warning Leif not to move from his current fixation.

"So why destroy the earth if you're not going to start anew?"

"I'm not saying an ending didn't occur. But as for Armageddon… well, how could it be? Jesus has not revealed Himself to us." He turned again to address me. "According to Scripture, a great battle between good and evil must still take place. From what we know, evil struck the planet nine years ago. Perhaps in those nine years Satan has been recruiting his army while God has been preparing His."

"You think there will be more?" I shuddered at the thought. "You think *this* hasn't been enough?" I was becoming visibly shaken. "Chaplain, how much *more* can we take?"

"God gives us strength, Sara. Take comfort in that, and in your son." He'd noticed my composure had taken a turn. His hands on my shoulders felt reassuring, but nothing would remove the fear I felt in *another* end, worse than the one we'd just lived through, *were* living through. My faith in something greater, something that was leading us to some kind of salvation was shaken to the core.

Chapter Forty-Nine

Ten days after my discussion with the Chaplain at the greenhouse, I walked through the halls en route to the mess hall. I was late to meet Leif for a movie.

The hall was sparsely populated with late afternoon movie goers and filled with the aroma of pop corn. I noticed that the feature would begin shortly as I scanned the building for my son.

Having spotted him I walked to where Leif was standing, staring out the window at the rain as it punched into the earth, his palms flat against the glass and his forehead pressed against the back of his hands. The rains had been relentless for three days and didn't show any signs of retreat. Leif was becoming despondent, aching to go outdoors. Any drawn-out duration of rain like that sent my heart plummeting to my stomach, reminding me of the first few months after the bombs fell. Sometimes I wondered how any of us survived it: that claustrophobic feeling you get when you feel caged in, the sameness of the day to day, same people, same problems, same solutions. Gil hadn't survived it. I forced the memories from my head and focused again on Leif.

To think that my son would ever have to know such sadness produced a lump in my throat. Still, those days were behind me. I had every confidence the sun would shine again as it had after every heavy storm during the past nine years. I put a hand on Leif's shoulder and squeezed. He tore his gaze away from the window and looked up at me. I offered a comforting smile and he returned the gesture.

"It won't last forever, Leif," I assured him.

"I know, but I want to kick the ball around." His face sank.

I knelt down in front of him and he turned to face me. "Hey, why don't we use this time to do something together, just you and me?" I suggested.

"Like what?"

"Well, we could play a game." My mind raced to think of ways to entertain him. Then something pinched my leg in my jean pocket. Remembering the contents - I realized it offered the perfect solution. "For instance, have you ever played the game… pendulum?"

"Pendulum?" He'd probably never heard the word before. I inched the delicate silver chain from my pocket and let the heavy ring threaded through the chain fall from my palm. The chain fell taut, stopping eight inches from my hand, wrapped around my index finger.

Leif's little hands reached for the pendulum, a gift from my witches. It was one of my prized possessions, bringing me back to that feeling of having some control over my own destiny. He rubbed the silver chain carefully between his thumb and forefingers, moving down to the ring that dangled at the end.

"This is a pen-du-lum?" he asked, still transfixed by the shiny metal.

"Yup, well, it's a kind of pendulum."

"What does it do?"

"It can answer questions." This seemed like the easiest way to give Leif a sense of what would be asked of him in the future. If he felt he could control something like this with his mind, maybe he would believe that in all things.

I watched as confusion entered his eyes, forcing up his thick eyebrows.

"Well, I mean, it can't *talk*, but it can answer questions if you ask them." I had piqued his interest. When I situated myself on the tile floor, Leif followed suit. We were seated cross legged, facing each other with the storm outside as our backdrop. I held the chain up and offered it to him. "Take it and hold it as I am holding it."

Leif gently removed the chain from around my finger and wrapped it once around his own.

"Good, Leif," I congratulated. "Now, hold it out in front of you…"

I continued to explain how he could make the pendulum swing at will and to decide a circular motion meant *yes* and back and forth meant *no*. Then I had him ask yes or no questions, some about things he knew the answers to and others he would like to know the answers to. We sat there for more than two hours while the movie played, all the while Leif learning about the abilities he never knew he had. Waiting to be found, and used.

Chapter Fifty

From our first "lesson" in the mess hall, Leif's curiosity about all things paranormal seemed to explode. He became hungry for knowledge and I only hoped our library at the base had something to offer Leif in his quest.

"You can access the digital files if you can't find what you're looking for in paperback," the librarian reminded us. Tina was a short woman with an olive complexion who had once lived north of the base. She had told us that the collapse of her hometown had been vicious. While not directly hit by nuclear missiles, the city imploded about a week after the toxic clouds arrived. Riots, gang wars, police brutality, everything you saw on the news in *life* when a city suffered a black-out in their poorest sector was experienced tenfold city-wide when the public realized that they were never going to recover.

Tina's duties in the library were far greater than organizing the books. She also kept records for the base: a day to day journal of all operations, including people entering and exiting. Hers was a position I found very intriguing. She was writing a new history. She used the Gregorian calendar, but also, secretly, began a new calendar beginning at year *1* from the date the bombs fell. She called it AA – After the Apocalypse. So, we were nine years into this calendar, 9AA.

"Can you look up Buddhism for me? Leif is really interested in reincarnation and stuff like that," I said, never alluding to his true interest. I didn't want anyone to think Leif was born for some great role. As long as he knew it, and I knew it, that was enough.

"Oh, we have some paperbacks on that subject, Sara. Last row, numbers 500 through 510."

"Perfect, thanks, Tina." The library wasn't big, but it was certainly a treat to have. I'd read much of what it had to offer. I had checked out a few books from the digital archives, but those you had to read in the library at one of the three computer stations.

I found the book I thought would most intrigue Leif and checked it out. Tina gave me a distracted smile on my way through.

"Goodnight, Tina."

"Mmhmm," she managed, typing frantically into her laptop.

On my way back through the barracks, I ran into the Sergeant just outside the family housing buildings. My heart fluttered and I felt the familiar heat escaping through my cheeks.

"Oh, Sara," he said as he saw me approach. "What a coincidence, I was just thinking about you."

The corners of my mouth immediately reached skyward, parting my lips in a ridiculous grin. I must have always seemed awkward to him. The game had gone on for so long. I didn't know how to end it.

"Hi, Jeff," I greeted in a high-pitched squeak. He grinned back at me, always in control.

"Sara." His hand touched my upper arm, closing gently, guiding me into him until we were inches away from each other.

"What's up?" Our eyes met and I quickly looked down at my book.

"I wanted to talk to you about something." His eyebrows pulled together as I snuck another look at his face. "Huh," he continued. "I completely forgot what I was about to say."

"Oh, well. Whatever it was will come back to you." I smiled shyly.

He shook his head, the mole I longed to kiss buried in the confusion on his forehead. I was happy to keep the connection going. I loved it when he touched me. I was blushing again, allowing myself to daydream. Not that I had spent my entire time at the base pining for the Sergeant. I'd had one partner after we'd first arrived. It wasn't love or anything, but we did enjoy a physical relationship for nearly a year. His name was Mike, and he'd been killed in an accident that had claimed the lives of four men on the base. I was starting to get a complex. Every man I became involved with seemed to find an early end. I'd kept to myself since then.

I looked up again to study the Sergeant's face. He was looking down at me with an intensity that kind of scared me, but got my heart pumping fast again, like when I'd heard him call out to me. It was as though he were working something out in his head, something he was desperate to tell me. He licked his lips.

"What is it, Jeff?" We were hidden from view, tucked into a tight corner positioned between two buildings.

"I need to tell you something, Sara." His voice trembled slightly.

"You're scaring me, Jeff. What's wrong? Is something wrong?" I placed both hands on his shoulders, I felt his whole body quiver.

A tear escaped the corner of his right eye. My bottom lip trembled. This was it. This was the moment. The electricity between us was indescribable. My mouth parted, my lips felt full, tingling in anticipation. His eyes shut hard releasing a river of tears as his face bent down to meet mine. Every part of me tingled now, my heart was in my throat, my breath mixing with his as our mouths inched closer and closer. His lips were softer than I could have imagined, his kiss deep and probing. I gave myself over to him, our lips sealing our fate. A warmth overcame me that I hadn't experienced since that first night with Joel many years earlier.

He pulled away after what seemed like ages. My lips felt hot, my body weak. I'd never fainted before, but was sure what came next qualified. My knees absolutely gave out, my eyes fluttered closed, the book fell from my hand and I collapsed at the Sergeant's feet.

Chapter Fifty-One

I awoke in my bed. Jeffrey was sitting at the edge, watching me. I smiled and touched his lips with my fingers. He smiled back.

"I'm sorry," he said. "I shouldn't have."

"No," I begged. "Please, don't say you're sorry." I knew if he meant it this was over. That all I would have experienced of our unspoken love would be that one and only kiss.

"Sara, I'm married. I have children." His face was the picture of despair. Was he unhappy with his life?

"Are you happy?" I asked.

"Right now I am happier than I've been in years," he admitted as he took my hand in his. "Sara, I've loved you for so long."

"I know. I mean, I've felt the same way."

"What do we do about it?"

Reality hit me. He *was* married. He *did* have kids. This was a small community. This sort of thing didn't happen here. "I don't know." I wanted to tell him I *did* know. That he should leave his lovely wife and family and be with me. But how?

"I shouldn't have," he began again and I heard a mournful groan that originated deep in his chest. His body shook to a convulsive, silent weeping. I sat up and threw my arms around him, squeezing him into me. I cried with him.

"We can make this work," I decided. "We can do this." I pulled his face back with both hands, unable to bear the thought of never kissing him again.

He kissed me then, harder than before, pushing me back onto the bed. He broke the kiss after too short a time and stared into my eyes. I didn't let him speak again. I drew my face up to his and kissed him in desperate successive breaths. My mouth veered from his mouth as I kissed his cheeks, his nose, the beautiful mole on his forehead, his neck. I was feral with emotion. Almost unconsciously I removed his shirt and unbuckled his pants. His boots fell to the floor with a satisfying thud as I realized he too was undressing himself.

Then his hands were on me, pulling at my shirt, pushing down my pants. I kicked off my shoes and arched my back in a race to be naked against him. His hot muscled flesh pressed up against mine and began to move rhythmically. My legs wrapped around his, my hips moving with him.

We made love for hours, until just before Leif arrived back from school.

I turned to look at Jeff. His eyes sparkled to life and he smiled. "I know," he said. "It's late, I should go."

"What are we going to do?" I smiled back at him sadly.

"Let me worry about that." I liked that he took charge, but this wasn't all on him.

"I don't want to be without you," I started. "But I can't let you leave your family for me." My head rolled to stare at the grey brick wall.

"This has been coming for some time, Sara. This isn't going to be a big surprise to her."

"I can't be the reason you leave your wife." I didn't know which would hurt more; living with the guilt of being a home-wrecker or living without Jeffrey.

"This isn't your choice alone, Sara." He raised himself on one elbow and looked down at me. "I *love* you. I'm *in* love with you and I can't hide it any more."

How I'd longed for this moment, for those words to come out of his mouth. Still, it was not perfect. Not while he was married to such a wonderful woman, a woman I respected.

"Don't do or say anything yet, Jeff. For me." I hated the words coming out of my mouth. I only meant to keep his wife from suffering this revelation tonight. I wanted to think of a way to not hurt anyone, but knew in my heart that was a silly dream. This would destroy his family and make us outcasts.

"I'll wait, but not forever. Not again, Sara." He kissed me gently, left the warmth of my bed, sweat glistening on his back. Once dressed he opened the door, looked down the hall and popped his head back in.

"I love you."

"I love you." My heart leapt as I spoke the words. With a cautious smile he winked and closed the door behind him.

I had only moments to lay in bed reliving the incredible event that had just occurred. Just as I was happily retracing his hands along my body, this body which had remained untouched for so long, Leif entered the room and began to undress for bed.

"Hi, Leif!" I caught him off guard.

"Mom!" He turned and threw his shirt at me. "Don't scare me like that!"

"Sorry, honey," I apologized. "I thought you realized I was back already."

"How would *I* know that?" He continued to change for bed, slipping a pajama top on next.

"Doesn't Blank Man tell you everything?" I kidded. Blank Man and I were a team now, with one direction: to instill a sense of destiny in my son.

"*You're* in a good mood."

"You think so?"

"You're practically *glowing*, Mom." That was as good an explanation as could be arrived at by an eight year-old boy.

"I guess so." I sat up gripping the covers tightly around my naked body. I patted my hand on the bed beckoning him over to sit. He walked over, and plopped himself down on the mattress. He touched my face with his little palms, tracing my features with his fingers. It was something he'd done since he was a toddler. When he came to my mouth I pretended to bite his fingers and he jumped back, smiling. We were both in a pretty silly mood.

"Mom, do you believe in love at first sight?" This was a timely question.

"Sure I do, Leif. Love can happen at any time, in any place. Are you in love?" His face scrunched up again and his tongue stuck out.

"No!" He continued to brush my hair with his fingers. "But someone told me they were in love with me."

"That's fun, honey. Who?"

"Sherri," he whispered, his head lowering as if he was ashamed to have told me. Sherri was his little friend from school. Sherri was the same girl who had lost her father in the terrorist raids.

"Sherri is a lovely girl, Leif. She is only six, a little young for you. But in ten or twelve years, that won't really make a difference."

"Mom! You're not helping! I don't *want* a girlfriend!"

"Okay." I laughed out loud. It was nice to see that the human condition hadn't changed so much. Boys and girls, whatever age, were still suffering the same drama as ever. "Just let her down easy though, okay?"

"But how do I do that? She's always grabbing at my hand in class and trying to kiss me." His little features crinkled up at the memory of her shameless advances.

"Leif, you just be *nice* about it. You tell her you're not ready for a commitment and that you would like some time to think about it. Trust me, this way she'll get bored waiting and pick another little boy to have a crush on."

"Okay, that might work. Thanks, Mom." He bounded off the bed and jumped up into his own.

"Sweet dreams, Leif." Sweet dreams. I couldn't remember the last time I'd had a sweet dream, but if ever I would again, it would be tonight. It had been so long since I had tasted true happiness, and tonight had left me longing for more. As much as I knew it was a torturous decision that lay ahead of us, all I wanted tonight was to sleep, feeling the warmth of Jeff surrounding me.

Chapter Fifty-Two

It had been two days since I'd heard from Jeff and I was becoming increasingly alarmed at the signals I was receiving. Every time our eyes met out in the openness of the parade grounds or in the crowded mess hall, he looked away. My heart fell sickeningly to the pit of my stomach each time. That he might have regretted our actions, gone back to his wife, told her he loved her and had decided to stay.

I had been on such a high the first day after our encounter. I had let him have his space while he decided on how to go about telling his wife, but had I pushed him away by not letting him break it off that same night? Did he think *I* didn't want to break up his unhappy home? I needed to talk to him, to tell him again that I loved him and convince him to do what was right for *him*. If that meant telling his wife everything and making a clean break to be with me then I had to believe that was the right thing to do. I deserved happiness too.

I was sipping coffee while sitting outside the hospital building between duties. Shielding my eyes against the sun, which had been burning up the clouds during the past week, I noticed Jeff strolling cautiously across the grounds towards me. I smiled automatically and thought I saw a smile on his face in return.

"Let's talk," he said abruptly, passing me on the bench and opening the door for me to enter.

My heart trembled and my stomach churned. My face sank as I passed through the open door and followed him down the familiar hallways and into the mess hall. He positioned us in an isolated corner. There were a handful of people milling about the hall. We didn't look out of place, but I felt very uncomfortable.

Standing across from him, I kept my head lowered. I found it difficult to look at him, hoping that if I didn't, I wouldn't read the bad news I feared he had come to give me. Then his hand was on my chin, lifting my head. I kept my eyes closed.

"Open your eyes, Sara. Please."

Tears escaped down my cheeks as I opened my eyes. His were hard, and all my fears were realized. My body shook uncontrollably and he took notice. I couldn't stop it. I was fighting the overwhelming urge to cry.

"Sara," he started, then paused. "Sara, please. You were right."

My teeth began to chatter, my chin quivering. The blood in my head pounded against my eyes, forcing more tears. Had I somehow convinced him to do the mindful thing and not follow his heart?

"Sara." He was reluctant to put his hands on me again for fear that the others in the hall might notice. I battled valiantly against crying out. My neck stiffened and a lump in my throat muted any attempt I might have made to speak. "Sara, please." He was embarrassed now by my inability to control my emotional response.

I wiped my face and sucked in a deep breath. I exhaled slowly and opened my stinging eyes. His expression oozed compassion.

"I love you," he whispered.

"But?" I managed, knowing full well something would follow.

"There's no 'but' about it, Sara. I *love* you." He paused. "And I love my wife." That was just as good as a 'but' to me. Where would I fit into that equation?

"You were right; she deserves more of an answer for my behavior. So do you." He leaned back and pushed his fingers through his short dark hair. "I'm confused."

"I'm in love," I said defiantly. "I'm in *love* with you, Jeff."

"And I'm in love with you, Sara."

"But," I said again, swallowing hard.

"Okay, listen, this is impossibly difficult for me, Sara. Yes, 'but'. But I love my wife. I went home after we – after, and there she was with the kids watching a movie and I realized I was not so unhappy. Not so much to ruin a whole family for my own selfish happiness."

"What about my happiness?"

"We can still be happy, Sara."

My brows met in the middle, confusion bubbling from within.

"I won't be a mistress." I blurted. I didn't want to sneak around, stealing a kiss or making love in secret. I would never get over the guilt of it. If he made a clean break, everyone could heal.

"What? No, I don't want that either. I want a solution. But I couldn't, can't do that."

"You *did* that already," I hissed.

"Yes, and I'm ashamed of it."

That was not what I wanted to hear.

"Then I guess we have nothing left to talk about." I couldn't imagine a more hurtful thing to say. With what little dignity I could muster, I left the mess hall, Jeff seated in the wooden chair. I didn't look back. I had been derailed from what truly mattered. My son, and his development into something great. That was my purpose here. I would never let my own petty desires for happiness intrude on that again.

Chapter Fifty-Three

The following week I made every effort to avoid the Sergeant while he made every attempt to find me. I found endlessly new and inventive ways of eluding his advances. I threw myself into teaching Leif the lessons I'd learned during my time with the old women in the bunker. It was all at once beneficial to both him and my state of mind. I spoke to the Blank Man, taking encouragement and information from him and relaying it to my son.

Spending so much time with Leif made me happy again. He had always been a source of happiness in my life. I'd look at him and I'd smile. It was just that simple. It was difficult to be depressed with a child who depended on your mood for their own comfort.

We visited the greenhouse twice a day and I let him sit with the Chaplain for hours at a time. He learned something new about the natural world every day and shared it with me over dinner. He also found comfort in the Chaplain's spiritual knowledge, pressing for more, asking questions and challenging him on his faith. The Chaplain was happy to engage Leif, and found their conversations very gratifying. One day in the greenhouse he confided in me that their conversations were as helpful for him as they were for Leif.

"It helps me understand my own faith when I can discuss it with someone as bright and curious as Leif," the Chaplain explained to me. "He is an extraordinary boy, Sara. He has questions that go far beyond his years."

"Leif has an old soul," was all I could reply. I wasn't sure if a man of God, based in Christianity, would ascribe to the idea of reincarnation.

"An *old* soul," he repeated. "That's an interesting concept. Not exactly what I preach. One soul, one life, one chance. That's the God I know."

"Is it limiting for you?" I asked.

"Was it for you when you *believed*?"

"I guess not. At least, not after the bombs fell."

"When did you lose your faith, Sara?"

"I don't like to say I lost my faith. It just evolved along with my experiences."

"It changed to suit your needs?"

I smiled up at him, his dark features thoughtfully smiling back at me.

"You know, I almost want to tell you a big secret," I nodded. "To get your take on it."

His eyes brightened. "But?"

"Well, the secret's really not mine to tell." My eyes fell to the cement floor which was slowly being overtaken by a crawling vine of some design.

"I won't press you, Sara. If you feel I could benefit you by telling me, you will."

"You're Catholic, so if I told you, you couldn't tell anyone else?"

"That's right. My confessional is absolute." He stopped and turned to face me. I stopped too to meet his gaze. "Sara, if you want to come see me tonight, I will sit with you and listen. If you'd like me to comment I will and if not, I will remain silent."

"I'll consider it." It would be nice to have an accomplice in Leif's on-going education. The Chaplain placed a hand on my shoulder and grinned widely.

"You let me know. It doesn't have to be tonight. I'm not going anywhere."

"Thanks." We walked towards where Leif and another boy were watching the fish dart back and forth in the raised pond as they flicked the waters' surface with their little fingers.

*****

That night, at dinner Leif questioned me about my conversation with the Chaplain.

"What were you talking about, Mom?"

"Oh, just the same kind of stuff the two of you discuss." I stacked our trays together and placed them on the neighboring table. I looked around and I could see Jeff and his family behind us. My face hardened as I turned back to my son. It had been excruciating being trapped in such close proximity to the man who had broken my heart, his wife, and his children. I had even thought about leaving. My primary concern was of course Leif and he was the only thing that kept me here. But every day I saw Jeff, the thought again reentered my head. Leif could apparently tell from the crease in my brow that I was preoccupied.

"Do you want to tell Chaplain about Blank Man?"

Jesus, was he reading minds now? I leaned into him and lowered my voice.

"What would you think of that, Leif? Would you want him to know?"

"I think he already knows actually." He finished the last of his granola bar and threw the packaging onto the trays.

"He knows? You told him?"

"No, I didn't tell him. But I have a feeling he knows. It's like he can sometimes see him, 'cause sometimes Blank Man sits with us when we're talking and gives me questions to ask."

"What makes you think the Chaplain can see Blank Man?"

"Sometimes he goes like this." Leif squished up his face, his nose shrinking as his cheeks rose and eyes squinted. "And looks in Blank Man's direction."

That was interesting.

"But Blank Man says not to tell."

I looked up turning in my seat.

"He's not here, Mom. He's just saying it in my head."

"Okay, honey. We'll follow Blank Man's instructions then."

"You *like* him now, huh?" A mischievous smile crept across his rosy cheeks. His head nodded as though answering his own question.

"Oh, yeah, we're like this now," I said with a smile, my fingers crossing. Leif smiled brightly and a giggle escaped his lips. I in turn snorted and we both started laughing. It was the kind of laughter that escalates the more you look at one another. People in the mess hall turned and looked, but this only made us laugh harder. Jeff was watching but I didn't care.

The muscles in my face ached after laughing so hard. I hadn't laughed like that in a very long time. I knew I had been wearing a frown almost every moment I wasn't with Leif. But right now I felt alive, and I would relish that moment in days to come.

*****

With the passing of another week I felt a little lighter. Time was healing my broken heart. I knew I couldn't feel this way forever. I had managed through my first love's death and this would be no different.

Leif was progressing brilliantly, becoming obsessed with meditation, taking a half hour three times a day to sit cross-legged, straight backed quietly humming to himself. How an eight-year-old had the patience for something most adults didn't have the patience to do I'd never know. I chalked it up to Leif being something special, something more. Just like the witches had prophesied. Like Blank Man had told me. Leif was going to be great.

It was in this state I found him one evening in our bunk room, seated on his bed, humming, eyes closed. But this time he did not break the meditation after his half hour was up. Nor did he break it at the hour mark. At two hours I became concerned.

"Leif," I said quietly from my bed, looking up from behind my book. "Leif, it's time to go to sleep, honey."

Nothing.

"Leif I need you to stop your meditation and go to sleep now." I put the book down and stood. "Sweetie, it's time for bed."

He did not acknowledge me at all. I gently placed a hand on his shoulder but was forced to snap it back. The electrical shock that I received was heart stopping. Amazingly, Leif did not budge. I positioned a hand above his head, afraid to touch him again. As my palm approached his crown, the hair on his head all stood on end.

"Leif," I continued, worried by this bizarre reaction. "You need to snap out of it, honey, please." I sat next to him and looked at his face. His expression exuded an absolute calm, the low rumble of his humming was hypnotic. I was careful not to touch him again but ached to hold him.

The humming got louder. Within a few seconds it was so loud I had to cover my ears. I got up and stepped outside the open door into the hall. I was scared to death at what was transpiring. There was no one in the hall to help me. I turned back to my son from the door way, his face glowing, radiating, and suddenly, as quickly as it had escalated, the humming slowed and with it the volume. I cautiously stepped back into the dimly lit room. Suddenly his eyes opened, the pupils tiny, as though he'd been in a very bright place far too long. I rushed to his side but stopped short of hugging him. I reached out a hand and it hovered. Something was pushing me back. We were like two magnets repelling each other. I could not get any closer to Leif. My palms felt hot and I pulled away. "What's happening!" I gasped, falling to my knees.

"Don't be afraid, Mommy." Thank God, his voice! "Don't be afraid." I stared at his face and realized the voice came from within him as his lips were not moving.

"Leif?"

His head turned slowly in my direction. His eyes found mine. Somehow I knew he was okay.

"What's happening to you, Leif?"

"Enlightenment."

REVELATION

The third book in The Judas Syndrome series

Michael E. Poeltl

To my family

And all my friends.

Memories are of the ethereal, and not the material world, that is how I know I am forever.

Leif Speaks....

I watch an army camp among the trunks of dead trees to the west from my vantage point at the edge of this rocky hill. The ruined forest offers modest privacy and even less protection should we decide to attack them before they do us. But the Sergeant and I have agreed that we are better suited to defend our position within the walls of our compound, rather than risk openly attacking a group so large and desperate.

My Blank Man is with me now. Blank Man is the name I gave to him when he first appeared to me at the age of six. I can feel his presence. Each time he appears the hairs on the back of my neck and forearms prick up. He is dark, and has no features save what I can make out of his silhouette. His voice is calm and soothing. Mom calls him my Guardian Angel, and he even has a halo of sorts. Not confined to his head, but surrounding his entire being. If I'd given him a face he would have one. But I have not in my twelve years of knowing him.

*****

Some months before I will be faced with the vision of an army at our doors, I find myself staring at the forests within our walls. They contain trees taller than our tallest building: pine, deciduous, fruit bearing, with birds and insects buzzing around. From the dust of my mother's Apocalypse, twenty years later, we have trees planted firmly in the soil. We have reestablished life where it was once devastated by a desperate, deliberate act of violence.

I have led a privileged life in comparison to those outside our fortified walls. To have grown up at all is a gift in the wasteland beyond our oasis. I have learned that life is a gift, and should be cherished, lived and experienced. Though experience often reveals itself as pain in this world, it is still purposeful, it still has its place in the evolution of our spirit.

*****

My name is Leif. I've been told that my father was meant for this end. But my father faltered in his attempt, afraid of this destiny, afraid of himself. It has been made clear to me that I was born to carry the torch - that the spirit of my father lives on in me. Though that phrase may seem cliché, it should be taken literally rather than figuratively. I am the reincarnation of my father. My angel has told me as much. And my mom has confirmed it, pointing out the bizarre birthmark on my right arm. It is a dark line that travels the circumference of the forearm, just below the elbow. Mom says this resembles a wound my father suffered not long before he died.

Part One
Chapter One

I feel that growing up here, on this military base, surrounded by protective walls and people, has helped foster my spiritual growth and make me the man I am today. It has allowed me the time and peace of mind required to meditate. It has given me the opportunity to learn from my long sessions of uninterrupted meditation, so that I can put what knowledge I pull from the spirit world to practice in this world.

For the moment, this tranquil existence must cease, as I have recently turned eighteen, and as a resident of this base, am expected to participate in a weekly military exercise. It consists of venturing beyond the walls of our stronghold, in search of other survivors. This usually takes two to three days, with the soldiers camping out in their vehicles overnight.

What weighs on my mind is that not every away mission is successful. There have been times which can only be described as disastrous: where they've returned with casualties, having exchanged fire with an unseen enemy, or worse, when we've lost the whole team.

I am to sit in on a 'ride along' with a battle-hardened group, some of whom are original members of the team assigned to this base twenty years ago. They have witnessed many horrors over the years: skirmishes beyond our perimeter, the defense of our walls, terrorist attacks that come in violent, random strikes.

I'm not looking forward to this experience, but know it is an obligation. It is a practice that has gone on since the bombs fell, and viewed as a necessary duty to bring in new blood.

My mom has gone as far as asking me whether she should talk to the Sergeant and have me removed from this rite of passage. I have told her no. Some of the residents see me as something of an outsider as it is, though I've been here longer than most. I do not want to give them anymore reasons to see me as different.

Anxiety over the possibility of a gun fight between my away team and an unknown enemy fills my chest. I breathe slowly and shake the adrenaline from my arms.

I have been trained in combat techniques: firing a gun, disarming an attacker, blocking a punch. These survival skills are taught to children ages thirteen through sixteen. Whether I am able to recall these learned skills when the time comes I can't say.

I arrive at the gates of the base and meet the men and women that will fill out our platoon. KC is to be our team leader. His small features and wire framed glasses paired with receding hair line and dark stubble create the appearance of being all at once menacing, yet approachable.

Four others complete our group. I am the only one experiencing this for the first time. Though I know virtually everyone's name on the base, they each extend a hand to me and introduce themselves.

"Gibson." A pale-skinned woman with dark short-cropped hair introduces herself first. I know her by her first name: Jillian.

"Hawkeye," a large, looming man tells me, grabbing my hand. I suppose this is a military nickname, as I know him as John.

Another man, one of the original military personnel, approaches me next. "Palisade," he tells me, "but you can call me Erick."

"I will. Thanks."

"Jasper," says a small thin man, reaching up to take my hand. "I'll be driving."

"Good to know," I reply, having a hard time placing this man.

"Now that you've met everyone, Leif, let's get you suited up." KC directs me to a building nestled under the east tower and takes me inside. Here I see stockpiles of ammunition and body armor. KC sits me down as he picks out a helmet, vest, fatigues and boots for me. I pull them on as they are offered.

"This will be your firearm, Leif." The gun is larger than I would have liked, but I know he would have reviewed my training records.

"A shotgun," I state, taking the heavy weapon from him.

"It gives you the best chance at hitting your target, should it come to that."

"Understood." The thought of firing at something other than an inanimate object gives me pause.

KC slaps my shoulder. "Don't worry, I haven't run into anyone or anything in my last three outings. I don't suppose we will this time either, but we need to be prepared for the worst." He winks at me.

"Thanks," I say timidly as he walks me out to the waiting Hummer.

*****

A few hours into our tour of duty we stop for lunch. We have travelled east today, following a monthly routine. The course we've taken is one of six surveyed eastern routes used since the inception of the away missions. Each plotted course has designated 'safe' spots where food, water and ammunition are stashed.

We exit the Hummer one by one, securing the parameter, careful not to make a noise. This safe spot is located at the center of a devastated village.

KC issues orders. "Hawkeye, take the rooftop. Gibson, you're on the left, Erick, to my right. Leif, you stay with Jasper and protect the truck."

I look at Jasper, who is rounding the Hummer. He grabs my arm and pushes me around to the back.

"Take up this position. Get on your stomach and slide yourself under the vehicle." I obey, thankful for the direction.

I wait, and watch. My heart is pounding against the pavement, my neck craning to offer me a better view of my surroundings. I study the buildings. I had ventured beyond our walls before, but never so far. Being in the middle of another settlement was strangely exciting. Reading about the past and seeing pictures don't allow for the 'feelings' I'm experiencing. Trying not to get too caught up in the anxious energy, I refocus on the mission at hand.

Not long after, KC returns to the Hummer, ushering Jasper and I out of our hiding places. "I've gotten confirmation from Hawkeye that the area is clear. We can eat if you're ready."

Jasper nods enthusiastically. I'm not sure I can eat right now as the excitement of the moment has replaced hunger with anxiety, but I will do my best not to seem rattled.

"Did you know, Leif, this is where the Captain is from, originally," offers KC.

Our Captain was a woman of great presence, but rarely seen outside of her home on the base.

"New Caesar, it was called. See the town hall beside us?" KC points to the dilapidated building to his left. "She was the mayor's daughter - comes from a long line of diplomats."

"That's why the base is still operational," says Hawkeye. "The Captain retained military efficiency, but gave civilians a sense of equality."

I like hearing about our Captain's past and enjoy listening to the soldiers speak so highly of her, and her accomplishments.

"The Captain thinks very highly of your mother, did you know that?"

I am a little stunned to get this information, but not for the information itself. "Okay."

"Strong women both," says Jillian, putting back the last of her water.

"And beautiful," adds Jasper. Jillian sends him a look.

I nod, embarrassed, if not a little confused over their affection towards my mom.

KC interrupts. "We all know the story of your mother's journey, and yours."

"No more heroic than any other survivors I'm sure."

"I wouldn't say that," KC disputes. "Your mother's story captured the hearts of everyone when they heard it, and even years later, when I arrived, it was one of the first I heard."

"Me too," Jillian chimes in.

"It's because it's more than a story of merely surviving, it's a tale of good versus evil!" KC jumps off the hood of the Hummer and swings around to face me. "And you're like this prophet or something, come to save us all."

I feel uncomfortable with his description, and with the others now looking on I feel I must defend my position.

"I'd be happy to see you all at my next meditation class, but don't expect any miracles." The group is silent, until I pull a coin from the back of KC's ear. Everyone laughs, including him.

With the mood now lightened, we pack up. Once we've refilled the rations at the safe spot I hop into the truck. Just as Erick is about to jump in beside me his back straightens and he turns abruptly around.

My heart skips a beat. I sense something is wrong. His aura shows him on full alert. He's heard something.

Erick shouts, "Go, Jasper. Drive!"

Jasper slams his door and fires us up the street. It's just Jasper and me in the Hummer. I turn in my seat to watch as the other four scatter behind a brick fence that lines the sidewalk in front of the town hall.

"We should go back," I say without thinking.

"We have our orders, Leif," Jasper replies dryly.

"Orders? What orders?"

"It may be nothing, Leif. Let them figure it out. We'll pick them up as soon as they've secured the area."

"I thought we did that already. Shouldn't we help them?"

"We have our orders," he repeats.

"What orders?" Frustrated, I go for the door and hear a click. Jasper has locked me in the vehicle. I pull at the handle. "What are you doing?"

"Just sit tight. It may be nothing."

Suddenly an explosion rocks the town hall, blowing what little glass remains out of the windows. I watch as my team huddles against the thin brick barrier, a shower of glass and debris raining down upon them.

"Shit," Jasper spits. He turns the car around.

I'd never seen an explosion like that before and the shockwave passing through my body leaves me stunned.

"Goddamn it!" Jasper is getting jumpy in the driver's seat. I blink and focus on the action beyond our windshield. KC and the others are focused on the town hall but I watch as a body rises out of the street.

Jasper notices too. "Jesus, they're coming out of the manholes!" He rolls down his window, opens his door, steps out and takes aim. Snapping one shot off after another, Jasper puts down the first figure sneaking up on our team. Then Erick turns to face the threat and fires on his attackers.

Soon everyone except me is caught up in the shoot out. I crawl over the bench seats and wiggle my way to the driver's side.

Jasper looks over at me. "Stay put!"

"I can help."

"We have our orders. Stay put." Jasper shoots me a look so hard I forget to ask 'what orders' this time. I lay my gun at my side and watch in horror as figures drop before our team's gunfire.

The fire fight does not last as long as it felt. Within two minutes the attacking sewer dwellers are downed.

Our group frisks the bodies and collects what useful tools they find. KC waves us over. Jasper nods at me and I get out of the truck.

"Don't forget your shotgun," he reminds me.

We approach cautiously. The smell of burning brick and wood permeate the air.

"We need to go down there," KC tells us. "They've obviously made a home underground. There could be more of them, but there could also be valuable items we could use back at the base."

"I'll go," I say if for no other reason than to get a reaction out of them.

"No, Leif," KC tells me.

"Why?"

"We have our orders."

"So I hear. What orders are those, exactly?"

"You are not to come into harm's way."

"A little late for that don't you think?"

"Perhaps, but let us keep you safe while we complete this mission."

"Why bring me out here at all?"

The five look at one another. KC explains. "If we had overlooked you for this you would have lost face with the others. Sergeant Jones insisted we take you out, but made it very clear that you were not to engage an enemy."

"So you're all here just to babysit me?"

Jillian steps forward, rubbing at the spot on her vest where she had been hit. "You're getting your experience, either way. You're out here."

"I guess."

"Let's get this thing done and move on," KC insists.

Hawkeye and Jasper disappear through the manhole. Jillian follows while KC and Erick remain with me.

"Erick, bring the Hummer to us."

Erick nods to KC and rushes past us. Our team leader looks thoughtfully at me.

"Leif, the Sergeant is only trying to protect the base's interests. You are a valuable member of our community."

"We're *all* valuable members," I retort.

"Sure, but there's more to you, and whether you know it or not, we're all counting on that." He lays a hand on my shoulder and ushers me into the Hummer.

I sit in contemplation. I know I'm being groomed by my Blank Man for some greater role. But I hadn't realized others were picking up on it. Perhaps since incorporating the deeper lessons I've learned from my angel into my meditation classes, people have talked.

A moment later Jillian emerges from the hole in the ground. Then, behind her, three small figures appear. She kneels at the manhole, shielding the children from the lifeless bodies of their guardians littering the sidewalk, directing them toward KC and Erick. They seem hesitant, but do as they are told. I step out of the Hummer and approach the children.

"This changes everything," KC says. "We go back to base."

I smile at the children. Their auras illuminate the grey day, though they each wear a grimace. I help them into the Hummer and sit with them. They are nonresponsive to my questions, but I believe they will be all right after a decent meal, dry clothes and a delousing.

After another sweep of the underground, KC is satisfied and Jasper takes us home. Nothing could be more welcome to our community than children.

Chapter Two

I regret the deaths of those children's parents, if in fact they were their parents. I couldn't have made it to where I am without my mom. In fact I am very grateful for all the men and women here. I am grateful for everything we have which those beyond these walls do not. I'm grateful for the new people that find us, either by way of luck or during an away mission. Mom and I were picked up on one of these missions when I was just a baby. *Destiny at work*, she has told me.

Each new survivor is tested and put to work where their talents best suit the base's interests. At the age of sixteen I was tested and given the role of morale officer. It is well suited for my talents and I find the work very rewarding.

I walk the inside perimeter of the base every morning, running my hands along the cool steel plating of the walls that keep marauders out, and those looking for salvation in. The buildings vary within our walls. A massive greenhouse has subsidized fresh fruits and vegetables for the freeze dried and frozen produce that stocks the kitchen's many storerooms and freezers. A stockade, which has housed many a criminal mind, sits adjacent to the front gates, which are heavily reinforced and have a tower guard on either side. The hospital and housing units blend into one another in a stream of dull gray brick. Nothing was built for its esthetic value, but rather for its sustainability and longevity. The material world has not interested me though, save those souls that suffer its harsh realities.

Mine is an old soul. Not only am I the reincarnation of my father, but I have lived many, many lives before this one. To avoid ego, my guide has not revealed those other lives to me, only nodding in response to my question of lives lived.

An old soul carries with it an unconscious knowledge cultured by their past lives. The vast majority of us cannot experience these teachings, but the knowledge is there, and can be drawn on through meditation. Wisdom of the ages refers to the wisdom gained by lives lived. Those that bring the wisdom of the ages to the waking world have learned how to capture that information, and pass it to the masses.

I am told that this knowledge, once gained, will excel the level of mental maturity in the person, causing them to exceed in all areas of study and seem enlightened. My own level of intellectual maturity has both amazed and frightened those around me. I know no different..

My enhanced state of consciousness upsets me at times, as my peers have a difficult time relating to me, and I to them. But I have found my stride, and hold meditation classes for all ages - helping them realize a similar goal of enlightenment. I can't help but wonder though, have I missed out on much of the human experience?

My Blank Man has spoken the names of great religious leaders that taught enlightenment through recorded history, referring to Jesus, Buddha, Confucius, Muhammad, Gandhi, Lao-tzu, Abraham and others. He mentions them, not to build my ego in linking me to them but, rather to build my confidence in their shared vision - *our* shared vision.

So much of what makes up this wisdom still waits to be discovered. The idea of it excites me. My angel has been a great source of knowledge, both that which is locked inside of me, and a wisdom that transcends my own.

Chapter Three

Besides my mom and angel, one other person has nurtured my spiritual curiosity. He is the one man I would like to have called father in my time here. Ironically, that man is a Catholic priest, *Father* Henderson. He is the Chaplain here, assigned this post just days before the bombs. The base itself was expecting a compliment of one thousand soldiers and their families to fill its newly renovated accommodations. But before that could happen, the Apocalypse struck.

In the Chaplain I have found a confidant who speaks at my level of spiritual understanding. Though his is confined to the limits of his Catholic religious tradition, he is a very enlightened individual.

We have enjoyed countless conversations and debates over the years. He has never treated any of my curiosities as trite or made me feel hesitant in asking questions about his own faith. He instead welcomes the arguments and questions, and enjoys feeding my hunger for knowledge. I respect him like no other.

We sit, as we have countless times before, in his greenhouse to discuss a vision, or a piece of information or method of meditation offered to me by Blank Man. The Chaplain doesn't know about my otherworldly mentor: Blank Man's existence is known only to my mom and I. But I suppose the Chaplain suspects someone or something is feeding me spiritually. Perhaps he assumes it is the figure he calls God. Either way he doesn't ask, and I don't volunteer.

"I've said it once, and I'll say it again, Leif. You are a gifted young man." He moves gracefully around a large potted fruit tree with his watering can.

I smile, embarrassed. Sometimes I really want to tell him all about Blank Man, but in sharing the knowledge my angel feeds me, I often do so in the guise of discussions and debate, questions and answers.

The Chaplain is a friend, though forty years my senior. His dark features hide in the shadow of the leafy tree as he rounds it a second time. His voice is deep and yet soft, the perfect mix in a speaker. He holds Sunday service in the mess hall to a large crowd of followers. Not all were Catholic, but they come to be a part of something bigger than themselves.

"You're not looking to steal away the rest of my congregation are you, Leif?" he asks, mock worry wrinkling his forehead.

It's true though. Many are finding my meditations and parables attractive, but this does not distract them from their Sundays with the Chaplain. I have no religion save the betterment of one's self. I offer enlightenment in place of heaven. I teach but never preach. My word has been heard before, but, like so many that have come before me, the words were bent to the will of man. Words thought to come from a God find power in men and power leads to want and want to war and, well, here we are. Nearly twenty full years into an Apocalyptic end. But, will it all *end*? I've only known this life. Aside from reading what paper books are available to me, and in the computer database of our library, I know nothing else.

I watch the Chaplain place the watering can down and manually pump water from one of a dozen wells drilled into the footing of the base.

"I think we should join forces, personally," I kid. He is a staunch Christian and though he appreciates my own brand of spirituality, could never consider leaving his church.

"We've had this conversation." He picks up the can again and moves around me. I turn to watch as he sprinkles the vegetable garden.

"You know, with the increasingly diverse religions I preach to, I think you're becoming more and more accepted by the masses."

"We're not in competition," I remind him. "We both work toward the same end."

"Saving souls," he proclaims, gingerly waving a fly from his tomato plant.

I nod and smile. The Chaplain rests his watering can on a table next to the raised pond filled with tiny fish, and we walk the length of the greenhouse.

"I see myself as something of a renaissance man," he tells me. "Like those great missionaries before me. Going to a strange land and preaching God's word."

Books have explained this process to me and though I respect Father Henderson, I have never found anything admirable in those men: missionaries riding a wave of violence against a "savage" race in a foreign land, destroying their spiritual histories, leveling places of worship and raising crosses in its place.

"You are a better man than those," I reply. "You have embraced other religions."

"Have I?" He stops walking and turns to me.

"You have allowed others to speak their mind," I remind him. "You do not turn them to your faith, but you feed their spirit."

He nods slowly, closing his eyes. "I learned long ago that pushing anyone into anything is counter-productive. If an individual wants to feed their soul I am available. If they want to rationalize God's word I will do my best to talk them through it, and if they want a funeral, I respect whatever faith they decide on and preside over it."

"You see? You're no missionary." My smile ignites his and he slaps me on the back, the sting meant as a reply to my – what he would call - cheekiness.

"If it's all the same to you, I'll do things my way, and you do what you do, because it seems to be working."

Father Henderson resumes his slow, deliberate walk and I follow.

"You know, Leif in all the time we've spent together, in all our conversations, you've never asked me why."

"Why?"

"Yes. Why."

"Alright." I cross my arms and lean against the trunk of an apple tree. The Chaplain watches me with a smile in anticipation of the question. "Why?"

"Why what?" His smile increases ten-fold. I break into a toothy grin.

"Maybe you don't have the answer then. Is that it?" I tease.

"If it has to do with my own faith, Leif, I can answer any question."

"Is that what this is about?" I push away from the tree, my arms unfolding. "Your faith? Why I haven't asked you why you chose the faith you follow?"

"It struck me just now." His hand wipes away beads of sweat forming on his forehead. "You've never questioned why I chose Christianity over other faiths. Why not Islam, why not Judaism, or Taoism or Hinduism."

"It doesn't matter to me. Your faith is all that matters. It has taken you this far, allowed you to preach peace. What difference would it make what you believed, so long as the basis of that faith was compassion and love?"

He sucks in a deep breath. "You are so very wise beyond your years, Leif." His head falls and shakes as he turns and walks toward the fish pond. "It's difficult for me to understand how more than one religion can exist. I mean, I've never been opposed to others' religious practices, but I always assumed I was right – that I was on the right path."

"So long as you follow your heart Father, you will never find yourself on the wrong path. You are a deeply spiritual person, and that alone will take you farther than most. What religion you believe is not what will deliver you into the light, but your actions in this life, and the reactions they set in motion."

"Leif, you make me question my very belief system." His voice becomes hard and distant. His hands grip at the edges of the raised plastic pond, dark skinned knuckles fading to white.

I touch his shoulder. "Father, don't compare one religion to another, or one prophet to another. Prophets are important, always have been. They are the teachers. To understand their words is to follow their light."

"Yes, and I understand my faith, and I understand that virtually all religions vie for the same end, to go to Heaven, or experience Nirvana – it's the same thing. But tell me Leif, why did I *choose* this path?"

"To each their own, Father. Your choice will see you through to that end. To introduce multiple religions is to introduce choice to the people, and all people of the flesh suffer the same end. We will all die, and if we've lived well and done good, as your chosen religion has taught, then whether we come back, or have achieved a level of enlightenment, our afterlife will reflect those actions."

"You talk of the afterlife *and* reincarnation. Which is it for you, Leif?"

"Both. Most will come back, and that too is an afterlife." I knew I was my father before I was me. Had my father followed Blank Man's guidance as I am, I suspect I would not exist as Leif, but rather exist in the spiritual plane.

"But, Leif, I don't want to come back." His back still to me, he hunches over the pond, staring intensely into its muddied waters.

"That will be determined by your actions in this life," I say decisively, leaving no room for discussion.

The Chaplain turns to me and nods slowly, his eyes alight with understanding. His hands float up and away from his sides.

Michael E. Poeltl

"We're all in this together."

Chapter Four

That evening I sit to meditate in the forest within our great walls and ponder the actions that have brought me to this moment in time. The sun falls behind the west tower, and summer is in full swing. A gentle breeze shakes the canopy of leaves above me. The air is warm and smells sweet as it pushes past my face. I inhale deeply, hold and exhale slowly.

A sharp sting cuts the serenity of the moment as something hard hits the back of my neck. I turn and see three men approach.

"Why don't you do that someplace else?" shouts Harry. He is one of two orphans found beyond Elle Lake just one year before I arrived. He is a hothead and was recently removed from military duty for insubordination. The two beside him are Chris and Monty.

A nervous smile grows on my face, and I wave them over. My heart races as memories of past bullying play on my nerves.

"Screw that," says Chris, wiping his shaved head, which is littered with long thin scars, a result of some horrifying ordeal he'd experienced while on the outside.

"You can take your fairy class and shove it!" Harry spits out.

They are classic bullies, though warned not to disturb me during classes, they are less inhibited when I am alone.

"Throw something back at me, you queer," taunts Monty. He wears a permanent scowl. Something he adopted at age six, after watching his parents be brutally murdered at the hands of rival survivors.

Each has a story. Each has adapted a personality to hide their pain. Fear rises in my chest. I hate that I can't control it.

Harry goes down on one knee and pulls up a chunk of asphalt from the broken road.

"Will you move if I throw this at your head?" Harry squeezes the fist sized piece of debris, and then hurls it at me.

I duck to avoid the flying object but it catches the bridge of my nose and I fall sideways. That's when something snaps inside me. I hear Blank Man in my head, but block out his pleas for a nonviolent outcome.

I grip my nose with both hands and stagger to my feet. Their laughter triggers in me a rage I have buried all these years.

They have come into the woods now, and as I listen to their footfalls on the forest floor I throw myself at one of them. We crash to the earth with a thud and I hear the wind escape the lungs of the man beneath me. I release the grip on my nose and feel a kick to my side, then another, and another. Monty and Chris are pummeling me.

I roll off Harry and kick at the legs in front of me. At the same time I feel a sharp pain to the back of my head as a fist lands a punch at the base of my skull.

Suddenly a roaring voice can be heard over the ringing in my head. The assault stops immediately.

"Step off!" the voice bellows.

"He started it," Monty lies.

Looking up, I see four black army issue boots shuffling the three away from me.

"Are you *shitting* me?" The voice rips into Monty's story. "Leif started a *fight*? Get these three under house arrest. I expected more of you, Harry."

I listen while lying on my stomach in the soft moss, mentally assessing the damage done. My ribcage hurts, but no more than a bruise or two. I pat my nose and pull my fingers away, wincing when I see blood.

I've never been hit before, and hope to never experience it again. A hand wraps around my forearm and pulls me to my feet.

"Jesus, Leif, you alright?" asks the soldier. It's KC.

"I'm okay. I'll be okay, thanks." I stretch and rub at my sides.

"What happened here?"

"I'm as much to blame as they are."

"I doubt that. I'll take you to the hospital and get you looked over."

"I screwed up," I insist, rolling my neck.

"Self defense, I'm sure," he suggests.

KC takes my arm and leads me across the compound and into the hospital.

*****

Why now did I choose to react in violence rather than allow it to pass? They'd never actually hit me before. They'd kicked dirt in my face, pushed me, but it had never escalated to this level of hostility.

Blank Man is as troubled by my reaction as I am.

"That you are distressed by your actions is important," he tells me. "You cannot lead others in peaceful meditation if you yourself exhibit fits of violence."

"I understand. Should I have taken the blow and bowed out?"

"You should have removed yourself from the confrontation the moment it began."

"I see." But I don't, not really. I mean, I'm entitled to sit in the woods just as much as anyone and be left undisturbed. I'm confused. I feel many things, shame, anger, but regret? I'm not sure about that.

*****

With my three oppressor spending a night in the stockade, I return to my corner of the woods to complete what I had started.

Gradually, I steady my mind and visualize Blank Man in front of me. He appears, sympathetic. I let my mind wander and, maybe because of my recent encounter, find myself lamenting my father's struggle.

"Tell me about my father," I say. Mom rarely spoke of him, side-stepping my questions even now. I used to think she was protecting me from some terrible secret when I was younger, but I'm eighteen now, and I want to know.

"Your father, Joel, was one of many chosen to lead in the time after. You are your father, and within you lives the same promise he rejected."

"I understand my father and I are one and the same. But why did he fail?"

"Your father failed because he fought the idea. He could not accept the concept of destiny. He felt he had been robbed of his free will. He attempted to veer from a pre-destined path, and with each determined move, his own destiny became clouded. "

"So he was capable of changing his destiny?"

"A destiny cannot be so easily side-stepped, and your father came to realize that. It is essential in a leader to understand structure and purpose, and that is what I was hoping to instill in Joel, so he could move toward this greater purpose."

"So then what? How did it end for him? How did my father die?"

"I was tasked with bringing him back to the idea of destiny, but failed time and again. I entered his dreams, I appeared to him in the waking world: I pleaded with him to see purpose in the tragedies that had befallen humanity. But he pulled further away from me the more I tried to connect, until the realization that he could never be *the one* was clear. You know of Gareth and the great struggle he brought to your mother's group. Your father had banished him and his followers from his home, the place where you would be born."

"Yes, mom has told me that much."

"Gareth led a group of survivors with a flag that embodied the world before. With this flag and the ideas it symbolized he was able to amass an army that went unchallenged wherever they went."

"Until they came upon my mother's group."

"Yes, Leif. But little did your father know Gareth would play a much larger role in his life. Joel's destiny had irrevocably changed from the path I'd hoped to show him, to the path he had made himself.

"Once we realized Joel could not be *the one* to lead, I planted in Gareth's head the vision of Joel's new path: where your father would come upon Gareth's group once more and offer a sacrifice. This sacrifice would be your father's friend. Driven by a paranoia that had been growing in him many weeks, fed by the narcotics he found himself hopelessly addicted to."

"He had lost his ability to see truth."

"Yes. And so, your mother with child a month prior to the event, we resigned ourselves to the idea of reanimating Joel's spirit in you, his son."

"But how did he die?"

"Once Joel had offered his friend to the will of Gareth, the outcome was clear. Your father would end his own life, and in doing so, allow us to start anew with his son."

This is what the scar on my forearm represented. For the first time, I understand my father had killed himself. The knowledge that my father was a coward stuns and confuses me. I break my position and slouch over. My head shakes from side to side in a slow, deliberate motion.

"I am not proud of the way I handled your father, Leif, but have forgiven myself. What good comes from *this* end is what matters now. What we build from the ashes of your father's choices are all that matters now."

"Does my mom know this?"

"She asked me once if your father was responsible for Connor's death, but before I could answer she withdrew the request to know. It is yours to tell now. If you feel it would serve her."

"I don't see the point, unless it is better to know the truth. Tell me what to do."

"I cannot. It has no bearing on your destiny. This choice is yours alone."

As I meditate on this question Blank Man offers more information.

"Do you remember Earl, Leif?"

Of course I remember Earl. Mom's sworn enemy. Earl had torn her small group of friends apart after my father's passing and forced her to flee their shared home. Then, eight years later, he turned up at our door, here on the base, having put together a rag tag band of desperate survivors. These people would test our defenses and attack our soldiers on scouting missions. Eventually Earl was taken prisoner, and while awaiting execution in the stockade, my angel directed me to talk to him, to 'know my enemy'. I didn't really understand why at the time, but a picture in my head was beginning to take shape.

"Yes, Leif, the events that will come to pass include many more variances than merely guiding you. I gave you that opportunity to meet and speak with your enemy when you were just a child. Now that you are an adult, you will be asked to face this enemy once more."

"Earl is still alive?" The question is more like a statement and I breathe deeply, thinking back to that night in the stockade.

*****

I was eight. The sky was beginning to darken, with stars appearing overhead one by one. Rumblings of thunder coupled with humid gusts of wind blew in from the west, slipping over the high steel walls of our fortress.

I had always enjoyed storms. Though anything longer than a few minutes usually scared me, a quick and powerful downpour was invigorating. I would run into the potholes that lined our streets and kick and jump as they filled with water. Flashes of lightening, rolling thunder and the sting of the driving rain always made me feel alive.

The night I met Earl, however, the rain didn't begin until I was already facing him, my enemy, through heavy steel bars, his hands and feet chained to the wall.

"Know your enemy," Blank Man had whispered in my head. From that moment I felt compelled to walk to the stockade, leaving the daycare, without my teacher's knowledge.

When I arrived, a vision of a key placed behind a loose brick filled my head. Once I had located the brick, I worked the key into the lock and let myself in.

In a dark corner of the stockade, a man sat in a cage. He was hunched over, his breathing ragged. A light in the opposite corner cast heavy shadows on the man and it was difficult to know whether he was looking in my direction or sleeping.

"Who are you?" he asked in a low rumble. I jumped at the sound.

"Your enemy," I answered, my voice pitching higher than I'd have liked.

The man offered a pained laugh at that. "Everyone is my enemy." He sat up and I could hear his chains rattle.

"I know that." I sat on a bench under the light.

"Who are you?" His head tilted to the right as he studied me.

"Leif," I answered.

"You're Joel's boy," he realized. "Sara's kid." He reached for his face but stopped short as the chains pulled taut against the wall. He lowered his face to his hands and rubbed at his eyes.

"You smart like your mother?"

"I don't know."

"She's a smart one, that Sara. You're a lucky kid to have found a place like this to grow up. Listen, we don't have to be *enemies*, you and me," he began. "Your dad and me were friends for a long time. Your mom too. We could be friends like that."

"No, I know that's not right."

"What do you *know*?" He leaned back, rolling his knuckles against his thighs.

"That you are my enemy."

"And where did you get that information? We were *friends,* your dad and me. The best of friends."

"I have a friend who tells me things."

"A friend, eh?" He laughed raggedly. "Listen, Leif, maybe talk to your *friend*, ask him to join us. I'd like to speak to him too."

"No, he won't see you." I stepped closer to the bars. Earl's face became clearer in the light as my eyes focused. He had a terrible scar on one side and a partial beard on the other. His red hair was slick and pasted to his forehead.

"No? Come closer," he urged as a whisper of a smile inched its way up the uninjured side of his face.

I felt myself wanting to obey him. It was a strange feeling. I knew it was dangerous to approach this man, but his eyes drew me.

"You know, your dad and me shared a lot of good times before this end came." He gazed at the ceiling. "We were friends." He looked at me again, still inching closer to the cage. "We did everything together. *We* should be friends."

I didn't doubt my father and Earl were friends at one time, as I could see Earl's aura shift when recounting his pre-Apocalyptic life. I found myself feeling sorry for him. I wondered if maybe we *could* be friends.

A moment later the door to the stockade swung open. A bright light shone in my eyes as two silhouettes pushed into the small space. One grabbed at me as the other shouted something through the bars at Earl.

I remember feeling grateful for having had a conversation with Earl. I felt a connection to my father that transcended the birthmark on my forearm.

*****

I break my meditation and stand. I'm lightheaded and stabilize myself by planting both hands on the trunk of a tree. Its energy feeds mine and I saunter off to my quarters.

Chapter Five

That night I take a detour to my room and walk through the compound. The air is crisp, and as I leave Father Henderson's visionary forest, I inhale the sweet scent of the spongy green moss carpeting the ground.

The night is quiet save the hum of the windmills, as it is most nights, allowing me to reflect. My thoughts tonight find me wanting. So many thoughts vie for attention that it is difficult to pin them all down. Blank Man had explained much to me, but there is more to the story of my father's life that I feel I need to know.

And that Earl is still a threat to our way of life, that he is someone of interest to the other side and that my own Blank Man has hinted at his importance in bringing about my destiny is disconcerting.

Back at my room I have trouble sleeping, tossing and turning as I try to piece together all that I now know of my father. I also find myself questioning my guide's approach to my father's difficulties.

"I've explained this to you, Leif. It is done."

"I'm just - I don't understand why it had to happen that way. Why did Connor have to die?"

"You are here, now, because of what transpired then."

I stare at Blank Man as he materializes beside my bed. Suddenly images of the Reaper, dressed in a heavy, dark cloak, bent over a large console of red and yellow buttons, flash through my head. A world map of hotspots lit up in front of him on a massive screen as his skeletal fingers push at the keys. I recognize the imagery as almost comical in its simplicity, but know the vision is more than just a farce.

"What *aren't* you telling me? There *is* something more."

"You've been struggling with the bigger picture." He'd read the images in my mind. "You're trying to put the pieces together. You feel there is more to the one called the Grimm Reaper; that his role has been somehow understated."

"His ideas – they were aligned with much of what you have taught me. They were noble, spiritually driven and, *enlightened*."

"They were."

"You *knew* this person?" My heart races: the story of the Grimm Reaper is about to be revealed to me.

"We have known of it a *very long* time."

Every hair on my body stands in anticipation. "Tell me."

"You know of what I speak." A pause. "You know what lengths evil will go to in order to perpetrate its own continuance."

"Even an enlightened mind such as his?"

"It's was *not* enlightened, but *enflamed*. It is no man, but spirit."

"Is there such a thing?"

"There is, and they are *many*."

"What spirit would inflict such horrors?" I feel suddenly sick. I feel that despite all I know, all I have been shown, that I've only experienced half of what the spirit world offers. That such an unspeakable evil could exist in a realm of such beauty… I focus again on my angel. The spirit's image twitches as I sense his energy spike.

"It is the great deceiver of man."

"Why wouldn't you tell me this?"

"What information you are offered is a tool for your ministry. Some information you are not meant to have."

"Then why answer my questions?"

"Because you ask them," he says matter-of-factly. "Mankind is such a curious creature. You are so simple, so material, yet so advanced in your processes. You question everything."

"It is one of our strengths."

"It is, and so I do not deny you the answers to your questions, but why question my answers? Why do you not simply accept them and move forward?" I understand his point, but that does not mean I will leave it alone.

"Is this spirit the *Devil?*" I ask.

"It may go by that name. It is *evil*. It is hate, jealousy, malice and guilt. It represents the opposite of everything good and beautiful. The spirit world is not so different from the material world in this respect. There is an opposite for everything, and *in* everything."

"So evil isn't just a facet of man? It's everywhere, in everything?" As the epiphany hits me I sit up straight in bed, clutching the sheets. "It's not the invention of man."

"No, it is not. But it is your choice, and it is your burden."

"Yes, as it has always been." I ball my hands up into fists. Then I release them and force myself to relax.

"Thank you, my friend. Thank you for always telling me the truth - whether I have to ask for it or not." I look up at him and sigh. "I appreciate your friendship and all that you have done for me, and for mom."

"All is as it should be, then."

"Yes. All is as it should be." I stand. "I'd like to meditate on what you've told to me." My angel bows and disappears from view. I sit on the floor and take deep concentrated breaths until I enter the light once more.

Chapter Six

With each new day, new opportunities to learn are revealed.

Today, three new arrivals from the outside world found their way to our door. As with all newcomers, once they have been questioned by our military body, they are turned over to the medical staff, examined and processed. I take it upon myself, as I do with all new arrivals, to introduce myself. As I walk through the hospital doors I see a small, pale man, thin, frail even, sitting on a stool as mom draws blood from his arm.

I learn that his name is Dieter and that he calls himself a physicist. I learn that he came from another land, far away, across an ocean, many years ago. His English is perfect, but his accent thick. It is hard for me to picture other lands – he is my only exposure to the fact other cultures and languages exist.

After a short conversation he makes an astute observation.

"You understand more than your years would suggest," he announces, flinching as mom administers a vaccine to his left shoulder, a preventative measure we continue to practice in fear of the plague that killed so many following the bombs.

"I might say the same of you, if you weren't so old," I tease. His eyes widen and in studying them, a knowledge that extends far beyond the material *now*, reveals itself to me.

He laughs and rubs his shoulder. Looking up to mom he smiles. "Thank you very much."

"You're very welcome." She smiles back at him. "Your wife and son are waiting for you in the mess hall. Would you like me to take you to them?"

"Could I have a moment with your son?" He turns back to face me, his eyes squinting. "I think we have many things to discuss." He pulls down the short sleeve of his shirt and stands.

"I would like that," I agree. Looking to my mom, I ask, "Could you let his family know?"

She nods and winks at me. I watch Dieter eye her up as she leaves the doctor's office. Mom is a beautiful woman. Her big eyes and long lashes have captured the attention of every single man on the base at one time or another, and some women, but mom turns them all down. Her dedication to my studies and now her own, under Doctor Bren, have left her precious little time to pursue a personal life.

I urge Dieter to sit once more.

"From what your mother tells me, you must vibrate at an accelerated level."

"I, *vibrate*?"

"Yes. Well, we *all* vibrate. *Everything* vibrates, just at different frequencies." He crosses one leg over the other and places his folded hands upon his knee.

"That's an interesting statement. Enlighten me."

"Oh, I'm rather certain I could not *enlighten* one so far along the path as you." The wooden stool lets out a squeak as he leans back. "Tell me, what method do you use?"

"What do you mean I *vibrate*? That *everything* vibrates?"

"Forgive me. It's a theory that infinitesimally small vibrating strings pervade the universe, their different frequencies the very building blocks of all matter and energy in existence."

"O-kay." I say drawing out my response.

"And you, my friend, I can only imagine are approaching that moment, where it all comes together, where the quantum world is finally realized in this world. Perhaps you have already?"

"Who *are* you?" I ask fighting back a smile, realizing I'm in a conversation I may never understand.

"I am a quantum physicist." He leans forward on his stool and plants both feet on the ground. "I came to your country to teach the young scientists here, before the bombs fell." He looks up, raising his palms to the ceiling. "Since then I have travelled many years to find myself here.

Yet no one I have met in all these years has expressed any interest in discussing with me the quantum world."

"Are you suggesting that you've found that person in *me*?" I must look incredulous at the implication.

"Yes."

"Why?"

"Your mother has told me you are a spiritual teacher here. She's told me you teach a form of meditation to your students and that you have been practicing since you were just a boy."

"Okay. And that makes me a scientist?"

"You are too modest." He wags a finger at me. "I have studied the effects of meditation on hundreds of people in congruence with my more 'scientific' research involving quantum physics, and have found similarities that may change the way we view the spiritual and scientific." Dieter pauses, and leans back on the stool once more. "I think you walk the line between this world and that. What you call the spiritual plane, I call the quantum plane."

"What is the quantum plane?"

"The quantum plane, or quantum physics, is the science of the very small."

"And you think the spiritual and quantum are one and the same?"

"That is my thinking. If God controls the quantum outcome, then He will determine *everything* in the end."

"You believe in God?"

Dieter runs his thin fingers along the stubble of silver hair framing a massive bald spot. "Maybe I do. You see, nothing is for certain at the quantum level. Space-time, or the physical realm, is ruled by four measurable forces, but something is working outside of space-time on the quantum plane."

"I'm not seeing the connection."

"What I believe, is that through your meditative practices, you leave the physical plane and walk with *God* in the quantum world."

I find myself becoming more and more involved in his homily. "So you think where my consciousness goes in meditation, and your quantum world, are the same place?" Dieter nods. "Why?"

He smiles. "Strings," he says, rising off of the stool. "The subatomic particles that make up every atom in the universe, which vibrate like the strings on a guitar when strummed, disappear and reappear all the time. They are not static here, in our physical plane, and we, as solids, bound by our three dimensions, could never experience them."

"But what of the mind?" I pose, beginning to understand what this brilliant man was alluding to.

"The mind?"

"Yes, in my teachings the mind is the spirit, and the mind is all knowing. If I am, as you say, walking with *God* in the quantum plane, shouldn't *I* be able to experience those other dimensions?"

"Yes, right, and I believe you *are*, when you meditate, shedding your physical self."

"Incredible."

"Indeed." With that Dieter stretches his lower back, arching his torso outward. "I should go. It is late and my family will be waiting."

"Of course. Let's discuss this further, another time. I am very interested in how your theory could be integrated with my own experiences."

"And I am very curious to discuss those experiences with you." He holds out a hand and I shake it. "Now, can you show me to my wife and boy?"

"Absolutely." I open the door and lead him down the hallway and into the cafeteria where his family greets him.

*****

Having grown up between worlds, living in the material plane while meditating in the spiritual, I have struggled with the approach I would take in order to pass the light of knowledge to others, as the two worlds seemed endlessly at odds with one another. But now that Dieter has introduced me to quantum physics, I am beginning to see how the two could co-exist.

*****

That night, hours after I'd gone to bed, a nightmare jolts me out of a deep sleep. My t-shirt and sheets are soaked in sweat.

My dreams and nightmares have carried warnings and premonitions in the past. If the jumbled images revealed to me tonight are any indication of a future event, I fear for myself and my community.

Chapter Seven

The following day the skies open up and release a torrential downpour. I invite mom to join me in the mess hall, pulling her away from her studies. For lunch we enjoy a slice of homemade bread and strawberry jam. It's a treat when the cooks prepare something fresh from our hydroponic gardens in the greenhouse. I watch as mom's face takes on an air of serenity. She chews each bite slowly, savoring the flavors.

She catches me smiling at her and smiles back.

"It's really good," I admit, staring at the thinly spread jam coating the thick slab of moist bread.

"You know what, Leif?" She looks at the piece of bread, turning it in her hands. "The last time I had strawberry jam was when I lived in the bunker, with my witches."

Mom and her witches. This was a recurring conversation between us. When I was a child they seemed more like a fairytale, a bedtime story. But then again, much of what she had taught me over the years was wisdom passed on from her witches. I still remember the first lesson, the pendulum. How empowered the exercise made me feel. That my thoughts alone could control the spinning of a weight at the end of a string was all at once magical and yet visceral. The idea that a thought was not contained in my head, but rather could be projected onto something real. The butterflies flutter in my stomach at the memory.

"Leif, I'd like to take you to see my witches, and I feel like they deserve to see you too, to *know* you."

"I would *love* to meet them." These women were so influential in my life, integral in my survival and in my teachings: Beth, Sally, Jenny and Carol. My chest stirs with excitement.

"Because, Leif, we wouldn't have made it here if it weren't for them," she continues, "and frankly, I've wanted to see them for a very long time."

"Of course," I lay a hand on hers. "Mom, let's go there."

She smiles up at me. I have towered over her since I was fourteen, when I experienced my biggest growth spurt. At eighteen I stand six feet, two inches.

"I'd also like to take you to your birthplace," she adds. "It's not far from the bunker."

"I'll talk to the Captain and have an escort take us there." I have no doubt the Captain will allow us this luxury. Though fuel is at a minimum, mom carries a certain respect among the officers and military personnel. Besides, one of the larger vehicles runs on electricity, of which we have an abundance.

*****

Once cleared, the Captain assigns soldiers to escort us on this day trip. It is an estimated two hours' travel to the house, and another hour to the bunker, allowing for a two hour return trip. We've been given an eight hour time allotment before we have to be back. That gives us roughly three hours to reminisce over mom's safe-house and sit with the women at the bunker and hope to bring them back with us.

The truck hurtles along at break-neck speed, weaving through a jungle of abandoned vehicles. It is an eerie thing, so many vehicles that had just stopped mid-journey; their occupants must have walked on to their deaths. I lean back in my seat, turning away from the window as I imagine entire families dying in this terrible aftermath. Mothers watching helplessly as their children give in to the ash and heat. Such scenes would have played out countless times the world over. A tear slips down my cheek and I wipe it away.

"Left here!" Mom calls from the front passenger seat. She reaches back to take my hand. I don't need to be an empath to sense we're close. We pull over slowly to the right at the top of a hill. Nothing indicates that there was ever a house here except the rusted cars and trucks that line the pot-marked driveway. Having burned down in a fire mom had set some eighteen years earlier, what remains of the house where she, my father and their friends had sought refuge, is only a hole in the ground where the foundation used to be. What timber that could be salvaged has been, and even the bricks and metal have been pilfered for some use. God only knows how anyone off our base existed for any length of time. I remember something the Sergeant told me once, about people, about how resilient our species is, and how driven we are to survive.

Mom walks down a slope in the yard approaching a pond. Her strides are long and determined. She is marching towards a memory. Behind the pond, which I'd been told was once a pool, she falls to her knees, her hands cradling her face. Then she bends further and touches her forehead to the earth.

KC walks past me, gesturing to his men and nodding at me. I nod back. As the soldiers rush past me to secure the perimeter I feel a sudden connection to the place where I was conceived and born. I imagine that the woods behind the house are green and alive and the fields stand high with corn stalks. The house towers above me, a massive brick structure. A gift from a memory of another life, my father's life before the end came. In reality, the forest now is spotted with only the strongest trunks - those with the deepest roots. They are not many and are black and bare. The fields to my right and behind me cultivate only dust now.

My attention again focuses on mom's sadness. I go and kneel beside her.

She looks up, wiping tears away. In her hand I see a bracelet. "This was Caroline's," she starts, holding the silver item up to me. "There's nothing else left of them."

This is where she had found her friends Sidney and Caroline after fleeing the fire. This is where Earl had ended their lives. Nothing remains but the bracelet now. But that is enough.

"She would want you to have it," I tell her.

Mom's bottom lip turns down and her chin trembles. "Do you think so?" Her teeth chatter. "Do you *know* so, Leif?"

I wrap my hands around hers and squeeze tight. "They are at peace now, Mom."

We walk the perimeter of the yard and even manage the trail back to a small cabin behind the house. The walk takes five minutes and we pass several grave markers. They rest beside a river bed, now dry and without purpose. She kneels down at each, placing a hand on the mounds one after another, whispering something inaudible. We spend a long moment at my father's grave, or what she remembers to be my father's grave. I find the sensation of being so close to the skeletal remains of my past life upsetting, and I move a few steps beyond the depression.

Then, a few seconds later into our walk, mom stops short in front of a branch connected to a thick trunk with a tattered rope tied to it. The rope has a noose at the end, like the ones we use at the base to hang criminals.

Mom's hands fly up to her mouth and a whimper slips through. I approach her and place my hands on her shoulders.

"What is it, Mom?"

Her head shakes. "Seth." The name materializes from a squeak at the back of her throat. Tears come next and I pull her into me and hug her hard.

After a time I release her and she smiles sadly up at me. "This is why we burned the house," she starts, pointing up at the gallows. "Earl had no right to do this… that bastard… cowardly bastard."

Mom approaches the noose and asks me to pull it down. I need to jump, but I get a grip and tear it down, the branch snapping away from the trunk. As we continue to move towards the shed, a sharp pain strikes me in my thigh. It's unlike anything I've felt before.

"Are you okay, Leif?" Mom asks, watching as my hands automatically grasp my thigh and the breath leaves me. The pain lasts only a moment, and I shake my head.

"I'm okay. Just a muscle spasm, I guess." I shake my leg, wondering at the intensity of the pain, and continue walking.

At the shed we come upon a strange sight. One that none after mom's Apocalypse has witnessed in the natural world. There is a single flower poking through the battered earth. Plants grew because we grew them, period, not in the wild. Not anymore. Mom bends toward the strange flower. She looks up at me and smiles. "It's Jake," she tells me. "This is where he died. He died protecting your father." Her head falls back to the flower and she inhales its scent.

"This is incredible, right?" I say. "This doesn't happen."

"No." Mom stands and crossing her arm, smiles. "No, it doesn't."

I lean in to smell the flower. I touch the earth surrounding the plant and it is moist. "Should we take it with us?"

"No." She doesn't miss a beat.

I rise and nod in approval, amazed at the mystery of the thing. We turn and head back to the Hummer. In my peripheral I see a soldier on either side of us, shadowing our movements, ever aware of their surroundings.

Chapter Eight

The drive from my father's family home to mom's safe-house gives me an hour to contemplate the feelings I pulled from the experience. Mom's stories became more real after visiting the place where my father once lived, the home my grandfather built, which had housed mom and thirteen of her peers for nearly two years after the bombs. I feel connected to my past both physically and spiritually. I meditate on the place, seated in the back of the Hummer, memories that are not my own race through my mind's eye.

I awaken from my trance as the doors to the vehicle are pushed open. The sun is falling behind the horizon, elongating the shadows of a distant forest. I step out of the Hummer and stretch. Mom walks toward a structure just a few feet ahead of us.

A veranda overlooks a large yard. A burnt out structure, long since reduced to its footings, lay behind it. Mom approaches the veranda with trepidation. I can tell that she is frightened of what she might find.

She pulls at a trapdoor at the base of the veranda and seems surprised when it opens. She looks back at me with her mouth open and eyes wide. I approach. Taking the door from her I swing it open, revealing a dark pit below.

"Bethany?!" She whispers into the abyss. "Jenny? Carol? Sally?!" There is no reply. Mom looks up at me and stands. "I need to go down there."

I wave over one of the corporals and ask for his flashlight. "I'm coming with you." She wraps a hand around my forearm and I switch on the flashlight.

"Can you guys wait for us up here?" I ask KC as he joins us.

"You're sure, Leif?" His eyes dart to the cluster of dead trees just a few yards north of us.

I look to her and she nods. "No one knew about this place."

"We're sure." I lay a hand on his shoulder and step onto the ladder. Mom follows.

Reaching the bottom I feel the grit of dirt under my soles. I turn with the light and shine it down a long narrow passage. The place smells damp.

"Beth?!" Mom calls out again. And again she looks up at me, her forehead creased.

"Maybe they've stepped out. We could wait for them."

She shakes her head and arm in arm we move through the darkened tunnel, and into a larger room.

Mom takes the flashlight from me and shines it frantically about the barrel shaped interior.

"Where *is* everyone?"

"Could they have moved on?"

She throws open cupboards and drawers. "Why would they leave? Look at this! There is still food here." She opens another trapdoor and climbs down a set of stairs.

"Wait! Mom!" I follow.

When I reach the basement of the shelter I stand in awe of the collection of canned and boxed goods. Everything from matches to jerky; dried fruit and juice boxes stacked in neat piles set on metal shelves; baby formula and diapers and toilet paper. All in what seems like a temperature controlled dry room.

"Why would anyone leave this place?" She ignites an oil lamp that hangs from the low ceiling. "I don't understand." She runs her hands along the jars and boxes.

"What would you like to do?" I ask, wondering if we ought to stay for a night and wait them out.

She nods as if reading my mind. "Let's stay a night or two. We can send the others home if they'd like to get back."

"They won't leave us here alone, Mom. You know that."

"I guess I do. But they might not let us stay."

"I'll talk to them. There's more than enough room down here for everyone." We reach the main floor of the bunker and close the door to the dry storage.

"Maybe I could clean it up a bit." She studies the place, her eyes flinching as they fall on objects and items of clothing.

"Everything okay, Mom?"

"No." She stares at the kitchen table. A Ouija board sits alone in the center. She shines the light over to a couch and coffee table adjacent the kitchen, where a deck of illustrated cards is laid out in a circular pattern. I watch the memories play out on her face, her eyes darting from one scene to the next. I approach her and gently lay a hand on her back.

"Can you tell me what's wrong?"

She bends down to pick up a piece of paper from the coffee table. "The horoscope…" Her voice trails off.

"Is this *my* horoscope? The one that Jenny researched for you?" I ask excitedly.

With vacant eyes she looks up at me, handing me a piece of paper. I take it from her and look it over. Flipping it in my hands, I notice nothing is written on it. I walk closer to the table and pick up the other sheets. All are blank.

"Did she not write down the information?" A shiver works its way up my spine.

"Of course, she did." Doubt creeps into her eyes as she pans the room for more details.

"Okay. Well, this must not be it then. Where would it be?"

"No, that's it."

"How can you be sure?"

"The corners." I study the corners of the paper more closely. They are turned in. "I turned them myself, to keep them together, but, that was long before I ever left here." She starts to pace between the kitchen and the living area. "I told you, we left abruptly. I packed our gear when the message came from your Blank Man, and left."

I remember the story. I sit on the armrest of the couch and watch her work through her memories.

"Ask him a question for me, Leif." She turns to me. "Ask him if they were *real*."

"Real? You think they didn't actually exist?"

"Once, yes." She studies her hands, her fingers interlocking.

"But not anymore?"

"Not even while I was here." Her head shakes slowly.

"Ghosts?"

"Yes." She stares straight ahead.

A moment passes, I focus on the question, not even sure I should relay the information Blank Man gives me to mom, who seems to be in shock. Still, when the answer is offered, I know that she must know.

"He says yes." I nod. "They were *earth bound* spirits. Free-spirits."

I watch as she shivers, and catch her as she loses her balance, placing her on the couch and sitting next to her.

"He's telling me that just weeks after the bombs fell, they succumbed to a virus just beyond the property line. In the woods to the north."

"The strain that killed so many?"

"Yes, the same." I answer. "But they'd made a pact. They would return. Free-spirits are powerful entities, living in this plane and that. They know they have passed, but are determined to see a thing through."

Suddenly I see the women in my mind's eye, a gift from Blank Man: the four witches, bathed in light. One chubby and kind, one with jet black hair and olive skin, another pale white and thin, and lastly, the one named Beth. She out-shines them all, and as they smile at me they turn, and walk out of sight, and into the light.

I look to my mom to tell her what I'd seen and notice a tear balancing on her chin.

"I saw them, Leif. Did you see them?" She wipes her face.

"Yes."

"Weren't they beautiful?"

"Yes, Mom."

"Thank him for me will you? Your Blank Man. That meant more to me…" I hug her and let her cry until the men that have accompanied us on this pilgrimage interrupt our moment with a shout down the tunnel.

"We've got company, Leif!" calls KC. "We need to get moving!"

"Be out in a moment!"

Mom pulls back from me and smiles, wiping her face. Then carefully she holds my face in her hands. "I'm so very glad you had the chance to meet them, Leif. They would be so proud."

I gently wrap my hands around her wrists and, smiling lead her out of the bunker to find the soldiers kneeling beside the trapdoor, rifles drawn.

"Get low." KC motions with his hand.

"What is it?" I whisper.

"Not sure. We heard rustling in the woods."

It is dark out. More time has passed in the bunker than I realized. The night sky is ominous, a great cloud blotting out the full moon. Then we see it, a pack of dogs emerging from the forest to the north, some one hundred yards from our position.

"Look at that," says one of the soldiers. "I've never seen so many at once."

The pack has picked up our scent, and curiously approaches.

"Let's make our way back to the vehicle," KC orders in a whisper. "No sudden movements. Just follow me."

We pick ourselves up and, crouching, make slow deliberate steps towards the waiting Hummer. The pack picks up its pace and breaks into a run.

"Move!" shouts KC. "Cover us!" He grabs my mother's arm and pulls her beside him. I follow, flanking left. It's obvious the dogs will overtake us before we make the Hummer. Three of the soldiers stop and turn to face the starving dogs, steadying themselves on one knee. Then their rifles shatter the silence, I hear the dogs whimper as they fall to the hail of bullets.

Once safely inside, KC slams the door behind us and fires his weapon at the beasts. I feel terrible the dogs were being gunned down like this, but they were starving and would not have hesitated to rip us to pieces.

As we look on, one solider trips as he runs backwards, expertly targeting one after another of the hungry dogs. Hitting the ground hard, his rifle fires into the night sky. KC and another solider rush to his side but not before one of the dogs has his ankle in its mouth. Then another is on top of him, tearing at his thigh. KC picks them off one by one with his rifle, managing to drag the man to the safety of the Hummer.

We shift to one side of the vehicle and assist in placing the wounded man on the folded seats. Mom goes right to work examining the wounds.

"Is he alright?" KC asks.

"He'll be fine," She tells us. "You'll be fine," she repeats to the wounded soldier.

I turn to KC. "There's a lot of food and accessories in that bunker."

"We should get Devin back to the hospital now," Mom insists.

KC nods. "We've mapped out the trip, so we can come back anytime to retrieve everything." He turns in his seat and gives the order to head back to base.

The Hummer speeds off.

Chapter Nine

A week following the field trip, the Sergeant and I sit in the cafeteria after Father Henderson's Sunday service, ready to assist in rearranging the tables and chairs to once again resemble a mess hall.

The Sergeant and I have a strange relationship. Mom avoids him, and has since I was nine. I'd noticed sadness in him, reflected in his aura when I would talk to him about her. But I always felt drawn to him, as a role model and the face of leadership on the base.

I shift in my seat as I watch what represents close to ninety percent of our residents shuffle into the hallway, discussing the sermon excitedly. The sermon dealt with what was the Holy Land; its purpose and its destiny. Its history is what most intrigues me: a violent, passionate history that spanned its entire existence.

"I can't imagine putting such stock in a *place*, in property," I say, the Sergeant looks to me, his eyes narrowing. "I mean; to attribute such worth to a *thing*."

"I would *die* for this place," he retorts. His wife lays a hand on his shoulder and joins the mass exodus. "Imagine our lives if we didn't have all of this."

"Point taken."

I had read extensive literature on the great and many religions of the world stored in the library's computer archives. I'd spoken at length with Father Henderson on religion, and its historical hold on humanity. From a very young age I found myself drawn to the subject and to the concept of possession.

"You know, Leif, what you speak about often reminds me of what the Grimm Reaper preached to the world before he ended it. We have records of his web logs and news articles. He demanded an end to organized religion and governments. He saw possessions as the devil's influence."

"Even the devil will quote scripture if it serves him."

Chapter Ten

My interest in my father's past tugs at my curiosity as I sit at a computer station in the library, considering his immoral act against his friend. I understand destiny, and so realize that there was more at work than just a paranoid mind acting irrationally.

Connor could see future events, and would unconsciously prepare graves behind my father's house, while in a trancelike state. But what really connected me to Connor was that he could *see* my angel.

These characters from mom's past were becoming more and more connected as I related the information: from the Reaper, to the flags, to the angel, to Connor, and to my father, and now, *me.*

I summon Blank Man. He appears before me as the dark figure I have come to trust, a *halo* of white light outlining his frame.

"Tell me about Connor," I ask.

"Connor was gifted with second sight. He found his gift to be a burden, but before his end came, he was given clarity, and so saw his own end."

"The flags," I interjected.

"Yes, the flags, and your father. Connor was gifted the future far beyond his own, and his friends. He saw *you*, Leif. He saw you take up your father's destiny, and so accepted his own, allowing his death at the hands of the flags, so that a future where you would complete the task he knew your father would forsake could be realized."

A sick feeling attacks my abdomen. "If my father could betray a friend, does that mean I may betray someone? I *am* my father, after all."

"You are and you are not, Leif. You are yourself, with your father's experiences to draw from. Most cannot draw from the experiences of their past lives, but you have that power."

"Why do you hold so much back? Why have you not told me this part of the story before?"

"It has no bearing on your destiny, but now that you have asked, and I have told you, you must be made aware. Begin the process of meditation." I cross my legs and place my hands on my knees, close my eyes and enter into the light. "Good, now see your father. Approach him and speak to him. He will offer you only truth."

I find my father in the light. He is young: my age. He smiles and I see myself in him. He is me. It is a difficult concept to grasp, but the closer we get to one another, the more his truth is revealed to me. I feel anxious at first, and then terribly sad, then strangely happy, and then numb. Then I feel anger, and jealousy and hate. Next I feel betrayal, then guilt and pain. Then there is light, and warmth and a sense of peace. All these emotions offer a story, and the story was deeply upsetting. But I understand it like I'd lived it. I understand my father.

"Do not make the same mistakes your father made."

As I ease out of my meditative state, I open my eyes and see Tina, the librarian, kneeling next to me with a glass of water in hand.

"Leif?" she asks. "Are you alright, honey?"

I smile, blink hard and unwrap my legs. "I am, Tina. Thank you." I take the water. "Have I been here long?"

Everyone on the base was used to my meditative 'moments' now, as they often struck me in odd, and unusual places.

"Not sure. I saw you walk in an hour ago, but how long you've been meditating, I couldn't say."

"Just an hour, then?" I stand and shake out my legs, allowing the blood to return to my feet.

"Yes."

Perfect, I was to meet mom for dinner in a few minutes. I thank Tina for the water and head for the mess hall.

*****

"I have something for you, Leif." Mom looks up from her plate. She seems preoccupied, moving the mashed potatoes around with her fork. "It's one of my only possessions and it's something your father wrote just before he died."

This was exciting: a physical relic from the past. Something my father had touched - something he'd written.

"You know how your father died?"

I nod.

"I didn't want to tell you."

"Of course, I know you don't tell a kid his dad killed himself." I lay a gentle hand on her arm.

"I was afraid one day you'd learn the truth. Does your *Blank Man* have to tell you everything?"

"There is a truth you wanted to know once."

She stares for a minute at me and shakes her head. "Once. Just for a fleeting moment."

"Okay, Mom," I say, letting it go. "Now where is this letter?"

She produces the paper from her pocket.

"I keep it with me at all times. So I never forget." She hands me the fragile artifact and I carefully unfold it on the cafeteria table. There are two pieces of lined paper with two distinctly different sets of handwriting. I look at Mom, who is watching me. I smile widely, my heart in my throat. The idea that Dad had left something tangible behind is exhilarating. Though I'd met him in my meditation and spoken to him and shared his experiences and emotions, this is something I could touch, and hold in my hands.

I hesitate, closing my eyes and inhaling deeply. I read the neatly handwritten verse first.

I know now that a single action can put in motion a series of repercussions. Should that action be positive, the repercussions are rewarding, but when that action is negative, so too are the events to follow. A single action can change you forever. Sometimes, if the deed is large enough, if the intent evil enough, the results can be disastrous.

I look at her again and can't believe what I've read. It's a suicide note.

"Are you okay?" She brushes my cheek with the back of her hand.

"It's Dad making sense of everything." I say, the gravity of my father's decisions weighing now on my shoulders. "He's explaining his actions, but also reliving the whole Grimm Reaper scenario in this one paragraph."

"You are a smart man." Mom runs her hand up and down my arm. "Read on."

I slide the top verse to the side and read the page with the sloppy print.

Blank Page, Blank Mind, Blank Brain, Blank man.
Blink and Blank man disappears, blink and Blank man disappears.
Blink, and nobody cares. Blink blinky, blink blinky, blink Bitch!
If I could, I'd blink, if only I could blink. I'd be Blinky, blinking.
Blank man would disappear.

After the fourth pairing on the first line I look back to her and mouth the words, *Blank Man.* She nods.

I read on. Once finished I read it again and again and again. The cryptic poem is filled with angst, but also carries a message of enlightenment with it.

To achieve a *blank mind* is to allow no thoughts, as in meditation allowing the participant to enter the light.

But the fact that he uses *Blank Man* spurs a question to Mom.

"Did Dad call his angel Blank Man?"

"No, that's all you. Joel didn't call him anything. He didn't have a name for him. Angel is about the only thing I ever heard him call it in his sleep."

"I'd like to copy it down, Mom. I want to go over it again."

"It's yours now, Leif. Do with it what you wish. I've held onto it long enough."

*****

Tonight another nightmare forces me from my sleep. My muscles are tense; I sit up, fighting to remember its message. Fear for one, fear of loss, fear of the unknown. These dreams are becoming more and more ominous. They are warnings. Something is coming, something sinister.

Chapter Eleven

Mary came to me in a dream. That was the first time I saw her, but in my dream she was leaving me.

The second time I met Mary was in the physical world. She, along with a half dozen other survivors, were escorted into the central parade grounds, then one by one marched into the infirmary. There they were disrobed and given showers and shots from the medical staff while mom and Doctor Bren supervised.

She was beautiful, even after going months, or maybe years, without a bath. Her hair was filthy, matted and pressed against her head, and her lips unnaturally pouty against her thin, malnourished face. As I stood beside the growing crowd that watched this new group shuffle into our lives her gaze met mine, and I was under her spell.

I make it a point to meet all new arrivals, to welcome them and explain our set-up. I make sure Mary is alone when I approach her in the mess hall. I watch as she cleans the last of her dinner off the plate.

"Hello." I say as I sit across from her.

"Hi." She seems distracted, pressing her finger against the plate, picking up the crumbs of bread and cheese.

My eyes had not deceived me earlier. She *is* beautiful. Even with her hair shaved to the scalp, as was the practice with new arrivals, her face seemed angelic. She catches me staring again, and I look away, red-faced.

"I saw you when we got here," she says shyly.

"Yes," I say clumsily. "It's always a big deal when the soldiers find new people."

"*We* found *them*," she insists, a smile playing across her flawless face.

I find myself smiling back. "However it happened, I'm very happy to have you here."

"I've never known anything like this place." She looks around the mess hall and inhales deeply. "Is this Heaven?"

I laugh aloud but stop myself. "I'm sorry," I say, watching her brows meet in the middle and her smile fade.

"It was a stupid question, I know, but if you knew how we've lived…" Her hands fly up to hide her face. Her body jerks violently as she sobs.

I stand and round the table, seating myself next to her, and carefully place a hand on her shoulder. She jumps and shifts back in her seat. I remove my hand quickly, realizing I've startled her.

"I'm so sorry," I whisper, careful not to upset her further.

"No, I'm sorry, I didn't – I'm sorry." Her head shakes as she lowers her hands, wiping away the tears.

"Don't be." I feel uneasy now. This isn't at all how I'd pictured this meeting going.

"Look, I've never been touched by anyone but my parents."

"I understand, really, you don't have to explain."

"You seem like a nice boy," she begins. "I – I'm just a little shaky. It's kind of a lot to take in, being here: new people and everything."

"I get it, I do. I'm sorry if I was too forward."

A smile twitches at the corners of her mouth. "It's alright. Let's start over." She extends a thin hand, lined with delicate veins. "I'm Mary Gardener."

"Leif," I tell her, feeling silly having not introduced myself immediately.

"Could you stay and talk, Leif?"

"If that's what you'd like." I feel giddy at the request.

"Please." She closes her eyes and seems suddenly tired. I wonder what this girl has had to endure. "It's been a little overwhelming for me. The others are catching up on their sleep, so I took the opportunity to just be alone for a while. I guess when you've spent so much time with the same people… well, I love them, but it's nice to have a break."

"Are you related to any of them?" I secretly pray she was not romantically linked to one of the younger men.

"One of the women is my mother, and the older man a sort of step-father to me. One of the boys is a cousin and another woman an aunt. The smallest of the boys we picked up a few months ago."

"How old are you, if you don't mind?"

"How old? I don't even really know for sure. We tried to keep track of the weeks and months and years, but gave up after the last of our journals was used up. That was a very long time ago."

"Do you remember how old you were in year one?"

"Year one?"

"Yes, the year of the bombs. We have a complete library of the weeks and months and years following, so if you knew your age then, I could tell you your age now."

"I was five when the bombs dropped," she says without hesitation. "What does that make me?"

"It's been about twenty years since that day. That makes you twenty five."

"Twenty years. I don't really know what that means. I'm not sure I ever did." It makes sense that someone who'd moved from place to place in search of food and shelter, with no semblance of structure, would have little use for concepts such as years or even months. Seasons yes, but months and weeks? The light of day would give way to the darkness and repeat. What else was there?

"Will you let me take you to see someone?"

She looks at me with wide eyes and I imagine she's sizing me up: friend or foe? I smile without thinking, studying her perfect features.

Mary nods and stands. I follow her lead and wave for her to join me as I walk towards the door of the cafeteria.

*****

Tina is dressed in her pressed army issue pant suit when we meet her at the library entrance. She takes her role at the base seriously, and works hard at keeping concise records of life after the Apocalypse. Tina came to the base from a northern city turned upside down after the bombs landed. When society failed and resources ran dry, she travelled alone, and was one of the first civilians to arrive at the base. From that point on she has kept the records.

"Leif, I was just closing up to get some dinner."

"Oh, that's okay, Tina. We can come back another time."

"No, don't be silly, you're welcome to use the library." She shifts her attention to Mary. "And is this one of the new arrivals?"

"Yes," I say proudly. "This is Mary." My new friend nods and smiles at Tina. Tina eyes me and a sly smile forms on her face.

"Listen, you're obviously here to talk to me. Come inside." She opens the door and I let Mary pass through first. I smile broadly, and Tina rubs my back knowingly. I wish Mary would pick up on my interest in her as quickly and effortlessly as Tina has.

"Has Leif told you about what it is I do here on the base, Mary?"

"He's told me some of what you do," she admits shyly.

"Come to my terminal and I'll show you the rest." Tina leads us to the desk where she spends much of her days. We gather behind her as she sits at the computer.

"I have kept records of this place in the time following the bombs," she explains. "But in addition to that, I have been recording Leif's life."

"*My* life?" I blurt, incredulous. "What, why?"

"Your mother never told you?" She turns to me, and my stunned expression is reflected in her bifocaled lenses. "Mary, you've made a very important friend in Leif."

I look at Mary and realize she has been staring at me. My face reddens and I smile at her awkwardly. I don't know if the stirring in my stomach comes from Tina's words or the intensity of Mary's gaze. It's a new feeling for me. Yes, I've noticed girls before, but the few women close to my age had become like sisters to me. This was new, exciting, and potentially devastating. It was more than mere physical attraction. There was a feeling in my chest that suddenly explained to me the expression 'heartbreak'.

Tina brings up a page of text on the screen and I read the title: *Leif. Years 1 – 10.* And then again as she scrolls down dozens of pages: *Leif. Years 11-18.*

"Leif is our moral and spiritual center here, and has been since he was just a child."

"I'm sorry, Mary, I didn't know." I feel she must think I'd brought her here to hear all about *me*. "Tina, what has mom told you?"

"Everything, Leif. She's told me everything."

"Why? Why would she do that?"

"She did it because she wanted a record of your life, so that one day your story and your words would reach others." She turns once more to face us both. "She did this for all of us, Leif."

I step back to sit on a chair a few feet behind me. Mary follows.

I knew her heart was in the right place, and that others could benefit from what I'd been talking about for years. My concern was personal. The ramifications were ego, and I had tried so long to avoid building one. With the release of something like this, would others get the wrong idea?

"I understand the purpose behind what you've done. I just have no interest in being *anyone's* center. If there is one thing I teach it's that meditation and spiritual realization happens within *you*, not through someone else. Please, Tina do me this one thing, and remove my name from the files. Let the words stand alone."

"Of course, Leif," she says. "I understand."

I reach out to her and she places her hands in mine. "Thank you."

My trip with Mary to the library had turned into something far different than I had imagined. I look up again and see she's looking right back, a renewed level of interest on her face, and a glow I could hopefully call something more than friendliness.

*****

I walk Mary to her room. Her mother and step-father are pacing about in the hall.

"Where were you?" her mom asks, rushing to meet us.

"Just at the library with Leif."

"Mrs. Gardner," I say.

"We were worried, Mary." Her eyes are red and swollen from crying.

"I'm very sorry. I had no intention of upsetting you," I apologize. "I just wanted Mary to know about the books."

"Leif, it's okay," Mary reassures me. "Mom, it's okay, I'm not even late for the Sergeant's tour."

"I know, I'm sorry." Her mother looks at me next. "I'm sorry, Leif, it's just, we've never been apart."

"It won't happen again without you knowing, Mrs. Gardner. I promise."

"Thanks, Leif." Mary brushes her hand against my arm. The sensation leaves goose-bumps in its wake. "I'll see you tomorrow."

"Yes, please," I say, barely aware of how silly I sound.

Mrs. Gardner walks her to her room, on the opposite side of the hall.

Mary's step-father walks toward me and lands a heavy hand on my shoulder.

"We're very grateful to be here," he starts. "Just know that we've been through a lot. You can't imagine." He stops himself, his head falling forward. Then he looks up at me again. "We're very grateful to be here."

I walk out of the family housing building and toward the hospital. A goofy smile plays out on my face as I dwell on Mary. The promise she would see me in the morning would make it difficult to sleep tonight. The morning could not come soon enough.

Chapter Twelve

Today is the day I discover what punishment Harry, Chris and Monty have been handed for their attack over a week earlier. I watch as an armed escort leads them to my meditation circle and nudges them to sit. They obey. None of them look up at me. They'd been held all this time in the stockade. So, sitting in on my meditation classes is to be their punishment. The irony and wisdom of the Captain's decision brings a smile to my face. I try not to take too much pleasure in their misery, but find it impossible to repress.

I use advanced yoga after our first round of meditation to further teach my oppressors a lesson, but am careful not to be cruel.

Warming down from the yoga I hold my pose and reflect on the night before. I feel awkward after Tina's surprise biography, but what I feel for Mary when I think on her is stranger still. I notice Mary in my peripheral, lingering just beyond the canopy of trees in the wooded corner of the base as the sun is just breaking the horizon. I ask my class to break and move to meet her.

"So, this is what you do with your days?" The smile on her face is genuine, and a little mocking. I like it.

My hands shoot into my pockets and my eyes fall to the ground. Her small top is too small I think, but would never bring it to her attention.

Mary touches my forearm. "Oh, Leif, I didn't mean it to embarrass you." A kind smile replaces the playful one of moments ago. My heart leaps at her touch.

"I'm not embarrassed," I say, pulling my hands out of my pockets. "Not about this anyway. I am a little embarrassed about what happened last night at the library."

"Don't be," she says, shaking her head.

"Please, Mary, I want you to know *me.*" I pause, wondering what my next words will be and then they surface. "Not someone else's version, but the *real* me."

"Is this not the *real* you?" she asks turning to the group behind us.

"It is," I nod. "But there is another me, and I'd like to share him with you." The words just keep coming; I feel I've lost control of my tongue. "Would you be interested in knowing me?"

A silence that I know is only one to two seconds feels like an eternity as Mary's eyes find mine and she answers.

"Yes." Her face ignites in white light as she moves to the right, stepping out of my shadow. "I would like that."

A buzzing in my chest erupts.

"Dinner?" I manage.

"Yes. Mess hall?"

"Yes." I answer. "Six?" I turn towards the group, reluctant for the first time I can remember to continue meditating.

Chapter Thirteen

The following week, Mary and I can't seem to spend enough time with one another. I encourage her to sit in on my meditation classes, and even to accompany me in my personal meditation. Mary is a quick study. She takes to the physical aspects of Yoga very quickly, allowing the mental facet of each session to fall in line. She is showing great promise in commanding her mind and body.

"I'm chasing the light," she says, patting her forehead with a hand-towel after an intensive mid-day class.

I laugh. 'Chasing the light' is Mary's new expression: a satirical description of her journey to enlightenment. She's very witty, which I have grown to appreciate.

"I think that's what we'll call your biography," I tell her. "'Chasing the Light: The Mary Gardener Story.'" She smiles back and whips the towel in my direction.

"Maybe I'll have a place in *your* story," she suggests, closing in on me. "But not my own." She is suddenly standing so close that the heat from her body feels as though it's enveloping me. I move backwards, and she follows, pinning me gently against the wall. My heels hit the steel with a bang, the sound startling us both.

"It was just the heels of my shoes," I blurt awkwardly. I'm not sure where to place my hands.

She pulls back. "Good, I'm glad you didn't bump your head." She was blushing now. Had I ruined a moment? She looks at the ground.

I know this is it, and I have to seize the moment. As if possessed, I place a finger under her chin and lift her face to mine. I feel my heart race. I lean toward Mary and our lips lock in a long, soft kiss.

Whistles and nervous laughter from the class enter my head like echoes, pulling me out of the moment.

"I'm sorry," I say, surprising myself once again. Mary's eyes pop open and her head jerks back.

"You are?" she whispers, her brows pushing up the middle of her forehead.

"No." I shake my head. "No, I don't know why I said that."

Mary smiles and takes my face in both hands, pulling me toward her. We kiss for a long time, eventually sitting on a bench.

Mary pulls back an inch or two and holds my face in her hands. She looks at me as if to say *I trust you.* I smile and my fingers find the line of her cheek bones and jaw. I trace them to her chin.

"Thank you for wanting this," she says, but I'm not sure what she means.

"I do," I assure her, regardless of the meaning.

"So do I."

We move toward each other again wrapping our arms around one other. Mary climbs on top of me, straddling me, and squeezes. I squeeze back.

After a time we stand. The class has dismissed themselves. I take her hand and we walk around the base. We say nothing. I find it difficult to quiet my mind. I want to kiss Mary again but feel suddenly shy. I want to tell her things, things that will make her smile and laugh and love me. Love me?

Is it so easy to fall in love? Why shouldn't it be? Why would it take any time at all?

Was I in love?

Chapter Fourteen

Tina has come to every meditation and assembly I've ever called, and now I knew why. She had been writing my biography.

"It's not just your words, Leif, that I'm capturing. It's your story," she explains, seated across from me in the empty cafeteria. It's three o'clock in the morning. I couldn't sleep and ran into Tina while walking the compound. I look up at her, putting aside the notes she had scribbled over the past 17 years. "And you've transferred all of these to your computer?"

Tina nods. "I'll print and bind them in a day."

I push the stack of paper back to her, having read my biography over the course of the last two nights. My neck feels tight and I rub it hard with my palm.

"Then why not tell the whole story, Tina?" I suggest. "Mom told you everything, you said." She nods again. "Then you know my story goes far beyond my years in this body. "

"What are you saying, Leif?"

"Tell my father's story as well. To tell only mine makes the story incomplete."

"How could I tell your father's story with any accuracy? Your mother knows her side only…"

I cut her off. "I know it intimately. You can listen as I meditate on my father's life and record everything I say."

"You can do that?"

"Yes."

"When did you want to start?"

"Right now," I say and she rises out of her chair. We walk quickly out of the mess hall and to the library where I have the privacy to recite the whole story.

*****

The work Tina and I had managed in the night was exhausting. I lament on the night before. Living my father's experiences, my past life, was devastating. We did get through it all though, and since Tina and mom had conspired to write my story, I felt it only right to be completely honest, offering the whole story from start to finish. Tina said she would interview mom next in an effort to collect a more detailed telling of when, eighteen years ago, she and I made our way here, to the safety of the base. That way she would have a complete tale up to the present day, to be added to as necessary.

So now Tina would have three books. Labeled as such: Book I A.A., Book II A.A, Book III A.A.

*****

Another nightmare leaves me at a loss tonight. Another warning of what will come to pass, another riddle to decode. The continuous assault on my sub-conscious by these distorted images and the emotions they carry with them have been hard on my nerves. I breath in, hold and release. I continue this practice until I settle down.

I haven't brought up these premonitions, if that's what they are, with my angel, but Blank Man has not approached me about them either. Though their imagery is muddied, their purpose seems clear. We are approaching an end that will not come quietly.

Chapter Fifteen

At dinner, Dieter sits next to Mary and across from me, his tray of food landing softly on the steel table. He is smiling as only Dieter does. His mouth, though sparsely populated with teeth, is never anyone's focus. His eyes shine brightly, projecting an extraordinary wisdom. I feel his excitement. It has been only two weeks since his arrival, but I already feel as though he will become a close friend. I am anxious to speak more with him, and I am sensing he feels the same.

"Hello, Leif." He turns to Mary. "And hello, beautiful Mary." She blushes, smiling. I wink in her direction and turn back to Dieter.

"How are you, Dieter?" I smile at him, my eyes darting between him and Mary.

"I wanted to continue our conversation," he says sheepishly. "I know that I talk above people on this subject – I told my wife about you and she thought maybe I was too forward."

"Well, you definitely had me at a disadvantage. But I caught the gist of it."

"Well, I wanted to just clear the air. I know we haven't had much contact since I got here, but getting settled seems to have taken more time than expected. You know, they have me working with the solar panels and windmills."

"I'm glad you've found something. We try to give people work that matches their skills, but pretty sure no one is hiding a physics lab on the base."

We share a laugh.

"This is fine for me." His hands wave frantically in front of him. "I've always loved sustainable power technologies. But, I did want to sit with you again and answer any question you might have since our last discussion."

"Yes, there are likely many more than I can think to ask on the spot, but maybe you could catch Mary up on our conversation." I ask as much for Mary's sake as my own.

"Certainly." He shifts in his seat to face her.

"I was five the last time I went to school," Mary admits. "My mom taught me things from books that we found as we moved from place to place, and I learned to read and write, but I wouldn't waste your time on me."

"It is never a waste to offer an education to someone willing to accept it." Dieter moves his tray of greens and bread to his right.

Mary nods and sits at attention. He takes up a roll in his hand and raises it over his head.

"What happens when I release this piece of bread?" he asks her.

Mary looks to me and then back to Dieter. "It will fall."

"Right, it will fall, but, why?"

"Gravity?"

"Yeah! Right again, Mary! Gravity is one of the four forces we can directly experience. The planet was created because of gravity, the solar system was pulled together by the gravity of the sun, and our galaxy was formed by the gravity of the black hole that sits in the centre. Everything we see is affected by gravity."

"Okay, I understand that," Mary says with a growing confidence.

"Good, Mary, so while classical physics describes the universe around us, or the very big, a physicist cannot apply it to the very small, the quantum world."

"Now I'm lost," Mary smiles. I laugh at her candor.

"Imagine something smaller than the smallest thing you can see with your eyes, Mary," continues Dieter, undeterred. "Now, imagine something a million times smaller."

Mary leans back in her seat at the thought, shaking her head. "I can't."

"And you are not alone. Few could. Allow me to take you to the hospital research area. They have a microscope there that is very powerful."

"Leif?" Mary looks for my approval.

I shrug. "I'd like to see where he's going with this too." I stand and we march out of the mess hall, Dieter stuffing the roll in his mouth.

Upon arriving at the hospital, Mary and I wait outside the research lab while Dieter speaks with Doctor Bren about using his microscope for a presentation. I watch as the doctor nods and waves us into the room.

Inside, Dieter places a flat glass panel with a red spot on it under the microscope's eye. "Mary, please, come and see what I mean." He points at his eye and then at the scope urging Mary to stare into the eye-piece. She bends over the microscope and places one eye on the scope. I watch as her mouth opens and a smile grows across her face.

"It is blood," says Dieter, nodding my way, his arms crossed. "Thousands of times bigger than you see with your own eyes."

Mary looks up and her eyes turn to Dieter. "But it doesn't even look like blood." Her head falls back to the microscope.

"No, so you can see how something that defines a universe we can see with our own eyes, the macroscopic, would have trouble defining a world as small as the one you are witnessing now, the microscopic."

"Could I see, Mary?" I ask, walking toward her. She nods and I lean in for a look. This must have been what Father Henderson meant when he said he'd *'found God'* in the intelligent design of all things, before he left his career as a biologist.

What I see in no way represents a drop of blood in my experience. It's not a liquid, but broken down into dozens of puck-like forms, opening my eyes to just how complex the physical world really is.

"That's incredible," I whisper.

"And that is not even close to what I was able to see when I had my own laboratory. So, you start to see that the very small make up the very big and this world of the very small is very different than what you see with your own eyes."

"It's amazing," says Mary, now holding my arm.

"It is that." Dieter takes a breath. "This is why quantum physics was realized. When you go another step, you see atoms, and then the subatomic particles, like hadrons and quarks."

I fear Dieter is starting to talk beyond his audience again and jump in. "But the strings you told me about? You can't see those?"

"No, sadly," answers Dieter. "These will remain a theory, a hypothesis, since I have lost the ability to scientifically prove their existence."

"What are Strings?" Mary asks.

"I believe they are the architects of all energy and matter in our universe. They vibrate at different frequencies, blinking in and out of 'existence'."

"Okay, I wanted to go back to the beginning with you anyways, Dieter, when you said that everything vibrates."

"Sure, let's start there." He pulls a string from his shirt pocket and ties a knot at one end. He then slips the knotted end into a cut in the wooden table pulling up on the string with his other hand. The string is now taut. Dieter begins to strum at the string, making it vibrate.

"You see how the more I flick the string the faster it vibrates?"

"Yes," Mary and I answer in unison.

"And do you see how it almost disappears from view, the faster it goes?"

"It's funny, I hear it too." I stare blankly at the buzzing string as Dieter continues to flick it.

"Everything vibrates like this on a quantum level. We are made up of vibrations, and so is this table, and this string." Dieter grins and closes his eyes. "Like music, yeah?"

I see a 'eureka' moment play out on Mary's face.

"I listen to music when I'm having difficulty with my meditation," she admits. "I *feel* the music and it helps to center my thoughts."

"Exactly!" Dieter's hand pounds on the table." You *feel it* because music *is* vibration and it touches you on a level that transcends the physical world. It interacts with those quantum vibrations that live within us all!"

"What does that mean exactly?" I ask.

"It goes to my point that we can be affected on the quantum level. If music helps send Mary into that plane of meditation where she may walk with *God* in the quantum dimensions, then my work is being realized as we speak!"

"Because…"

"Because you *feel* music." His fingers point frantically at his ears. "You hear sounds. Sound is not a tangible thing, but a wave of energy, you *feel it*. And that it is the vibrations from the music which helps send Mary into a meditative state, those vibrations are affecting her own frequency propelling her spirit, into the quantum level!"

"Perhaps you should learn to play an instrument," he suggests.

"I would like to learn to play the piano, but I'm told it is out of tune,"

"You have a piano here?" Dieter perks up.

"In a room off the library, but it needs tuning and no one here knows how." Mary's face drops.

"I know how." Dieter urges us to move. "Please, show me this piano and I will fix it for us."

Mary and I rush out after an almost delirious Dieter, anxious to hear the ancient instrument brought back to life. Mom had spoken of my grandparent's piano, and how it used to soothe her to sleep as a child. A gift of music was always welcome, and if Dieter could really tune the piano, it would be a great gift for the entire community.

Chapter Sixteen

Mary, I am certain, has found herself here by way of destiny, not only for her, but for me as well. I sense during every moment with her that epiphanal feeling that it is 'meant to be'. These stirrings have alerted me to what I have been missing: love, on a physical plane. Not the love of a friend. Not the love of a mother, though no one could replace her for me. This is altogether different. I feel it in a very physical way. There is a tingling in my chest when I think of her. Electricity excites the hairs on my arm when we touch. I smile without thinking, feel a sense of independence in her presence and a freedom I have only known in deepest meditation.

In the mess hall, mom is resting her head in her hands, grinning from ear to ear as I tell her what's been happening to me during the past couple of weeks with respect to Mary.

"Yup!" she exclaims. "That's love." Her hands reach out for mine. "I've been wondering when it would happen."

"Well, then, what do I do about it?" I ask finding it hard to catch my breath.

Mom's face turns suddenly serious. "Do you know if she feels the same?" I know mom was once in love with the Sergeant. She called it unrequited love. A sad story, and it shows now in her face.

"I think so. But, how can I be sure?"

She squeezes my hand. "Leif, you just ask her then. There is no joy in not knowing. There is less joy than in knowing she doesn't, but then you can get over it, or work on it. But ask her."

"How do you ask someone that, Mom?"

"Tell her how you feel." She's squeezing harder now. I let her nails dig into my palm without a word. "She will be more than happy to tell you if she's feeling the same."

"And if she isn't?" I can't say I'd thought about it much from that angle, but saying the words aloud took the tingling sensation from my chest and landed it firmly in the pit of my stomach.

"It's early still," she says, leaning back. "Maybe it's too soon to ask something like that." I must look confused. Was she changing her plan because she thought it unlikely Mary could have fallen for me as quickly?

"Maybe," I say looking down at my hands.

"You do what you think you should do, Leif. Don't listen to your silly mother." She's smiling again as I look up at her. "Young people fall in love quickly like that. I remember." Now she is looking at her hands.

"I'll know what to do the next time I see her. I'll just know." I wish my feelings were as sure as my words.

Chapter Seventeen

The sanctuary is well hidden by Castle Peak, the towering three hundred foot-high mass of jagged rock jutting up just a few yards north of the base, creating a sheer cliff along the south-west expanse of the lake. Elle Lake itself, which cuts around the trees and gardens in a long semi-circle until it comes to the hills rising up in the east, offers only a southern passage and potential eastern approach, both of which are heavily guarded.

It is ideal. The fishery is directly off-shore and there is netting laid a hundred yards in every direction to fence in the fish, preventing them from disappearing into the areas untouched by the zebra mussels, which were employed to clean the lake floor of the fall-out.

Elle Lake is where the Chaplain's efforts to rebuild our world are really beginning to shine. His work in populating the indigenous fish that once teemed through the waters and planting such a variety of vegetation, the majority of which once thrived here, have paid off.

The blossoms bloom in the summer sun and their perfume is exhilarating. It is a crime to pick a bloom, as these will one day be edible fruit, and I fight off the urge to hand one to Mary.

The day is warm and the sky a brilliant blue. The lake carries with it a breeze that catches Mary's new growth of hair.

She has gained a little much-needed weight since her arrival and looks even more beautiful than when I first laid eyes on her. Even her lips have grown fuller and her skin more radiant. I love to hear her laugh and as the wind picks up she laughs louder.

I take Mary to my sacred hollow that sits in the center of a small pine forest.

"This is gorgeous, Leif." She spins around.

"Sit with me a moment, Mary." I pat the soft forest floor in front of me. Mary sits and, closing her eyes, takes a deep breath.

"This is more fragrant than the forest on the base."

"We have very few cedars and pines behind the walls. The Chaplain says they do better out here, close to the water."

"Can we drink the water?"

"Not directly. Not yet anyway."

"But it works for the trees." She touches a white pine's rough trunk and smiles.

"Yes, the soil from our compost is rich in minerals and helps to filter the water so the tree isn't poisoned. We get our drinking water from underground wells."

"What's your favorite fruit?" she asks playfully.

"I don't have a favorite fruit."

She smiles and leans in to kiss me.

I meet her lips. My heart is racing. Can she hear the thumping in my chest? Mary puts her hands on my knees. I feel her touch throughout my entire body. I hope for the moment to never end. Just as this thought occurs to me, Mary pulls back. She looks at me intensely for a moment. Then, as if almost frightened, she speaks.

"I'm happy, Leif," she says. "I'm so happy with you." A shy smile appears and her face reddens.

I'm so sure I love her. I feel as light as air, yet the trepidation I feel in my stomach when I think to tell her… it's all very confusing.

"Leif, do you think we were meant to meet? I mean, you believe things happen for a reason, right?"

"Yes. I always have." I hope she's going where I think she's going with this line of questioning.

"I think I believe that too. I think if we weren't meant to meet and be a part of each other's lives we wouldn't have."

I nod in agreement, though my enthusiasm is underwhelming. Not because I disagree in any way, but because I feel myself leaving my body.

"Don't you?" She looks at me, tilting her head.

"I do," I reply. And with that the impulse strikes me.

"I love you." I feel the heat in my cheeks burn to the surface. A beacon of my humiliation; I think. What's wrong with me? Mary straightens and there is a pause as she looks me in the eye. I've made a very pleasant moment tense for her, I think. She doesn't feel the same way. This is all falling apart. I'm an idiot. Just when I feel I can't possibly last another moment without another word being uttered, she springs forward, wrapping her arms around my shoulders and forcing me back into the spongy soil. She then proceeds to kiss me in short explosive pecks all over my face and head and neck. I giggle as her tickling breath accompanies each kiss and am overjoyed at her response to my declaration.

We roll around among the pine needles and I kiss her passionately; our tongues rolling over one another's. Then she slides on top of me and pins me to the ground.

"I love you, too," she says very slowly, her lips swollen and pink.

Her shifting weight on my pelvis excites me and I pull her down to my left to avoid any further embarrassing affirmations. My vision is blurry and my words now stick in my throat. I can smile, but that's about all I can do. She leans in to kiss me again and the urge to fall into her, recklessly, and without thought of our surroundings, ignites a fire inside me.

Mary pulls away from me. "Do you want to?" she asks in a whisper.

I know what she's asking, and yes, oh *god* yes, I *do* want to. I nod like an imbecile. She stands up and offers me her hand. I grab it. We rush through the sanctuary, past the guards, the vegetable gardens, the brick oven, row upon row of apple and pear trees, the blueberry bushes, every new obstacle seemingly placed to make our escape more difficult. Running the perimeter of the base we rush through the gates and push through the residence doors, Mary leading the charge.

When we arrive at her room she fumbles with her keys. Once the key turns in the lock Mary shoulders the door open and drags me inside. The door slams shut, the key still in the lock. Mary hurries off her outer layers of clothing and I stand there watching her reveal herself to me, dumbfounded. Mary slows and then stops.

"What are you waiting for?" She grins at me. I snap out of my stupor and burst three buttons on my shirt, tearing it off. My pants fall away and we're on Mary's bed kissing and pushing our bodies against one another. Her flesh is hot. I feel like I have a fever and the only way to quench it is to satisfy this intensifying urge to bury myself in Mary. Her under-things are now on the floor and she's pulling at mine. I let her. We're both trembling. The thrill of connecting like this with another person is unlike anything I had imagined.

I am present. I am Mary and she is me. We are one.

Chapter Eighteen

I've always known love. My mother's love, the love I feel when enraptured in meditation, the love of my community. Though these affect me on a physical and spiritual level, there is something infinitely more substantial about the love I feel when I look at Mary. I feel out of control. It's exciting and new and addictive. I love being in love with her, and it makes me feel amazing that someone so incredible feels the same about me. I have found my bliss in Mary. She is my soul mate, and I tell her this every opportunity I have. I do not want to be away from her, and when I am my focus is on when I will see her again. I see her face when I meditate and feel her arms around me. The physical aspect of love is far greater than I had imagined. When we are intimate in that sense I am present, in the moment, enjoying her and enjoying the life of a physical 'now'. I had never imagined the 'now' in the physical world being so perfect.

"Mind your feelings, Leif," Blank Man whispers to me. "You're drifting dangerously out of sight."

"What's that supposed to mean?"

"Your destiny, Leif. Your dedication has been misplaced as of late."

"Have I not done all you've asked of me?" Irritation rises in my voice.

"You have."

"Then let me have this. What harm can come from this?"

"Do not ask the questions if you do not want to hear the answers, Leif."

"Fine, don't answer then." Blank Man simply wants my undivided attention. After everything I'd done for him, living my life the way he'd wished, didn't I deserve a little happiness of my own? And wasn't the point of all of this to rebuild the human race? If I couldn't fall in love and have a family, what is the point?

"You still haven't *seen*, Leif. Your father's destiny is yours now and you must see it through."

"What do you want from me now?"

"You require more time spent in meditation and less in other activities before you can learn this."

"Just answer the question, please." I am becoming angry.

"You will learn your true destiny in meditation."

"I meditate five times a day!" My hands turn into fists. I was happy in every aspect of my life, but now Blank Man is trying to disrupt that.

"Why!? Why can't I have this? Why can't we be happy together?" I am thankful Mary isn't in the room to witness this outburst.

Blank Man leans toward me from the mirror. His head cocks and I throw a fist into his silhouette, breaking the mirror and cutting my knuckles.

Chapter Nineteen

I am angry with Blank Man and send him away each time he calls on me. I do not understand his disapproval of my newfound relationship. Am I nothing more than a workhorse to him? Plowing out his plans to the crack of his whip? Am I to have no life but that of servitude? When was *I* given a choice? I've been prepared by the Blank Man for some great purpose he won't reveal to me, yet I'm supposed to just accept it?

This night I sleep poorly. My 'Angel' constantly tries to push through the boundaries of my mind, to discuss this disagreement between us, but I force him out – for now, my thoughts will be my own.

*****

I do not sleep through the night. A new nightmare finds me. They are becoming more and more frequent. There is an urgency in this recent manifestation. A darkness approaches.

Chapter Twenty

The next morning at the greenhouse I find the Chaplain tending a new crop of indigenous fish. To our left there must be a hundred saplings - pine, fruit trees, deciduous. These will further fill out the forest by the lake in years to come.

"Good morning, Leif."

"Hello, Father."

"I hope you've come with conversation this morning."

"I have, actually," I say, as though that were something atypical. My arm rests against the plastic pond as I watch the tiny fish dart through the water.

"Wonderful." He picks up a mug of coffee from the pond's plastic ledge. He never starts the day without a coffee. Luckily, the base had enough freeze-dried coffee in its underground storage facilities to caffeinate one thousand soldiers for five years. The absence of those soldiers left enough coffee to serve the one hundred or so this base has housed at any one time for at least fifty years.

I enjoy watching the Chaplain sip at his cup. The look on his face as he holds the bitter liquid in his mouth and swallows always makes me laugh. He grimaces as I smile at him; this one vice he should be allowed to savor.

"You were a botanist before you became a religious man." I open the conversation with a statement we both know to be true. I am nervous about my line of thought.

He nods and I continue.

"And I assume you never married?"

"No, never truly." He closes his eyes, allowing the coffee's aroma to permeate his senses. "I did have several relationships with women though."

"Was it easy to give that up? I mean, have you ever been in love?" I look down at my hands so he cannot see how much his answer matters to me.

"When the spirit of the Lord entered me, all others became secondary. It was a calling."

"But you knew what love was before you were called?"

"I did. I was with someone for eight years when I was called."

"And were you in love with this person?"

"I was. I mean, I had fallen in love with her and we lived together for five years as I worked as a botanist." He pauses. "Was I still in love with her eight years later? I'm not sure. Love is a powerful emotion at the onset, but it fades over time. Being called upon by God to serve is not a love that diminishes, and for me it was an easy transformation."

"So you gave up the love of a woman to love *God* and serve *Him*." This was a difficult pill to swallow, if the Chaplain could give himself completely to his religion, should I not also feel this connection to the purpose laid out for me by Blank Man? But Mary… My heart skips a beat at the thought of her. I love her.

"Father…"

Before I finish my thought an explosion bursts in my ears, the glass wall beside us shattering into thousands of pieces.

Chapter Twenty-one

I waken to the sight of mom hovering over me. I am lying in one of the hospital bunks. When she sees my eyes open, she springs to my side and strokes my forehead.

"Thank God," she says.

I sit up and see that my right arm is bandaged from wrist to shoulder, and a wrap covers my chest. "What happened, Mom?"

"The terrorists are at it again." Her face is a maze of lines. I feel an urge to trace them with my fingers.

"*Earl*?" His name is still with me after all these years. Earl, mom's enemy and leader of a group of terrorists that has tested our bases defenses time and again. But, that was many years ago.

"No," Mom answers. Her brow pulls downward. "He wasn't among the dead, and those left alive didn't seem to know who the Sergeant was talking about before they were hanged."

"But you're alright?" She runs her hand delicately over my bandages.

"I am, Mom." I grasp her moist palm with my right hand and flinch at the many tiny sharp pains that travel up and down my arm.

"Oh, Leif, don't move your arm."

"Yeah, bad idea," I agree. I look at her again and see a sadness that goes beyond my superficial wounds. "Is there something else?"

"Oh, Leif." Her head bows and eyes close, and she stays that way for a time.

"What, Mom? What is it?" My heartbeat speeds up and my stomach drops. Something was very wrong.

Her head turns to her left, and I follow her gaze. In a bed three cots from me is Mary. She is still, lying under a grey sheet with her head bandaged and a brace around her neck. I instantly attempt to go to her, but find the pain of moving too great.

"What happened?"

"They found her lying behind the northwest watch tower. She had fallen." Her hand moves to her mouth. It is a twenty foot drop from the crow's nest to the ground.

"Is she unconscious?"

"It's more than that, Leif." I feel her hand softly rest on my shoulder. "She was gone for nearly three minutes."

I swing around and stand. "Gone? *Dead*?"

"It was all we could do to bring her back, Leif."

"Is she…" I couldn't finish the sentence.

"We don't know that."

Tears escape down my cheeks and she wipes them away.

Putting on a brave face I say, "She will."

I am able to travel the short distance to Mary's bedside without too much discomfort. I sit, reading a book of meditations aloud. I feel at odds with my own theories and truths. That my destiny would steal away the woman I love makes me question everything. I am finding it difficult to fight away feelings of anger and discouragement. I should be happy for her, should she cross to the other side. But was she ready? I have so much more to teach her. I want her to be prepared for this end. And I, perhaps selfishly, want her with me longer. The love I feel for her is so different from all others, and that we love each other, total strangers, is incredible.

My leg involuntarily bounces on the ball of my foot. I continue to fight back the negative thoughts causing the unwelcome emotional responses.

"Leif," a small voice whispers. My heart leaps.

"Mary," I say, bending to face her. I leave the book and take her hand in mine. "Mary."

"Leif," she says again in a weak whisper. "Leif, I saw."

"You fell, love. You fell and hit your head. But you're fine, you'll be fine."

"Yes, everything will be fine," she assures me, nodding in spite of the neck brace. There is such a peaceful look on her face that I am unprepared for what happens next. Mary suddenly begins to blink wildly.

Her eyes roll up into the back of her head.

I stand, not relinquishing my grasp on her hand. "Doctor!" I shout. "Nurse!"

A nurse rushes to my side and sees that Mary is awake and in distress. "I'll get Dr. Bren," she says, rushing out the door.

I sit again and gently kiss Mary's face. "Stay with me, Mary." Her eyelids cease their flickering and she stares at me.

"I saw, Leif. I felt it. It's beautiful."

Dr. Bren rushes in. He immediately takes Mary's blood pressure, tests her reflexes and shines a small flashlight into her pupils.

"Leif, let us do our work here," he orders sternly and I realize I haven't let go of her hand. "I'll come get you when we're done. Go get a coffee in the mess hall or something."

I nod blankly and back off. I turn and walk with a slight limp out of the hospital building, blindly following the Doctor's orders.

Chapter Twenty-two

I wander aimlessly through the streets that line the base walls. My heart races. The first thing Mary did was explain to me that she had experienced something marvelous. What did Mary see? I ponder this for three laps of the base. The thought had instantly occurred to me, but I let it roam around in my head: Mary has been to the other side.

I double back through the center of the complex, reaching the library. I throw open the door and burn a straight line to Tina, who is positioned where she always is during open hours: at her desk, her frameless lenses reflecting what information she is typing into her monitor. Tina's head pops up over her screen. "Leif!" she says, alarmed at my obvious distress.

"Where can I find anything on near death experiences?"

Tina gets out of her chair and rounds her desk to take my hand, and noticing the heavy bandage on my right arm, changes her plan and waves me forward.

"There are two hard-bound books here, but there are many more on the server, if you want to use the computer stations." She leads me to an open computer and begins typing the keywords into the base's intranet. A myriad of titles reveal themselves.

I watch her type frantically on the keyboard and study the screen as a dozen more titles appear.

"This is great, Tina." I scan each of the titles, deciding which to read first.

"Has something happened, Leif?"

"It's Mary, Tina," I say, "She's been to the other side."

"Dead?" A look of horror appears on her face.

"Yes, but back. She's come back!" I can barely contain my excitement.

"Thank God," she says, her hand falling on her heart. "Are you okay?"

I nod to my bandaged arm and shrug. "I'll live! But, I need to do this now. Can I stay here tonight?"

"Whatever you need, Leif. I'll be leaving in a couple of hours, but you stay on as long as you need to, honey."

I quickly flip through the two books Tina brings me and discover some very interesting information about the experiences others have had with this phenomenon. I need to know everything I can. Then I will be ready for this conversation with Mary. An inevitable conversation I'd always hoped I'd have.

Chapter Twenty-three

My duties as morale officer require me to visit with the friends and families of recently deceased members of our community. I have read up on the subject and trained myself on the approach. Though the Captain had no living relatives, and made no attempt to build a new relationship after her husband and children had died, the other three soldiers who had perished in the recent car bombing did have families who needed consoling.

After a few hours at the library I stand and stretch, resigning myself to the task of visiting with those distraught individuals, mourning the loss of their loved one. It's not something I relish, but I do feel as though I make a difference when I sit with them.

I step out into the warm summer night and watch a crowd of people rush past me. I stop Luke, a man of about forty, to ask what's going on.

He answers me excitedly. "Someone's lost their mind and climbed the big windmill!"

"Climbed it? Why?" We had several windmills on the property, but only one we called the 'big windmill'.

"That's what we're going to see." When I release his arm, he hurries off.

I naturally follow the crowd, my curiosity piqued. When I arrive at the scene I can make out a silhouette climbing off the last rung of the ladder and sitting atop the turbine. There is no breeze, thank goodness, so the blades are not turning.

"It's my brother," a woman tells the crowd. "He's sick: he told me he was going to kill himself." She's frantic. I watch as two men climb the ladder to the roof.

I shout up to them. “Don’t rush up there.”

“How else do you suppose we’ll get him down?” One of the men shouts back from the roof top.

“If you charge after him like that he’ll throw himself off. He’s suicidal.”

“There’s no other way.” Peter, the smaller man shouts back. “We’re going up.”

“What will you do once you’re up there?”

“I dunno, grab him and drag him down.”

“He’ll never let you get that close.”

I remember the woman, but I can’t remember her brother’s name. “What’s your brother’s name, Serena?”

“Marcello.”

I move to the ladder, climb it and join the men on the roof.

“Peter, Jason,” I address the men. “Marcello needs to be talked down, not forced.” I thought if he was truly suicidal he’d have thrown himself off already. But if he’s not, and is tested, he may jump anyways.

“Be my guest.” The man steps off the ladder and on to the roof top.

Sergeant Jones appears on the roof a moment later with KC and two others.

“You’re not going up there,” the Sergeant tells me.

“Yes, I am.”

“It’s sixty feet up, if you fall.”

“I won’t fall,” I insist. “Besides, who’s better suited to do something like this?” I’d have volunteered the Chaplain, if her were thirty years younger, and it dawns on me that I haven’t seen him since the explosion.

The Sergeant looks at KC and has to concede my point.

“But your arm, Leif.” KC motions towards my bandage.

I bend my arm in the thick wrap to show how much movement I have. I bury the pain and smile through it.

“Give Leif your harness,” the Sergeant orders one of the other two soldiers. “And here is the spare, for Marcello.” He hands me both. I nod and KC helps me with mine.

“When you get up there, Leif, place this pulley assembly on a flat surface. It’s magnetic and will act as your life line. We’ll have the other end of the rope down here, understand?”

"I understand."

It takes only two minutes for me to climb to the top and once there I slow to a crawl.

"Marcello, it's Leif." I've seen Marcello at my classes once or twice with his sister. I had the feeling he had been coerced into attending.

"Oh, no, no, no, no, please don't do that. I'm not up here to talk to anyone."

"I just need to know you are okay, Marcello."

"I'm not."

"Why?" His nervous energy was beginning to get to me. I feel his angst and fight it off.

"You can't understand why."

"I will listen though." I watch Marcello pace along the hood of the turbine, and gently place the magnetic pulley system on the steel casing.

"That would be a first," he says, his hands balled into fists as he moves from one end of the turbine to the other. "No one listens to me, not my sister, not the people in the kitchen I work with, no one."

"Could I sit with you up here and listen?"

"What difference would that make?"

"Okay, then it's alright if I come up?"

"Doesn't make a difference," he assures me. So I climb the last rung in the ladder and sit on the high perch. It doesn't look this big from the ground, but it's actually very spacious: ten feet long and five feet wide.

"You're making me nervous pacing like that, Marcello. Would you sit with me?"

"I'm not doing this to upset anyone."

"Then why are you up here?"

"To jump."

"And you don't think that would be upsetting to anyone?"

"Who would miss me? I'm invisible."

"I see you fine, Marcello."

"Okay, I'm not invisible, but I might as well be. No one listens to me. No one lets me do anything. I'm useless here."

"No one here is useless, everyone's role is important to the community."

"I can't go back there now, look at them all watching me. I might as well jump and save myself the humiliation."

"Your sister is down there. Do you want her to see you hit the ground? Would you like her to live with the image of her brother, who she loves, slamming into the earth?"

"Goddamn it." He falls to a seated position and rocks back and forth, his fingers pulling at his hair. "I can't even do this right!"

"That's not a bad thing."

Surprisingly, a giggle escapes his lips.

I laugh as well hoping to encourage more laughter from him. It works. I crawl over to him and sit once more.

"Do me a favor would you, Marcello?"

He looks at me, quizzically. "Do you a favor?"

"Yeah, a small favor."

"What?"

"Talk to me. I'm a little nervous up here."

He nods.

"I'm not up here to tell you how to live your life, but you should understand the consequences of your actions."

"Consequences?" He begins to pace once more.

"Yes, well, your sister for one."

He steadies himself and breathes in deeply. A shudder can be heard through his throat and chest as he exhales.

"I didn't want to hurt her."

"But you know you will if you jump."

"I wasn't thinking of anyone else."

"That's the trouble when people act out of selfishness."

"I'm not like that."

"I know that, that's why this is so hard for you."

"I just can't exist like this anymore. No one listens to me."

"Well, you've got my attention, Marcello, I'm listening!" A smile pulls up the corners of my mouth.

"I feel useless!"

"You're not. You have to believe that. Look at all the people that have come to your side. They want to help. They're worried for you."

"They're here for a show." His eyes widen as he stares down at the crowd. "Why now? Why care now?"

"Because we're all in this together, and when one of us is hurting, we're all hurting." His nervous energy is spiking. He gets up and makes two more passes on the turbine and I am honestly getting a bit scared of how this is going to end.

"They pick on me."

"They pick on me too, Marcello." I pause. "But how you deal with it makes all the difference. This isn't dealing with it. This is running from it."

"I guess."

"You know that's what you're doing."

"It's so hard."

"It doesn't have to be." I motion to him. He flinches and moves further from me.

"Come down with me," I show him the harness. "Hug your sister."

"I'm sorry." He tells me, shaking his head.

"You don't have anything to be sorry for. We all have weak moments."

"No, I'm sorry, Leif."

I have little time to react as he bolts for the edge of the turbine. I grab at his ankle and his heal connects with my chin. My grip fails. In a last ditch effort I lunge at him with my wounded arm and manage to pull him down. Sergeant Jones and KC join me and secure the other harness to Marcello.

I am upset it went this way and sit on the turbine to ruminate over my approach. Tiny spots of red pepper the bandage on my right arm. I've reopened some of my stitches.

As the Sergeant hauls a struggling Marcello over the edge, KC manning the rope, I watch them land to cheers and applause.

Chapter Twenty-four

After the attack on the base, we count our losses. The Captain and three soldiers were killed in the explosions. An explosive device was thrown into the cab of their jeep while on a routine sweep of our parameter. The force of the explosion pushed Mary off the watch tower and onto the forest floor.

The second explosive, which put me in the hospital, had sailed over the walls, exploding on impact with the greenhouse.

The Sergeant was having a harder time than he wanted to admit. All of this was wearing on him.

I watch as he approaches from the east. I am cross-legged, nursing my newly bandaged arm on the forest floor where Mary had fallen. He is dressed in full military regalia, armed to the teeth.

"Do you mind if I join you?"

I nod and motion for him to sit. I look at his red and swollen eyes.

"How are you coping?" I ask.

"Not well, Leif," he admits, wringing his hands.

"Can I help?"

Sergeant Jones stares at me a long while, long enough to make me feel uncomfortable. He sucks in a deep breath and exhales roughly.

"It has become very apparent to me these past few months that you are a leader, Leif. I say this with conviction. The people love you. They are connecting with your ideas. You are meant for something greater than this." His hand shoots out in front of him, panning the landscape, the ruined greenhouse beside us.

"Well, not everyone is so accepting, but I appreciate your kind words, Sergeant."

"These are more than just words, Leif. This is a request. I'm asking you to share the load of leadership."

I stare at the Sergeant, dumbfounded. "Wouldn't that honor fall to you alone, now that the Captain is gone?" I respond tactfully.

"Yes, of course, I will take command of the soldiers and run the military aspects of the base but, I am not the politician the Captain was. It is because of her we enjoy the relative peace we do inside these walls. Leif, your mother has told me what you're capable of. She's told me you could change everything, and I believe her. The way you live your life is very attractive. You have *disciples* for Christ's sake." He stops himself and studies the ground.

"I'm impressed at how you handled the jumper last night. It was inspired. You have it in you to lead."

"I failed Marcello last night."

"You didn't, Leif. He's with his sister now, he's alive."

I appreciate the Sergeant's words, and I allow myself the peace they offer. Understanding the path my destiny is leading me down with his offer of leadership I tell him: yes.

The Sergeant's eyes blink wildly. A grateful smile lightens his mood. "Yes?"

"Yes, I will share the load." I watch as Blank Man hovers over the Sergeant, a blinding light pulsating from his now brilliant silhouette. My heart fills up with a heat that penetrates the visceral, teetering on the spiritual. My destiny has been realized, and is now in motion.

Chapter Twenty-five

In the hospital, I catch Dr. Bren moving through my peripheral. "Doctor," I whisper, rising slowly from the chair next to Mary's bed, my hand never leaving hers. "Could I speak with you?"

"Please."Doctor Bren motions for me to follow him.

"Back soon," I promise her, kissing her hand before resting it upon her chest. Mary nods and smiles weakly at me, blinking twice and then closing her eyes.

As we enter the doctor's office he waves for me to sit in one of the worn, plush leather seats. I remain standing.

"I would like to know the extent of Mary's injuries."

"Of course," he takes his seat. "Mary's reflexes and other motor controls are perfect, Leif. Her speech and memory and problem solving abilities are all excellent. She has recovered completely."

"That *is* good news."

"Yes." His eyes narrow. "But you knew all that, didn't you?"

"I figured."

"Then the question is not about her mental and physical recovery."

"I was hoping you might have some information to offer from past events. Have any other patients had a similar… experience?"

Dr. Bren moves behind his desk and opens a drawer. He carefully places a folder three inches thick on the desk's smooth metallic surface. "This has been something of a pet project of mine." He taps the folder with his palm. "When you lose a patient on the table, you lose a part of yourself. Then you start looking for answers. First you look for the mistakes, you look at procedure and you wonder if you could have done something differently. Then, when all avenues have been exhausted, you look beyond the factual. You look for something more. Some point to it all."

"And this is your research?" I point to the blue folder laid out on his desk.

"Yes. I have had patients die on my table, but some of them came back. Like Mary." He sits and opens the file. "What those people said to me, about where they went, and what they saw and felt, has intrigued me." His long, narrow fingers trace the profiles of dozens of case studies on the subject of 'near death experiences'.

"Then you believe?"

He straightens up. "I'm a doctor, a surgeon. Though these accounts are inspiring, I'm a man of science. I believe in the visceral. If I can see it, touch it, if I can feel it, then it's real to me."

"But your file: you must believe on some level if you've carried this file with you all these years."

"No, Leif, I *don't*. These files challenge the statements from those people." He closes the folder and looks up at me. "Whatever it was your Mary experienced, it was not life after death. Not in my opinion. My research says her experience was that of an oxygen starved brain, calming the mind and preparing it for death."

"And how do you justify that explanation?"

"Through the research of great surgeons: those who've dedicated their time to the study and mapping of the human brain." He sits back in his chair. "I know what you believe, Leif. I respect your beliefs, and I believe in meditation, but I cannot tell you I believe in life after death. Consider what science knows. As the brain gets closer and closer to death it only fires in areas which are very basic to survival, closer to the brain stem: a fundamental and primitive part of the brain. So, when the visual cortex, the back part of the brain, or the superior colliculus, which is considered part of the brain stem are activated; *all you'll see is light.*"

I sit forward in my chair, fascinated by his clinical explanation.

"And that point of light is surrounded by darkness. Our best interpretation would be of being in a tunnel. *Everyone* that has had a *'near death experience'* has shared this vision. It is much like dreaming, disjointed images, nonsense dialogue, it pulls from the same place. In near death, the central nervous system reanimates our most primal memories, our most deep-seated life experiences You could say your whole life passes before your eyes."

"So what about 'out of body' experiences. I mean, you're telling me the 'near death experience' is the brain putting a person at ease, but it is often accompanied by an 'out of body' experience. How can that be explained?"

"I can't explain that, Leif. I won't even try. I can only comment on the science, not on the spiritual."

"But you understand a man laying flat on an operating table, for all intents and purposes, dead, who can describe how many people were in the room and even what they looked like once revived isn't experiencing a hallucination."

"I'm not qualified to answer that, Leif."

"You are if you have an opinion, Doctor."

He laughs and shakes his head at me. "Sure, Leif, if I had to answer that I would say no, he's not having a hallucination, he's dead."

"What then?"

"Perhaps another look through my notes will produce a satisfactory answer, for both of us." He opens the folder once more.

"Thank you for your time, Doctor." I turn and open the door to leave.

"Leif," he calls after me, his tone pleasant. I turn. "Either way, she's back."A broad smile lightens his face. I smile back.

"She is, Doctor, thank you for that." I smile and return to Mary's bedside.

Chapter Twenty-six

The Sergeant and I walk toward the greenhouse, where Father Henderson and I were talking when the explosion happened. I take in the damage. The north side of the building has been shattered. The metal skeleton is bowed in the middle, all the windows gone. The vegetation and gardens inside seem unharmed save the thousands of pieces of plastic that litter the soil. Dozens of volunteers wade through the vast gardens picking out the plastic, careful not to disturb the plants, many of which are ready to bloom.

"It's a damn shame," the Sergeant says as he tosses a shard of window pane into the walkway where the volunteers are stacking it. "I'm sorry about the Chaplain."

I turn to meet him. "What?" I ask dumbly. "What about him?"

"Oh, Leif, didn't your mother tell you?"

"No."

He takes a moment to wipe away a pained expression. "I'm not sure I should be the one to then."

Anxiety rises in my chest and I realize I am holding my breath. I choke out a response. "Tell me, please."

"It's not my place." He explains.

"Sergeant," I take him by the arms. "What's happened to Father Henderson?"

"It's just, well, of the two of you, you were the lucky one." He squeezes my shoulder. I step back and shake my head. I hadn't felt so light headed before. The Sergeant's arm falls to his side as I move out of reach.

"What?" I manage. "Where?"

He approaches me with a look of concern. "I'm sorry, Leif, I should have let Sara - your mother - tell you."

I back into one of the raised ponds, my left arm sinking in the water. I let myself slide down to the concrete floor and sit. The Sergeant joins me.

"How?" I look at him. His head shakes slowly back and forth.

"They found him on top of you. He'd taken the brunt of the explosion."

"He saved my life." I whisper, my eyes darting from one crack in the concrete to another.

"Yes, you would have both been killed if he hadn't been standing where he was and you where you were."

"Can I see him?" My voice cracks with emotion.

"He's in the morgue."

We walk to the Hospital where the morgue is located in the basement. My legs feel as though they may give out under the weight of my building sadness as I stumble down the steep staircase. The Sergeant opens a steel metal drawer and there I see my mentor's earthly remains. His eyes are closed, his lips sealed tightly in an attempt to conceal his over-bite.

I hear the Sergeant move up the steps behind me, leaving me alone with my friend. I stand over him until my legs can no longer hold me up. I crouch down and steady my breathing.

Now I rest a hand on his arm and speak to him. I place a hand on his cheek, while a tear rolls down my own. "I'd never told you this, but I imagined you as my father." I am getting weepy now, but feel compelled to express how deeply our friendship touched me. I pull in a deep breath and continue.

"It has been a great honor to have known you in this life." I touch his chest and rest my forehead against the back of my hand. "And I will see you in the next."

*****

The funerals for our fallen take place over the course of one day. It is an opportunity for those that knew them to offer their remembrance, their love and their goodbyes. The funeral for Father Henderson came at the end of the day. Mom spoke eloquently for ten minutes; recalling her relationship with Father Henderson, and how her own conversations with him had given her great peace of mind. I carry out the Catholic rites as he would have wanted, and as he had asked of me some time ago should he die here.

Chapter Twenty-seven

The days after Mary's fall and her miraculous return to the physical plane were difficult. She slept most of the day and when coherent she would require assistance at meal time and during infrequent trips to the bathroom. Her family and I stayed by her bedside, as she recuperated.

*****

Terrible thoughts of Mary suddenly dying plague me. Though I should know better than to be sad for her should she suddenly pass, if she did die I would feel a great hole in my life, in myself.

So I decide to forego any meditation classes and all public appearances in favor of being by Mary's bedside. And when the doctor gives her the green light to come home, I roll her out of the hospital in a wheelchair, back to her room in the common housing sector.

"The doctor says you'll enjoy a full recovery," I tell her as we detour into the wooded corner of the base. "You'll be back to your old self in no time."

She reaches back and places a hand on mine. "Thank you for your love and support, Leif. I'm so grateful for you."

My heart soars as it does each time she professes her love for me. I want to hear that all the time now, and I am anxious to show her again how much I love her.

"And when can you take your bandages off?" She gingerly strokes my arm.

"Tomorrow," I tell her. "Mom's going to remove them and check the stitches. I have a lot more movement now than I did a week ago."

Tyrell greets us as we stroll slowly into the canopy of trees, escaping the heat of the day. “Hello, Mary.” He bows to her and then looks back to me. “Will there be any classes this week?”

“No,” I say with conviction. “All my focus is on Mary now.”

Tyrell is stunned.

“When can we expect you back?” he stutters.

“Please let the others know I will return when Mary is well.” Tyrell looks at us and bows again.

As we continue our walk in the woods several others approach Mary and I. They ask the same question Tyrell did. In order to deflect their concerns I decide to announce who will take my place until I return.

“Please, speak with Daniel,” I say. “He can lead the meditation during my absence.” Daniel is only sixteen, but a quick learner, taking to the concept and practice of meditation from a very early age.

“Daniel is so young,” says Jessie, stepping forward. She is in her thirties, a survivor from the east, who joined us when I was only six.

Mary looks up at me and I can tell she is uncomfortable with the attention.

“Daniel!” I call as his slight frame moves through the crowd. He joins me. “Daniel will lead the classes until I return.”

Daniel turns and looks up at me, confused. “Me?” He whispers.

“Yes, Daniel.” I take him aside and lower my voice. “You will do fine. I need this time with Mary.”

“Please hold meditation three times a day as I have. Repeat what you know.” I place a hand on his shoulder and squeeze lightly. “You’re ready.”

Daniel is apprehensive at first, but nods at me.

“If that’s what you want.”

“That’s what I would like.” I explain.

“Okay, Leif.” The anxiety leaves him and a genuine smile replaces the nervous one of a moment ago.

*****

"Will you tell me about your experience, Mary?" I ask softly as I put her to bed. The ambiance in the room offers an aura of calm, the corner lamp producing a supple yellow glow.

"I think you know what I saw, Leif," she says coyly, as she lays her head down on her pillow.

"I want to compare notes." I sit next to her. Taking her hand I lightly trace my fingernails over her forearm. She closes her eyes and I watch as her pupils move underneath the thin skin of her eyelids. Her mouth parts as she remembers.

"There was a light." I think back to Dr. Bren's soulless description of what the light meant in his case studies. "It was beautiful, but not just the light, the warmth. I felt like I was being embraced by love." She pauses.

"That's the sensation I get when in deep meditation. Cloaked in a light so perfectly white and warm that you just want to let go, and allow a breeze to take you with it."

"I wanted that," she says, her eyes still closed. "I had no intention of fighting it." Her eyes dart open.

Mary's free hand rises to my face and strokes my cheek. "Forgive me, Leif. I don't have the resolve you do. I could not imagine fighting that feeling. I am happy to see you again, and happy to be alive, but I would have let it take me..." She stops herself, turning her gaze to the grey brick wall.

"If the doctor and mom hadn't fought for your life and brought you back," I say, finishing her sentence. The warmth of her hand leaves my face.

"Yes," she smiles again, but this time there is no joy in it.

"I just, I would have liked to have had more time there, in the light." Mary pauses a moment. "I saw my dad. He reached out to me, you know? I really wanted to take his hand. I have very few memories of my father. Mom says he was overseas when the bombs fell. I didn't know I'd never see him again."

Now she weeps openly, abandoning all attempts at composure. I lean close and place an arm around her shoulders.

"I hated it when he went away. Sometimes for weeks. I told him I *hated* him when he went out the door for the last time." She takes a deep breath and wipes the tears from her face with her knuckles. Her chin turns upward, trembling, and she again cries into her hands.

"You were only five, Mary. Your dad knew that. He knew you didn't really hate him." I say, rubbing her back. The convulsions ease after another minute and she wipes her face with her shirt.

"I know that now. I was floating on a river for some reason." Her eyebrows thread together as the memory rushes back. "He was on the banks of the river. I called out to him, asking him to join me on the raft. But he shook his head. I screamed for him to come with me. He said he'd be waiting and disappeared from view."

"Be grateful you've been given this gift, it's a glimpse into your next life. It is a rare thing."

Mary smiles at me. "Your mother said I was the only one on the base who had ever done it."

"You see, my Mary, you *are special*." I smile.

"There's more, though," she says timidly. "As I fell out of that world and back into this one I saw your mother and Dr. Bren and a nurse working on my body." A chill visibly shoots through her at the memory.

"I can tell you what they were wearing, what they said, everything. The lights on the equipment blinking, the feeling in the room as they beat my chest with their fists…"

"It's incredible what you've experienced, Mary. But you're here, with me now."

"I love you, Leif." she says, her face deadly serious, and if it weren't for her piercing eyes I fear I might laugh. I quell the urge and lean in, kissing her. Mary in turn wraps her arms around me and pulls me into her. Pushing away the covers I lift the oversized night shirt above her waist. Again and again we make love, our hearts adoring, our bodies entwined.

Chapter Twenty-eight

As I wake next to Mary I find her propped up on one elbow, staring at me.

"I'm fine, you know Leif." She smiles and brushes a finger across my cheek. "You should be with the others now. Don't stay cooped up in this room with me. The doctor says *I* need to rest, not you."

I sit up and cross my legs, taking her hands in mine. "I *want* to be here, Mary. I want to look after you, be here for you."

"I know, and I appreciate your kindness, but I can't allow you to separate yourself from the others. Your work is important and you need to continue it. It's been two weeks. I'm feeling much better. *Much* better. You need to get back to what you do."

I am steadfast in my refusal.

"They will be fine. They have lots to meditate on, and you are my number one priority. You are *everything* to me."

"Listen to yourself, Leif." Her eyes narrow as she takes my face in her hands. "This isn't what you preach. You know better than anyone that this is an unhealthy connection for the mind. Don't center your attentions on me."

"Mary. I won't abandon you in your time of need." My head shakes as I speak, unable to comprehend her warnings.

"Leif, you have to leave me here and go to them."

"No," I say without thinking. I turn away, stand and make myself busy at the dresser rearranging the limited possessions she has brought with her.

"Please, I don't want to be responsible for you veering off your path."

"You have nothing to worry about," I say, still occupied with the trinkets. "I'm fine, everyone is fine. They understand why I'm here,"

"But do you?" she interrupts. I turn to meet her gaze.

"Of course I do,"

"When is the last time you spoke to your Blank Man?"

"I've blocked him out so I could be with you."

"Don't you see what you're doing, Leif? You've made *me* your *center*."

"So?" I shout, not meaning to raise my voice. Mary is caught off guard at my response. Frankly, so am I. I lower my tone. "I have given all of my life and myself to him and want only this time with you."

"To what end?" She rises from the bed and walks toward me. "Don't ignore your destiny for me. I'm no one."

"Don't say that!" I shout again. "Why would you say that? You're my *everything*, Mary. I *love* you. I never thought I could have this, but with you I can. Please, let me do this for you."

"That's just it. It's not for *me* that you're doing this. It's for *you*." She pauses to take a breath. "Can't you see that? Is your mind so clouded with love for me that you've lost your way?"

I turn and charge out of the bedroom into the common hall, anxious to get away from this conversation. She stops at the doorway and calls out.

"Leif, I love you, but don't lose sight of what's most important."

I stop a few feet down the hall.

"Please, *understand*, Mary, that *you* are most important to me." I feel a lump lodging itself in my throat and continue down the hall.

"Leif, we need to talk about this!" Her voice cracks and though part of me wants to turn back and embrace her I push through the outer door and into the grey day.

Chapter Twenty-nine

I'd spent the night at mom's after storming out on Mary. I complained that Mary was pushing me away when all I wanted to do was take care of her. This aroused emotions I had never felt. I *resented* her. It felt like the blood had turned acidic in my veins, my muscles hardening, filling up with the poison. A weight fell on my chest and I felt disconnected. Mom talked me through the alien emotion and settled my nerves, massaging the stiffening muscles in my neck. I fell asleep on her bed and awoke to see her sleeping on the couch which sat in a corner my childhood bed once occupied. Feeling a sense of peace seeing her sleeping there, I slipped quietly out of the room.

I return to face Mary. But now I am ready to face her accusations and uncertainties. I enter her room, which is dark and silent. Mary is not on the bed, where she should be. Instead, a note lies in her place.

Now, faced with this note, my muscles are set ablaze with the poison once more. I rub at my neck as I bend to retrieve the letter.

I've seen the light, Leif. I know your path is true. I cannot allow you to lose yourself in me when so many need you to find the light I have found.

Our time is over now. I see that. We have loved each other so much in such a short time. But we have loved blindly, recklessly.

Please understand why I am writing this and why I know I have to leave. My heart breaks for us, but I know I am doing the right thing, and I know you will see that in time.

You've shown me so much. I am eternally grateful. In this time of darkness you've opened my eyes, my heart, my mind. You are a blessing to everyone that meets you and I know you will do the right thing, as I know I am doing.

Don't let this act be in vain, my love. Go back to the people, for me, for yourself, for those that would follow you.

I am gone away.

I love you, always.

Mary

I realize I've fallen to my knees and am shaking. My sight blurs as the tears well up.

"This is it," I whisper through chattering teeth. The tears come in torrents now. My cheeks are soaked in moments. I drop the letter and it floats to the floor. My neck and back ache as they never have before. The tension building in my muscles is unbearable. My throat feels the size of a pin hole as I begin to convulse. I am weeping, howling now. Curling up on the floor by the side of our bed I wrap my arms around myself and draw my knees up to my chest. I want to run. Run out of the front gates and into the cruel wilderness after Mary. Chase her down and tell her she's wrong.

How has it come to this? What have I done? How will I survive this? I'm losing everyone. First Father Henderson, now Mary, who's next? Mom? The idea haunts me as I lay on the floor for hours, re-reading the letter, looking for something that offers a glimmer of hope that Mary would return. But I find no trace of such hope, and so I fall into hopelessness.

Chapter Thirty

The following days are bleak. I remain in my room, only occasionally opening my door after mom has knocked and left. She leaves food and water each time. I drink the water but find I have no appetite.

I read Mary's letter endlessly, aloud at times, hoping it will reveal some hidden meaning, something I've missed. I am ruined, I'm destroyed.

I question everything now. Did she ever love me, really? How could she leave me if she loved me? Were they just words? What's wrong with me that she would go to such lengths to separate us? The questions break me down, each one a little sharper than the last.

"Drama deconstructs love." Blank Man's voice sounds distant.

What has happened to me is unfair, I tell myself.

"This is self-indulgent," Blank Man retorts.

I am not speaking to him. My walls are down and so his words come through, but I refuse to acknowledge them.

I fear I am letting Mary down though. She asked me not to let her sacrifice be in vain. But what place was it of hers to sacrifice *our* happiness?

"She was right." Again Blank Man is in my head, defending Mary's rash solution.

Why couldn't I have both? Why couldn't I have everything?

"You know the answer."

In order to make sense of Blank Man's incessant input I would need to have a conversation with him. But I don't feel ready for that. In fact, I doubt the whole point to any of it now. Was I not to experience love in this life?

"That gift has been granted."

But it was taken from me.

"This too is a gift. You know the lesson. Meditate on your anger, your sadness, and your solitude."

Daniel is at the door now.

"Leif?" I hear his head rest against the metal door. "It's been four days, Leif." There is a pause. "Mary left another letter."

My heart jumps at this and my feet land on the tiled floor.

"It was to her parents."

This news is impossible to deal with right now. Her parents, her family, she's left them too.

"She told them why she left." Another pause, "Is it true?"

What could she have said? The fallout of this act would affect many more lives than just mine. But mine was all I could focus on now.

I listen as he pushes off, eventually. His footfalls travel down the hall, slowly, probably anticipating me throwing the door open and ushering him in. But I don't.

My thoughts turn from Mary's parents back to my own grief. My heart is broken. I'm in pieces. I was more when Mary was with me than I ever was alone. Her very presence was a gift. And that gift has been stolen from me.

"Mary's purpose was clear." Again the Blank Man disrupts my thought processes.

"Mary's *purpose*?" I finally react.

"Mary has served in the development of your destiny. It is now for you to understand to what end."

"Mary was sent to *teach* me something?" I chuckle ironically. "A lesson? I don't believe that." I pace the narrow space between the bed and the desk.

"Meditate on this, Leif. You will understand."

"Don't tell me Mary was nothing more than a lesson to learn. What was it all for? To learn about loss? To experience emotions no one should have to? What? WHAT!?" I scream. My hands fly to my head. I lock my fingers together and crouch on the ground. I rock there on the balls of my feet for a long moment, slam my hands down so hard on the tile floor that they instantly sting to life. The sudden pain sends me to my feet and I shake my hands out.

"Do not dishonor what Mary embodied," he tells me. "Meditate on her and know what she knew. See what you refused to see in her presence. Be the man you were meant to be."

Rage now builds in me. Rage is unlike anything I have felt before. It is unnerving, dangerous. I want to shout and scream and tell the Blank Man to go, to leave me and never come back, but then it hits me. The rage passes, my fists unclench and I sit, cross-legged and breathe deeply. I have to control this monster inside of me.

Blank Man appears in my mind's eye and shows me a meadow. It is beautiful, more so than even our gardens at Castle Peak. I see Mary there. She is radiant as the sun ignites her pale skin. A smile grows across my face.

"What is this?" I ask my angel.

"Does it calm you?"

"Yes," I answer.

"Mary's image calms you?"

"It does." My chest is no longer heaving, my face no longer hot.

"Good," he replies. "Use her to focus your thoughts and emotions. Now consider what she's taught you. Once you have grasped this lesson, share it with Daniel and the others. It is paramount to everyone's path."

Chapter Thirty-one

After another three days and nights meditating on Mary's image, her purpose, and my life's path, I open the door to Daniel and invite him in.

Mary was the embodiment of impermanence. She was my lesson, my teacher, but she was much more than that. Mary knew that I was becoming too involved in the physical world. She knew that she was the cause and so the effect of distancing myself from my one true path. I love her more now than ever knowing she could sacrifice her own happiness and mine in this life so that I would not fail in my destiny as my father had. That she could leave this place for the unknown hardships of the world beyond was truly heroic. But that she *knew* the hardships she was taking on by leaving, speaks even more of the courage she possessed.

"My biggest fear is that I have condemned Mary to the worst life imaginable simply by risking loving her," I tell Daniel. For all his youthful appearances, his is an old soul as well, and so we are drawn to one another.

"Don't say that, Leif." The soft tone of his voice comforts me. "She made her decision. You didn't ask her to leave."

"No, but if I'd known this end was promised her, I would never have made an attempt to meet her."

"What would have come of that? What could have been learned from that?" He stands and circles me. "Impermanence, it's the foundation of your teachings, the core lesson you've preached to all of us, and for some reason, you have been given an example in your own life to draw from."

"It has been a difficult lesson." I remain on the bed. "But as you say, it has reminded me of the importance of impermanence in this life. That nothing in the here and now is forever, that everything goes away, in the end."

"Everything," he repeats. "An idea, a thought, you, me..." Daniel stops himself.

"Yes, but Mary is so much more than a lesson," I stumble with my words. "She is the person I love."

"What will you do?"

I take a deep, cleansing breath. "I could have her followed. Send soldiers out to search for her." A tear escapes me. "They could bring her back, and I could stay away from her if I knew she was alright."

"You think so?" Daniel pulls up the desk chair next to me. I look up at him, smiling sadly.

"No," I answer.

"And so ends the lesson."

Chapter Thirty-two

Though I have accepted Mary's leaving, her parents insist they will never recover.

Seated in the hospital, where Mary's mother has suffered a stroke, and her step-father has spent the better part of the week, I beg their forgiveness.

"If I could take back the last few weeks and return Mary to you, I would." I tell them.

Mary's mother is lying on her back, unable, or unwilling, to move. The only sign of life is her sporadic breathing, and the trail of tears that shows no sign of slowing. She is an emotional wreck, and I feel one hundred percent to blame for her predicament. Though I thought I was doing them proud by looking after Mary, spending every waking hour at her side as she recovered, I became the catalyst for her decision to leave the base, her family and myself.

"Please, Leif," Sam, her step-father says through clenched teeth. "Please, just leave us. We've asked the Sergeant to send a team out to find her days ago."

This news excites me, but days ago? She's hiding from them. She doesn't want to found. "I want you to understand why she's done this. Why she left us."

"It was you, Leif. We all read the letter!" Sam was becoming animated now. "This place was filled with promise. It was the light at the end of a long and winding road. And now…" He pauses to catch his breath. "Now it has accomplished the one thing we worked all of these years to avoid."

"What was it all for anyway?"

I bow my head, knowing the answer may not give them any peace. It has given me peace and reaffirmed my purpose in this life, but is there a chance these deflated people will see purpose in their daughter's disappearance? I must try to make them see that there is.

"I would offer you a reason, if you would listen," I say quietly.

Mary's mother sits up.

"Tell me then."

Sam is startled by his wife's unexpected reaction. Mrs. Gardener waves him away. Her aura is dark.

"Mrs. Gardener," I begin with a heavy heart. "There is more to Mary's letter than you may know, and more to our story than you may believe."

"Then tell me why my baby is out there in this cruel wasteland. Tell me why she's left her family." Her voice is raspy, and it carries with it a terrible pain.

"You did this!" She shouts. "It was you!" A sharp finger points accusingly at me.

My heart falls into my stomach. I feel horrible. She's right, it is my fault.

"Please," I plead with her.

"You should leave, Leif." Sam tells me.

My mind races to find the words that will console them, but I only stutter out the same plea time and again.

"No," Mrs. Gardener says loud enough to be heard by everyone in the room. "No you go! Nothing you say will bring her back. Nothing you say will change what has happened!"

Tears rush down my cheeks as I stand and obey her wishes. Fighting the urge to plead with Mary's family again I remove myself from the hospital and push through the door, utterly defeated by the sorrow that fills the place.

*****

That evening I hide in my room once more. I weep over the devastating reaction from Mary's family. Why did the words not come? Where was my Blank Man?

It takes hours for me to calm down long enough to center myself and steady my mind. I am exhausted. I sit cross-legged on my bed and rest my palms on my knees. My back straightens and my head falls forward, eyes closed.

Suddenly I feel a tug on my spirit. I am being pulled out of my body. I allow the energy to guide me, and steer my consciousness. A feeling of foreboding overcomes me. It is reminiscent of my recent streak of nightmares. I've never experienced this sensation when in the rapture of meditation.

It's Earl.

Part 2
Chapter One
Earl Speaks…

My trip through the second floor window of a burning building nearly twenty years ago wasn't exactly graceful.

I remember awakening to the thick smell of burning wood and drywall, which replaced the delicate scent of the bud we'd smoked moments before. I stood up in a panic, slapped Freddy on the head, stirring him out of a drunken slumber, and scanned the room for Kevin.

"What?" Fred shouted, sitting upright on the couch, blinking madly.

"The house, it's on fire!" I gathered a few personal items and placed them in a backpack. He stood and stumbled into the coffee table. "Where's Kevin?"

"I don't know. Last time I saw him he was complaining about a smell and left the room." Fred waved away the smoke that was filling the room above the three car garage.

"Right." I remembered that. I walked to the open staircase that overlooked the car port. "Shit, there's no way we'll make it through that." The flames were climbing the stairs. I turned and coughed violently as the smoke caught me in the lungs.

Freddy was at the door to the second floor. As he grabbed at the handle he pulled back quickly, his face contorting. "Jesus Christ!" The door knob was red hot. He waved his hand, blowing on the bubbling flesh. "What the fuck! What are we going to do?"

I looked at the windows. It was easily a fourteen foot drop from any one of them. Freddy followed my gaze and shook his head.

"We'll break our legs."

I threw the backpack over my shoulders and approached him. "We could try the stairs." I said sarcastically.

"Fuck." Fred repeated. Suddenly an explosion from below hurled us both into the west wall, and Freddy went flying through one of the windows.

Now the fire was racing through the addition, lighting up everything it touched. I realized it was now or never and attempted the door that led into the second floor. Wrapping my shirt around my hand I approached the handle. Then another explosion burst in from outside, shaking the whole house and sending glass flying everywhere. Suddenly I felt the scorching pain of a burning curtain mixing with the flesh on one side of my face.

Screaming, I flung myself through the same window Freddy had been thrown from. I landed hard on the earth below, narrowly missing the patio stones which lined the back of the garage. Looking ahead, I could see that the fuel tank had blown.

Pulling at the foreign material still burning its DNA into my own, I felt the skin of my face give way and screamed. I soon realized my mistake in crying out.

Gunshots coming from inside the house fired off sporadically. Knowing no one would shoot their way out of a burning house I realized that our ammo depot had been lit up by the heat.

"Freddy?" Cautious not to shout over the roaring flames in case this had been an attack from some unknown enemy, I crawled on all fours toward the back of the house. Looking up into the night sky, I watched as smoke billowed out of the windows, and realized that none of the house would be spared. I pressed the burnt portion of my face to the ground, rubbing some of the cool mud into the wound to stay the pain. Tears blurred my vision. Lying on my stomach I struggled to find Fred. Where had he gotten to in such a hurry? The pain in my face trumped the newly acquired shin splints, but I rubbed at them all the same, face back in the mud.

Then I saw them, two figures crouching behind the pool house. Squinting against the light of the inferno, I pulled my pistol from its holster. I began to crawl towards the pair.

The closer I got the more disturbing the vision. These weren't enemies per se, they were my house mates! The one darker than the other: Sidney!

And the other one: Caroline! The whites of their eyes danced in the light of the flames. I watched them a moment and wondered whether they had just escaped the same fate I had. Then I saw they had two heavy bags with them, and water rations. They hadn't escaped at all! They had set the fire.

"*Sara*." I decided to wait for her to appear before I shot them all dead. Baby or no baby, Sara had made a choice, and she would die for it.

*****

From the moment the first vote was cast, I knew I should have been the one to lead. Joel was unprepared. Shell shocked. A leader sure, but a leader for easier times. The Apocalypse wasn't exactly something every man was cut out to survive. It should have been me they voted for. Why Joel? The fact that we took shelter in his house was one of the deciding factors, I remember. What kind of quality was that in a leader? But we were just kids, and Joel was our mutual friend. Almost everyone knew Joel on a personal level. So it was decided. Joel would lead us. At least he recognized in me the ability prepare the defense of our stronghold.

When I consider the contributions I made, when Joel died, the house should have automatically passed the responsibility of leadership onto me. But they didn't, and the house divided. Why couldn't they see that it was *me* that gave our friends the level of comfort they enjoyed in the time after? When everything went to shit, *I* was the one who brought the artillery, *I* was the one who set up posts around the house and built the barricade, and watched the rain levels slowly drop. It was *me* who gave them hope!

I find myself dwelling in the past more and more these days, wondering how this end might have played out if I had been crowned leader instead of Joel. But that was all so very long ago. Eighteen years… nineteen maybe? Much has happened since then.

Sara, for example, *Sara* happened. Eight years after she'd lit the house with the intention of burning me and Kevin and Freddy alive, she walked back into my life. Running into her again eight years later blew my mind, and meeting her boy, Leif, Joel's son, was a trip. I saw them both in turn, from my cell in the base's stockade, where I was being held as a terrorist. First, Sara walked in to question me. *Where was my base, what were our numbers?* I was stunned at first to see her. I'd assumed she'd died with her unborn baby in the wilderness. But there she was, that superior look about her, holding her head high, smirking down at me. Christ, I'd like to have smashed that look off her face. I dream about it. I fantasize about killing her. My hands around her throat, squeezing and then, just when she's chasing the light, releasing, letting her regain consciousness and then squeezing again so she can feel death approach time and again. I can't help but smile at the thought, how I'll relish the moment.

Then surprise, surprise, her eight year old son walks into the stockade late one night, alone. He sits across from me; the iron bars all that's separating us. That was an interesting conversation. Although I did most of the talking, I still wonder what possessed him to go to the trouble of unlocking the door and sitting with me.

None the less, once the army had found my hideout, killed the men and brought the women and children back, my escape plan was in full swing. Sara thought she'd pulled the information from me, but I offered it under the guise of having let it slip. If I hadn't given up the location, my woman wouldn't have been brought into the base, thus locating and freeing me. We scrambled under the wall at a point in the base's defenses where the earth could be dug out enough that we could slip our thin frames under, undetected.

Now, after ten years in a strange land, just a few day's journey from the base - where I can say in no uncertain terms - my arch enemy - my nemesis resides, I have rebuilt my army, and it is many, and it is hungry.

Chapter Two
Leif

I have seen the beginning of the end of our time here. A great army writhing in desperation, anger and jealousy approaches from the west like a plague.

"Earl," I tell myself, waking from the nightmare. My sheets are drenched in sweat, my heart is pounding fiercely. We are soon to be overwhelmed by an evil with an appetite for destruction.

I must speak with the Sergeant. He needs to know what is coming.

Chapter Three
Earl

I want to meet Leif again. It's a strange feeling I have fostered since I escaped the base. Something compels me. Strange whispers in the night, his name repeated in my dreams. Why did he come to see me all those years ago? The questions have tormented me. I'm not losing my mind, I'm too strong for that. No, it's more than that. A destiny I have to fulfill.

We set out a month ago to return to the base. Perhaps they are all dead from another round of the plague? Perhaps they are stronger than ever. Either way, I've made it my mission to return. And I will meet them on neutral ground, with an army behind me.

Just days from my goal, the troops are restless with the promise of battle and the potential locked away in that place. Food and water await, and if I can't have it, then no one will.

*****

I see the skeletons of the past as I look upon the forest separating my army from the base. All seems still. Castle Peak towers over the plains to the north, and hidden behind it, Elle Lake. A hill climbs skyward just beyond the fortress' east wall. I approach from the west.

With twelve of my best men, I march through the woods, a white flag tied to two of my soldier's arms, our weapons hidden behind fallen trees a short distance behind us. Soon the base's west wall is barely twenty yards away.

"Stop!" A sharp voice calls from above and we obey. The pair of guards in the tower have their automatic weapons trained on us. "State your business."

"I am Earl," I shout back. "I've come to speak with Leif."

"Circle round to the south gates. You will need to be searched before entering the compound."

I watch as one picks up a communication device and speaks into it. He waves at us to move towards the gate. I nod to my men and we cautiously make our way round the tall steel walls I had tested time and again so many years ago.

At the front, between us and them is a repaired version of the gate my men had slammed through ten years earlier with one of the base's own trucks. It was a failed attempt to take the base, but a learning experience all the same.

There, looking out at us, is Sara. She, of course, is not alone, flanked by a dozen soldiers, weapons drawn.

"*I can't believe it.* Why would you return? Why shouldn't I gun you down right now?" she screams at me.

"Sara." I speak through clenched teeth, faking a smile. "Good to see you too." I bow, not taking my eyes off hers. She looks good: that dark hair, those big piercing eyes, and that body have not changed with the years. Jesus, she has kept herself up. I should like to ravage that body before I choke the life out of it.

"Enough with the bullshit, Earl, *why are you here*?"

"As I explained to your watch tower, I'm here to speak with Leif."

"Why would you need to speak with my son?" She is rattled at that. I am enjoying this.

"It does not concern you, Sara."

"Everything about my son concerns me." She pauses. "Shoot them."

I raise my arms. "Are you ready for war?"

Sara's hand rises from her side. "Wait," she orders. Her ability to lead these men impresses me. She has grown formidable over the years. "What do you mean, war?"

"What I mean," I say slowly, dropping my arms to my sides once more, "is if I do not return to my men within the hour, my army will attack this base with extreme prejudice, destroying as much and as many as they can with no thought for their own lives."

"You've rebuilt your army." Leif's voice rings out as the gathering crowd parts to let him through.

"Leif." My hands go out to him, my smile as sincere as I am capable, after what damage his mother's fire had done to my face. He is tall, like Joel was. In fact, it's a bit disarming that he looks so much like his father. But I know my enemy when I see him, and this kid is my enemy, whether he wants to believe it or not.

"We do not want a war with you, Earl. We want peace, but if war is all you offer, you will find no peace here." Even his mannerisms remind me of his father. The way he carries himself, the way his head tips sideways when he speaks.

"I must speak with you, Leif."

"So speak."

"No, not here, not like this," I approach the gate and shake its bars. "Could we meet on neutral ground?"

"We could. There is a patch of woods on the north side of the base, by the lake. Meet me there in two hours."

I point beyond the base, brows raised, and Leif nods confirmation.

"You remember Castle Peak," he says to me. "Just navigate around to the east side and follow the wall of rock to the lake. I will meet you there."

Sara grabs his arm and whispers something. I see Leif nod and whisper back.

"We'll see you there." I wave my men away from the gate.

As we march back into the woods I feel a warm glow on my face. I wonder if he will come alone. I will kill him if he does. But it is unlikely. The thought lingers though. Killing Leif, Sara's son, would devastate her. It would be better than killing her. She could live another forty years with the pain of knowing I took him from her.

We reach our weapons and gather them up.

"What's your plan?" asks Kent. He is nearly fifty and one of my earliest recruits.

"My plan is to meet Leif in his forest and *understand* him." I throw my rifle over my shoulder. "Know your enemy!" I say, kicking the dead earth. We change direction and march north. I send Kent back to the army to report on our progress, with the promise of victory.

Chapter Four
Leif

Seated on the forest floor, I watch as Earl and eleven others march into my sacred circle. Earl's aura burns like his dark red hair, but with a muddied green underlying the red. His slender frame looks ravaged by malnourishment as his ragged clothing sways around his torso, the scar on his face strangely appropriate.

My mother and seven armed soldiers form a semi circle behind me. Two more perch in the trees, guns trained on Earl's party.

"Welcome, Earl." I offer him a seat. He chooses to stand.

"This is some greeting." He is suddenly very aggressive, pointing at the soldiers. "And you claim to preach peace." His burn allows only a pained attempt at a smirk.

"I only offer guidance."

"And where does this 'guidance' come from? Is it the great beyond? Chasing spirits like your daddy?"

I ignore his contempt. "I'd like to offer you to a new path, a path of least resistance."

"Yeah, sure, offer *you* the least resistance so you can finish us off." He turns to his men and laughs, they respond in kind.

"In resistance there is pain, and suffering." I know Earl was nowhere near ready to respond to this message. All the same, I will only engage in a peaceful dialogue with him.

"You're as crazy as your father was." Spittle flies from his mouth as he speaks.

"Why would you deny yourself an opportunity to learn a greater purpose to this life?"

"This life is to live, to grow old and fat on the backs of others. Survival of the fittest, right? That's why we're here, to live *our best* lives." He turns again to his cronies for approval and they nod.

"And how is that working out for you?" I ask.

"My day will come." A bright lemon-yellow spikes in his aura.

"You have misled yourself and your group."

"I am what I am," he says, arms flailing. "The great I AM! That's what it is to be human: to exist, to excel, to know *yourself*."

"You distort everything to serve your own interests."

"So *enlighten* me." His arms stretch out beside him as his face pushes forward. His sarcasm is so thick; I feel it come at me in a wave.

"There is a new end approaching. You should listen, Earl, all of you." I address the men flanking him. "With this end, there is a new beginning on the horizon. You could be a part of that new beginning, or you could continue on your path, and be left behind."

"You're the one who's been misled, my friend. You're confused and you're confusing everyone around you. *This* life is all there is. Wake up!" He taps a palm against his temple.

His narrow vision of life is his greatest weakness. "If all you can see is what is in front of you, then you are lost."

"Fuck you, little man."

At this I stand, signaling the end of our conversation. My six feet two inches towers above his five foot ten. He backs up unconsciously, turns, and in a huff leaves the sacred circle with his eleven followers.

Mom calls after him. "What you do in this life will determine how you live in the next." He dismisses her words with a wave of his hand, not bothering to turn around.

I face mom and the soldiers.

"There is too much conviction in his words. Ego has overwhelmed him." I bow my head. There can be no doubt now, the end I have foreseen is the end we will meet.

Chapter Five
Leif

With the realization that Earl's army is here, now, I speak to the Sergeant concerning my vision.

"It's Earl," I tell him, seated on a tattered floral print chair in his family's quarters. "My vision saw a great army overthrow us, and I'm sure that Earl's men are the threat I've foreseen."

"This is it then? This is our last stand?" His eyes narrow.

"Yes, I feel certain of it."

He had trusted my ability to 'feel' the future for years now, and today was no exception."We'll determine a defense strategy." His face is void of emotion, his voice stern and ridged.

"You're not understanding, Sergeant. I didn't just see an *attempt* to overthrow us, I saw it *happen*. We need an escape plan, not a defense plan."

"We can't flee our homes… it's too risky."

"We will all die then."

"A good death, one long overdue."

I'm stunned by his reaction.

"And your children? Is this a *good death* for them?"

He shifts uncomfortably in his chair. "What is there out there for them but a slow and painful death? A wasteland beyond our gates?"

I had never heard the Sergeant so negative, but understood we all have days where the future seems dim. Still, today was not the day to forfeit optimism. Today we needed a leader with hope.

"We have the lake; and the forest beyond our walls now. We could make a life there," I remind him.

"It's too close, if Earl's men take the base."

"They *will* take this base. That much I know for certain."

"If you're certain, I will consider this option." He stands and I with him. "If we run, then we take all we can. We leave them with nothing. Destroy the generators, the windmills, the solar panels, everything."

"A good plan," I agree.

"But, if they find no one, they will pursue us." I see scenarios working their way through his military mind. A smile flickers across his face a moment later, and he turns to me.

"We'll make a bomb."

Chapter Six
Leif

As the daylight fades, I walk the perimeter of the forest within our walls. It is an exercise I practice two or three times a day now. Here, I run into others on the base, all of us attracted to the life that inhabits the woods. Today especially, I contemplate a life beyond these walls. Dieter catches up with me.

He seems out of breath. "You know Leif, I just realized something and I'd like to share it with you."

"Please." I invite him to walk beside me.

"Whether your mother knows it or not, she is an anagrammatist." Dieter has that playful, whimsical look about him that always makes me smile.

I slow my pace. "That's a new word for me."

"Yes, and very cleverly done, actually, from what I know about you now."

"What is an anagrammatist, exactly?"

"Someone who can spell out a word or phrase and by rearranging the letters, pull another word or phrase from it. Sometimes this practice was used to pass on secrets."

"Why do you say that? Why is mom such a person?"

"Look at your purpose in this life, Leif. What are you here to accomplish?"

"To enlighten," I respond without hesitation.

"Yes, but it's more than that, and it is much simpler than that: you are to bring the people to grips with a life outside this one."

"Yes, to teach them what I know."

"Yes, but the message you bring is *life*." He stops and grabs my shoulders, looking me directly in the eye. "Your message is only this."

"That there is no death, save the transition from this life to that. Yes."

"Exactly, *Leif*." He winks then smiles at me, as though he were enlightening me to some great mystery. But as he speaks my name with a slow, deliberate, drawn-out pronunciation, I quickly rearrange the letters in my own name.

"*Life*," I say aloud. The veil of mystery Dieter had so expertly crafted lifts.

"Hah! Yes, Leif. *Life*!" He slaps me on the back.

A sense of purpose once again electrifies me.

*****

After dinner I find mom in the post-op. She is three years into her training as a surgeon under Dr. Bren, and as a result could be found day and night in the hospital, studying, or performing a simple procedure on a patient. She is in love with her new career path.

"Mom," I call out across the room. She looks up and smiles at me. I wave and walk toward her.

"Leif, what a nice surprise." She stands and we hug.

"I just had the most interesting conversation with Dieter." We sit at the desk and she clears away the books. "Do you know what an anagram is?"

"Is it a play on words?"

"Yes, at least, as I understand it, it can be. It's where one word or several can be broken apart and made to mean something completely different."

"Okay, sure, I know what you mean then. Tina has some games like that on the computers in the library."

"When you named me, why did you give me the name Leif?"

"Your grandfather's name was Leif. Why?"

"So you didn't pick it for its double meaning?"

"Well, I know it's Scandinavian, and that it means *loved*. Why the sudden interest in your name, honey?"

"Dieter pointed out that when you move the letters around, as in an anagram, you get the word *life.*"

She connects the dots right away and again places her hands on mine. "That's destiny at work for you."

"Isn't it amazing? How you can find purpose in something like a name?"

She nods again. "And just as you were doubting yourself."

"Yes." A lump forms in my throat. I had been so preoccupied with Mary leaving I had abandoned myself, and in doing so inadvertently abandoned my destiny. I stare at the desk, my head down.

"Leif, if Mary was meant to stay, she would have, you know that right?" Her hand wraps around my forearm.

I look up, nod and wipe away a tear. Though the logic is obvious in what mom says, I've held on to the feelings of loss and guilt. I keep them as a reminder of her, of Mary. Morbid, maybe, but I am having a difficult time letting go altogether.

Chapter Seven
Leif

I take Daniel up to the highest point of Castle Peak. An armed escort remains below us keeping a watchful eye. I have brought him here to practice a method of meditation I had not yet introduced to anyone.

Seated precariously on the rocky outstretch, I ask him to close his eyes and quiet his mind.

"Find the silence behind the noise. To embrace the silence you are embracing your creator. Experience the absence of sound. Hear only my voice now. Let my voice carry you forward. Let time dissolve and dimensions melt away. Find truth and *see*."

In our time on the mountain's crest, Daniel sees events unfold and an end so shocking he is thrown out of his meditation.

"It is our destiny to see this through, Daniel," I tell him. He is dazed and looks horrified. His head shakes slowly from side to side.

I nod at him. "Yes, Daniel. But remain hopeful, the best is still possible."

Chapter Eight
Leif

After my meeting with Earl and his group at the edge of Elle Lake, the Sergeant decided to double the guard. In the meantime, he carefully crafted a plan for the future. Unfortunately, my vision couldn't pinpoint an exact date, but the immanency of the attack had us both on edge.

Our men carried the most advanced weapons: fully automatic machine guns, grenades, even a rocket launcher. They were set up in crow's nests along the sides of Castle Peak's rugged cliffs and in bunkers that surrounded the man-made wonder.

*****

The Sergeant is a cautious man and skilled strategist, and whether he will admit it or not, quite clairvoyant at times. Just three nights passed before Earl's army attacked. The attack took place under the cover of night, the blackened sky making the gun bursts that much more dramatic.

The fighting was fierce, but short lived. Earl's men were quickly overcome, some killed, others captured.

The blasts woke the base, and many made it up the north towers, overlooking the bloody battle as it unfolded. I too watched as our soldiers gunned down the retreating group of twenty or more.

*****

The following day I get an idea. Having captured six men last night, an option I'd overlooked occurs to me. I pull the Sergeant out of the interrogation room, leaving the prisoners in the company of three armed soldiers.

"I want to speak to Earl's army."

"I'm not letting anyone from *his* group in this compound unless they're prisoners of war. None of them can be trusted."

"But there are children and women. I'm sure there are others that don't want to follow Earl, but do out of fear. Earl has manipulated them."

"Exactly, Leif, just like he had manipulated the girl who released him from our stockade all those years ago. Do you honestly think we could tell one apart from another?"

"I could."

"How?"

"If I concentrate on their auras, I can read intentions."

"You're a lie-detector now?"

"It's worked for me in the past. Please, Sergeant, you offered me a leadership role for a reason. I'm asking that you to get behind me on this."

His brow furrows. "And you can guarantee to me, *swear* to me, that you won't let a single person cross our gates unless you're fully confident they are done with Earl?"

"Yes."

"Because, Leif, as much as we're all very happy to have you lead us in our day-to-day, the protection of this base and its citizens still falls on me."

"Sergeant, I have every confidence in your abilities to defend us. Please, believe in mine."

He concedes. "Well, at the very least it may plant a seed of rebellion in his ranks. It can't do any harm to preach to them."

"Everyone should have their shot at salvation. These people are no less entitled."

"Can you see anything with these six?" He waves an open hand in the direction of the deflated and demoralized group behind the glass.

"I can tell you the two on the end want nothing to do with Earl. The others support their leader, but those two…" I point at the young men on the far end of the bench. "They are ready to leave him."

He nods, as if I'd just confirmed his own suspicions after hours of interrogation. "How do you want to approach the others? I'd suggest using the loud speakers, what with their squatting just beyond our walls."

"Perfect."

"This way you can get your point across without ever endangering yourself. When would you like to start?"

"Tonight, if you can arrange it."

"Let's speak to Salem about it."

*****

Salem, a forty year old man who maintains the electrical equipment on the base, sits up when he sees the Sergeant and I approach.

"Gentlemen," he greets us, sliding a palm across his shaven head and adjusting his glasses. "Is there something I can do for you?"

"There is, Salem."

"Does the intercom still work?" I ask. "I'd like to send a message over our walls."

"To the terrorists?" Salem is alarmed; his right hand unconsciously moves to the sidearm at his hip. "Why?"

The Sergeant interjects.

"Leif would like the opportunity to talk them down."

"Oh, stirring up some shit, eh?" He chuckles. His other hand moves to his chin, digging at the deep dimple. "I'm on it. Though we haven't used the loud speakers in a few months now, they ought to work." He scrambles back into his shop, where all dead electronics come to life again. He resurfaces with a component, holding it up for us to see. "I might need this," he says. "Let's go."

We follow Salem through the parade grounds, passing the grave markers, and find ourselves in the control room. Salem slides under one of the panels and, cursing, slips back out.

"Something the matter?" Sergeant Jones asks.

"This thing might make a bit of noise is all." He flips a switch, picks up a headset, and blows into the mike. I notice someone walking past our window flinch and cover their ears. Salem then points for me to exit the building and confirm that I can hear him outside. I can.

Tonight I would offer salvation over suffering.

*****

Several speakers line the exterior walls of the base. A number of speakers also sit upon the rooftops of our buildings. I hear a low crackle of static in the air as I approach the control room.

Sergeant Jones stands at the door and opens it for me to pass through. He follows closely.

"We have doubled our guard in the towers should this cause a sudden uproar."

This news upsets me. My purpose is not to cause unrest, but to appeal to their sense of self.

"I'm not going to approach them in a threatening way."

"Just letting you in on what's what, Leif."

"Okay," I say and sit. I turn to the control panel. My arms go up as if to say what now? Salem assists me by placing the headphones over my ears and arranging the microphone.

"Just flick this switch whenever you're ready, Leif. You'll have no trouble being heard for literally miles just speaking at your normal level." He gives me a thumbs up and steps back, smiling.

I begin my appeal for the souls of those trapped in an impossible scenario, in purgatory.

Chapter Nine
Earl

The nerve of this kid. Who does he think he is? His words penetrate every inch of the woods. I run through the encampment, ordering everyone to cover their ears.

My generals do the same.

I'm panicking, I'll admit. This was not something I'd expected or prepared for. A fucking sermon! He was good, Leif. He understood the same basic principal of leadership as I did. Fear. I had them fearing for their lives and their family's lives, but this little prick was trumping me with an immortal soul. This would ruin everything. After our defeat at the lake, if even twenty percent of my army decided to leave, I don't think I could take the base. I expect roughly that percentage to die in the initial rush. I was foolish to have made that earlier attack. I hadn't expected them to be prepared, and my people were hungry, but regret now the impulsiveness of that decision.

And what if they do decide to leave me? I'd have to kill them myself. We'd have a rebellion in my own camp! What would the great leaders of the past have done?

I stand, my chest heaving as much from the running and shouting as from the anxiety of the moment. My head turns from side to side, watching my army listen to the propaganda.

"Cover your ears!" I shout again at one of the women and point my pistol at her and her child. They obey.

My generals surround me and shout the same order again and again, but I know I can't force this upon everyone. Many will obey, but many will listen to him. How I deal with it when it is over is what will make all the difference.

I listen now as Leif repeats everything he just said. Or has he recorded it and will now loop it again and again until it drives us mad?

“Should we shoot out the speakers?” asks Karl. He is the youngest of my generals, but every bit as ruthless as I need him to be.

“No,” I answer, unblinking. “We can’t let this rattle us.” I wear my mask well. “They have the high ground and will decimate us. No, we won’t be provoked into a fight. We wait until we are ready.”

“When will that be?” I see the lust for blood pumping through his young veins.

I turn to him and slap him across his face. Karl staggers back, surprised, his hand shooting up to shield himself from another.

“Lower your hand,” I order. He does, revealing a scarlet mark matching the back of my hand. I smirk.

“We attack when I say we attack. Not a moment before,” I tell him, my voice rising over the loudspeaker, my finger now in his face. Karl lowers his head and turns from me. I look at my other generals. They have stopped shouting orders to watch the spectacle.

“Make it known they are not to listen to this propaganda!” I say, my voice steady and stern. All four walk off, repeating their orders to the masses. My attention returns to the base, whose west wall is just one hundred yards from our camp. Through the broken pillars of trees separating us I watch as the tower guards survey our reaction to this attack on the senses.

Chapter Ten
Leif

Sergeant Jones' son, Jasper bursts into the control room and reports his findings from Tower Two. "They're scrambling to regain control, Sergeant." Jasper is Jones' oldest, and a soldier at twenty two. The Sergeant has asked his son to address him as such while on duty, and Jasper doesn't seem to mind the formality.

"Thank you. It's working."

The recording Salem made is working perfectly. It is a brilliant idea, allowing the message to go on indefinitely. I have stated my position on this life, what they can all achieve if they walk my path, and explain the results of living the path they are on in the next life. I realize many of them have been too brainwashed by Earl for this to work on a large scale, but the few that may yet have the strength and presence of mind to leave him, will. They may do so at their own peril, but in dying for a decision as important as this, they will find peace.

Chapter Eleven
Earl

By morning, the recording has stopped. Had it played all night? My dreams were haunted by Leif's voice. Had the damage been done? I stand, scanning the grim landscape, and hope that my army is still intact. My orders before I slept were to form firing lines along the east and south of our encampment; guns turned inward, firing upon any deserters. The equipment we'd been working on in secret was almost ready. My offensive on the base would be quick and deadly, and it would be soon.

Three women are brought to me.

"These three attempted to flee last night with four others: three men and a child," reports Curtis, my third-in-command.

"Where are the others?" I ask.

"They were shot."

"Dead?" I ask, stone-faced for clarity.

"Yes, dead," Curt answers.

"And why have these three survived?" I approach the women, who are being restrained by the other three generals.

"We don't throw women away so easily," Karl answers. "As per your orders."

I nod. "And which of these has produced a child in the past?"

"I – I have, Earl," answers one, the desperation in her response palpable. I eye her up.

"And where is your child now?"

"They took him from me."

"And you two, you don't have tongues? I don't remember cutting them out." I laugh sadistically and my generals join in. The women are frightened and visibly shaking.

Without hesitation I cut the throat of the one to my left. She gasps a last breath, eyes bulging, and I watch as her pupils turn upward, her body falling forward.

The other two are now trembling, crying for their miserable lives.

"Go back to your child," I tell the toothless one, waving for Karl to release her.

Turning to the remaining woman my eyes narrow. "This one we make a public spectacle of."

"No!" Her voice is cracked and dry. But she has no energy left to even kick up the dirt under her feet. She is dragged to a central point and tied to a tree. There she will remain until dead, her pleas for mercy killing the sense of rebellion Leif may have planted.

Chapter Twelve
Leif

It is my hope that many of those lured into Earl's camp through a basic need for survival, will take my words to heart, keep them close, and find the light in their darkest hour. I see their suffering from my vantage point in the tower, but hold onto the hope that I have done more good than harm.

*****

Daniel approaches me in the greenhouse to revisit the meditation we'd had on Castle Peak days before. It's time to convince him that his role is every bit as important as mine.

We talk under an apple tree. It gives me a sense of well-being to continue conversations here.

"Because we have seen what may come to pass, I need to know you are capable of carrying it out," I remind him.

His expression falls. "It isn't as easy as that, Leif."

I lay a hand on his shoulder. "You are my friend, Daniel, and I know what I'm asking of you will be difficult, but it is for the greater good. You understand that don't you?"

He nods reluctantly and looks up at me. "I understand." Tears fill his eyes and rush down his gaunt face, tracing the hard line of his cheek-bones.

I place my hand on his head now, a lump forming in my throat as I come to terms with my destiny. "You have doubts. You fear the unknown even after all that I have told you."

"No. I mean, yes." He looks guiltily at me.

"Do this for *me*, and you do this for *all* of us." I state taking his shoulders in my hands.

A look of determination suddenly plants itself on his face. "I would do anything for you. I just wish it wasn't this."

I release my grip on him. "But you will," I reassure him.

"Yes."

"Be clear in your mind that you must be prepared for this end, Daniel. If what we have seen is to occur, be ready, be strong." I am losing my composure. Turning my back on him I walk to the edge of the greenhouse. Turning once more, I smile at him.

"You can count on me." He nods, sucking in a deep breath. "I am that I am."

"You are that and more." I leave him, standing in the warm light of the greenhouse, as I march into a misting rain, and towards my destiny.

Chapter Thirteen
Leif

Mom sits, hunched over, on one of the cement benches that lines the north end of the hospital. Her blue surgical fatigues are coated in blood after assisting in yet another still-born birth. The rain has advanced from misting to spitting, but she does not budge.

"I'm so sorry, Mom," I tell her as I take a seat.

Mom just shakes her head. "That's six in a row, Leif," she tells me. Of course I know this, as does everyone on site. A pregnancy was rare enough the last few years, but a live birth was much more so.

"Do you know, Leif," mom continues, her head still down, hands crossed, forearms resting on her thighs, "the youngest person on the base now is three?"

I nod silently. The news is dire now. With no new births, everyone fears we will be the last. The doctor had predicted this long ago, and fed pregnant women what limited vitamins were left in the vast storage lockers underground, but they were proving not enough.

"Don't despair, Mom." I take her hand and she looks up at me, her tears mixing with the rain.

"Where do we go from here?" she asks, shaking her head. "If no more babies are born, what's left?"

I couldn't tell her what suspicions played out in my mind. Not now, not after what had just happened.

"All is as it should be, Mom. Trust in that." I offer a reassuring smile. Mom offers a sad attempt at a grin and pulls my head to hers. We bump foreheads lightly and I pull her up, walking her into the cafeteria, out of the driving rain.

Chapter Fourteen
Leif

I sit on my bed, preparing for my last meditation of the day, and find I am still thinking of Mary. Everything is for a reason, I tell myself. I lost her because I couldn't see what I was doing, I didn't *want* to see. I loved her so much I lost myself in her. I gave myself to her. I lost sight of my destiny and cloaked myself in her love.

I meditate on her image, I see her in my mind's eye as she was the day she left me. Sometimes I think I'm seeing her for real.

I wonder about her always. I feel responsible for her leaving. I have forgiven myself my ignorance and ego, but it is difficult not to wonder how she's coping in the world and want to go looking for her.

I find myself meditating on Mary exclusively today: her face, her hair, the color of her skin. I feel the heartache of her leaving, the anxiety over her safety, the depression over losing her. Strangely I feel I am losing control of my session: Mary's image is penetrating every corner of my mind. The sensations continue on a physical plane now as Mary's touch is remembered: the soft embrace of her lips, the scent of her skin. My head tilts back as Mary runs her fingers through my hair, her hands not stopping at my neck but tracing my spine and rounding my hips. Excitement builds to a climax as the vision melts into me and the sensation of being one with Mary overcomes my senses.

I open my eyes, lying on my back in my bed. Mary floats above me. She is dressed in a white, flowing gown, her face angelic. A smile works its way across my face as I reach up to touch her. But as I do, Mary drifts slowly away from me, landing silently on her feet on the floor beside my desk. She is smiling. I start to rise but she holds up a hand. I sit again.

"Mary," I say, my heart leaping out of my chest. But as I watch her flowing gown move in a non-existent breeze, I realize what's happening.

"Oh, Mary." The smile leaves my face and I fall on my knees, weak from the realization.

"All is as it should be," she says in a quiet echo. I feel the touch of warmth embrace my head, her weightless hand resting upon it.

"How did it happen?" I wonder through a tightening throat. "Did you suffer?"

"We all suffer, Leif," she answers cryptically.

"Please, I couldn't bear it if you suffered." I slide off my bed to my knees and my forehead falls to the tiled floor. I want so desperately to hold her in my arms, but know I cannot. Not yet.

"I am at peace, now." I look up from all fours and see her light barely contained by her apparition.

"You are beautiful."

"I had to see you again, my love."

A shiver rushes through me. I stop breathing.

"I love you," I say, speaking from my heart. Her light pulses. My eyes close and my head falls back once more. To be enveloped in her light is like a thousand gentle fingertips caressing every nerve ending.

"And I love you, Leif." Mary's light is fading fast, her features disappearing.

"No, please, don't go," I beg. "Talk to me, Mary, please!"

"My time is short here, Leif."

"Did you find your father?"

Mary's smile outshines the rest of her. "Yes."

"Good," I say. "What can you tell me of the other side?"

"Nothing." She shakes her head in slow motion, her hair moving as if submerged in water.

"Why?"

"It is not for the living to know."

"The Chaplain?" I ask. I must know.

"He is here."

"He knows now." I smile at the memory of his kind face.

"Yes, he knows."

Chapter Fifteen
Leif

Tonight I have a most disturbing dream. Horsemen charge toward me. A backdrop of blood red sky mixes with thunder clouds, spitting a thick, paralyzing rain from the west. A dark figure commands an ink black steed. I feel smaller the closer they get. Then they pass over me and I watch helplessly as the rider charges past.

I wake up with a start. My hands fly up in front of me, protecting my body from the pounding hoofs. I have never seen a horse outside of a movie, or picture book.

Did I see Earl's mangled face on the rider's head? I fear I did.

"They are coming," whispers Blank Man.

"Is that what that was?" I ask, swinging my legs out from under the sheets and hurrying out of bed.

"Your vision will be realized in hours."

"Hours!" I shout, looking about the room for my Angel. "Can I get everyone to safety in hours?"

"If you begin the process now."

I stand and rub my eyes. "What time is it?" I trip on my sheets as they wrap around my ankles.

"Damn it. Where are you?!" I ask, angry at his timing. "I could use your light!"

My guide appears at my desk and my room immediately ignites in a warm white light.

"Thank you!"

"You're welcome," he answers, his silhouette bowing slightly.

The clock reads 3:33am. I hear a pounding rain on the metal siding. It has been raining for days.

"He would attack us in this?"

"He will."

"Then let's get started." I get up off the floor, grab the head-set of my land line, and punch in the Sergeant's number.

"Yes," a faint voice answers on the other end.

"It's time," I say. I hear a click and my receiver goes silent.

The base has emergency procedures for several different scenarios. But this particular emergency has never been put into practice, until tonight. A level of calm must be observed in order to keep the retreat a secret. No lights blink or sirens sound. Instead, a group of ten will now be summoned to the control room and briefed on our next task. That task is to knock on each resident's door and escort them to the mess hall for a warning of what is about to transpire.

*****

Once everyone is assembled, I take the podium.

As I look into the crowd of survivors my heart goes out to them. Children cling to their parents, still half asleep. Some are restless. Others are angry, knowing what is coming, knowing they will be asked to either defend their home or leave it for an uncertain future.

What do I tell them?

"You've probably guessed why we're here, in the middle of the night," I start, my voice thundering over the fearful chatter of the congregation.

"The group of desperate people that have been living beyond our walls these past few weeks have decided that tomorrow they will begin an assault against us."

This stirs the crowd into more frightened noise.

"Please," I say, lifting my arms to invoke a sense of control. "Please, listen to me. We've prepared for this time. We know what to do. Please gather up your belongings, and meet back here in twenty minutes. From here we will head east: at the top of the hill we have dug out covered shelters into the earth. Remember, we must do this quietly."

Groans erupt from the audience. No one wants this. The Sergeant stands up next to me, taking the podium.

"Listen," he tells them. "I agree with Leif on the importance of placing everyone in our eastern bunker until this thing is won, but I want to call upon anyone that can and will take up arms in this fight to join me in the armory. I have sworn to protect this base, and I will do just that."

Cheers now ring out. I find mom in the crowd and watch as she spins, slowly, taking in her surroundings and those men and women cheering on the fight. I'd told mom what Blank Man had said to me. She knows that anyone that stays behind will die defending this base. She also knows about the bomb, and the plan should the Sergeant fail in his attempt to beat back Earl's forces. But any effort to talk anyone out of the fight would only deflate their morale, and I know many of the people here are ready to make the transformation.

I am at peace with the decision to allow it. Some were born for this end, as I am mine, and Daniel his, and mom hers.

I see fight in mom's eyes too, caught up in this whirlwind of emotion. She looks up at me, and we catch each other's gaze. She smiles sadly at me and I back at her. She nods and joins me at the podium.

"Let's get them ready to go," she says.

"Twenty minutes!" I shout and the group thins out, most of them rushing back to their rooms to collect what limited possessions they hold dear. They'll bring some food and water, though the bunkers have been outfitted with life's necessities for a few weeks.

Those who remain have committed to the fight. I see Salem. His enthusiasm over the defense of his home is inspiring. I also watch as Harry, Monty and Chris join the group. Harry frowns. He nods at me and I raise a hand. I watch as the Sergeant leads the men and women out of the mess hall toward the armory. Before he slips through the door he turns and motions for me to follow. I kiss Mom on the cheek.

"I'll be back to lead everyone out the front gates, Mom. I just have to help the Sergeant with something first."

*****

I follow Sergeant Jones and his company to the armory and notice that his wife is among the fighting few. Both her children have also joined the fight.

Once the group is outfitted, the Sergeant orders one of his sons to brief them on tactics until he returns.

We move through the halls to the kitchen, open the trapdoor to the basement, and descend. There, resting on a steel table is our bomb, and a simple counter set at one hour sits atop the monster.

"It will have enough force to disintegrate everything in this room, and the burst will take out the base right to its walls. No one will survive. If it's hopeless, Leif, I will set it after a few minutes. This watch will sync up with the timer on the bomb as soon as it self-activates the countdown." He straps the watch to my wrist. "This way you'll know how much time you have to *duck and cover.* I will light this flare if I determine that we have Earl's forces in retreat and then I will dismantle the bomb." He waves the flare in front of me. "If I succeed in shutting it down, your watch will tell you that too."

I study the architecture of the room briefly. It seems to vibrate around me. The energy waiting to be released is overwhelming.

The Sergeant slips the flare into one of the many pockets that line the legs of his battle fatigues. "We'll start pulling the components out of the generators and motors now. We'll meet you in the mess hall so you can take the bags with you. If we win this thing, it won't be any problem replacing the parts. If we don't, and the bomb doesn't work, and your plan B fails, at least Earl will never be able to produce a single kilowatt of energy."

I nod and move toward the door, hopeful this fight would not depend on my plan B. The Sergeant grabs my arm and gently pulls me to face him.

"We *can* win this thing, Leif," he says, looking for some affirmation from me.

I take his hand and squeeze it between my own. "Good luck, Sergeant."

"It's been an honor to know you," he tells me. "Tell your mother I'm sorry. Tell her -"

"She knows."

He smiles broadly and I watch as a warm, white light envelopes him.

"I will see you soon."

Chapter Sixteen
Earl

This is it. I inhale deeply, sucking in the rotten scent of the dead trees. Its slick floor is thick with mud as the rain falls hard at a forty-five degree angle. I had hoped to attack yesterday evening, as the sun set, blinding their watchtowers as we approached from the west, but a driving rain would suffice for cover now. Rain is all we've seen for the past three days and my army has become demoralized. It's now or never.

I'm not sure that I believe in destiny, but I know I was always meant to lead. Desperation breeds a need for stability, for leadership. In these uncertain times if you are not a leader of men you are nothing. I have little respect for those who would follow, and am comfortable labeling them expendable. It's good to be King! Lead with fear, and respect will follow. These people have lost everything: their families, their friends, and their self-respect. It is easy to lead a people so devastated. They are already fearful for their lives and the lives of those they love. They are starving and have no direction or purpose except to stay alive. So you bring that fear back, the fear of loss, of death. What do I have to offer? Purpose, for one. Protection in numbers and governance, something many of them remember from before the bombs. People want to be ruled. They want to be told they're doing a good job and that they are giving back to their community. They want to know there is a reason to go on, and that reason is the promise of something better, and that something is a base, packed with food, water, energy and shelter. When rallied, a group feeds off its leader, and off each other. And with the promise of salvation, they will follow you into Hell. But promises expire, and I see my army is restless. The time is now. What I've worked towards all these years is now upon me. My great purpose waits to be fulfilled.

Under a rudimentary tent of tarps tied securely to four tree trunks, I meet with my generals.

"Your teams are ready?" I ask them, my voice rising to be heard above the rat-a-tat-tat of rain slamming onto the taut tarp.

The four men nod in unison. Jonah, the oldest of my generals and approximately twenty years my senior, speaks up.

"I'm worried our plan won't work in this weather."

I glare at him. "This is not *our* plan, this is *my* plan, and if I say it will work, who are you to question that?"

Jonah steps back and straightens. "I meant no disrespect."

"Does your team share your concern?" I circle the four men.

"No." As he says this I can smell the fear on him. Good, I like that.

"This is no time to be making examples of my generals." I stop to face Jonah. "Do the rest of you feel my plan is flawed?"

"No, sir," they ring in. I keep my gaze on Jonah.

"You see, Jonah, you are wrong to be worried."

"I see that now." He avoids my stare.

"Good, good, then we will proceed as planned. Recall the scouts." With that, I order the men leave the security of the tent and rush back into the torrential weather, shouting orders. I had four scouts sent to the west wall, or more precisely, to the fox holes dug along the forest-line just twenty yards from the walls. They were dug under cover of night the past week and our scouts have been watching the towers for three days. We have been erecting siege weapons for the past month. I remembered the ancient siege tools that would launch dead enemies over the castle walls, as well as dead cattle and pigs to spread disease and fear among the residents. Though effective, we could not survive such an extended campaign, nor do I have the people to spare. Instead, I opted for siege towers and ladders to be built.

The scouts now back, they give us details concerning numbers at the towers, their shifts, and the best placement of our siege equipment. I discuss this with my generals and order the siege towers dragged just beyond the forest-line. The rain was falling so heavily now that it was becoming difficult to navigate the woods. But this was perfect, offering a visual distraction as well as muting the sounds we were making pushing over tree trunks as the equipment rolled clumsily through the sticky muck of the forest floor.

Upon passing the trenches we knew we were in place. Visibility was limited to about four or five yards, the west walls all but hidden behind sheets of rain. This bode well for the secrecy of our attack, but the scout's suggested points of entry were equally hidden.

My generals and I meet once more before the final charge. With four siege towers and a dozen ladders, we would be able to put one hundred soldiers inside the base before anyone was the wiser. The difficulty in this rain would prove itself once inside. Though each soldier has studied my rudimentary maps of the interior and been given a role in the attack, this rain prevented us from carrying out the plan to any degree of accuracy.

"Have each soldier stay put once they've landed inside. Unless we're made, we'll wait for the rain to let up." I say. "Let's make sure to take out any guards in their towers quietly," I make a quick gesture with my thumb running across my neck. "You pick the man in your teams to do the work. Let's do this shortly. Wait for the signal." With that we split up once more and I return to the siege tower which I will command personally.

The towers were made mostly of wood, a classic design I borrowed from medieval times. Four wheels sit under a heavily supported base and on that base walls are built along the front and two sides. Within the enclosure are two levels and ladders that go right to the top. At the top is a plank that will fall on hinges meeting the top of the wall and act as a bridge for my men to scale the wall and climb down on ropes.

The signal they wait on before beginning the siege would be a loud cracking sound, meant to mimic a falling tree, echoing through the woods.

My army was now at the walls and ready to pour in upon an unsuspecting community. I licked the rain water from my lips and thought of Sara and the things I would do to her before I let her die. A spastic smile works the muscles in my cheeks, the skin warming over from the action.

'SNAP'.

The signal sounds and echoes through the forest as planned. The siege towers move forward immediately and within a few seconds the equipment is in place. Silently we breach the walls and slide down on ropes. A thud indicates that a tower guard has been taken out.

Mid-siege the rain begins to taper off. The sheets of rain fall away like a curtain, revealing the base in all its detail. Moments later the sun shines down on the central parade grounds, a fog lifting, beckoning us on.

Chapter Seventeen
Earl

The sun burns up the fog, lifting it up and away, revealing the base in all its abundance. I am ready for action. I look to my right and see that my army is eager for the fight to begin. My generals are walking the line, their index fingers pressed up against their lips. On my signal we will move forward as one and fire at will.

Crack. Crack, crack, crack. My line scatters for cover as gun shots rain down on us. A siren sounds. The battle has now begun.

I duck behind a tree and take a moment to smell the bark and feel the rough surface. I smile, knowing that soon I will own this tree, and everything inside these walls. Then I detect a different scent, one familiar. Gasoline! As I make the connection, a flaming arrow lands a few yards from me in the soft forest floor, sparking a raging inferno. *Not again.* I scramble across the road and behind a large building, avoiding sporadic gun fire, and watch as others seeking refuge in the woods are flushed out by the fire and shot down.

"They're in the towers!" I scream to my platoon. We open up on the two eastern towers. Two bodies from each tower plummet to the saturated earth.

"Hold your fire!" I shout again. My orders are repeated four times down the length of the wall.

With the exception of the raging forest fire, the base goes silent once more. I listen for movement. I hear a metallic footfall, and reason that there are more soldiers on the roof of the building I am under. I whistle to my generals and point my finger to the sky. I then walk my fingers through the air to indicate that I hear men on the roof. They nod and prepare the pipe bombs. I throw one onto the roof of the hospital. Three more are lobbed up and I watch as the others toss theirs on the rooftops of the housing buildings and mess hall.

Explosions rain shrapnel onto my enemy. The sound of men screaming and shrapnel hitting the metal roofs excites me. Three soldiers fall from their high perch.

"Fire!" I scream. The three fallen soldiers have no time to react and are dead in seconds.

I send ten of my men to the roof to finish off anyone left, and report on our success. My generals follow my lead.

It's time to secure the grounds and move indoors.

More gun shots from above confirm that there were survivors and that they too are now dead. My group Captain leans past the roofs' overhang and I motion to him to send five men back and secure the grounds from his elevated position. As he obeys, more shots. I step aside in time to watch my Captain slam into the cement beside me with a sickening thud.

My men scatter again and fire into a Hummer which is now charging at us, a gunner on the big machine gun ripping my men apart. I steady my nerves and line the gunner up in my sights, snap off two rounds, and penetrate his helmet. I watch with satisfaction as he slumps over his gun and the Hummer slams on its breaks. Four doors open and gun barrels poke through the windows. I see a similar story playing out at the south end of the base as I slip behind a generator to avoid the hail of bullets. My men on the roof fire down on the unsuspecting soldiers, ending the exchange swiftly.

"Regroup!" I yell to my people still on the ground. As they huddle around me I realize I have lost a considerable number and am worried for the outcome. Either way, if I die today or take this base, today is the last day I want for anything, ever again.

"Let's move inside. I need you to remember your training. One kicks in the door and the other moves in. Then the kicker follows. Do this with each door you find, closets, anything." The men nod and kick in the back door to the hospital. I feel good about how the assault is progressing. Though worried I lost as many as I did right out of the gate.

Looking south I see my generals have begun the same process of flushing out anyone in hiding.

After twenty minutes the hospital is secure, but eerily quiet. I have confirmation from my generals that their buildings too are secure, and so

I order men to the towers to lock down the perimeter. But where is everyone? The majority of the base's population - they must be hiding somewhere, the cowards. But they can't hide forever. We will find them. And take what we came for.

Chapter Eighteen
Leif

The majority of our people are safely situated on the eastern hill. The rain opens up rivers of mud on the hillside and impedes our view of the battle, soaking us through to our skins, but the sun now breaking through the clouds illuminates the central parade grounds, offering a clear picture of what is transpiring.

"Why did so many stay?" Mom steps out of one of the bunkers.

"The Sergeant told me, if he could save the base, he would try." He'd done what he had promised, rendering the generators useless, removing items Earl's army could never replace, and sending them up with our group. But his insistence in fighting the good fight, hoping to avert a full scale retreat, was either brave, or incredibly foolish if what I'd seen in my visions would come to pass.

In a short time the bomb would self-activate. If the Sergeant was left alive to stop it, he would send the flare. If not, the bomb would begin its countdown of one hour. I check my watch, which is synchronized with the bomb's timer.

My heart races at the possibility of the Sergeant actually turning the tides of destiny. He is a competent soldier and a good man, but the odds are stacked against him. Earl's forces are counted daily by the tower guards and the count holds at approximately two hundred. This number does not include the children, of which there are ten, none under the age of six. These children are currently being removed from Earl's camp by a separate task force, who will hide them in our lakeside gardens.

Blank Man has left me to my destiny. I see his light atop Castle Peak, waiting, watching.

The sound and smell of gun fire resonates over the wall of the base and climbs the hill, finding us, seventy refugees, watching the flashes of light pepper the landscape of our stronghold. Smoke begins to cloud our view of the battle as the woods and rooftops ignite and countless bullets leave hot barrels. I look at my watch. Five more minutes and the bomb will start its countdown. Five more minutes, Sergeant, to change our destiny.

"All is as it should be," I hear Blank Man whisper.

Daniel approaches mom and I. His expression is hopeful.

"How long?"

"Five minutes before the countdown starts." I am not without hope. But I am not without fear over my own end.

Mom hugs me, pressing her face against my back. "No flare yet."

"No flare," I repeat.

Chapter Nineteen
Earl

I am in the kitchen with my generals. We pull open the large fridges and freezers, our mouths watering. They are filled with food. I smile as I have not smiled in many, many years. My eyes squint as my cheeks burn at the unfamiliar act. I hide this reaction from my men, returning to my trademark scowl as I turn to meet them.

"Well, we've done it!" I pronounce, arms outstretched. The three men congratulate each other.

Suddenly the sound of gunfire in the kitchen sends us scrambling to the floor. Kent is shot in the chest, which spewing a cloud of blood in all directions. His body lands inches from Jonah, who's found shelter behind the metal island. The artillery fire ceases and I slip the pistol from my holster, slowly, quietly.

"Who's that?" I call out.

"The last voice you'll ever hear."

"We've got ourselves a live one here, boys!" I shout out. I need to flush this lone wolf out.

"Curtis?" I yell out.

"I'm here," he replies.

"Cover me!" I shout back.

Curt's head peers around the corner of the same island Jonah is hiding behind. He can see me too. I'm under the counter facing the line of industrial fridges, where I suspect our shooter is hiding.

Curtis looks questioningly at me. I point for him to stand and scan the area beyond me. Uunbeknownst to him, he will draw the shooter's fire.

I watch as he slowly rises to the level of the counter.

Pow! One shot and I hear Curt's head pop, and a split second later his corpse hits the tile floor behind me. I slip back behind the counter, having located our sniper's position.

My heart is racing now, but my nerves are steel. My excitement mounts as I deliberate on my next move.

"Jonah!" I call out. Nothing. No reply. This pisses me off. "Jonah, goddamn it, answer me!"

Three shots fire into the stainless steel counter inches from my head. I slide along the tile floor on my belly the length of the counter, spacing myself from the shooter.

"I'll fucking kill you myself when I'm done with this asshole if you don't answer me." I swear to Christ, I will too.

"I'm pinned down, Earl, what do you want me to do about it?"His voice is shaky.

"I want you to take out the shooter, Jonah. It's just one guy up there. He ain't goin' nowhere, either."

"I can't see him. Did you see what happened to Curt when you ordered him up?"

"Yeeeees, Jonah, I saw that. But you're not an idiot like Curt, now are you?"

A moment's pause. "No."

"So, what are you waiting for?"

I hear movement from behind the island. Jonah struggles to his feet, hoping to hit the shooter before he's shot himself.

"Where did you say he is?"

"I didn't say. He's above the fridges. Jammed back there like a sardine. All you have to do is let that automatic of yours do the work."

Once he starts firing I'll be able to pop up and zero in on the sniper, hopefully taking him out with a well placed shot.

Jonah starts counting. "Okay. One, two…"

"Jesus, don't count it out." I slam a fist into the steel cabinetry. "Are you dense or something?"

"Sorry."

"When you're ready just do it." I have no delusions that Jonah will live through this experience but Christ, he should at least give himself a fighting chance.

Then it happens. The automatic snaps off wild rounds, and I pounce. In my peripheral, I see Jonah's head snap back as the shooter finds pay-dirt. But this gives me the chance I need to line him up and fire two shots into the darkness above the cold storage.

I fall back below the counter tops and wait. Looking over to my right I see Jonah's head release a puddle of blood onto the white tile.

I wait another five minutes before picking myself up and inspecting my kill. I am leery of this, but without another general available to me, I do the work. I climb the metal ladder attached to one of the ice boxes to discover that my expert marksmanship has not let me down. It's a young man, shot in the face. I hit him with both shots! I slide the rifle from his death grip and hop down.

Once my feet hit the tile my knees buckle as I am struck in the face by a fist.

I stagger back and through blurry eyes see the face of an older man, dark hair layered with grey and a giant mole on his forehead. I shake my head trying to regain some semblance of equilibrium and narrowly escape another swing at my ringing head.

I pull my knife from its sheath on my leg and jab it at my attacker. Though I could skin a man alive, my fighting skills with a knife were amateurish at best.

My pistol, and the rifle I had just retrieved were lying on the floor, out of reach. Where did this guy come from?

I continue to swing my knife haphazardly and the man grabs my wrist, and twists it at an unnatural angle, snapping it. I suppress a scream. My free hand swings at his head but is expertly blocked. As my vision clears I realize who this man is.

"Sergeant," I say uncomfortably, one hand swaying uselessly at my side while the other remains in his grip.

"Earl," he hisses at me. The last time we saw one another was in the stockade, here on the base some ten years earlier.

"Did you know that guy?" I ask, realizing he was punishing me rather than just trying to kill me. But with this realization comes an opportunity. If I can talk to him, maybe one of my own people will charge in and shoot him down.

"My son," he says through clenched teeth. He follows through with another thundering punch to my temple and I go down. My head is buzzing so loudly now I don't know if I can keep up conversation.

"My family died defending this place," he continues. Then a boot comes down on my ribs. I groan at the pain. I remember a similar treatment ten years ago as his men worked me over for information.

"How did you know?" I manage to ask him, not sure that he'd know what I was talking about.

"Never mind how we knew, how you're going to die should be the only thing on your mind right now."

That was grim. Things are definitely looking grim for me right now. I'm not even sure I could stand to face him, and I truly believe my life depends on it.

"I don't care how I die, Sergeant." I swallow a mouthful of blood. "I only ever cared about how I lived."

The doors to the kitchen burst open and three of my men charge in, guns drawn.

"Get away from him!" one of them yells.

I hear myself laugh. My eyes close and I want to sleep. I lay down completely and watch the Sergeant's face screw up into a hate I know too well.

He pulls his weapon and fires on my men. In turn he is shot a dozen times. Some hit his body armor, but others find his shoulders, arms, legs and finally, his neck. He falls gracefully to his knees and as his head tilts forward, his chin tucks into his chest and blood rushes out of his mouth.

"Are you alright?" The remaining soldier bends over me.

"Help me up." I lift a hand and he takes it. I am beyond dizzy, but can manage. I realize there may be others embedded in the tight spaces and dark corners waiting to ambush my men.

As we move outside a hush comes over those gathered. They see me bruised and battered, my wrist unnaturally bent to the right.

"You should see the other guy," I say in an attempt to lighten the mood. They laugh, still giddy in light of our victory.

"We have rats in the walls," I announce. "They may all still be here, waiting to ambush us, to divide and conquer. This war ain't over yet. I want groups of six to run through every inch of this base. Be smart, be silent and flush them out."

*****

As I watch the groups, twelve in all, set off to flush out what infestation may remain, the realization of what I have accomplished excites me. The throbbing in my wrist subsides. From such humble beginnings I now hold the ultimate position of power. I have overthrown my enemy; taken control of the most sought after piece of real-estate within a thousand miles and am the leader of a great army. Pride cannot describe what I am feeling. I no longer have to ask myself whether it was dumb luck that landed me on that camping trip so many years ago, surviving the initial end my family suffered. There is no question now that destiny has led me here, that my actions and the actions of those who subsisted with me blazed this path. After the vote had been cast to make Joel our leader, after the fire Sara set at the house, after months living at the barn garden and the numerous attempts to disrupt this base's infrastructure, I am victorious. After my confinement here and my escape, after another ten long years of scraping by and building my army the end I knew I was fated to realize, has been.

*****

Another twenty minutes passes and I count only three gunshots. Perhaps they have fled.

Chapter Twenty
Earl

Where is *Sara?* They must have rushed everyone out to the lake. Are they hiding in their gardens? How did they know I would attack today? These questions plague me, taking away from this great victory I should be enjoying. I want to *kill* Sara. I've wanted that as much as I have wanted to take this base. Well, one out of two ain't so bad, considering. But that snot-nosed kid of hers, Leif, I wanted to take him out of the game too. Preachy little prick. Okay, one out of three is nothing to be proud of. We would finish securing the base and I would send a platoon to the lake to be sure.

My face and wrist have been dressed with what was left in the hospital storage lockers. A splint would have to do for now, where my broken wrist is concerned.

The Captain from Kirk's group runs up to me. "Earl, the equipment is missing components."

"Missing…"

He rushes me to the open generator, and I realize what he means by *missing.* A particular component that is crucial in the operation of these units is gone. And it is very clear that it is not something we could just replace. All of the generators were missing the same piece and so all of the windmills and solar panels and even the gas powered motors were utterly useless.

"Goddamn it." I'm so pissed off. This is half a victory. They've robbed me of power. "How in the fuck did they know we were coming?"

The four men were dumbstruck. I knew none of them could produce an answer.

Chapter Twenty-one
Leif

I spot Dieter as he emerges from the bunker.

"Dieter," I greet him, tapping nervously at my watch.

"Leif," he replies with a tired smile. He takes me by the arm, guiding me toward a large flat stone and seating us there.

"I had - how do you say - an epiphany!" Dieter tells me excitedly. "Just last night."

"Like an idea?"

"Yes, but more than that, it's like an idea has just been confirmed as fact, rather than just a theory." Dieter's aura is pulsating a golden hue of inner knowledge.

"Tell me, can it help us now?" I wave Daniel over.

"It will help you further understand the connection science and spirituality share. It might not help us out of our immediate danger, but if we should survive… Even if we don't…" I prepare myself for another revealing lecture from this brilliant man. Daniel kneels in front of us and listens.

"You experience visions, yes?" I nod affirmatively. "What is a vision?" he asks.

"A future event. Something that could occur based on all that has led to that moment." I think back on all the angel has shown me.

"Exactly. And what are you doing in order to see this information?" He shifts excitedly on the stone slab.

"It's shown to me in meditation, by my guide in the spiritual world."

"Right, exactly. And what have I told you about the spiritual world?"

"That it is the same as the quantum world, the very small."

"Right. So, let me explain my epiphany. Before the bombs fell, we, the scientific community, were just beginning to experiment with the idea of time travel. Actually passing information through time via neutrinos."

"Neutrinos?" Another new word.

"Yes, they are an invisible particle that lives in the quantum world. In fact, we are being bombarded by millions of them right now, passing through us at the quantum level." He waves his hands wildly. "But, I digress! You see, the experiment had been tested many times, and the results were always the same. Every time a group of neutrinos were fired from a source to a specific destination, it was confirmed that they had travelled faster than the speed of light! And if something can go faster than the speed of light, it becomes a future event. Suddenly Einstein's theory that nothing in the universe can travel faster than light is questioned. All of physics is suddenly being put under the microscope, so to speak."

I am stunned by this incredible description of what mankind was on the brink of discovering about the natural world, and that we had been so close to understanding so much. Dieter notices my state of awe and slaps me twice on the arm.

"Do you see how this further develops my theory on the spiritual plane and the quantum plane existing as one idea, one unified theory? Think about it, Leif, nothing should be able to travel faster than the speed of light. So where are the neutrinos going? Another dimension? A wormhole? They must be taking an alternate route to the destination than the rest of us. Nothing travels faster than light. This is what we know. But the neutrino says differently. And *you*, my friend, say differently. When you leave space-time during meditation to travel into the future to experience your visions, events not yet realized in the material world, your consciousness is traveling faster than light - reporting on a future event!"

I close my eyes and shake my head. This is truly inspiring.

"Isn't it amazing? Even after science had lost the ability to experiment with new theories, years later, I come upon you. Living proof."

"Everything is for a reason." I say, a sense of purpose taking hold. I fill up with the overwhelming urge to live, to keep going.

I watch a tear track the deep lines in Dieter's face. He looks past me and then up to the sky, where a perfect blue is framed by the rising smoke escaping the base.

"I have proven my theories work, without so much as a laboratory." A rising lump in his throat can be heard in his speech. "I have found the theory of everything."

Breaking the moment, Mom takes me by the arm and leads me away. We walk a few yards and stop. The sounds of gun shots still pierce the air intermittently. Shouts from Earl's army are vulgar and filled with hateful elation.

She turns me to face her, grasping my arms in her hands as I watch tears well up in her eyes.

"We've lost the base, Leif. We've lost everything."

"Not everything," I grab her arms and squeeze. "We still have our lives. And we have each other."

"I *love you*, Leif," she says. She's said it a thousand times before, but this time is different. This time she says it with a sense of finality that makes me heartsick.

"I love you, Mom." I nervously look at my watch, realizing the bomb should have blown the base sky high. But it hadn't. The digital output is frozen at nine seconds. I move to leave, but mom grabs my arm.

"Leif, don't." She pleads.

I turn and face her, she is crying now. I didn't want this moment with her. I didn't want to say goodbye.

"Whatever it is," she pauses. "Whatever it is you're going to do, don't. Please." She takes my face in her hands. What is it she thinks she knows?

"Mom," I manage. "Mom, please." Now I'm the one doing the pleading. "I have to go." I shake my head and she pulls me close and hugs me. I hug her back.

"I love you." She says again, pulls away and takes my hands in hers. "You're my baby." She tells me through heavy sobs. "Let me do what needs to be done."

"It's not yours to do, Mom." I insist, trying to keep from crying. "It's alright, Mom." My voice lowers to a whisper. "All is as it should be."

"Leif, please. You're just a boy."

My heart hardens at this final appeal. I've never been just a boy. I've never felt like other boys my age, ever. I'd been born into servitude. Reared to complete a destiny I couldn't carry out in a past life. To hear my Mother say 'I'm just a boy' is heartbreaking, but also exactly what I needed to hear.

"Mom, you know I'm not. You've always known." I squeeze her hands and let go. "I love you. And I will see you soon." I smile at her, turn and walk away.

Chapter Twenty-two
Leif

The bomb has not ignited. Daniel's face is set in stone. Swallowing hard, he looks back at the base. "This is it then," he says, looking at my digital watch.

"Yes," I nod. The realization that I had been bred for this end was bittersweet. Especially in light of what Dieter had just discovered. I so desperately want to continue my spiritual journey here, on this plane. Teach the science behind the spiritual and appeal to everyone's sense of purpose.

"It's just as we'd seen."

I concentrate on my aura and let it envelope us both, giving him strength.

"Stay with our friends and family now, Daniel. They *need* you."

"They need *you*, Leif! Not me! Who am I?"

"Who am *I*, Daniel?" I grasp the back of his head and pull him closer. "*Who am I?* I'm just like you," I whisper. "I'm *afraid*, Daniel." I release him once more and back off.

I take up the binoculars and study my route to return to the base. My plan B. Earl's forces are crawling all over the base now, but I have a secret infiltration point, one the Sergeant and I had mapped out when the bomb had been constructed. Should I make it down the hill undetected, I would make it to the bomb.

I pan the temporary bunkers, where supplies have been dumped in preparation for this possible end. I see fear on the faces of the crowd gathering at the hill's crest.

Turning back to Daniel I tell him what he already knows. "Keep them here. Keep them safe. Teach them what you know."

Daniel nods. I lay a hand on his shoulder, then cup the back of his neck and squeeze. "You're ready."

Chapter Twenty-three
Leif

On my descent towards the base my face flushes with fear. Thoughts of fleeing, of turning back, of returning to my life, plague me. The closer I get to the base, the stronger the impulse is.

The Blank Man can be heard in my head once more as I question this path one final time.

"Death brings an honest response," he says.

Had I heard this before? I continue down the slope on all fours to escape detection, sliding in the mud on my hands and knees."What are you saying?" I whisper. What response should I have in death?

"Remember what death is."

Death is a release from this life, from pain, sadness, angst and hate.

"What else?" This is a strange time for a conversation, but I'll bite.

It is an opportunity to live again, either in this life, or in the next. To know death is a gift. To know what it is, and to understand it allows you to approach death as you would a friend.

"How will you greet death?"

I will meet death with arms open, heart full and the knowledge that this life is fleeting, impermanent, but necessary and important. My response to death is to embrace it, to respect it and to understand it. As life is full of purpose, so is death. Memories are of the ethereal, and not the material world, that is how I know I am forever.

Soon I am back at the east wall, the sounds of gunshots still exploding over the victorious shouts from within. I open a trap door that takes me beneath the watch tower and follow the underground crawl space for ten minutes, fighting off bouts of claustrophobia, until I enter the dry storage directly under the kitchen. I push through the ventilation hatch and climb on to the smooth concrete floor.

The bomb sits a few feet from me. Its size is comically massive. As I approach the monstrosity I see that sure enough, the yellow wire has popped off its position behind the timer, stopping the process at just nine seconds. I wonder, perhaps for the final time if this is my only option. So much death. Could we not perhaps live? Continue running, fleeing Earl's army, hoping for and expecting much better for the future. No children had been born in years. I know the human population is already on the brink of expiring. But still, was it not our inherent nature to hope? Were we not given this ability for a reason? Even if 'death' could bring peace, should we not still choose life?

A realization overcomes me: I am standing in my final resting place, my mausoleum. My life would end precisely nine seconds after I replace the wire.

I take several deep, cleansing breaths, then climb up onto the steel table and sit directly behind the bomb.

"*Son of a bitch!*" The voice is Earl's. I look up, past the bomb. He is poking his head into the stairwell, which descends from the kitchen floor.

My destiny so clear now, I can taste purpose in the very air around me. I know there is nowhere he can run.

Our eyes lock as he watches me place the wire to the back of the timer, and the clock move backwards from 9, 8, 7…

Epilogue

In that short time afforded me, I relive my final conversation with my angel. The moment so still, and poignant, as the timer continues its countdown: 6, 5, 4… I am standing once more on Castle Peak, Blank Man having just revealed my destiny.

"So, this is to be my end? Like my father's end."

"This end was never in question, Leif. Your father carried it out prematurely and without purpose."

"I'm having some trouble with this end, friend."

"But you understand it is the end you were meant to arrive at."

"I do."

"Then rejoice, and know that everything you have accomplished brought you to this end."

"I understand. But I am afraid."

"Why? After all you know, all you've been shown?"

"Human nature I guess." I smile up at him.

"Leave this behind you."

"Enlighten me again, friend. What was it all for?"

"Our identities have been hidden in the flesh and blood and ambition of humanity long enough. Those who have come back again and again and not learned their greater purpose will be discarded in this final exodus from the flesh."

"To have lived so many lives, how could every soul not know love?" I ask, dumbfounded.

"It is a question those souls will be asking themselves for an eternity."

"We cannot save them?" I plead.

"They have made their choice," he replies, his voice soft and sad.

"We're finished then."

"You've only just begun."

ACKNOWLEDGEMENTS

Thanks again to Rose and Lisa. My editors.

Thanks also to my fan followings and friends on Facebook, Goodreads, and Amazon.

Thanks to friends and acquaintances, strangers and reviewers who asked: *What happens next?* Which spurred me on to build a trilogy out of the ashes of book one.

Additional Resources:

www.the-judas-syndrome.com- official website for the series

www.mikepoeltl.com- official author website

Find Michael Poeltl on Twitter @mpoeltlauthor, Linked-In and with his own Facebook fan page

Made in the USA
Charleston, SC
09 June 2012